PLAGUE SEARCHERS I

RED WANDS

ROB WILLS

PLAGUE SEARCHERS I

RED WANDS

ARCADIA

First published 2022 by Arcadia
the general books' imprint of
Australian Scholarly Publishing Pty Ltd
7 Lt Lothian St North, North Melbourne, Victoria 3051
Tel: 61 3 9329 6963 / Fax: 61 3 9329 5452
Email: enquiry@scholarly.info / Web: www.scholarly.info

ISBN 978-1-922669-95-7 (Volume I)
ISBN 978-1-922669-96-4 (Volume II)

Cover design: Sarah Anderson

To ancient women

My grandmothers & great aunts
Edna, Ethel, Aunty Pat, Bertha, Gwendoline

My mother & my aunts
Muriel, Phyllis, Winifred, Grace, Dulcie

My mother-in-law & her sisters
Patricia, Kathleen, Lorna, Mary

My wife
Suzanne

'Item, paid for 2 redd wands for the searchers in the sykness tyme 00 00 04 [fourpence].'

Oxford English Dictionary, citation dated 1625/6

'When any one dies ... the Searchers ... (who are antient Matrons, sworn to their Office) repair to the place where the dead Corpse lies ... and ... examine by what Disease or casualty the Corpse died.'

J. Graunt, *Natural and Political Observations Made upon the Bills of Mortality*, 1662

'If we were all taken with the same thing, there could be no living in the World.'

Mrs Jane Sharp, *The Compleat Midwife's Companion: Or, the Art of Midwifry Improv'd*, 1671

ACKNOWLEDGEMENTS

I am, as always, grateful to my publisher, the energetic and supportive Nick Walker of Australian Scholarly Publishing. And I owe thanks to a great many scholars, in particular to Richelle Munkhoff for her crucial 1999 article, 'Searchers of the Dead', in the journal *Gender & History*.

Many of my 'informants' are dead – recent and long gone. I gratefully acknowledge them on my bookshelves, stored in my computer, and through this novel, but have to single out Samuel Pepys for his Diary.

A comprehensive list of the sources I've drawn on would be a chore to compile and intrusive at this point, but perhaps to be posted later on a website.

AUTHOR'S NOTE

Begun in March 2018, the book had reached Chapter 16 when Covid-19 struck the world in 2020. As the pandemic progressed it became clear that there are many similarities – and not so many differences – between two plagues raging 350 years apart.

Two and a half years into the pandemic, *Plague Searchers* has reached the point where I can say, like Searcher Joan Brokefild, *finis*. I hope the same can be said very soon of Covid.

Rob Wills

Brisbane

June 2022

CHAPTER I

*'When a man does die they should not cry that his glass is run ...
but his pipe is out!'*

'The worst thing of all is – Aagh!' Goodwife Joan Brokefild's back finds a sharp nubble on the wall. She turns and sees a lath poking through crumbling plaster. Shrugs herself down into a more comfortable place. The day is hot, and flies and stenches assault them from the cesspit in the yard, and from inside the house.

Fellow Searcher, Widow Margaret Hazard, says nothing. Goodwife Brokefild's likes and dislikes will soon come without prompting. She delves for the tobacco purse and hands it to the Goodwife. They fill their pipes, strike a flint, and sit on the ground side by side, companionably smoking. Leaning against the house wall. No-one will come for them there or chide them for their lack of busyness. Although they are busy thinking, because there is more to do.

Widow Hazard sends smoke from her right nostril only. She hums a low murmured 'Mmm'. Her left nostril, like much on that side of her face, was cruelly damaged, melted, by a brand from the hearth when she was small. Her left eye put out for ever, her cheek moulded into fleshy, protruding folds, her nose twisted.

They are smoking for their health. The tobacco not only protects them, its pleasing odour masks the stink of shit and death and corruption. It is also, Widow Hazard admits in honesty, but only to herself, pleasurable. Which gives her some unease because she has convinced the Church Warden to pay for tobacco not only for the Searchers but for the Viewers and the Keepers as well. The Warden is open to notions that are for the good of the congregation and the parish, and open to doing a favour where he might expect one back.

Agreeing to the Widow's request the Warden said, as if it were normal, natural, 'The parish of St Cyneswide and St Tibba: Our Commonwealth: A Tobacco Covenant made.' The Widow found herself warmed by the fellowship, the complicity, offered. Found herself pleased to hear the word Commonwealth. Acknowledged all this to the Warden with several sharp nods.

Goodwife Brokefild must talk but she also sings. She is a boisterous ancient matron with a loud tenor voice, 'There is a catch that sings of smoking – *Good, good indeed, the herb's good weed.*'

'Not now. Not singing now,' Widow Hazard in her flat voice dampens her friend, the smoke whisping from her good nostril. But she often likes the things that Goodwife Brokefild does and says that she herself would not do or say.

Lips together, Goodwife Brokefild can still sing inside herself about the good weed and smoking it and how good it is to sing while smoking it. How the Learned say *vita fumus*, and how we say to the Learned *if life's a smoke as they maintain, if life's a vapour without doubt, then when a man does die they should not cry that his glass is run ... but his pipe is out!*

The last words float from her mouth, like smoke, 'His pipe is out.'

'My pipe is out,' Widow Hazard replies.

'Now for searching,' Goodwife Brokefild says energetically, moving with difficulty away from the wall. Her vigour, her sanguine nature, cheer the Widow, reminds her of her good fortune to be paired with the Goodwife.

They help each other to their feet, leaning on their red wands. Long, red-painted staffs. 'Almost as high as an ancient woman,' the Church Warden says, grinning. Often says. Goodwife Joan Brokefild and Widow Margaret Hazard are ancient matrons of the city parish of St Cyneswide and St Tibba, and chosen Searchers of the dead. Elected Searchers of the dead. Widow Hazard silently runs the words, her lips moving:

Viewers of the dead corpses of such as should die in this parish.
Viewers of the bodies of such as shall die in the time of infection.
And to give true knowledge unto the Clerk of such as should die of
the plague.

They re-enter the room where the man lies dead. Lying spread on the floor, bowels and bladder released by death. His death by the infection is clear. By the grace of God, the body with its blaynes, botches and buboes, has left no doubt of that. They hold the still warm bowls of their pipes close to their noses.

They know him. Of course. He is a member of the congregation of their parish. They know all the parishioners. All the houses. All the bodies, living and dead, that they visit. Bodies who they have sworn, under Oath, to search. He is Will Barrett, a journeyman joiner.

Their smoking pause told them there is more to do in this house. Will Barrett was a married man with three children. In a dark corner of the room – most of the room is dark – they find a tumble of clothes that are his two sons, dead. And his wife Goody Barrett and small daughter Mary, alive. All show the plague signs.

Widow Margaret Hazard and Goodwife Joan Brokefild know that yesterday the Viewers of the Sick were here. And the Keepers brought food and drink and other necessaries. The plague marks on living and dead are clear, yet no-one has been told. There is no red cross on the door.

Close neighbours – the loud, curious, suspicious family of William Sutterwhit – had been listening carefully, and hearing nothing of the Barrett family that morning had called for the Searchers.

The Widow and the Goodwife go out the front door and nod a 'Yes' to the watching Sutterwhits, who back fearfully away. The women set off to report to the Parish Clerk, who will call for a watchman and for the red cross, one foot high, as the city orders, to be painted on the door. The pious entreaty will be added above the cross 'Lord have mercy upon us.' Later the corpse bearers will come for the bodies.

The widow and her small daughter will need the Lord's mercy, and the help of the parish, to survive their month locked in the house.

Widow Margaret Hazard and Goodwife Joan Brokefild walk slowly, leaning on their red wands. As required by Order, they make their way beside the drainage channel in the middle of the street.

'The worst thing of all is that the playhouses have been closed,' Goodwife Joan Brokefild says in a whisper, she cannot help herself. Of course she knows it is not the worst thing of all. But she can say such things to Widow Margaret Hazard, who tolerates her mad fancies because they are friends who have worked well together, paired as Searchers, for many years. The Widow gets wry amusement from the Goodwife's animated chatter. Has defended her against parochial suspicions of disorderliness, flightiness, excess.

'You do not go to plays,' Widow Margaret Hazard says comfortably.

'Oh no, I do not. But I like them nonetheless. The players quickening the tales and songs into life, dressing and moving and speaking as someone they are not! I think it a marvel.'

If Widow Margaret Hazard acknowledges this with an 'Mmm' Goodwife Brokefild does not hear it.

'I *have* seen the puppets. I love the puppets,' the Goodwife says enthusiastically, reminisces about the hand-puppet plays she saw as a child. The bright red, pointy-horned devil with his claw hands and long tail. The hilarious exchanges.

'We often, so often, saw the play of Noah and Goodwife Noah and the Ark. Goodwife Noah made us laugh and laugh. What of when he asks her how she be and she answers *All the worse now I see thee. We women may be wary of all ill husbands, I have one who loosed me of my bands*' – at this Goodwife Brokefild with sly movements shakes and wriggles, as if her bands were being loosened – '*but with game and with guile I will smite him and smile, and should he then smite me so he shall rue, for I shall smite back, three for two!*'

Goodwife Brokefild's husband Isaac is a feckless, sour man who rarely finds work and cannot keep it. At times he will fetch and carry for whoever will pay, or take simple digging work. But labour does not agree with him nor he with it. There is only one who smites in their house and it is not the Goodwife.

Widow Margaret Hazard is not listening to the scene from Noah and the Ark. Her mind runs on the small girl, Mary Barrett, still alive. She will press the Church Warden to make sure food is brought today, then every day for the next thirty to the Barrett house. She will pray for their good recovery, but not now while she is walking beside the channel. And she will keep close watch on the Keepers to make sure they do their job.

When the Widow returns to listening, Goodwife Brokefild is talking about Bartholomew Fair and the Italian string puppets. She has seen them, too.

Widow Hazard also likes the Italian puppets. Her Sara hopping with delight at their bowing and waving and stalking along their small stage. Squeezing her mother's hand and bouncing and bowing and waving herself. The Widow held her close. Watching the people as well as the puppets. Watching from a distance so as to remain separate from the assembled crowd. Later she had heard Sara retelling the play to her friends, 'And then See-your Polchello, and then he,' the child is overwhelmed by laughter. Continues 'the See-your he, he, hits the devil on the bum with a big stick! Hits him on the bum and whacks him into Hell!' Her mother has heard the parish children, shrieking with laughter, re-enact this moment many times.

The streets are thin of people. Strangers take note of their red wands and keep close to the walls, hurrying away. Fellow parishioners recognise the matrons and some wave or nod a greeting but do not approach. They slowly follow the gutters back towards the church. It is early June and the days have been stinking hot. The channel gutters are sluggish, almost dry. Widow Hazard thinks that if she were blind she could follow the channels' smells to find her way. Except, she thinks, if blind and walking near the gutters she would certainly fall. She must guard her remaining eye.

Both ancient women reach the end of their separate puppet reveries.

Goodwife Brokefild confides, 'Oliver Protector could surprise. He stopped Christmas but allowed the puppet plays to continue.' She likes to speak of the Protector, but only to Widow Margaret Hazard, and when they are alone. The Widow also remembers the Protector with strong regard.

'What will we say of Barrett? What will we tell the Clerk?' Goodwife Brokefild asks, suddenly deferential. Widow Margaret Hazard is older and has been a Parish Nurse.

'What we always tell him. What we saw. That Will Barrett and his sons died of the infection – the signs are clear. That Widow Barrett and daughter Mary have the signs but are alive.'

'Yes. Yes. But what more? That Viewers Anne Abowen and Widow Ursula Chaukley and Keepers Goody Susanna Parsons and Widow Dorothy Bullen, who've all been to Will Barrett's house, went only yesterday, but made no report, no report, of the signs, of the sickness? The signs are clear and must have been for days. What will we say of this?' What, the Goodwife thinks, of any corruption or false reporting by the Viewers and Keepers? 'What,' she asks Widow Hazard, 'of any corruption or false reporting? What will we, you, say of that?'

'I will say,' Widow Margaret Hazard replies, 'that the plague is in Will Barrett's house. That the house must be sealed, a cross painted, and a watchman posted. The corpse bearers must come. But the Clerk knows to do all that of course. I will say that Widow Barrett and the child Mary must receive food and drink, and we pray they come alive from the house in thirty days.' She pauses, 'He will know all that too.'

'And say nothing of the Viewers and Keepers?'

'What would we say? What would you say of them? Would you tell the Clerk and the Vestrymen that the Viewers and Keepers have been disorderly and neglectful? Have made false report and should be removed? They are women of our parish,' she says indignantly.

'I would not say anything like that. Oh no.'

'No, nor I. But they *have* been disorderly and neglectful and it is a disgrace. The Clerk will know that too.' The Widow stops walking. A slow thought has surfaced, 'But Oliver closed the playhouses.'

'Yes. Yes he did. And he let the puppet plays continue. The Protector could surprise.'

They turn into the small square in front of the church of St Cyneswide and St Tibba. The parish is proud of the church with its three arches facing the square. Which other of the city's churches has three arches? Which other London church has two saints, apart, of course, from nearby St Anne and St Agnes? In the porch, newly pasted upon a board, is the Notice that Widow Margaret Hazard would normally stop to read, well pleased that she knows her letters. Today she doesn't stop, but this does not matter as she can cite it by rote.

> *That in or for every parish there shall be appointed two sober Ancient Women, to be sworn to be Searchers of the bodies of such as shall die in time of Infection, and two other to be Viewers of such as shall be sick and suspected of Infection: which women shall immediately, upon such their views by virtue of their Oath, make true report to the Constable of that precinct where such persons shall die or be infected, to the intent that true notice may be given both to the Alderman or his Deputy, and to the Clerk of the parish, and from him to the Clerk of the parish Clerks, that true certificate may be made as hath been used.*
>
> *And every woman so sworn, and for any corruption, or any other respect, falsely reporting, shall stand upon the Pillory, and bear Corporal pain by the Judgement of the Lord Mayor and court of Aldermen.*
>
> *They, at their going abroad, to bear red wands, go near the Channels, and shun Assemblies as before. That every woman or other appointed to any service for the infected and refusing or failing to do that service, shall not have any Pension out of the Parish. And the parish shall have in readiness one or more sober discreet women, as the case shall require, as Keepers to be providers and deliverers of necessaries for infected houses and to attend the persons sick and infected.*
>
> *Order to be used in the time of the Infection of the Plague within the City and Liberties of London, June 5, 1665*

The old Notice had faded and had been up in the church for so long that the congregation no longer saw it. Philip Carter, Parish Clerk, insisted that this newly issued Notice be printed, not hand-lettered, because printed words carry the greatest authority, great authority being needed in sore times.

The Parish Clerk is a squat, hot stove of a man, himself giving off the fierce heat of authority. The two women find him in the vestry, where he is usually found. A short, broad-shouldered, thickly muscled man whose arms and trunk have grown to do the work of his spindly, wasted legs. Legs crushed by a toppling stone. He sits on a small stool, his back against the vestry wall, the parish chest to his left, his crutches to his right. His writing box on his lap. Anything else needful is spread on the floor around him, easily dragged to hand by his crutch. Among themselves the ancient women call the vestry the Parish Clerk's nest, his sty.

The ancient women stand and Widow Hazard reports on their search at Will Barrett's, names the three dead and the cause of their death, names the two living and their infection. Despite her strong words to Goodwife Brokefild, Widow Hazard does not tell the Clerk what he should do now. It is for the Clerk, not an ancient woman, to tell parish officers what is to be done. He takes notes of their report and will summon the Constable and a watchman to go to Widow Barrett's house. The information on these three plague deaths will go to the Alderman, and to the Clerk of the Parish Clerks. The cruel numbers from St Cyneswide and St Tibba joining those from other parishes in the weekly Bills of Mortality.

The two women wait quietly, grateful for the support of their red wands, while he writes slowly and clearly, focused on quill and paper. His taut stillness dominates the small room. He is not a relaxed man. He is devoted first to his plump wife and second to leading the congregation in psalm singing. Finishing his document, he takes two pay-tickets from his writing box and letters the first: 'Wid Haz iiii^d x 3' and does the same for 'Gdy Brok'.

The tickets left on his writing box, he stabs a large angry finger at the Widow. 'You. You taught those women, Viewers and Keepers, you taught them of infection and illness and death. They failed. You failed. Plague has been in that house for how many days? Now teach them again. Teach them again. Teach them the signs. Where on the body to find them. What the signs tell them. Teach them again. You are sure it is plague?'

'Yes,' they reply. Confident in what they saw.

The Clerk rummages and pulls out the latest Bill of Mortality. 'This is for 30 of May to 6 of June. No plague deaths for the 97 parishes within the Walls. None. Just 43 for those beyond. Are you sure?'

They are. 'There will be at least three within the Walls for the 6 to 13 June list,' the Widow says.

Only then he hands them their tickets. 'Wait outside, and when I have given my running boys their messages send me the Viewers and Keepers.'

They hear his shrill whistle and move as quickly as they can out of the way so as not to be bowled over by four boys dashing into the vestry. Standing outside they hear him give his messages and issue the boys with their small black rods of office. When appointed Clerk he had taken the Church Warden's advice, 'Since you can't move easily yourself, use small boys as runners for your messages. Your running boys. With some little token of office they'll gladly serve. We had messengers in the army. Fast, eager boys.'

The small black rods of office work better than any other reward. Sometimes they need to be replaced after battles between the runners, or from clashes with other boys, but that is a small price to pay – the rods cost almost nothing. And sometimes the Warden can find a copper farthing for each boy.

'We should call the Viewers and the Keepers now?' the Goodwife asks, but Widow Margaret Hazard is fixed on stopping Harry Shute, one of the running boys, with her red wand.

'Where is the Church Warden, boy?' she asks. The child raises his black rod as if to strike her wand away but thinks better of it.

'Down in his closet,' the boy shouts then weaves past and runs on his way. The Widow goes into the church, making for the stairs to the crypt. She assumes Goodwife Brokefild will follow: she does.

The heat of the day has crept even into the crypt. Seeping in through the small, barred wall openings. Pressing its way down through the stones. The first door into the crypt is unlocked – the Warden is known for his doors and locks – and Widow and Goodwife make their slow way towards Warden's closet at the far end. He comes out to meet them.

'The weather is hot, eh, eh? Some say the hottest day! Welcome to my cooler closet,' but he stands at the closet door and does not let them in. 'Cooler down here in the underworld. I can always hear the approach of Searchers, your red wands give you a third leg! Pace, pace, bomp. Pace, pace, bomp,' he laughs. 'Two ancient women of the parish coming to the Church Warden's closet.'

Frances Barrow is a genial, charitable, talking man. He has told Widow Hazard he likes her soldier's face. He was a soldier once himself but has no wounds that can be seen. He's not London-born but comes from the flat fenlands to the east. A trooper during the three civil wars and ever loyal to dead Oliver and the late Commonwealth.

'Have you heard news of the grand burial? Wednesday past? The funeral of Sir Thomas Vyner goldsmith. President of Christ's Hospital.'

'We were not told,' Goodwife Brokefild laughs. 'At least I think we were not,' she laughs again, 'but I shall ask my serving girl if there were any callers while I was out.'

'Or perhaps your footman will know,' Frances Barrow quips.

Widow Hazard does not have the quick wit to join in but can see the joke.

'Well,' says the Warden, 'well. The procession was the Lord Mayor, all the Aldermen, the Blue-coat boys from the Hospital. And, and here is something, leading before the corpse were seventy six old men to number his years. Seventy six. A few pennies for each of them I'm sure. So there could be some pay for ancient women to mark the years of his wife, his third wife Alice, when she dies. Will you do it? Oh no, you can't, red wands must shun assemblies. He was buried at St Mary Woolnoth. I didn't see the procession, only heard of it. Sir Tom was a moneyman friend of Charles the dead king, then of the Protector, and of Charles the king now,' he raises a quizzical eyebrow while listing this mix. 'Money has many friends of different stripes. That is money, and that is why you are here. Money, pay, to get some pay. Will Barrett's death. Have you your pay-tickets?'

Frances Barrow turns back into his closet and they hear the sounds of keys and metal scraping and other interesting noises. They know he must be opening his strong box but no-one has seen this happen. Few are allowed into his closet and those who've been there say there is a small wooden chest, hooks on the wall, and sometimes a writing box, but no sign of his strong box.

He comes out holding a small bag and counts out six pennies and twelve halfpennies into the Widow's hand. 'There Captain, your pay. A soldier's pay. I was never a Paymaster although I would have been a good one. Would have been a good honest one, more honest than most. I would not have made any dead pays. Dishonest Paymasters numbered dead men on their payrolls and kept their pay!'

The Goodwife has her own preferences for payment, and the Warden tells out three silver groats for her.

Coming from the church the Searchers see the anxious faces of the Viewers and Keepers. Widow Hazard knows that the Clerk will be angry because she did not immediately call them as he ordered. The Clerk will hold this against her, but it was more important to collect her pay before the Warden locked his closet, and in any event the Clerk's anger is a black storm that passes quickly.

She rasps at the Viewers and Keepers, 'You have shamed me, shamed yourselves, shamed the parish. If you cannot see signs of the sickness ask me. Call me to come and see. The Clerk will scold you and I scold you, and I will teach you again. Tomorrow.' The four women look at her sourly, sullenly, but say nothing. She dismisses them, summarily waves them towards the vestry and the waiting Clerk as if she were the Clerk herself. Goodwife Brokefild stands solidly beside her fellow Searcher, nodding.

The Widow worries, 'I did not do as I said I would. I said I would tell the Clerk what he should do for the Barrett house and I said nothing.'

'But there was no need,' Goodwife Brokefild soothes. 'You said yourself he knows what to do. And he does. There was no need for you to say more than you did.'

'And my teaching has failed.' The Widow is despondent.

Goodwife Joan Brokefild shrugs, 'Sometimes it's all honey, and then all turd. You over expect.' The Widow begrudges her a smile.

Then, with drama, Goodwife Brokefild declaims, 'The event of things is not in our power. By time, and Counsel, do the best we can, Th'event is never in the power of man.' She pauses, adds, 'You, we, we do the best we can.'

Goodwife Joan Brokefild prizes a battered book of poems bought cheap from a rag-seller hawking old paper to use for spills, for the house of office, or for whatever the buyer likes. The Goodwife's library is her bible, the poems, and a handful of penny chapbooks.

The Widow grunts rudely at the poem but listens anyway. They part with a God be w'ye, the poem's words still working slowly through the Widow's head.

William Northage the bell-man is walking the parish. His bell rings and he cries out the deaths of Will Barrett, Joseph Barrett, John Barrett.

Home, the Widow gives her daughter Sara thrupence ha'penny to go and buy a loaf of bread, a pound of cheese and a jug of small beer. Snaps at her to be quick, not linger or loiter. Sara runs, knows the times when she must immediately do as she's told. The Widow takes off most of her wearing clothes, hangs up her hat, her bodice, kicks off her pattens, but leaves her overskirt on until the child returns and the door can be bolted.

They sit to table. The child, as taught, serves her mother. Carefully pours the beer into their two cans. Spillings in the past have brought her mother's sudden hand, especially when she is brooding like this. Sara cuts the bread against her chest. Leaves the knife sticking in the cheese so her mother can take the slice she wants. Conscious of her mother's mopeish humour, the girl is cautiously silent.

The Widow is slowly soothed by food and drink and finally says, 'Talk to me.' An easy job for Sara who chatters of friends, street play, who she saw and who she expected to see but didn't, how everyone says how hot it is. Who was buying bread and cheese and beer. Who was buying meat, fish. Who was seen taking a coach. How Mr Smoote the coal-man said the thunder heard the other day was not thunder but guns from a great sea fight with the Dutchman. Or the Frenchman. And how Mr Hillcocke the broom seller said it *was* thunder.

Now quiet of mind Widow Margaret Hazard tells Sara to bring her bible and read psalm the ninety sixth. Sara knows to turn to the back where the psalms in English metre, the psalms as sung in church, are printed:

> *Sing ye with praise unto the Lord new songs with joy and mirth:*
> *Sing unto him with one accord all people on the earth.*

Sara's reading is more like singing, her voice faithfully mimicking, in much higher tones, the Parish Clerk's loud, deep, Sunday psalm leading.

Mother and daughter lie down to bed, Sara sleeping instantly. The night is still oppressively hot and Widow Hazard, not finding sleep, gets up carefully to avoid waking the child.

She takes her usual comfort by opening the shutter and looking into the smoky night. The great heat of the day has brought dry lightning that slashes the heavens. Then one great shower of rain.

> London, Bills of Mortality for 130 Parishes
> from the 30 of May to the 6 of June 1665;
> Buried, in all – 405; Plague – 43
> Parishes clear of the Plague – 123; Parishes Infected – 7

CHAPTER II

'Foul water as soon as fair will quench a fire.'

The two saints who name the parish church are not well known in London, or in most parts of the land. It is the Church Warden who knows most about St Cyneswide and St Tibba. As a man who served in Oliver's New Model Army he has no time for popes, bishops, or saints. He is a man who expresses dissenting religious views at odds with the Church of England. But he is also a man who took the Oath in the year 63 and so kept his church position. At the assembly where the Vestrymen and church officers made their oaths he shrugged, was ready to mutter with bluff, old trooper's bravado to his cronies, 'A man must eat. And drink,' but choked instead, on shame and deep humiliation. So he and they all swore before the bishop, chanting the Oath slowly, liturgically:

> *I Frances Barrow do declare that it is not lawful upon any pretence whatsoever to take Arms against the King, and that I do abhor that Traitorous Position of taking Arms against His Person or against those that are commissioned by Him, And that I will conform to the Liturgy of the Church of England as it is now by Law established, And I do declare that I do hold there lies no Obligation upon me or on any other person from the Oath commonly called The Solemn League and Covenant, to endeavour any change or alteration of Government either in Church or State, And that the same was in itself an unlawful Oath and imposed upon the Subjects of this Realm against the known Laws and Liberties of this Kingdom.*

With an Amen. But during the Oath, and after, the words that rang truest for Frances Barrow were those of Article IV of the Solemn League and Covenant of 44:

> *We shall, according to our places and callings, in this common*
> *cause, not suffer ourselves, directly or indirectly, by whatsoever*
> *combination, persuasion, or terror, to be divided or withdrawn*
> *from this blessed union and conjunction, whether to make defection*
> *to the contrary part, or to give ourselves to a detestable indifferency*
> *or neutrality in this cause; but shall, all the days of our lives,*
> *zealously and constantly continue therein against all opposition,*
> *and promote the same, according to our power, against all lets and*
> *impediments whatsoever.*

When he was not long turned eighteen Frances Barrow had so sworn Article IV. An oath which he had not kept all the days of his life but had, after twenty years, openly rejected. Defecting to the contrary part, yielding in cowardly fashion to lets and impediments. Worse, his recanting was done before a bishop; and did not Article II of the Solemn League and Covenant have him endeavouring the extirpation of popery, archbishops and bishops? It did. All he could offer himself was, 'A trooper knows when to retreat. Retreat is not surrender.' But it was his shame that carried the day and remained the victor within him.

Frances Barrow knows of the parish's two saints because he is, so to speak, a fellow countryman. Which is how he also knows why (so he says) the church front has three magnificent arches, space for three saints, but which only acknowledges two. The three are Kyneburga, Cyneswide and Tibba. Three saints, three sisters, three princesses, daughters of old King Padder, who no-one has heard of. All were ancient women, the Church Warden explains, from the cathedral city of Peterborough. The Church Warden, born in the nearby hamlet of Dosthorp, knows the city well.

This morning he comes across Widow Margaret Hazard in the square, leaning on her wand, staring at the church front. He is happy with an audience and launches into his story of the church and its saints. She's heard this before, but good stories thrive and grow with repetition.

'Their father, the king, was a heathen,' he pauses ingenuously, smiles – who could accuse him of making a sly reference to the world of 1665 and the king's rumoured popish sympathies? – 'but his three daughters were all good Christians. With their father's money, and force, they founded an abbey at Castor for monks and nuns, with Kyneburga as the first abbess. Then her sister Cyneswide was abbess, and after her Tibba. Saintly women who have their own chapels in Peterborough cathedral.' He smiles at this.

'Yes,' says the Widow, who has no knowledge of these chapels but says Yes anyway. 'Yes, but there are only two of the three sisters here. Why isn't Kyneburga with them?'

'Monks running riot. The monks left Castor to join their fellows at Peterborough Abbey and the nuns had the Castor house to themselves. But the monks missed the nuns and made a garden path from the Abbey to the nunnery. A deal of passing to and fro along that garden path. And some drinking, and more. The Abbot ran riot. Visited his gatekeeper's wife. Everyone in the city knew. Even off in Dosthorp. Some of the nuns, shamed by all this loose living, left for London to set up a new house here. Sensibly taking some treasures with them. Why not? So here you see today our splendid, fine church of St Cyneswide and St Tibba.' He flings out a theatrical arm.

The Widow is still not satisfied. 'But where *is* St Kyneburga? Why is she not here with her sisters? One arch is empty. In a way empty. Three arches on our church and only two saints.' She is annoyed by this inconsistency.

'Because,' the Warden explains with satisfaction, 'because Kyneburga has her own church, in her own country. She does not need a church in London.'

'Then why build a church here with three arches if you only have two saints?' She is offended by the untidiness of it. The waste and confusion caused.

'The nuns wanted their London church to have the look of Peterborough cathedral. To bring Peterborough with them. The good of Peterborough anyway. Smaller here of course, but the same. Peterborough has three arches. Big arches. Big saints. Three saints. Peter, Paul and Andrew.' He shrugs, 'Peterborough cathedral is much bigger. Big enough to stable a troop of horses. Two shillings a day we were paid for man and horse – *when* we were paid! You couldn't stable many horses here. In the cathedral we stabled next to the saints' chapels.' He is not looking at her but listens carefully for any response to this. Hears none.

The Widow is still thinking about his explanation of the two saints, which she finds both too simple and too complicated.

'That's all I know, and now you know all I know,' he says. 'St Tibba is the patron of falconers. Not many of them in this parish. Haven't seen a falconer here for days. The three saints share a feast day in March. Popish practices. Now you know more than everything.'

'If St Tibba is for falconers, then Kyneburga and Cyneswide, who do they patron?'

He laughs. 'Masters of foxhounds? Of ratting dogs? Of pigeons? I don't know.' He offers her tobacco and they light their pipes.

Half way through her smoke she asks him, 'How do you know this? Nuns and monks and abbots? That was not yesterday.'

'Oh,' he says airily, 'everyone in Peterborough knows that. We all know that.'

Then she asks, 'How many horses could you stable in our church here?'

'Well … about ten. Why? How many horses do you have?'

Her 'Mmm' is half snort half laugh. As they part she has one more question, 'In the cathedral, in the church, when they are stables, who cleans out the horse shit?'

'We troopers do,' he calls over his shoulder, pointing to her and himself.

Widow Margaret Hazard is waiting in the square for the Viewers. This morning she was called to the vestry to be shouted at by the Parish Clerk who believes he can make people do right, be good, do what he wants, by shouting at them.

Yesterday why did she not call the Viewers and Keepers to him when he said? Was collecting her pay more important? The Widow knows two things: that this storm will blow itself out, and that collecting her pay was more important. The storm passes. The Clerk has thought on it and decided that the Keepers do not require further instruction. Their job is, he quotes, 'to be providers and deliverers of necessaries for infected houses and to attend the persons sick and infected.' They are not Viewers. Widow Hazard replies mildly that if a sick person being attending shows signs of plague, then the Keepers need to know the signs. 'No,' says the Clerk, 'if they see signs they don't know they call for the Viewers.' He wins.

The Widow will visit houses with Viewers Anne Abowen and Widow Ursula Chaukley. Despite what the Clerk has said, Keeper Goody Susanna Parsons has determined she will come too. Widow Margaret Hazard is glad of Goody Parsons' presence. The two Viewers, in particular Anne Abowen, are not the Widow's friends, but Goody Parsons is a gentle, well-disposed matron who quarrels with no-one.

The households they visit have griping of the guts, fever, spotted fever, childbed, quinsie. None have signs of plague. Widow Hazard is not deterred. She points to groin and armpits and describes the bubo swellings that will be found there in case of plague. This causes great consternation to Emmanuel Bird, an old man with ague whose limbs she has used for her demonstration. She is then hard pressed to convince Emmanuel Bird's wife and daughters that she is not saying he has plague. Nor is she saying he will get it. Although he might. The four visitors leave the household in uproar. Anne Abowen shares a smile with Widow Chaukley. The morning lesson has turned out surprisingly well.

Widow Margaret Hazard calls a halt, fills her pipe and walks away. She wonders how the visit ended this way. Goody Parsons also walks away, but she returns to Emmanuel Bird and tries to convince him that he, his body, was but an example, a slate on which the lesson was told. He does not have the plague she reassures him. But calling him a slate unsettles him further.

Smoking and thinking, Widow Hazard leans on her red wand. Thinks that she, a Searcher, with her red wand, only comes to search the dead. The living would not like, would not want, a visit from a Searcher. So, when next she searches a corpse she will take the Viewers with her and show them – should it be the plague – the purple tokens, some as small as a flea bite, some as big as a penny; the blue-coloured blains, blisters full of filthy matter; the botch or bubo, a hard swollen lump that grows in the groin, armpits or neck, as big as a walnut or a hen's egg. Then they will know and understand. No more searches of the living. Satisfied, she walks beside the channels back to church square.

* * *

Goodwife Joan Brokefild is stirred by the great naval victory over the Dutchman and has seen the bonfires burning in celebration. She exalts that the victory is doubly welcome because, as all know, bonfires are an excellent protection against the plague. Widow Hazard can tell Sara that Mr Smoote the coal-man was right and Mr Hillcocke the broom seller wrong. It was guns, not thunder. Sara, whose ear for news is as keen as Goodwife Brokefild's, knows this already.

Sara and the parish children delight in the bonfires. Running and dancing by them, feeding them, warming hands that don't need warming in this hot June. They eagerly hope for more fires, more victories against the Dutchman.

For adults, and the children too, it is the bloody death by chain-shot of the Earl of Falmouth and one Richard Boyle (a name nobody knows) that is most talked about. How their blood, their flesh, their bones and very brains, were torn from them by the shot and flung in the face of our Admiral the Duke of York, brother of the king. And even more, the blown off head of that Boyle was dashed violently against the Duke, which is another game for the children to retell around the fires, now become the burning vessels of the Dutch navy, destroyed by our brave English fire ships. Sara, with the liberty of being out of her mother's sight, is an English fire ship throwing twigs into the flames. She manages to avoid most of the mud and muck – which, she is told, are really brains and flesh and blood – flung about by an enthusiastic John Clapshaw.

Her mother knows many old saws about fire and heavily imposes these on Sara. The one the Widow says most often is 'The burnt child fears the fire,' but there are others and Sara can chant them off in a string, in a stream:

> Fire and water are good servants but bad masters.
> Foul water as soon as fair will quench a fire.
> No smoke without fire.
> No fire without smoke.
> Out of the frying-pan into the fire.
> All the fat is in the fire.
> Fire in one hand and water in t'other.
> Water, fire, and war, quickly make room.

The other children have picked these up and join in, always starting with 'The burnt child fears the fire,' as they laugh and poke at the bonfire and dash in close to its fearfully enticing flames. They know they will not be burnt.

Sara knows another saw about fire, learned not from her mother but overheard from Nicholas Troute, the angry, moon-faced carter who was damning Constable Samuel Snow to coal-man Smoote. 'The man is a hog-high twattling fool who does not know he's a fool. "Here will be a good fire anon said the fox when he pissed on the ice!" That is Samuel Snow.' It does not make sense but she thinks the pissing fox very funny and it is a favourite with the children, who chant it vigorously.

* * *

London, Tuesday, 13 June 1665

The days following uncover no new cases of plague within the bounds of St Cyneswide and St Tibba. Yet the parish still feels its effects. People with business at the Smithfield beast markets have been warned to take the long way and now go by Duck Lane rather than risk the parish streets. So far, few parishes within the walls have felt the plague. St Cyneswide and St Tibba is known as one of the unfortunate few.

The hackney-coachmen who live in the parish – Robert Loe, John Pooly, Richard Undnay – share the dilemma of all coachmen. If they carry a passenger with the plague they must obey a city Order to lay up their coach and leave it air for six days. Few coachmen, except the very foolhardy, or those who want to trust in magic – amulets, or scraps of paper with strange writing – are tempted to take a fare who shows signs of the plague. But if by ill luck they do so, then … they have to balance life against livelihood. Goodwife Brokefild is yet to see the hackney-coaches of Robert Loe, John Pooly and Richard Undnay sitting still, laid up. So they must have been lucky, she thinks, she hopes, and have avoided infected passengers.

A running boy comes close, but not too close, and calls out to the two ancient women that he has a message from the Clerk. He stands still in place, waiting, throwing up and catching his black rod.

'Well,' Goodwife Brokefild asks, 'what is the message?'

'A building fall. A man has fallen.' Someone has fallen. Is dead.

'Where? What man, Jemmy Pooly? What place?' the Widow calls back.

Jemmy Pooly thinks. 'Bell Street,' he shouts, 'Little Bell Street. Not Little Bell Street. Near Little Bell Street. A man is dead, the Clerk says. The house, the new house that is building. He's dead. Near the resting stone for the back carriers.'

In Little Bell Street a carrier is resting his basket on the stone, watching with interest the collapsed scaffolding, the man lying under it, the efforts of a small crowd to rescue the fallen man from under the timber, the arrival of the two Searchers. The Searchers stand away, far enough away so when the front of the new building begins to slowly topple forward they are safe. The house leans out gradually, first from the top story where the painter was working – 'Run! Run!' the Widow roars, 'Run!' – then the top pulls out the ground floor with it, and the whole collapses into the street with a rush of dropping bricks and great beams and clattering floor boards and mortar dust and the smell of wet paint.

Many of the rescuers can run to safety. Some are splintered, brick-grazed and bleeding, but most are whole, just dusted, like bakers. Two, those who were working closest to the fallen painter, dragging the tumbled scaffolding from him, have caught the full force of the collapse and all three are lost beneath.

It is hard to see through the dust haze and there is a long, still pause before the rear of the building plummets down into the rubble. The two chimneys are still standing on either side. The next door neighbours stare at the tumbled chaos, the surviving chimneys, and shout and weep and call on God to save them and their houses.

Samuel Snow the Constable arrives with two watchmen, Simon Gurry and Barnard Clapshaw. His officiousness to the fore, and necessary, the Constable shouts at the neighbours to stand well back – 'Back! All back!' – organises a gang of men to move the bricks and timbers – 'Quickly! Carefully! Quickly!' – and orders the Searchers to watch the two chimneys and shout again if they see any, any movement. Any movement at all.

The straining workers yell instructions at each other, mutter abuse of the Constable, ask him if he'd like to come and help rather than giving orders, and clear enough of the collapsed building away to pull out the painter, dead, and Henry Huchenson, pewterer of this parish, dead, and Nathaniel Huett, living, but badly injured. His head and hands torn messes of blood and flesh.

The Constable calls the Searchers to view the corpses. 'Easy money,' he says earnestly. The cause of death in both cases is not in doubt. Henry Huchenson, the pewterer, his shop is close by and he was one of the first to come at a run when the painter fell. Nathaniel Huett is a knife-sharpener who'd been passing, calling his trade, 'Ha' y'any knives to grind! Grinding! Sharp-ning!' The Constable has set a watchman on his abandoned grinding barrow.

They do not know the painter. The neighbour to the right, George Lumme, tells them the painter is Ralph, but Ralph is from outside and he does not know the man's family name. No-one does. He is called Ralph, he is a painter, and now he has died in the parish of St Cyneswide and St Tibba. George Lumme is more concerned about the now almost free-standing chimney, barely clinging to his house wall.

'What are you going to do about that?' he demands of the Searchers. 'What? My house, me. My family's in peril. If that falls it will bring my house down. My house! What are you going to do?'

The Searchers are not going to do anything about it. The Goodwife is tempted to tell him that if the chimney does fall and he is killed then they will, of course, return to view his corpse. She later tells the Widow this, who agrees that Yes, this is naturally what they would do. But instead the Goodwife calls the Constable to listen to George Lumme.

Constable Snow listens impassively then tells George Lumme that the two bodies will be placed in his house until the bearers come for them.

The ancient matrons walk away and follow the channels back to the church to make their report, knowing that the Clerk will be angry because an outsider has died in his parish. 'Ralph? Who is Ralph, this painter? Why didn't you get his full name? And he dies in my parish. This … this Ralph.' It is no good. No good at all.

The Widow, who listened closely to all the talk at the collapsed building, tells the Clerk that Ralph the painter was working high on the scaffolding, that a footboard shifted under him and so he fell, that the scaffolding then fell against the building, dislodging bricks and the new windows, this all bringing the whole house down. The Widow knows that the Clerk likes full details.

The Widow adds, 'I say, we say, there were bad bricks and bad mortar. Mmm.' Goodwife Brokefield agrees, 'The mortar was powder and the bricks were no better.'

The Clerk nods, slightly appeased. 'This Ralph, dead Ralph, and poor Henry Huchenson.' He writes out the Searchers' pay-tickets. 'Find who this Ralph is for me,' he orders the Widow. 'Must be buried in his own parish.' He adds firmly, '*by* his own parish.'

The Widow rumbles a long 'Mmmm,' nodding agreement even though she doesn't understand. She has to think. What has she to do with this Ralph and finding out who he is?

The Clerk waits. When she says nothing he explains, 'We will bury him, this Ralph, here. Tonight. If it was winter we could keep his corpse in the crypt until you find his parish, his name. In this hot June we'll bury him tonight. Bind the corpse well, bury him in paupers' corner and when you find his family they can have him and I can issue the Certificate. His family will want to bury him. You're a Searcher. Search out his family. Well?'

Now the Widow understands.

The Clerk is pleased and counts out on his right hand with evident satisfaction. 'Then two things, two forms.' The Clerk always stresses the importance of forms. Forms filled out properly, completely, correctly. Signed and dated. 'One, the Coroner will sit on this Ralph so there will be the Coroner's written Warrant on his death. Two, when you give me his name and parish I can send my Certificate to the Clerk of his parish. I wonder who it is?' Philip Carter knows his fellow Clerks.

The Widow is not sure if he is talking to her or himself. 'If the Coroner does not find that he died in an accident under a collapse of bricks and beams …' she trails off.

'If he does not then you will be amazed? And lose your reputation as a Searcher?' The Clerk asks in good humour. 'I don't think you will be amazed or lose your good name.'

Goodwife Joan Brokefild, following all this closely, laughs. The Clerk smiles at them both and waves them away.

The Church Warden is nowhere to be found so they will have to collect their easy money later.

In the long summer evening three ancient women sit on the low wall that belts in the churchyard. The shadow thrown by the church tower shields them from the still hot sun and here they can smoke and rest and talk and, if they want, flap and waft underskirts to cool themselves. Their chosen place for these dusk gatherings is at paupers' corner where few ever come. By tacit agreement the congregation has accepted that if Searchers and Viewers and Keepers have to have some outdoor gathering place then this far, undesirable, corner of the churchyard is where they should gather. Their red wands rest against the wall, declaring their possession and warning others to keep away.

In recent days Goody Parsons the Keeper has joined the two Searchers for their end-of-day smoke and talk. Goodwife Brokefild always greets her and makes her welcome. Widow Margaret Hazard who does not like new things, new ways, has been cool and sometimes abrupt, but now does not mind Goody Parsons so much. The Widow knows Goody Parsons tried to mend things with Emmanuel Bird because she told the Widow of her efforts to explain. The three women agreed it was the fault of Emmanuel Bird and family – well known to be difficult, prickly, obstinate people – that the teaching visit had not gone well. Goody Parsons states that at the very least the three gathered here are all blameless. The Searchers agree.

They share tobacco, and their talk turns to the collapsed house. It was to have been the shop and dwelling of Robert Holt, glover and leatherworker. Did he try to save money by using inferior bricks and mortar? Or was it the builder's fault by trying to skimp on materials and bump up his profit? Robert Holt is a long-time member of the congregation of St Cyneswide and St Tibba. The builder Alex Norden, like his painter Ralph, is from outside. The alien builder is surely to blame.

'What parish is the builder's?' the Widow asks. Perhaps Ralph the painter belongs to the same parish.

'Frances Barrow the Warden will know,' Goody Parsons suggests eagerly. 'He knows everything that happens here, and outside.'

'Mmm,' the Widow nods to Goody Parsons. 'Mmm. Yes.'

Goodwife Joan Brokefild also nods happily, pleased with this contribution to the growing harmony among the three. 'That is good. Good.'

Widow Margaret Hazard is content with companionable silence. Not so her companions, who prefer talk.

'It looks such a fine house. It is a fine house,' Goodwife Joan Brokefild uses her pipe to point to the rectory across the square. The rectory is a handsome building and glows brick-red bright in the late sunshine. 'Full of Walter Hall's kin. His two brothers–'

'Their wives, and his uncle, and his nieces,' Goody Susanna Parsons offers.

Yet Walter Hall himself is rarely there. Except for Sunday services, and often not then. The rector of St Cyneswide and St Tibba is a gentleman, a flowing man, whose smooth unhurried walk is a constant source of fascination in the parish. It is not known how he manages to cover ground in such a liquid way – some have declared his walk to be 'beautiful.' This in grinding contrast to the way the Parish Clerk levers himself forward with great and dangerous speed on his crutches. Young John Barrett, now dead of the plague, had given great joy to the parish children with his mimicry of 'Walter Hall's walk.' Many adults had also enjoyed it, although not so openly. In his five years as incumbent the rector has seen no need to win supporters, made no effort to do so. He knows it is the duty of parishioners to support the established church, and thus their duty to support him as the church's representative.

If the congregation of St Cyneswide and St Tibba – apart from Frances Barrow, the Church Warden, who comes from outside – knows nothing of the foundation of their church or its saints, they are closely familiar with its history during the several overthrows and turmoils they have lived through.

Widow Margaret Hazard lays claim to being the most ancient of all the ancient women in the parish. This is not uncontested. Her birth took place, her mother told her over and over, 'when our English Bible was first printed.' The Widow has strong proprietorial feelings for our English Bible. As for Goodwife Joan Brokefild, she is some years younger, being born during the Great Snow, when *her* mother had despaired of the new infant in the cruel, bitter cruel cold. Travellers were lost in the deep snow and froze to death, their bodies not found for months. The frozen ground could not be sown, and there were shortages of grain, of all crops. Those who survived the cold faced starvation. A dreadful time. Goody Susanna Parsons is not as ancient as these two.

'I can't remember the name of the rector here when I was a child,' says the Widow, staring at the rectory, 'he was a small, bald man, not very loud, it was hard to hear his sermons, but I can't remember his name. Peering over the top of the pulpit. I thought he should stand on a box. Then there was John Gifford who was good enough. Each year it was the same sermons.

He did not have many and you could tell the month by the sermon. "The excellency of the Christian revelation as it removes the guilty fears of sinners," that was February – or March – and later in the year "A sad prognostic of approaching judgement, or the happy misery of good men in bad times." I can remember them. All good sermons, good Christian sermons, but heard too often. Familiarity makes the mind idle and thoughts turn to other, less worthy matters. Mmm.' She must rest and smoke after this long speech.

Goodwife Brokefild has her memories, is bursting tight with them, but waits for the Widow to stop talking and draw on her pipe. 'Gifford,' says the Goodwife quickly, 'Gifford was a refuser of the Solemn League and Covenant, a double refuser to subscribe.'

'Did he double refuse or neglect to appear?' asks Goody Parsons.

None of them are sure, but know certainly that twenty years ago 1,000, or 5,000, or 10,000 Church of England Ministers, John Gifford one of them, were expelled, or resigned, from their livings for not subscribing to the Solemn League and Covenant for the Preservation of the Reformed Religion.

'The congregation here strong for the reformed church,' says the Widow with satisfaction, 'most men in the parish subscribed. They put their names, their marks, in a book.'

'The Clerk and the Church Warden, not today's Clerk or Warden, signed and urged others to,' Goodwife Brokefild says.

'Parish Clerks always have loud voices,' Goody Parsons says, 'it is their job. Like bell-men. Strong loud voices.'

A loud voice comes from the approaching fat chicken man. He sees their red wands and gives the ancient matrons a wide berth, calling 'Fat chic-kens! Buy my fat chic-kens!'

Goody Parsons says, 'I like a fat chicken. Cut in pieces, stewed with pepper and mace and an onion. Then wine, white wine – a few pence worth of French is cheapest – and marjoram and thyme and parsley.' She is known to be a good cook and the Searchers ask her to repeat her receipt while they sit and listen and smoke.

The Widow is frugal. 'How much wine?' she asks.

'Only enough to cover the chicken,' Goody Parsons reassures her.

The Goodwife, whose mind is elsewhere, laughs, 'George Lumme's face was a black storm cloud when the Constable ordered the corpses be put in his house.'

'Why should he worry?' snorts the Widow. 'Henry Huchenson and Ralph the painter were crushed, not infected. The parish of Norden the builder, I must ask Frances Barrow.'

They tamp out their pipes and refill them. It is now a little cooler.

'If I was a man I would have subscribed,' the Widow muses.

'If above the age of 18, the law said.'

'I was above the age of 18,' the Widow points out.

'So was I, so would I,' says Goodwife Brokefild.

Goody Parsons says, 'I wasn't the age of 18 then.'

'Nor a man,' the Widow makes her deep voice even deeper, manly. This causes guffaws.

Surprised at herself, and pleased, the Widow is talkative again.

'After Gifford they put in the Scotchman, Angus McMisery he was known as. With so many old rectors gone any man in orders with the right view of religion could get a place. St Cyneswide and St Tibba got McMisery. McManus was his name. Angus McManus.' She briefly tries then quickly abandons a Scotch accent. 'Hated it "down here" he said. Too hot, too crowded. Our food was worse. Our fish tasted bad. He was a miserable man. Had three children here. One lived. His wife better than him, grateful when you spoke to her. A kind word. Gave birth easily.' She stops to inspect her pipe. Remembering more.

'He died,' the Goodwife offers, encouraging.

'Yes, he died. Kept saying he was going back to Scotland, but he died. I searched his corpse. Impostume. In sore hard pain for months but bore it well. Bravely.' She points to a grave close by the niche for the parish coffin. 'Not Scotland, he went over there, buried beside the two children, boy and girl.'

'Then,' the Goodwife cannot wait, her face bright with pleasure, 'then came in Thomas Dugdale, a Congregation man. Elected by the congregation. Elected! No more bishops, the Prayer Book gone, the parish under the congregation, the congregation the parish. Remember the Prayer Books gathered up and taken away? No more empty words read and said every Sunday. Instead full words from Minister Dugdale, speaking the Bible truth.'

'And singing the psalms,' adds Goody Susanna Parsons. 'Worshipful psalm singing.' She has a good voice. 'He always joined in the psalm singing.' She does not add that he did not sing well.

They fall silent, all knowing what comes next. The Great Ejection.

'The new king comes in.'

'The bishops come back.'

'And the Prayer Book.'

'The Prayer Book,' the Widow says. 'Thomas Dugdale refused the Oath to it. Went out with all the other good men on Great Ejection day. St Bartholomew's Day. He wasn't here then, off at some other parish, he was deprived of that parish, deprived of that and doubly deprived, first sent on his way from here in 60 when Walter Hall came in with the king. That is Minister Thomas Dugdale, ejected.'

'St Cynswide and St Tibba deprived of Minister Dugdale, and Thomas Dugdale twice deprived,' agrees Goody Susanna Parsons.

The ancient women share a fondness for Thomas Dugdale, an earnest, prophesying man who could preach for hours and lose few listeners.

'Then,' says the Goodwife, 'comes in here Walter Hall with his nose-in-the-air wife.'

'Margery.'

'Yes, Margery,' the Goodwife agrees. 'He says when courting her:

My person is divine,
My parsonage fat and fair:
Then let us join in love,
And make a loving pair

She says –
Your person is divine

Your parsonage during life;
But if the parson die,
Pray where's the parson's wife?

Goody Parsons is shocked, 'Did *he* say that? Did *she* say that?'

'No!' the Goodwife laughs, 'it's a merry verse only.'

'From your poem book?' the Widow asks.

'No, a chapbook. From a merry penny chapbook.'

'Say it again,' asks Goody Parsons and the Goodwife is happy to do so.

Off to their right they see the Parish Clerk make his way with familiar speed down the vestry steps. 'Old, says the Widow, 'him becoming an old man now.'

'Twenty years and some as Clerk,' Goodwife Brokefild says, 'came in the same year the reformed worship came in. And the Prayer Book went out.'

'Came in after Clerk Edward Mortingdale. Stopping of the stomach took Edward Mortingdale off,' says Widow Margaret Hazard, getting in before the Goodwife can offer this.

'His wasted legs got Philip Carter made Clerk,' the Goodwife laughs. 'Vestry said they could pay him a parish pension for the rest of his life or they could pay him as Clerk in Mortingdale's place and not waste pension money.'

'He wanted to be Clerk,' the Widow says. 'Before his legs healed enough for him to crutch himself about he had the bearers take him to church in their sling. Wanted to show out to Vestry his strong will, his virtue.'

Goody Parsons thinks this harsh, 'But he *is* a virtuous man, surely he is!'

'Yes, enough to be made Clerk,' says Goodwife Brokefild comfortably.

'The bearers. The bearers who carried him then. Dead now. The bearers would say, with him in their sling, "Much harder work than corpses" they'd call out when they took him of a Sunday from house to church. "Much harder. Much heavier, *and* he moves." They thought it a fine joke,' says the Widow.

'And say it again as they carried him back,' adds the Goodwife.

'He is a man who loves singing the psalms,' says Goody Susanna Parsons. Singing the psalms is that part of worship the three women most look forward to. That part of worship that brings them closest to God.

The Clerk, crossing the churchyard, sees the three sitting on the wall and unexpectedly jerks his crutches in their direction and comes to sit with them. Lowering himself down beside the Widow he pushes her red wand aside to do so.

He breathes heavily and wheezes, 'My bent broke legs, your burnt face, and here we sit.' He finds his pipe but also finds his tobacco pouch is empty. The ancient women all reach for theirs but the Widow is closest and quickest. He nods a thank'ee that for him is gracious. Pipes are filled.

'We talked of you leading us in the psalms,' Goody Parsons says brightly. She knows this will please the Clerk. It does.

He says pompously, as Parish Clerk, 'Psalms that sing his praise please God.'

'Yes, God. Of course they please God. And these are psalms, not sinful songs, and so they cheer the singers and make us more worthy and, and, psalm singing is … is … good,' says Goody Parsons, suddenly scared of saying something that the Clerk will find is not good.

But he nods and almost relaxes. 'When I was first made Clerk The Directory for the Public Worship of God was new issued. The year 45. Minister McManus pushed it into my hands and told me I must learn this reformed way of worship. I did,' he pauses to draw with satisfaction on his pipe, then intones in his booming Clerk's voice:

> *It is the duty of Christians to praise God publicly, by singing of psalms together in the congregation, and also privately in the family. In singing of psalms, the voice is to be tuneably and gravely ordered; but the chief care must be to sing with understanding, and with grace in the heart, making melody unto the Lord. That the whole congregation may join herein, every one that can read is to have a psalm book; and all others, not disabled by age or otherwise, are to be exhorted to learn to read. But for the present, where many in the*

congregation cannot read, it is convenient that the minister, or some other fit person appointed by him and the other ruling officers, do read the psalm, line by line, before the singing thereof.

He smiles in admiration at the greatness of it. 'So clear. Sing with understanding. Making melody unto the Lord. That the whole congregation may join in.'

'Yes,' says Goodwife Joan Brokefild, 'yes. And all who cannot read are to be exhorted to learn to read! I did.'

The Widow is silent. It took longer for her to learn to read. Much longer. Her reading is recent, but now she can find her way in her psalm book and bible.

'That was many years ago,' says the Clerk, his joy ebbing out. 'These times are different.'

'Different,' croaks the Widow.

But the Clerk re-finds his joy, pushes himself up on his crutches, holds up his pipe and nods at it in thanks for the tobacco, nods at them, and makes his customary farewell, 'And so home.' Now a happy man he moves off into the arriving night.

To his departing back the amused women chant quietly, sardonically – as they customarily do – an expanded version of his farewell that pays tribute to the Clerk's uxorious nature, he being a very married man: 'And so home and to bed.'

The Widow stands, wishes God be w'ye to her fellows, and shouts 'Sara, come!' The child quickly darts away from the other children who continue with their squealing game of chasings. The Widow takes Sara's hand.

London, Bills of Mortality for 130 Parishes
from the 6 of June to the 13 of June 1665
Buried, in all – 558; Plague – 112
Parishes clear of the Plague – 118; Parishes Infected – 12

CHAPTER III

London, Sunday, 18 June 1665

'The King and Rulers of the earth, conspire and all are bent,
Against the Lord and Christ his Son, which he among us sent.'

'Lord have mercy upon us. Lord have mercy upon us. Lord have mercy upon us.'

Sunday morning and the three ancient women sit on their wall outside the church, waiting and smoking.

'His song has changed,' Goodwife Joan Brokefild says, head-pointing at Walter Shute, who is standing and swaying near the church door. The parish of St Cyneswide and St Tibba has several buffleheads. Walter Shute is the loudest.

'Yes!' Goody Parsons quickly agrees. 'Sunday last it was "O ye lightning and clouds bless ye the Lord, O ye seas and floods bless ye the Lord." He has many "O ye-s" and "Blesses," Walter Shute.'

The Goodwife laughs, 'He hears Walter Hall in church and some, a few, of Walter Hall's words find their way into Walter Shute's mouth. The two Walters,' she mimics Walter Shute's excited finger pointing at the rector, at himself, back and forth, to and fro. 'Walter, Walter, Walter,' she mocks, dismissing at least one of the Walters.

'Their voices are so different,' Goody Susanna Parsons says, 'one harsh and coarse, the other fine, refined.'

'Walter Shute's tongue, his poor head, had him calling on the fowls and beasts and cattle and whales of the air. Of the air!' This odd combination is a source of mirth to Goodwife Brokefild and the rest of the parish, and is repeated often.

'The air. Walter Shute must have some understanding,' the Widow ponders, 'some. With his "Lord have mercy upon us" Walter Shute must know the plague has come, is in the air now, all around.'

The Goodwife's view is that Walter repeats, like a bird, with no understanding. The Widow murmurs 'Mmm.' Goody Parsons agrees with both.

A coach stops at the rectory. It is of interest. It arrives at this time on some – by no means all – Sunday mornings. Rector Walter Hall steps out, first to greet his kin in the rectory and then, later, to lead them in family procession to church. No-one in the family has his smooth, flowing walk. They straggle and stroll. Nor can they match his fine clothes. The parish knows (some proud, many not), that he is one of the king's chaplains and was with him during the years of exile.

Sometimes his wife Margery arrives in the coach with Walter Hall, sometimes not. Something to look out for. Today, the three ancient matrons see, it is Not. She is said to be frequently ill, of a frail disposition. It is also said that Margery Hall's preference is to worship at the Chapel Royal. Walter Hall himself prefers the Chapel Royal. His absences from St Cyneswide and St Tibba are for an excellent reason. As a divine in royal favour he often assists the Court in its worship at Whitehall. As recently as last Sunday he was at Whitehall by the Thames rather than in St Cyneswide and St Tibba near London Wall.

The Church Warden says that Walter Hall's clothes are rotten rank with incense. The Widow is not sure if the Warden is jesting, her nose is no good with smells. When she mentions this uncertainty out loud Goody Parsons reassures her that the rector's vestments have a most beautiful smell. Whatever might happen in the Chapel Royal at Whitehall Palace – and those whose sympathies persist with the reformed church have heard stories of popish practices – incense is unknown in the church of St Cyneswide and St Tibba.

The reform faction has wondered why, if Walter Hall is in the king's favour, was he settled in St Cyneswide and St Tibba? The Church Warden, as usual, has answers. 'Because the parish endowment is large, and the rectory is a roomy warren for all his kin. And Whitehall is not so far away.'

'Again, when the wicked man turneth away from his wickedness that he hath committed, and doeth that which is lawful and right, he shall save his soul alive.'

In celebrating divine service Walter Hall prefers, in his bible readings and prayers, brevity, ease, and speed. To commence he is fond of Ezekiel Chapter 18, Verse 27. It is the first option listed in the Book of Common Prayer; it is brief; and it is fitting – before him in church he sees many wicked men and much wickedness. In particular those boys, even men, who he has heard use the horrid insult 'Porridge' for the very Book of Common Prayer. Possibly Robin Kerton, and certainly his son James. Two weeks ago he had caught the boy at it and beaten him. The monstrous child claiming, 'Borage, sir, borage. I was just saying to Daniel Stiles my grandmother told me to forage for borage. Good against the melancholy sir. The old saying sir – "Have you no courage? Revive your soul with borage" – gives courage. Borage, not porridge. No.' Walter Hall did not believe him and beat him again.

The Parish Clerk, propped up against his desk, loudly Amens at the end of prayers, leading the people in these and the other responses. He is equally loud in the Lord's Prayer, and his responses throughout the service ring forth. The people are ragged, often slack, in taking their part. Although more enthusiasm is sometimes heard in the reply to Walter Hall's 'O Lord, open thou our lips.' A few of the parish boys, with sidewards smiles, daring each other, vary this part of the liturgy from time to time with, 'And our mouth shall spew forth thy praise.' This gives them unholy delight, but they are cunning enough not to do it every time. The silliest child, who once thought it a good joke to imitate spewing, received sufficient clouts and cuffs and blows from the Clerk after the service to discourage others from following his example. The boy, Christopher Northage, was grateful the Parish Clerk cannot kick. If he could have kicked he certainly would have kicked.

Philip Carter needs the boys, at least the biggest of them, to do for him what a Parish Clerk has to do, bodily reverence, but which he cannot because of his crushed legs and his crutches. The spoken responses the Clerk does vigorously, but he cannot, by example, so direct the people when to stand, when to kneel. Even his bowing at the venerable name of Jesus is more clumsy, more makeshift, than reverential. So a tall lad – he chose the tallest – is at his side to fall and rise and nod and bob as required for the worship of God according to the Church of England's Book of Common Prayer. Tall Thomas Snow does this well. 'The lad does a good job stirring the porridge,' Robin Kerton chortles to his mates.

'Here beginneth,' says Walter Hall, 'the reading of Verses the first to the twenty-fifth, of Chapter 10, of the First Book of Kings.' This is a reading that gives him great satisfaction. His voice is round and rich and warm with the splendours of the attendance of the Queen of Sheba upon King Solomon. His voice slows down in the measured unveiling of treasures.

'She came to Jerusalem with a very great train, with camels that bare spices, and very much gold, and precious stones ... And she gave the king an hundred and twenty talents of gold, and of spices very great store, and precious stones ... And the navy that brought gold from Ophir, brought in from Ophir great plenty of almug trees, and precious stones. And the king made of the almug tree harps also and psalteries for singers ...And he made three hundred shields of beaten gold ... a great throne of ivory, overlaid with the best gold ... all the king's drinking vessels were of gold ... the navy bringing gold, and silver, ivory, and apes, and peacocks ...'

The congregation, too, relish the sumptuousness, their faces soft with imaginings. Images of glowing gold, of silver, of ivory thrones, of apes. They have seen a dancing ape led on a string, and know of peacocks. They have spices but their own stores are small. The almug tree is a mystery.

The Searchers and Viewers and Keepers sit separate in a pew in the side aisle, Sara beside her mother – a rare concession for her. Sit by what was once, the Church Warden has told them, St Tibba's chapel. As the Queen showers the King with great gifts the ancient women exchange small smiles of shared pleasure. This is Walter Hall at his best. And the luxury he is laying out before them is legitimate, biblical, not popish.

Before the first psalm is sung Walter Hall turns to leave. The congregation see his pursed lips as suggesting distaste for what is to come. He has made it clear the singing is nothing to do with him. He leaves to refresh himself, to recover his breath after the fatigue of reading the lesson.

Philip Carter shunts himself around to face the congregation, his back to the departing priest. Walter Hall is gone and the glorious time of singing is now upon the Clerk, upon them all. The congregation – children, women, men – worship God in their way, with no need of Solomon's harps or psalteries. Or of Walter Hall. They have the old way of singing.

The Clerk's voice bellows, 'Let us sing to the praise and glory of God psalm the ninety first.' He gives the tune, St Mary's. Then with tuning pipe he sets the pitch, and the congregation, in a great and boisterous 'Aaaahing,' do what they can to match their voices to it.

According to long custom, and for the benefit of those who cannot read or whose fecklessness has meant they have no book in hand, the Clerk reads the first line of the psalm from his Sternhold and Hopkins: The Whole Book of Psalms Collected into English Metre. He knows the psalm by rote, but holds up his book as an example for the congregation to follow. As taught and encouraged by his fellow Clerks in the Company of Parish Clerks, he reads the first line tunably, in a singing tone, after the manner of chanting: 'He that within the secret place, of God most high doth dwell.'

The Church of St Cyneswide and St Tibba is filled with great sound as the congregation sing the line slowly, very slowly. To keep the due quantity of time from bar to bar the Clerk makes an even up down motion of his right hand: the count is one, two, with hand up, three, four with it down. Many in the congregation do the same. Hands move slowly up and down in solemn, satisfying, clockwork-mechanical unison: a great, gratified, machine of sacred song.

Then the Clerk moves to the second line: 'In shadow of the mighti'st grace, at rest shall keep him well.'

For some of the verses the Church Warden stands with the ancient women – the kind friends, as he calls them, of the ailing, the dying, and the dead – his good voice and the good voices of Viewer Anne Abowen and

Searcher Goodwife Brokefild are bold enough to offer slight harmonies. The Widow's voice rumbles on, young Sara pipes.

Steadily, line by line, each laid out in turn by the Clerk, the congregation with stately pace sing their loud slow way through the psalm's sixteen verses. The ninety first psalm suits the times. 'He shall defend thee from the snare, the which the hunter laid: And from the deadly plague & care, whereof thou art afraid.'

After many long-held crotchets and minims, they end in cheery optimism to confound the deadly plague. 'With length of years and days of wealth, I will fulfil his time: The goodness of my saving health, I will declare to him.'

Glad with their songful worship, sweating from the heat of the day, and hoarse from singing, the congregation settles to wait for the return of Walter Hall, now rested, refreshed and finely vested, for his sermon. Which usually disappoints. He cannot live up to his first efforts of five years before, when, new to the parish, he dazzled with his beautiful voice. One outstanding sermon is still spoken of, where he laid out before the congregation what awaits the godly in the world to come after this.

In late summer 1660 Walter Hall still carried with him warm impressions of the luxury seen at the courts of Europe during the king's exile. The comforting embrace of these places of refuge so coloured his sermon that the parishioners of St Cyneswide and St Tibba caught a glimpse of that softness, richness, effortless ease, that would be the lot of the godly in the next world. They felt, while he spoke, a skin-warming shiver of eternal happiness. They saw and smelt and tasted the milk and honey, the great loaves of white bread, the abundant table, the settles with soft cushions. The restful beds. They shared a wondrous feeling of satiation, of never being in want.

Today's sermon is a poor effort, on the duty of all to imitate the lives and practices of Christ and the saints departed. Walter Hall's examples of those who have done so dwell at length upon the nobility, upon bishops, and many in the congregation are unmoved. There is a rustle and adjustment of bodies in relief when he finishes and again leaves the church.

There is one more psalm. Once again St Cyneswide and St Tibba belongs to its congregation, and one of them is presiding, the Parish Clerk in his surplice. At these times the congregation is united, safely at home in its sacred building. Even those who accept the return of bishops and the Book of Common Prayer are joined in this. However the service is conducted, whether by the Directory of the reformers or the Prayer Book of the Church of England, the slow sung psalms have always belonged only to the people. All of them.

Philip Carter declares, 'Let us sing to the praise and glory of God psalm the one hundred and seventh. The fourth part.'

'Was that one hundred and eleven?' Simon Gurry calls out. The congregation chortles, nudge each other. If it isn't Simon Gurry then it's Nicholas Troute who doesn't hear, has to check.

The Clerk, more amused than exasperated, flaps his hand against his ear and shouts, 'One Hundred and Seven, Simon Gurry. One Hundred and Seven, Part the fourth.' Simon, unconcerned, waves his hand in thanks. For many years a coppersmith, Simon Gurry's strong right arm has beaten most of the hearing out of both his ears.

The Clerk has chosen this psalm for the great heat they are enduring, and 'the many plagues that compass them about.'

> *The wilderness he often makes, with waters to abound:*
> *And water-springs he often turns, to dry and parched ground.*
> *A fruitful land with pleasures deck'd, full barren doth he make:*
> *When on their sins that dwell therein, he doth full veng'ance take.*

The psalm sung, the congregation wait patiently, talking, enjoying their enforced leisure, until Walter Hall returns and the tight reins of the Book of Common Prayer steer their worship through to its end.

The service done, slender, elegant Walter Hall flows through his church to the vestry, taking with him brewer Gilbert Swaile. Philip Carter follows them, and his message boys, with arms full of gathered prayer books, follow him. Remembered pleasure filling his precise, gentry voice, Walter Hall rejoices to the brewer about the beauties of the Chapel Royal.

'The organ ringing out, sonorous, magnificent. The singing men in surplices. Oh, very fine music. Very fine. A brave anthem sung. His Majesty was well pleased. And viols playing a symphony between every verse. Every verse. The magnificence – the word, the very word – the magnificence of this elevated worship. His Majesty shows the way. Such a privilege. The Chapel Royal. So magnificent. Art displaying its glories throughout. Art in the painted decorations, art in the magnificent music. All of the highest taste,' Walter Hall smiles with genuine pleasure at the brewer, pauses, then adds sadly, 'A pity, a great pity, the heady zeal of misguided and peevish sectaries who decry this worship, this music, as popish and anti-Christian.' He shakes his head in sorrow, but happier thoughts soon prevail.

'And the sermon,' Walter Hall laughs lightly and gives the brewer an askew, quizzical, smile. 'The sermon was upon the words "He that drinketh this water shall never thirst." A most excellent sermon made by Bishop Hacket. But one that might not appeal to brewers.' Another light laugh.

'No, no,' laughs Gilbert Swaile in turn. Now, happily, on more familiar ground. 'A brewer lives by thirst, and not for water. Ha!' He is flattered by the minister's attention but it is unusual. Walter Hall never lingers after a service. However news of the Court is always of interest to a rising man, and Gilbert Swaile is a rising man. Perhaps he is being considered for some office?

Walter Hall has his back to Philip Carter but knows he is still there, in the vestry. The Clerk is clattering around on his crutches, busily engaged, directing the boys who are stacking prayer books into the chest, counting off the books.

The rector slightly lowers his voice, only slightly. 'Good music is a particular concern of His Majesty. A concern I, we, I am sure, all share. There is much more to be done. That *we* can do,' he says with significance and emphasis to Gilbert Swaile, who knows something important is being put to him, but has no idea what.

'There is a most amusing epigram, most amusing, by my Lord Rochester which is very *on point*. Amusing.

Sternhold and Hopkins had great qualms
When they translated David's Psalms
To make the heart more glad;
But had it been poor David's fate
To hear thee sing, and them translate,
By God! 'twould have made him mad.

'Made extempore,' he confides to the brewer, lowering his voice to little more than a whisper, 'to, and about, a singing Clerk. Of course.'

Shed of his vestments, Walter Hall escorts Gilbert Swaile out of the vestry, still talking. The Clerk now left behind and out of earshot.

The Clerk steadies himself against the wall, spits out in fury, 'Fuck Lord Rochester! My Lord Rochester. Fuck him and fuck the Chapel Royal!' This causes the messenger boys unbearable delight, they look at each other with great smiles of wonder. The Church Warden hears the Clerk and comes quickly into the vestry, shooing the boys out. They are saying over and over, unable to stop, 'Fuck my Lord Rochester! Fuck my Lord Rochester! Fuck my Lord Rochester!'

The Warden clouts and cuffs them with savage back-handers. 'Stop. Now,' he orders in his trooper's voice, and they do, for the moment. The Clerk, brought back to himself, stops too.

'No foul words in church,' the Warden says to him cheerfully, 'come out and smoke a pipe.'

In the churchyard they find a familiar place, old pipe ash underfoot. No words during the soothing process of filling pipes, lighting, taking in the smoke and seeing it float out.

The Warden thinks it worth a try to distract the Clerk, says, 'I saw the boys putting the porridge book in the pot. Walter Hall beat James Kerton for saying porridge. The boy said,' the Warden laughs, 'it was borage he said, not porridge.'

The Clerk does not want to be distracted, says bitterly, but a little quieter, 'The Chapel Royal. Music. Cathedral music is what they have at the Chapel Royal, cathedral music. Abominable. Cathedrals, they sing anything. Unlawful litanies and creeds, and prose not framed in metre fit for singing. The congregation don't sing at all. They do not! A cathedral congregation neither sings nor understands what is sung. Chapel Royal is all battologizing. The singing men battologize, quaver over a word. And they do not all sing together! First one sings an anthem, then half the choir – choirs! – then the other half sings, tossing the word of God about like a tennis ball. Then all yelling together, making a confused noise. Most unlawful.'

'Cathedrals,' the Warden has his own strong views on cathedrals. 'Good big barns to stable horses. Not fit for much else. We used them for armouries, warehouses – large spaces to keep stores.'

'Not fit for worship, cathedrals, Chapel Royals,' the Clerk has not finished. 'Not fit for congregations. My Lord Rochester. Fit for him. Fuck Lord Rochester! Chapel Royal and organs. Fuck them. We don't have organs. Don't need them don't want them. The right thing was done by organs. All of them destroyed. Now they're creeping and wheezing back.'

'We sang psalms,' the Warden reminisces, 'waiting in the wet fields before Marston Moor fight.

> *The King and Rulers of the earth, conspire and all are bent,*
> *Against the Lord and Christ his Son, which he among us sent.*

The Clerk joins in:

> *Shall we be bound to them, say they? Let all their bonds be broke:*
> *And of their doctrine and their law let us reject the yoke.*

When they are done the Clerk says, 'The second psalm. Easy enough to find in the book.'

'Simple troopers. We need such things to be as easy as they can. And we sang the twenty seventh. Not so many pages away from the second.

> *Though they in camp against me lie, my heart is not afraid;*
> *In battle strong if they will try, I trust in God for aid.*

'In the year 44, rain pissing down. Then Oliver leads us off, the Eastern Association, down the hill in brave order. We do well until Rupert cuts through us. We cut back at him.' The Warden stops himself and laughs, elbows the Clerk, 'You've heard all this before. Oliver said "an absolute victory obtained by the Lord's blessing upon the godly party principally." And here I am, still, one of the godly party. Principally.' The Warden pauses for some time, adds, 'Battologizing – not a word I hear said every day.'

The Clerk grunts, says, 'Repeat repeat repeat, again and again and again, over and over and over. Battologizing. A word of scorn, heard at our Parish Clerks' meetings. When *we* sing we do *not* battologize. And we scorn those cathedral choirs that do.' He draws deeply on his pipe. 'Good meetings, good singing, every Tuesday without fail. At full strength 130 good voices. All the Parish Clerks. Of course we never are at full strength.'

The two linger in silent clay-pipe comfort. The Warden with fair thin hair, a round flat face. His mother called his face a smiling pie. The Clerk with black coarse hair, hairy arms, hairy everywhere.

The Clerk smokes away his anger, his breathing settles. He armpits his crutches, nods a sort of thanks to the Warden, and levers his way back to the vestry. The Warden sits, lingering back in the grand, bright, days of hope of the Eastern Association. Oliver called them his 'lovely company.'

He sees Widow Margaret Hazard and calls her over to smoke a pipe. 'Our Clerk was put out. Mightily put out. By our rector.' They can see Walter Hall and Gilbert Swaile talking by the rectory. 'But I have something for you that will bring Philip Carter some cheer.'

The Widow, busy with her pipe, wonders what this could be, murmurs, 'Mmm?'

'The dead painter Ralph. Ralph Eackles of the parish of St Martin Vintry. South of here, down by the river. Two brothers and a sister still living, William Eackles and James Eackles and Mary Watkins. Philip Carter can make out his Certificate and send the corpse off to St Martin Vintry. The vintners church. So, good wine at the funeral feast for Ralph Eackles.' He smacks his lips.

While Widow Hazard is thinking this through with help from her pipe, the Warden adds, 'Don't tell the Clerk you had this from me.'

'Why don't you tell him?' She has been pondering on this.

'He asked you. Now you know and you can tell him.'

'He'll ask how I found it.'

'Will he? You're a Searcher, you search. That's why he asked you to search Ralph the painter. You search. You've found people. Mothers who left their babes in the streets. And if he does ask you how, you can say you were lucky. By luck you were told what you were looking for. True. He won't think it luck because you're a good Searcher.' He waves his pipe. There's no more to say.

The Widow thinks there is more to say. 'Mmm. Ralph Eackles, with brothers William and James, and sister Mary–'

'Watkins.'

'Watkins, all of St Martin Vintry.'

'Thankee Frances Barrow. Thank you.'

His pipe waves away her thanks. 'Wait a day or two before you tell the Clerk.'

'Why?'

'Why? He'll think it too easy if you give him a quick answer. Wait a day or so and show that it took some time, was hard work.'

'It didn't and it wasn't. There is his family ... brothers and his sister. A day or two?'

'Then tell him when you think best. Now or later. For me, I'd wait.'

Confused, she manages an 'Mmm.'

The Warden, not at all put out, smiles and again waves his pipe, now empty, and turns back into the church.

Walter Hall and Gilbert Swaile stand talking outside the rectory, the minister speaking with enthusiasm of music and of organs.

'These sectaries who replaced, still replace, the fine old hymns with songs of their own alterings and composings. Sternhold and Hopkins remade the sacred psalms into common songs. Common songs unspeakably crude. Sacred poems meanly expressed. They took the psalms, sacred words from our English bible, and forced them, twisted them, beat them into rough shape to fit bad music. And these *psalms* are sung by companies of rude people. Cobblers and their wives and their kitchen maids and all. Low people who have as much skill in singing as an ass has in plucking a harp. Barren dull poesy, but the people will have no other. My Lord Rochester has the right of it.'

The brewer, like all in the congregation of St Cyneswide and St Tibba, like all parish congregations, knows only the Sternhold and Hopkins psalms, readily found bound at the back of his bible. Like all he cherishes them as familiar, comforting monuments of religious life. The essence of Sunday worship. He is shocked by Walter Hall's irreverent criticism of the sacred songs.

Gilbert Swaile knows that the king is back, the Court is back, the Book of Common Prayer is back, and that the Church of England and its ministers – like Walter Hall – are back. Yet for most of his adult life he has worshipped according to the Directory for the Publique Worship of God, not according to the rituals and litanies of the Book of Common Prayer. And he has sung, with devotion and uplifting pleasure, from *The Whole Book of Psalms collected into English Metre by Thomas Sternhold, John Hopkins, and others.*

A man confident of his own opinion, Gilbert Swaile says disapprovingly, 'Lord Rochester. Not a very Christian gentleman. Not at all.' Thinking Rochester a scandalous whoremaster, a wicked man whose many sins are public, while Gilbert Swaile's own carnal transgressions are private.

The Vicar smiles a small smile, shakes out his sleeves and their flounces, 'Amusing nonetheless.' Remembering he is courting the brewer's support, then adds in the sober tones of a divine, 'Certainly. Rochester, his Lordship, is doubtless a good poet, but regrettably a man of reprehensible character and actions. Let us talk more of organs soon. A mighty, noble, sonorous organ. St Cyneswide and St Tibba sorely needs one.'

Gilbert Swaile is not listening to Walter Hall's organ talk but thinks of the scandalous court, the scandalous king, the scandalous whoremasters – Rochester only one of them. The brewer has a very clear image – one he cannot wipe from mind – of Sir Charles Sedley, in open light of day, up on the balcony of *Oxford Kates*, Bow Street, showing his arse, acting all the postures of lust and buggery. Worse, abusing scripture with a mocking, mountebank sermon. Then, like some charlatan street seller, offering the watching jeering cheering crowd a powder that, he said, 'will make all the cunts in London run after you.' Sedley's very word. Cunts.

Walter Hall, unaware that it is not church organs but wicked bodies that are preoccupying Gilbert Swaile, vigorously promotes his subject. 'The glory, the magnificence of the diapason – only the organ, running through all the compass of the notes. Only the organ!'

Sedley, further delighting and outraging his audience, then washed his cock in a glass of wine and drank it off, toasting the king's health as he did so.

Yet what lingers most for Gilbert Swaile, brewer, what he thinks about most, is the powder. Gilbert Swaile knows it is a falsehood. A coarse, stupid jest. There is no such thing. But?

* * *

One of the older children, Nell Girling, is leading a large band of young ones in a game. She stands in front of them and lines out a favourite rhyme. 'Mary, Mary.' They all sing 'Mary, Mary.'

Nell stops them with raised hands, and continues with her lining out, 'Quite kertrary.' And so, line by line, through, 'How does your garden grow – with silver bells an cockle shells – an pretty maids all in a row.' With the last line she sets all the girls in a row – it is mostly girls but there are a few very small boys present, in the charge of older sisters. There is a move by two girls, Dorothy Damport and Annis Richbell, to expel the small boys, Michael Clapshaw and Sam Stiles, because the lads are not maids. The little boys cry, and small Sam Stiles shrieks 'Mamma mamma!' Then everyone is immediately allowed to be a pretty maid for fear angry mothers will come with their heavy hands. 'Shut up cry-baby Sam,' Dorothy says and with ill grace pushes him into place to join the others. He stops crying. All the pretty maids parade, smiling graciously.

Sara Potts follows all this closely. She is ever interested in mothers and children and what mothers are like. She knows – has been told frequently

– that her own mother is not her own mother. Not like other children's mothers. But her mother is her own mother. If there is a difference between her mother and other mothers Sara can't see it. Sara greatly fears and loves her mother. The same way the other children fear and love their mothers.

CHAPTER IV

'Music the medicine is for discontent,
Heart's joy, ear's food, man's honest merry merriment,
Man's honest merry merriment.'

'My rope of onions! White St Thomas onions!' The seller walks slowly through the square, crying to her right, to her left. 'My rope of onions! White St Thomas onions! My rope of onions!'

Widow Margaret Hazard lingers in the churchyard, her mind working on Ralph Eackles' name, and his parish, and the names of his brothers and sister. Now she knows these names she cannot keep them to herself for days. Not for two days, not even for one. When – she tells herself – there is a death to be searched Searchers are promptly called and by their Oath they report their search without delay. She cannot change this and does not want to. Why should she? To betwattle the Clerk? To please the Warden?

The onion seller's cry distracts the Widow, calls to mind a rhyme from her young girl days:

Good St Thomas, do me right,
And see my true love come tonight,
That I may see him in the face,
And him in my kind arms embrace.

She remembers wrapping a St Thomas onion in a piece of her linen and putting it under her pillow as girls do, even girls with burnt, twisted faces, so she could dream of her true love. She shakes her head at the silliness of girls, of young women. Frances Barrow made no mention of a wife and children but Ralph Eackles might have been a married man.

True love. Marriage. The Widow wants to talk to Goodwife Brokefild. Not to ask what she should do about Ralph Eackles, rather to tell her what she is going to do about Ralph Eackles. But the Goodwife has gone home and will not have anyone, including the Widow, call on her there. The Widow also wants to ask the Goodwife if she ever laid her head on a white St Thomas onion to dream of her true love. But the wedded state has not been kind to the Goodwife, who often carries the smell of St John's wort balsam on the fresh bruises that overlay older ones.

Another street noise breaks in: a band of children circle dancing and singing 'London Bridge is broken down.' Sara and the others shriek as the circle breaks and two of the dancers face each other, joining outstretched arms for the rest to pass beneath. When their arms descend and some squirming child is captured under the broken Bridge, high yelps of joy fill the square.

Despite her odd 'mother,' Sara is in good standing with the parish children. She is among the older ones, and her strange mother is a person of fear and fascination. They say that her mother – her non-mother mother with the dreadful face – can still see with her blinded left eye. See what? Things others can't. Things folk don't want to be seen. And there is also her ominous red wand. An object of awe. Has Sara ever touched it? Held it? Has she? She has learnt from her mother the power of silence.

'Stay Gypsy stay!' the bell-man growls. His lurcher is crouched, ready to savage the children's circle game. A swift boot up the arse makes Gypsy stay. The dog has learned not to growl back. For William Northage summer is the easiest, the best, season. Short nights, mostly warm nights, as he walks the parish of St Cyneswide and St Tibba, crying the hour, watching for fires. This summer of the year 65 is different, he says to Robert Loe. The bell-man's son Christopher works in the livery stables where Robert Loe hires his horses.

'The infection,' the bell-man, who has a clear role in these evil times, doesn't lower his voice, doesn't know how to lower his voice, 'the plague. More dead and dying. More corpses to lead with bell to burial, more names to cry to the parish. More work, more walking, more crying.' He is not unhappy or put out by this. It is his job.

'More work for you,' Robert Loe, the hackney-coach driver is unhappy, spits, 'less for me. People fleeing the city. Passengers afraid of who might have been in my coach before them. Of course if I see someone with the signs I don't stop for him. Whip up and I'm off. Gone quick. But that's another fare lost. Sometimes you can't see the signs. They cover up. And *if* you carry an infected man and *if* they know you have – if the Mayor's men know – then that's it, your coach's laid up for six – six – days. No fares, no money for six days.'

'Some are starting to leave even from here. Hear talk of people going. Starting to see the loaded carts leaving,' the bell-man sees many things.

'Me and my coach are all over the town. I see the carts. Carts! Slow, get in the way. Driven by fools. Carts on the road. And people flying by boat, up river and down.'

The bell-man nods, repeats, 'Some are starting to leave, even from here.'

'Only those who've got somewhere to go,' Robert Loe snorts. 'Have you got somewhere to go? I don't. Who does? I'm here until my coach is laid up for six days and then I starve. You,' he says, half envious, half joking – who'd be a bell-man? – '*you* get more and more work in dying times.'

William Northage nods his commiseration, and his satisfaction, 'Evil times, these,' he says with pity for his friend, but glad he's a bell-man and not a hackney-coach driver. Later William Northage will tell his wife and son of Robert Loe's plight, and how bell-men are better off than hackney-coach drivers. Young Christopher Northage doesn't believe this – working with horses is better than tramping the streets shouting and swinging a bell – but he has learnt there is no point in having this argument, again, with his father.

Father and son also disagree on the fineness of a verse about a bell-man that William Northage has heard from Goodwife Joan Brokefild. William Northage is convinced that the worth of the verse should be obvious, even to his son, but he can only remember scraps when he tries to quote it, never does it full justice. There is something about fires, and a goblin, but at least he keeps two lines in full, and he is always ready to say them:

> *Past one o'clock, and almost two,*
> *My Masters all, Good day to you!*

Walking the night streets he thinks, again, he must ask the Goodwife to say the whole verse, slowly, so he can get it all. Each time he asks she doesn't seem to mind. He has heard of fellow bell-men who themselves can turn a handsome verse, skilled in finding rhymes for 'clock' and 'sun' and 'night.' William Northage finds this hard but trusts he *will* learn the full verse from the Goodwife, and hold it firmly in mind.

Failing to find a fitting word to rhyme with 'Four,' the bell-man resigns himself to simply calling the hour, then thinks that 'poor' might work:

> *Past three o'clock and now 'tis four,*
> *Good day to you all, rich and poor!*

Pleased, he repeats it until the half hour comes. Pleased.

The Widow, awakening to the loud four and poor verse, leaves the bed. She sleeps on the outside, Sara against the wall, and the child sleeps on. She uses the chamber-pot then unshutters the window and empties the pot. At table with a heel of bread and some of last night's beer, she breaks her fast. In the new daylight she reads her bible, the book falling open at the familiar pages of Proverbs.

Widow Margaret Hazard yearns for what the Book offers, what Proverbs offers: wisdom and instruction, to perceive the words of understanding. To receive the instruction of wisdom, justice, and judgement, and equity. She knows she, and many like her, are numbered among the simple and looks to the Book to give her subtlety. Thomas Dugdale had helped her, and others, to understand the words, to receive instruction. Thomas Dugdale spoke of equity, and while he was speaking she had a clear and exhilarating understanding of it. She had the subtlety. But later, when she tried to recall that understanding, her subtlety failed and she needed him to explain again.

Early morning and she is smoking by the churchyard wall when the

Clerk arrives at the vestry. He unlocks and gestures her in.

He's in a good humour, says, 'A Day of Thanksgiving tomorrow for the victory over the Dutch. Some good victory psalms.' Leaning against his wall he leafs through Sternhold and Hopkins, 'The ninth is very fitting,' and he sings forcefully:

> *For that my foes are driven back, and turned unto flight:*
> *They fall down flat, and are destroy'd by thy great pow'r and might.*

They sing on until he breaks in, 'Now the last –
Lord, strike such terror, fear and dread, into the hearts of them:

> *That they may know assuredly, they be but mortal men!*

Clerk and Widow are pleased with the psalm, and themselves. He even smiles at her, says very loudly, 'The Order of Service, contrived and printed for the Thanksgiving, appointed to be used in and about London on Tuesday the twentieth of June. Fresh printed,' he waves a booklet of some thirty pages. 'As always, the Scripture be read with a loud voice.'

She wonders briefly if she should smile back, but says, 'Ralph the painter is Ralph Eackles of St Martin Vintry. His brothers William and James, his sister Mary Watkins.'

The Clerk's face lights up even more. When the great stone crushed his legs it also splintered him into sharp shards of frustration, of anger. But his temper has – mostly – been soothed and salved by a warm marriage. 'Good!' he says, 'Good. Eackles. St Martin Vintry. William Orrell. The Clerk there is William Orrell.' He thumbs through his Form Box. She waits while he, with concentration, fills out the Certificate for the Removal of a Corpse to be Buried in another Parish:

> *These are to Certifie, That Ralph Eackles Died of Crushed under*
> *Fall of Bricks & Timber as our Searchers report; you may therefore*
> *interr the Corps at your Discretion. Witness my Hand this*
> *nineteenth day of June 1665.*
> *Philip Carter* CLERK

He writes his name, applies the parish seal, leans back, and his face settles, 'More deaths to be searched. Reports of deaths,' and counts on his fingers, 'Robert Sedgwicke, John Sly, Francis Woodhouse, Henry Gipps, Thomas Dorbridge, Frances Aspiner, John Shipley. And the Widow Barrett. No-one answered when the Keepers came to the Widow. The watchman has knocked and still no-one.' He repeats the names again for her then sends a running boy to fetch Goodwife Joan Brokefild.

'The hundred and eighth, the other psalm for the Thanksgiving,' he tells her while she waits for the Goodwife. Together they sing, and the Goodwife arrives in time to join in an emphatic roaring of the last verse:

Through God we shall do valiant acts and worthy of renown;
He shall subdue our enemies, yea, he shall tread them down.

The Clerk will have his psalms loud. He calls a repeat, then dismisses them with a jerk of his head and the command, 'Do valiant acts.' They do not know if this is said in earnest.

'Is searching a corpse a valiant act?' the Goodwife wonders as they pause in the churchyard to gather their thoughts. The Keepers and Viewers are arriving to see the Clerk, slow moving Widow Ursula Chaukley lagging behind, pausing at the wall to take breath. They greet Goodwife Joan Brokefild and ignore Widow Margaret Hazard, who does not notice.

'Done it for long enough not to think so. I never thought so. But many do. Think it a valiant act I mean,' the Widow replies. She then recites the names they have to search, adding. 'Widow Barrett and child first.' The Goodwife agrees, though both know there are others on the list who are closer.

'Mmm,' this Mmm has a dubious tone. The Widow stops by the churchyard wall. 'John Sly. His house is close by Thomas Dorbridge. So swap John Sly around with Frances Aspiner. We will search in turn Widow Barrett, Robert Sedgwicke, Frances Aspiner, Francis Woodhouse, Henry Gipps, Thomas Dorbridge, John Sly, John Shipley.'

As they walk the Widow tells how the bell-man's repeated call of his 'four' and 'poor' rhyme stuck in her head until psalm singing with the

Clerk drove it out. The Goodwife laughs, 'Yes! So loud and so often, over and over!

> *Past three o'clock and now 'tis four,*
> *Good day to you all, rich and poor!*

Goodwife Brokefild cannot share such jokes, share anything, with Isaac Brokefild, but she can with Widow Margaret Hazard. She smiles affectionately at the Widow, who replies with a half grin and, 'Mmm. Rich and poor.'

There are few people in the streets and those that are give the ancient women and their red wands a wide berth. The stagnant channels the ancient matrons follow have an evil stench, tempered at intervals by the unobjectionable pong of fresh horse droppings.

Watchman Barnard Clapshaw is not to be seen but his son John is across the street from the Barrett house and half calls an uneasy greeting to the women, showing that he's the Clapshaw on watch at the moment. The Goodwife nods an acknowledgement, the Widow doesn't.

The carefully lettered 'Lord have mercy upon us' on the door greets them. Inside, they immediately see, and smell, and hear, that death now has possession of the whole family, and must have taken Widow Barrett and her daughter some time ago. Rats patter away. Their rat stink mingling with that of the corpses. The persistent loud buzz of flies. The Searchers should have been called yesterday. The flies are reluctant to be brushed away. Swollen, discoloured buboes, other lumps and lesions, declare that Widow Barrett and Mary Barrett will be recorded with fellow plague victims on the Bills of Mortality.

'The plague is inside. All dead,' the Widow calls to John Clapshaw, who stays pressed against the wall across the street. 'When your father comes you go and tell the Clerk bearers are needed here. Don't leave until then. When is he coming back? He is coming back?'

John Clapshaw pauses to think, but this doesn't help. He shrugs.

'We'll come back this way,' the Goodwife tells him. 'If you're still here we'll send for the bearers.' She closes the 'Lord have mercy upon us' door with its large red cross.

'And tell the Clerk to send us two of his running boys,' the Widow calls to John Clapshaw.

'Now?' he asks eagerly, ready to run away. 'I shall go now?'

'No,' the Goodwife says patiently. 'Wait until your father returns.'

John Clapshaw slumps back.

The ancient matrons walk on. 'Rat bites,' says the Widow, bumping the cobbles with her red wand. 'Keepers should have called for Searchers yesterday.'

'Should have,' the Goodwife agrees. 'Some are hard to teach.'

One of the verses from the ninth psalm she sang with the Clerk comes unbidden to the Widow's head and she sings, not loudly:

> *He is protector of the poor, what time they be opprest:*
> *He is in all adversity their refuge and their rest.*

The Goodwife sings with her and they find solace in the verse, in the singing. Comfort, refuge, and rest in God who protects the poor.

Robert Sedgwicke's room is on the first floor of a tenement. Jane Eburne, looking out of her door at the ground floor, shows the Searchers a face of fear and resentment before she locks herself in.

'It's not the infection, not the infection,' Robert Sedgwicke's daughter Katherine Grinle tells them as they come up the stairs. 'Not the infection. Old. He's old.'

The corpse of old Robert Sedgwicke has been laid out carefully on his bed mat. The Searchers examine it slowly. Check armpits, groin, legs, chest. No signs, no lesions, no boils.

'Were there convulsions?' The Goodwife asks.

'No!' Katherine Grinle answers firmly, fearful this might be a sign of the plague, but confident her father did not have convulsions.

'Fever? Bleeding?'

'No.'

'What did he have?' the Widow asks.

'A gripe in his guts,' Katherine Grinle says with tears. 'He always had a gripe in his guts.'

'Mmm. It's not plague.'

'Not? No cross on the door? No shutting in?'

'No,' the Goodwife says, 'no. Not the plague. It's griping in the guts.'

Katherine Grinle weeps heavily, with sorrow and relief both. One burden lifted, she moves to give the Goodwife a thankful embrace – but stops herself in time and backs away, embarrassed. 'Tell her downstairs it's not the plague. Not.'

As they go down the Goodwife says, 'She needn't have feared touching me. I would have moved back if she hadn't.'

'And I would have stopped her with my wand,' the Widow says, holding it outstretched as a barrier. 'But she wouldn't come near me. My face.'

'And your red wand.'

The Widow wonders which is … stronger? 'I don't know. I have had this face for most of my life. The red wand only for thirty some years.'

'Good for scaring folk. Both.'

They stop at the bottom of the stairs. 'Yes,' says the Widow, and with her hand stretches her deformed face even more, amusing the Goodwife. She does this to Sara, who always laughs uncontrollably.

As they leave the Widow calls through Jane Eburne's locked door, 'Not the plague.'

'Did she hear you say "Not"?' Goodwife Joan Brokefild asks her friend.

'My "Not" was just as loud as my "plague",' the Widow answers.

They go back to the channel, both cheered – like Katherine Grinle – that it was not the plague. Their spirits lift, and they bang down their red wands and repeat 'Not. Not.' Life has taught them that even if their behaviour is unseemly, verging wicked, it does not matter. The two ancient matrons are invisible, can do or say – mostly – what they like. No one wants to see them.

The Widow remembers something she meant to ask the Goodwife.

'Did you dream on a St Thomas onion as a girl? Dream of your true love? See him in the face?'

The Goodwife is silent for some time. 'No. If I had had a true dream then, a true one, of my wedded life I'd have choked myself on the St Thomas onion and been glad of it. Or welcomed strangling by the Night Mare.' She recites morosely:

Here we are all, by day; By night we are hurl'd
By dreams, each one, into a sev'rall world.

Even so, the Widow can hear that saying the verse helps her friend. 'Hurled and world,' the Widow repeats, liking the rhyme.

'Dreams,' the Widow says, 'the dreams we're hurled into, they're understood by opposites. A dream of shit means money coming. I've never dreamed of shit.'

'No, never had money coming.'

'No, I never. Dreams yes, but sleep, it's sleep I don't understand. How strange to, to sleep? Here, then not here. Then here again. Odd. I don't understand it.'

The Goodwife has never thought about sleep. Her friend the Widow can be odd herself. 'To dream of gathering up gold and silver signifies deceit and loss,' the Goodwife recites from one of her penny chapbooks.

'Yes, opposites,' agrees the Widow. 'Shit is a better dream than gold and silver. Here is Frances Aspiner, his house. Widow Barrett and Mary Barrett plague. Robert Sedgwicke griping in the guts.'

'Then when we have searched Frances Aspiner,' the Goodwife teases, 'you can add his name to your list of those searched.'

'Yes,' the Widow agrees earnestly, 'I can.'

The house of Frances Aspiner is large, ten hearths.

'A small tailor Frances Aspiner, one hearth as was,' the Goodwife gossips. 'Married better than he could expect, Elizabeth Spencer a widow from Salisbury. He traded in broadcloth thanks to his wife's money; had his wife's family in Salisbury sell him broadcloth at kinfolk price; used his own fox-cunning to market the cloth here in London, overcharging, I have heard Roger Easewell the chimney-man say. That is Frances Aspiner, ten hearths.'

'Mmm,' the Widow thinks out loud, her thoughts keeping pace with her slow steps beside the channel. 'So he has done well. He is fortunate in his wife, in her family. He has gathered up his crumbs and done well. He is, has become, a merchant who sells for profit. Merchants do. Is he an uncharitable man? Ungodly? Harsh to the poor, to his servants?'

The Goodwife is stumped, does not know. She likes Roger Easewell and has listened sympathetically to his stories of difficult dealings with householders who have many hearths. She shrugs, 'We will soon see.' Her friend can be something of a chore at times, hard work.

What they first see are seven carts in the courtyard, some already full of chests, some loading, a maid calling from a window that they will have to take off the bedroom chest and re-open it, there is still more bed linen. 'No! Not that. The big chest with the three bands. That one, yes.'

'All right, me handsome!' a small carter calls back, waves his cap to her and laughs.

At least out in the courtyard it is a busy, even cheerful, household, with death confined indoors.

The cheeriness is dampened by the arrival of the ancient women and their red wands. The carters, their voices marking them as coming from the west, nod knowingly at each other.

The small man says to the youngest of his fellows, 'See Tom, we told you when there's a death in London the red wand widows come to search the corpse. The Lord Mayor himself sends 'em. See there.' Tom, bowed beneath a heavy roll of rug, stares at the two ancient matrons. Their black bodices and overskirts, their high, flat-topped hats, are unremarkable. Their red wands are worthy of remark, and he does.

'I see them! I see them!' he calls, and stops still, balancing his load. He remembers his gammer dressed like that. Many women in Salisbury still do. But none carry red wands and search the dead.

Widow Hazard and Goodwife Brokefild ignore this prating. They are taken inside to the Widow Aspiner, a slight woman with a twisted neck and a lame left leg.

'You have taken your time coming,' she says with flat resignation in her tear-weary voice.

The Widow disagrees, 'No. The visitation of the plague means searching takes time. Yours is the third house we will search today. There are six still to come. Where is the corpse?'

'Laid out in his bed. The plague,' she says with irritation, 'there is no plague here. My poor husband is dead from a fall.' She leads them a halting progress up the stairs. Servants with bundles and boxes stand back on the landing, fall silent, let them pass, then their loud talk of packing and travel resumes. The three women enter a bedroom empty of everything except a grand bed and the corpse that lies on it.

'How did he die?' the Goodwife asks.

'A fall down the stairs. He was carrying his – carrying a weight, a heavy thing, caught his foot at the top and tumbled,' she stops and stares at the body. Frances Aspiner is older than her. A tidy, lean man. The Searchers move closer and see the mortal bruising on his head and body. They have seen many deaths from falls. These are familiar signs. His neck is twisted, broke. Widow Margaret Hazard thinks it not as twisted as that of Elizabeth Aspiner. She looks at her to check. No, not as twisted.

'We ran to help, all of us,' the new made widow says in listless despair. 'All of us but we were no help. He was dead. Is dead.' She turns and leaves the room, weeping again.

'What was he carrying?' the Goodwife idly asks Widow Hazard, who does not know.

They can hear the servants in the long gallery talking of Salisbury, of flying from London. Of the plague. A manservant, standing listening outside the bedroom, comes in.

'Master was starting downstairs carrying his strong box, small and heavy with, with, with what was in it. He would have only himself carry it. The box started to fall from his hands and he reached better to hold it then fell himself.'

'You saw this?' asks the Widow. The manservant shakes his head, but others have joined him in the bedroom and agree that this was how it was.

As they do when a staircase has a banister, the Searchers hold on with care going down. Widow Aspiner is not to be seen and out in the yard the cart loading continues with shouts and jokes.

'All off to Salisbury,' the small carter calls to them, waving them a good-natured God be w'ye. 'Leaving soon. When we're all packed up. If I can get these dozy boys to load a balanced cart. Weight over the axles, weight over the axles. What I always say,' and turns back to his work.

'Now Francis Woodhouse,' the Widow announces.

Francis Woodhouse is not dead, his wife Anne is. His son John is. Francis Woodhouse is frantic. He does not want his family dead. He does not want to be shut into his house. He does not want the plague.

'Go!' he shouts at the Searchers, and weeps. Rips at his clothes, his hair, both already torn. Crouches in a corner. The ancient matrons ignore him and search the two corpses. Both dead of plague. The signs are also clear on Francis Woodhouse.

'Your son, your other son Edward. Where is he?' the Widow asks. Francis Woodhouse sobs, does not look up.

'Your son, your son Edward. Where is he?' the Widow repeats stolidly. Francis Woodhouse folds himself into a small weeping ball.

'The bearers will come for the corpses,' the Goodwife tells him, 'and Keepers will bring you food and drink.'

'More watchmen needed,' the Widow says when they are outside. They squat in the small lane beside the house and relieve themselves. Back in the street they rest against the wall and take out pipe and tobacco, waiting to see if any of the running boys will catch up with them.

'His pipe will soon be out,' the Goodwife points her pipe back at the house. 'He needs,' she pauses, 'that is who he needs.' She can see Edward Woodhouse coming in the distance and calls out to him. 'Edward Woodhouse!' and waves him to her. He is unhappy but comes. A small lad of fourteen, uncomfortable.

'Your mother and brother are dead. From the plague. Your father is still alive. Must be cared for.'

He nods. Tries to speak but can't. Nods again, and goes into the house.

'Widow Barrett and Mary Barrett plague–' Widow Margaret Hazard begins her listing once again but the Goodwife stops her.

'No need to say it all again. Now, Henry Gipps. The children have always been sickly. We've searched here before.'

'Yes, the child Kate. Dead of fever.'

Now two more of the sickly Gipps children, Bartholomew and Anne, are dead and it is the plague. Father Henry, mother Agnes, son Giles, and daughter Margery, all have the signs. Ten year old Helen does not. Except for Margery and Helen, those Gipps still living sit or lie groaning, staring. Margery and Helen help where they can. Fetching drink or a chamber pot. They avoid their dead brother and sister, laid out at the end of the big bed.

'What should we do?' Helen asks. 'What?'

'What you are doing,' the Goodwife answers. 'The bearers will come for the corpses, the Keepers will bring you food. You'll be shut in but the Keepers will still come. Keep coming. There'll be food and drink.'

The Widow confirms, 'Doing right. Mmm. You're doing right. The watchman outside will hear if needs be. If another death, tell him.'

The Goodwife tells all the living Gipps, 'The bearers will come.' Outside, two of the runners, Jemmy Pooly and James Kerton, are waiting. The Widow sends Jemmy Pooly off to the Clerk for bearers and watchmen.

'The Warden,' Jemmy Pooly answers back before he leaves, 'the Warden, the trooper, he's doing all the bearers and watchmen and all that business. All that. Just like in Oliver's army he says.' Jemmy Pooly finds the time of plague and infection exciting. 'The Warden knows everything of levers and the Clerk's crutches. He was at Marston Moor fight. Marston Moor fight!'

The Goodwife waves him away, says to James Kerton, 'Stay near, we have three more corpses to search, three houses.'

The boy bounces up and down on his toes, ready to run when told.

The women stop to rest and smoke near the water house in Water Square. The square has another name but has always been called Water Square by the parishioners of St Cyneswide and St Tibba who come to fill their jugs and buckets and bottles, and pass the time of day while they wait their turn at the spout. On the other side of the square a coach is ready for trade at the hackney-coach stand. The ancient matrons find a comfortable wall in the shade where they can rest and smoke, keeping their distance from those at the water house who are wary of red wands.

> *Fine Seville oranges, fine lemons, fine,*
> *Round, sound and tender, inside and rine!*

The orange seller does good business with those waiting at the water house. The ancient women have been walking and working and are hungry, but not for oranges at six pence for two. The Goodwife summons the lurking James Kerton and throws him twopence to buy bread and cheese. On his return he holds back the food, makes as if to eat it himself. The Goodwife glares, slowly raises her red wand. The boy quickly hands her the food, 'A joke, a jest,' he says placating.

'Yes. No more jokes,' she nods a neutral nod and gives him a small share of bread and cheese. The Widow thinks the Goodwife too soft-hearted. She would have beaten James Kerton with her wand, but it is not her business. It was the Goodwife's twopence, and the Goodwife does not like beating or being beaten. The boy, content with his food, sits at a sufficient distance to show that he is with them, and not with them.

The orange seller moves on, starts her cry again. The Goodwife remembers the bell-man's morning cry, 'Now 'tis four, rich and poor. I told him a better cry but he's another one who's hard to teach.

> *From noise of Scare-fires rest ye free,*
> *From Murders Benedicitie.*
> *From all mischances, that may fright*
> *Your pleasing slumbers in the night:*
> *Mercy secure ye all, and keep*
> *The Goblin from ye, while ye sleep.*
> *Past one o'clock, and almost two,*
> *My Masters all, Good day to you!*

The Widow snorts, 'Mmm. William Northage remembers the last rhyme. Over and over that one. The full verse is very fine.' From his distance

James Kerton agrees – the Goodwife has a good, clear voice, and the boy enjoyed it. Especially the Scare-fires, the murders and the Goblin. He is sure he could get it all to memory quickly. Better than William Northage.

The Widow's one good eye sees and her one good ear hears a commotion at the waiting hackney-coach. It is Isabella Undnay, shouting, distressed. She crosses over to those at the water house and the two ancient matrons can hear her loud question. 'Richard Undnay, have you seen him? Have you seen him?' Heads shake, people say No.

She sees the two women and runs over, comes up closer than is usual. Asks the same question. No, they haven't seen her husband Richard Undnay, the hackney coachman.

'The horse brought the coach back without him. Without him. Empty.' She stops and gulps and weeps, helpless. 'You,' she says to the Widow, 'you search well. A good Searcher. Not just the dead. You found the mothers who left their babes in the streets. Found them! You can find my Richard Undnay.'

Widow Margaret Hazard holds up a hand, shakes her head. Feels too old. Is too old.

'That Ralph Eackles, the dead painter, you found his family. Not even in this parish. You can find Richard Undnay. You can.'

The Widow shakes her head again. She can't find him, and weeping Isabella Undnay goes off to look and ask elsewhere.

Holding firmly on their red wands the two walk down to the channel.

'Wasn't me. I didn't find the painter's family,' she tells the Goodwife, 'that was Frances Barrow. He told me of the brothers and sister and St Martin Vintry. Said it should be me to tell the Clerk.'

'No, but you did find mothers of babes left in the streets.'

The Widow did, through low cunning and dogged persistence. Wonders about the most important mother of all, Sara Potts' mother. Mother of baby Sara Potts who was found in Potts Alley in the year 57. The year Parliament asked Oliver Protector to be king, offered him the crown. Oliver said No. No crown. No king.

'You found five of them, the mothers.'

'Some, yes, five. Many I didn't,' the Widow says, thinking again of Sara Potts' mother, of the motherless foundlings she cared for until the Vestry sent them out of the city to a country wetnurse – Richard Swan, Mary Bell, and all the others long gone.

'I don't understand,' the Widow says, 'to leave, to desert, a newborn child. Mine died, four of mine. All died. Who could leave a helpless newborn babe in the street? I've no time for such mothers who are no mothers,' the Widow is bitter, hard.

'They wanted them found,' the Goodwife says, 'the babes weren't tipped down a cesspit or into the river. They were left where they were sure to be found. Left in streets quiet at night and busy by day. Bell Alley, Swan Street, Potts Lane, Bear Street, Friars Close.'

'Some cared, cared a little,' the Widow says grudgingly, 'they were the mothers I found. Found because they hid themselves where they could see their babe safely taken up. Got to know where they hid, saw their hiding places. I found five mothers, no more.'

'Sara is a good, obedient girl,' Goodwife Joan Brokefild says, knowing this will please the Widow. It does.

'Sara Potts, found in Potts Lane. Sara Potts.' The Widow softens with remembering. 'Small, bawling. Little tiny mop. Took my finger and sucked. Margaret Allchurch, I got her as wet-nurse. I said I would have the child, keep her. I did, I have.' The Widow struggles between not wanting to say too much and being overwhelmed by motherly feeling, joy in her Sara.

'Philip Carter was a good help. Made Vestry agree Sara should be with you. Didn't need to shout at them.'

'No. He said to them, he told me, I was a good servant of the parish. A widow. No children of my own. I would look after Sara now and in time Sara would look after me. I had long service in the parish as a, as a reliable Searcher. A –' she stops, hearing herself talk like a bragging woman.

'Vestry knew that. They easily agreed.'

'Mmm. Not so easy. The Clerk said benefit to the parish purse was his best argument. Then Vestry did agree. Said Yes.'

'You have done well with Sara. A dutiful child.' They both think of Goodwife Joan Brokefild's adult sons and daughter, who are not. The daughter Hannah absent, married into another parish, and sons who are like their father. Jacob is a carter, Joseph a lighterman on the river.

'Vestry said Yes, Oliver Protector said No,' the Widow says, thinking aloud of the other good thing in the year 57. 'No crown. No king. No king for him.' She slowly stands, groans with her aches, helps the Goodwife to her feet. 'Thomas Dorbridge, hatter as once was. Ancient, and ill for years. His Abigail is his blessing, the way she tends for that miserable ancient man. Mmm. As is only right. As she should. Her duty.'

The Goodwife has her own views on wives tending to miserable old husbands. Is tempted to offer an ironic 'Mmm' herself. But forbears. The Widow thinks in her own way, the Goodwife in hers. They do not always agree, nor need to. The Widow's face is stern. The Goodwife gives her a friend's smile and the Widow responds with the same. They walk along the channels to the house where live Thomas and Abigail Dorbridge.

'Lived,' says the Goodwife out loud, for they have been told by the Constable that Thomas, or Abigail, or both, are dead.

'It is my mother,' Katharine Briggs tells them, weeping, as she opens the door. 'My mother. I feared it was him, my father, so old and ill. But it is my mother.'

Katharine is still young. She looks imploringly at the two ancient matrons as if there is something they can do to make things better. She herself cannot. Her father cannot. It is up to them. They say nothing, waiting to get past her into the house.

'I prayed they would both stay healthy. Be spared the – the, the …'

'Plague. The plague,' says the Widow helpfully. 'I prayed for my children, my four babes that they would not die. They died. God's will.'

They push past Katharine and inside find Abigail Dorbridge dead of the plague. Thomas Dorbridge sits on the other side of the room, angry with his dead wife, his daughter, the ancient women, everyone.

'Your father has the signs,' the Goodwife tells Katharine. 'The house will be sealed once her corpse is taken by the bearers.

'Sealed? Who will look after my father?' Katharine asks.

'You will,' says the Widow. 'You have the signs too. But whether you have them or no, you cannot leave a plague struck house. You will stay here with your father.'

Katharine cannot speak. The old man continues angry, saying nothing, his face flushed and furious.

Katharine finds her voice. 'I am Katharine Briggs, wife of Christopher Briggs the hatter. I must go to my husband. My family. My children.' She is able to say this calmly. It is obvious to her and must be obvious to these old, poor women.

The Widow waits until she has finished, then says what is obvious to her. 'You cannot leave. This is a plague house. A house like other houses that have the plague in this parish.'

Katharine Briggs says confidently 'No,' and finding this gives her comfort repeats it as she moves slowly around the house, from room to room. 'No no no no no no,' adds, 'I shall not.'

Thomas Dorbridge shouts, 'Get out! Get out! Get out!'

His daughter says firmly, resolutely, 'I shall not. I shall not. Not be shut in!'

The Goodwife calls to her and her seething father, 'The Keepers will come. Bring you food. Drink.'

The Widow says to the Goodwife, 'She shall. And he shall convulse himself to death. Shall not,' she snorts. 'The wife of a hatter, the daughter of a hatter, does not mean she can shrug off the Orders.'

The Goodwife herself shrugs, 'She does not want the plague in this house or in her house. Does not want to suffer from the plague. Does not–'

The Widow breaks in, impatient, 'No one wants the plague in their house. We stop it spreading by sealing up the houses that do have it. She should know that. Everyone should know that.'

Outside, a gang of parish boys, and a few girls, have collected like assembling pigeons. The boys are playing a boisterous, loud, game of Warny Egger, piling one upon the other until the pile collapses, to triumphant jeers, yells and hoots. The girls watch, egging them on. Sara lurks on the fringe, excited, but carefully inconspicuous. Her mother's hand has made it clear that Searchers are respectable ancient matrons and that their family, their children, must be respectable too. Sara does not think Searcher Goodwife Joan Brokefild's husband Isaac Brokefild is respectable. He is a shouting, beating, drunkard, but she does not dare point this out to her mother. And there is no need to. The whole parish knows of Isaac Brokefild.

The Widow points to Daniel Stiles with her red wand. 'You, Daniel Stiles, to the Church Warden for a watchman and bearers to come to this Dorbridge house.' She points to the house. The Widow knows messages must be made quite clear to boys.

There is nothing for the Searchers to search at the house of John Sly, linen draper. No corpse.

'The maid,' John Sly explains, 'her family came and took the corpse. The maid Doll Matthews. I said wait for the Searchers but they took her anyway. George Matthews, her father, a gardener. St Giles Cripplegate his parish.'

The two ancient women stand silent. What has happened here in John Sly's house – no corpse to search – is irregular, improper, wrong, and they all know this. The Searchers wait to see if silence presses more information from John Sly. It usually does. Here it doesn't. He too stands silent. He knows, everyone knows, Searchers are old, poor women. Parish pensioners.

'Her death,' the Widow asks, 'what did you see of the cause of Doll Matthews' death?'

'I don't know, I wasn't here. The cookmaid found her.'

'And you sent for her father?' the Goodwife asks.

John Sly shrugs. 'No. One of the servants must have done that. The cookmaid? I don't know.'

'Is the cookmaid here now?'

'No. Sent on messages,' John Sly turns and walks from the room.

The two old, poor women go outside, close the door behind them.

'If she had the plague–' the Goodwife starts.

'If. We tell the Clerk, the Constable, what he said.' The Searchers have dealt with unhelpful householders in the past and expect to see more in this time of plague. No one wants to be sealed up in their house with a red cross on the door.

The running boy, James Kerton, showing bold, comes closer to the ancient matrons and their awful red wands. 'Messages for the Clerk? Watchman needed? Bearers? Any messages?' he asks hopefully. Like Jemmy Pooly he finds these stirring times.

The women know that a report on the removal of the maid's corpse is too important to be entrusted to a running boy.

'No,' says the Widow, 'no messages.'

The Widow is tired. The Goodwife is tired. Another boy, Daniel Stiles, comes running up, full of energy and cheek, gives James Kerton a punch. James Kerton kicks him.

'What is it, you Daniel Stiles? What is it?' the Widow snaps in ill humour as the two boys wrestle.

'Please,' Daniel Stiles lets go of James Kerton, says boldly, 'please to know Clerk says "Where are those poor old women? Where are they?" and sends me to see.' He keeps his distance.

The Goodwife breaks in ahead her friend, 'Tell Philip Carter Parish Clerk that the two ancient and respectable matrons, ancient and respectable,' (the Widow nods and Mmms approvingly) 'are now to the house of John Shipley, the last name on his list, to search the corpse there.'

'Ancient and respectable,' says the Widow. 'Tell him that, but only tell him that if, Daniel Stiles, only if the Clerk said "those poor old women" and I think he did not, you jingle brains boy.'

The boy laughs, wobbles his head as a great joke, punches James Kerton again and runs off.

The ancient matrons trudge on, heavy steps. The Widow has been thinking, says, 'Psalm the seventy third sings on the prosperous state of wicked men, how they seem to prosper but at the end they do not.'

'Yes,' says the Goodwife wearily.

'We sing "how thou settest them upon a slippery place, and at thy pleasure and thy will thou dost them all deface." That Frances Aspiner a wealthy merchant, a prosperous man, was set upon a slippery place at the top of the stairs. Yes?' She looks enquiringly at the Goodwife.

Exasperated, Goodwife Brokefild says, 'So you now say Frances Aspiner was a wicked man, not a good man, not a good merchant?'

'I don't know what he is, was.'

The Goodwife flicks her wand to strike a halt to this talk, says nothing.

'Thomas Dugdale would know,' the Widow says optimistically.

'He would.'

John Shipley's house is two turned corners away. Big, six hearths, but not as big as Frances Aspiner's.

Widow Margaret Hazard pauses, regrets her recent words to her friend Goodwife Joan Brokefild, thinks they might have sounded sharp, unfriendly. 'I meant no offence. About Francis Aspiner. No offence to you.'

The Goodwife laughs, 'I do not take offence from you.'

'Good. I meant none.'

In the courtyard of John Shipley's house there is a horse and cart, and an open coffin, waiting. The two ancient women hurry their steps. They are met, blocked, at the door by Hester Shipley.

Widow Margaret Hazard breaks the silence, 'Widow Margaret Hazard and Goodwife Joan Brokefild, we are parish Searchers here to search the corpse of John Shipley. Sent here by the Parish Clerk. To search the corpse.'

Hester Shipley does not move. Widow Hazard presses her melted, rippled face and her red wand close. Widow Hazard is not tall. Widow Hester Shipley is a handspan shorter. Widow Shipley flinches but holds her ground, stares back at Widow Hazard's stare. The Searchers can hear movement, voices, in the room beyond. Widow Hazard tries to push past Hester Shipley, who stays in place, blocking the way with her small body and the half-closed door.

The movement and voices in the room stop. Hester Shipley looks behind then stands back, with a tight smile lets the Searchers into an empty room.

'We are to search the corpse of John Shipley,' the Goodwife says, her cheeks flushed, her voice high with excitement.

'There is no corpse here. See.'

'Where is it?'

'Gone. Gone already. Taken for burial.'

'The coffin and cart are still outside in the yard. Waiting.'

'A mistake. Stupid mistake. Two coffins, two carts were sent. Only one needed. The other is gone with my poor husband. I am not dead.'

The two Searchers think on this. Widow Shipley, still with her small smile, waves her arms briefly to show how alive she is.

'Why did you stop us at the door?' the Goodwife asks, fired after a day of hard grind by the occasion for a discussion, a dispute.

'A room, a house, is a mess after death. The mess was being cleared away. See, now it is all gone.'

'I can still smell death,' Widow Hazard says, sniffing loudly with her good nostril.

'A hard smell to be rid of, as Searchers must know. But you are here and to no purpose so we will have a bite of something then you can go.'

A bite of something sounds good to the Searchers. It is some time since bread and cheese, and they have searched many houses, many corpses. Widow Shipley gestures them to sit on the window seat and calls for cherry tarts and small beer. She keeps her distance from them while they eat and drink. Wants no more talk with these ancient, poor women.

When they have refreshed themselves they rise and Widow Shipley goes to open the door for them.

'Now we will search the house,' Widow Margaret Hazard states.

'There is no need. The corpse is gone. I told you. Gone.'

'We will search the house or I will stay here while Goodwife Joan Brokefild sends for the Constable,' the Widow says flatly.

'There is no need. No need for searching or Constables. You are tired and need to rest and need some reward for your pains.' Widow Shipley takes out her purse and offers each of them a new Guinea, the gold bright and enticing. 'Take these and go to your houses and rest. Take them.'

Widow Hazard ignores her and with little difficulty finds the shrouded corpse in a dark corner, covered in rushes.

'Take the guineas!' Hester Shipley shouts. 'There is no plague here, only spotted fever. Here are the guineas.'

The Searchers brush the rushes aside and unwrap the body.

'See, spotted fever, spotted fever. The spots. Spotted fever.'

'Plague. The infection,' the Goodwife says, 'we have seen many like this today. And other days. It is plague. Do you have the signs? Others in the house have the signs?'

Hester Shipley has nothing more to say, sits down, even smaller folded into herself, and picks at a cherry tart.

The Searchers find the servants gathered in the kitchen. The cook has the signs.

Widow Hazard sends the lurking James Kerton to fetch a watchman and tells the carter he can wait til night before taking the corpse for burial.

Their walk back to the church square is slow, with rests and pauses on the way. As they come closer the slow tolling bell gets louder.

Most of what they have to say to Philip Carter he knows already, after a fashion, having already made some sense of the excited and often confused messages brought back by the boys. He takes the full details from the ancient matrons, jotting notes in his shorthand.

'The corpse of maid Doll Matthews was taken from John Sly's house before we could search it,' the Widow tells him, 'and Widow Shipley offered gold to say it was not the plague.'

The Goodwife thinks she would have kept this last bit to herself.

'Was it the plague?' the Clerk asks.

'Yes,' both women say.

'Today we have searched ten corpses, eight plague, a fall, and a griping of the guts, and the maid Doll Matthews who we did not search, could not,' the Widow says. 'That is St Cyneswide and St Tibba today. What of the other parishes? Parishes nearby. How bad is their infection?'

The Clerk looks in his chest for the Bill of Mortality for 6 June to 13 June. Finds it, reads aloud, running his finger down the columns.

'St Alban Woodstreet, three burials, one of them plague, Allhallows Honeylane, no burials. St Maudlin Milkstreet, one burial. St Michael Crooked Lane, two plague. St John Evangelist, one burial.' He scoffs, 'That's something at least, one burial. No-one dies in St John Evangelist.

May be it is plague, but not listed as such. Without the Walls it's growing on, the plague. St Sepulchre, twenty five burials, ten of them plague. Ten. Worse in St Giles in the Fields, 120 burials, 68 plague. There, you see,' he holds up the paper.

There is nothing more to say but he adds, 'Buried 206, plague 112. Out of the 130 parishes 12 infected. And that was the Bill before this week.'

Outside the ancient women take their customary places on the churchyard wall. The Goodwife sits, relaxes, slumps, in loose-limbed leisure. The Widow is not a slumper, sits up straight.

'Deaths. The dead,' the Widow says, lighting her pipe and waving an arm encompassing the church-yard, the parish.

Goodwife Joan Brokefild shakes her head, shrugs, and sings, not too loudly:

> *Under this stone lies Gabriel John, in the year of our Lord one*
> *thousand and one,*
> *Cover his head with turf or stone, 'tis all one, with turf or stone,*
> *'tis all one,*
> *Pray for the soul of gentle John, if you please you may, or let it alone,*
> *'tis all one.*

The Widow has not heard this song before and considers it, testing the sentiment, 'tis all one.' Then says cautiously, 'Praying for the soul of the dead is papist. Thomas Dugdale said, his sermon: "The dead need no prayers. The dead may in no way be helped, though we would help them ever so much, because the sentence of God is unchangeable, and cannot be revoked again. Every mortal man dies either in the state of salvation or damnation. There are no jurymen to be swayed by special pleading, by prayers. There is only one stern judge, who has made his judgement." Thomas Dugdale's words.' The Widow can, at times, recall a sermon, a speech, a conversation, word by exact word. 'Is this then a papist song?' she asks.

'I am not sure. I don't know. The song says pray for Gabriel John's soul if you please, or let it alone. One or the other, it does not matter. I do not think it is a serious song. It is not.'

'Who is gentle Gabriel John?' the serious Widow asks. 'He died long ago. What do you know of Gabriel John?'

'It is only a song,' the Goodwife replies, 'a song. A song that is good to sing but only a song.'

'It sounds pleasing,' the Widow concedes, and from the one hearing sings it true to word but less to note, '"Under this stone lies Gabriel John, in the year of our Lord one thousand and one." Mmm. Pleasing. Where did you find it?'

The Goodwife hesitates then says, laughs, 'I heard it at a tavern. It was sung at a tavern, and I heard it. I was not in the tavern, but the singing was loud.'

'What tavern? The *Three Tuns*?' the Widow asks – her friend's life surprises her: it often does.

'Not the *Three Tuns*. The *White Hind*.'

The Widow knows the Goodwife is reluctant to go home to Isaac Brokefild, with good reason, and is sometimes seen out late, moving purposefully as if on Searcher's business. 'You hear good singing there?'

'Yes. Good ones, clever ones, lewd ones, drinking ones. The *White Hind* singers like drinking songs. Our Warden is a sometime singer there. I hear the singing from outside. Outside the tavern.'

'Our Warden?'

The Widow has to digest this, and they smoke in comfortable, cogitating silence. The Widow thinking 'songs good, clever, lewd, drinking, our Warden;' the Goodwife sings in her head: 'Music the medicine is for discontent, heart's joy, ear's food, man's honest merry merriment, man's honest merry merriment.' Music and verse a balm for her discontent.

A gaggle of children wander into the square, Sara is among them talking, laughing, with her good friends Nell Girling and Dorothy Damport. The Widow beckons her over and grabs a tuft of hair. 'Sara Potts I saw you today.'

The child not sure what to say, how much to say, what her mother saw, says nothing.

'Hear your good mother,' the Goodwife says in warm support, 'hear her,' but glad she does not have an eight year old child.

'Remember, I have the eye that sees everywhere, everything,' Widow Hazard taps the flap of skin that covers her left eye socket.

Sara tries to recall doing those things that would anger her mother, but she has not stolen or taken the Lord's name in vain. Pride: she does have pride, in the number of words she knows, in her reading, in the way she can out-talk her fellows, but her mother shares this pride. So Sara nods submissively, in the hope this response will satisfy. It does. Widow Hazard gives the child a half affectionate slap and lets her go. Calls her back and pushes a scrap of cherry tart into her mouth.

The Goodwife watches all this with interest. Her friend the Widow is a good mother.

They sit and smoke and smoke, protecting themselves against the infection, and watch as the bell-man sets his face to mournful. With a solemn nod to the Searchers he moves off through the parish streets, swinging his bell and chanting the names of the dead loudly, dolefully. The dog Gypsy slopes along behind.

'Widow Barrett. Mary Barrett. Robert Sedgwicke. Frances Aspiner. John Woodhouse. Anne Woodhouse. Bartholomew Gipps. Anne Gipps. Abigail Dorbridge. John Shipley.'

'He asked the Clerk about Doll Matthews, John Sly his maid, whether to include her name,' the Goodwife tells her friend. 'Philip Carter said the body had not been searched so it is not known if she is dead. She might be dead or she might not be dead.'

'Mmm.'

CHAPTER V

London, Thursday, 22 June 1665

'Delicate cowcumbers to pickle.'

The Church Warden is as pleased as a trooper can be without a horse under him, so he tells everyone. He has set himself up with his campaign table in the church porch, a folding side-table salvaged – he says requisitioned, commandeered – from one of the victory bonfires of weeks ago. 'Too good to burn, even to celebrate against the Dutchman. You can see it still has good use in it.' The table is uneven, wobbles.

He hums and whistles the *Zealous Soldier*, a favourite, and when Constable Samuel Snow arrives sings to him with full voice:

> *God hath no doubt a purpose to bring on*
> *A work both for his glory and our good,*
> *You'll say it hath been the confusion*
> *And cause of shedding many thousands' blood:*
> *'Twas for our sins that God this war did bring,*
> *But know we may have cause, rejoice and sing!*

The Constable enjoys the show and would join in but is not confident of the words. Samuel Snow likes a song as much as the Warden, as much as any man in the parish, but his appreciation of the enthusiasms the Zealous Soldier sings of are not as great as they were in days past. He is the parish Constable, has taken oaths, and he knows his current ruler is the second king Charles.

The Warden is working with the Constable in commissioning and despatching the many watchmen needed. He gives the Constable a comradely clap on the shoulder, as one old soldier to another. The Constable is not, but is grateful for this bluff, trooperly attention which makes him feel he might have been an old soldier.

The Constable eyes the Warden's lists and weekly rotas and wishes, as he often does, that he was better with his reading and asks the Warden to read them out if he would, to help him put them into memory.

The Warden is a sturdy man of arms, a man Samuel Snow admires, but Samuel Snow is the Constable. He best knows the streets, houses and people of the parish of St Cyneswide and St Tibba, and knows there are problems with the rota and says No, he will not have the Warden's rota allocating Thomas Billington and Robert Tomlinson to share a watch on the Dorbridge house.

'It's not possible to have Thomas Billington and Robert Tomlinson share a watch. Share anything. They're never of the same mind on anything.'

'They won't watch together,' the Warden explains patiently, 'one replaces the other. They don't have to be good friends. They take turns to watch over the house.'

'Yes,' says the Constable, well aware of how the watch works and well aware that the Warden has not lived long enough in St Cyneswide and St Tibba to know why Thomas Billington and Robert Tomlinson cannot stand each other.

'This is how things are between these two. Thomas Billington said – this is ten years ago or more, at least ten – he made a secret first promise of marriage, said, she says, Jennet Bladwell says he said, "I shall marry Jennet Bladwell" but he said it in secret and he never did, never did take her to bed and make it a proper wedlock between them. Then weeks later he made an open promise to Mabell Copland. Jennet Bladwell is cousin to Robert Tomlinson.'

It is a history the Warden likes, 'So Thomas Billington did not say "I marry her"? And there was no, no – what do the lawyers say? – no copulation of their bodies?'

'No, no bedding, no *copulatio corporum*, and he said "I *shall* marry her," and he never did. And Thomas Billington denies he ever made any first promise to Jennet, any promise at all. So Jennet Bladwell hates him as do her family and friends. So her cousin Robert Tomlinson hates Thomas Billington and will not share a watch with him even if the business is so arranged that they do not meet or see each other. And that cannot be done.' Drained by this long speech, the Constable reaches for his pipe.

The Warden nods, taking in this parish history with interest, and the Constable recasts the watch so that Thomas Billington is now paired with William Hawkins and Robert Tomlinson with William Tailer.

The lists and rotas settled, the Warden makes his report to the Clerk. The two sit outside with their pipes. The Warden would prefer to take a turn around the churchyard, stretch his legs, but the Clerk needs both hands to work his crutches and although he can grip his pipe between his teeth he has bitten though too many pipe stems to want to walk and smoke and talk, so they sit and smoke and talk.

The Clerk is in a good humour, pleased with the conduct and content of Tuesday's service of thanks. He delighted in its martial departures from the well trodden paths of the Book of Common Prayer, in the triumphal, trumpet words, in its celebration of routing the Dutch fleet. From the Thanksgiving book he reads out with relish the gratifying words:

> Our enemies compassed us about on every side. They were many, and did rage horribly. They intended mischief and had marked us out for ruin. Out of the deep of the sea we cried unto thee O Lord, and thou didst hear us. It is not our own strength that hath helped us, not the number of our ships, nor the courage of our soldiers, nor yet the conduct of our Commanders, but thy alone wisdom and power that hath defeated the counsels and broken the strength of our adversaries in pieces, hath purchased us this victory, a victory beyond all example great and glorious, complete and cheap, in the preservation of our ships, and sparing of our persons.

He pauses, draws on his pipe, observes, 'True. Only a small bill of account. A cheap victory, our persons spared. Only two Lords sunk. One Admiral gone and another going down with the gangrene.'

The Warden, who owns all battles, whether on land or sea, breaks in,

'*Vice*-Admirals. One of those Lords was a new-made Earl, Charles Berkeley, a loud windfucker by all accounts. His head was blown to pieces. It gave the only proof that he ever had brains,' he guffaws at this highly popular witticism, adds confidently, 'the great ships are the ships do the business.'

The Clerk half listens, pages ahead through the service looking for more about the victory, leafing past the fat burnt-sacrifices, the horn exalted like the horn of a unicorn, the heathen who have no knowledge of his laws. He stops at that itching, irritating part of the service where God is praised for 'rescuing the people from the miseries of a civil war at home.' He, and others, baulk at these words and he draws the Warden's attention to the passage.

The Warden is in no doubt where God's sympathies truly lie. High words form in his head but he keeps them in there: 'It is the papists, the French first and foremost, who have sat Charles Stuart back on the throne. The king's mother, a French woman, is a papist; the king's sister is a papist, married to the brother of the French king; the king's wife is a papist; the king's brother openly favours the papists. And the king? The king? Ha!'

But he does say out loud, 'The Lord's blessing is upon us, the godly party,' then he sings again, the Clerk being a new audience:

'Twas for our sins that God this war did bring,
But know we may have cause, rejoice and sing!

The Clerk waves his pipe to the tune.

'The *Zealous Soldier*,' the Warden explains, 'a favourite troopers' song.'

'Not only psalms then?'

'Psalms, and more. Here's a campaign story for you. Our men in Canterbury cathedral in the year 42, one of them banged out the *Zealous Soldier* on the cathedral great organ, banged it out with such soldierly zeal that the Canterbury organ's never been in tune since. Never since!'

This story is perfect for the Clerk, who has never heard better, and he laughs and roars until he is doubled over with a coughing fit.

'Don't cough too much,' the Warden says with callous humour, 'or the Searchers will find you dead and the bearers will call.'

'The Searchers,' the Clerk says, 'there is this business with the maid Doll Mathews, the corpse gone. And talk of corruption, bribes offered, at the Shipley house. A purse of gold I heard.'

The Warden shrugs at this gossip, says briskly, 'No bribe taken that I have heard of. Money offered by Widow Shipley – a guinea, no purse of gold – but this was refused. And it was reported to you by Widow Hazard herself.'

The Clerk is less certain, has heard something different. 'It's said that the Widow would have accepted the purse, or the guinea, but the Goodwife was not of the same mind.'

The Warden is sceptical. 'It's said? By who? Not I think by Widow Hazard or the Goodwife. The Widow is tight with a coin, makes certain she gets every farthing – every half farthing! – she is due, but no more than she's due. Not a bribe-taker. A respectable ancient matron, she would be the first to denounce bribe-taking.'

'Searchers have been known to take bribes,' says Philip Carter. 'At Parish Clerk meetings you hear things, you do hear things. Some old, poor woman Searcher who takes money to conceal the criminal death of a babe. A gold coin can turn a capital crime into a sorry accident.'

The worldly Warden knows such things do happen, shrugs again.

The Clerk suddenly laughs, 'Henry Sharrow the Clerk over in St Benet Fynck says he had a Searcher they called Silent Sarah. Quiet as the grave at midnight, never opened her mouth except to report the result of a search. Or to drink, and she opened her mouth often for that. They found she was a bribe-taker, kept the coins in her mouth! There's corruption for you. For money she would tell a suspicious death as a mishap. Would tell a bad infection – even plague – as something else. Those with means will pay not to have their house shut up. Not to have it known theirs is a plague house.' He shakes his head, laughs again, 'Silent Sarah.' Falls serious once more, 'And then there is the removal of the corpse of Doll Mathews from the house of John Sly. Was he warned the Searchers were coming? Saw the plague signs on her body and had it borne away?'

The Warden finds this a fancy too far. 'Of course John Sly knew the

Searchers would come. Someone dies, the maid dies, the Searchers come. No need for forewarning.'

'Yes, of course, of course,' the Clerk says sharply, and persists, 'but I have heard that the order of the Searchers' visits to the houses of the dead was told to John Sly. He was forewarned that there would be many houses searched before his. Giving him time.'

'Why would the Widow, why would anyone, do that?' the Warden asks.

The Clerk jingles coins in his purse.

As the Warden stands to go he pulls a printed sheet from his pocket, says, 'Those sea lords of ours who died against the Dutch,' he reads:

> *Some great ones fell, t'instruct us by their fate,*
> *We honour love, which our base enemies hate.*

'A good verse, here, from a new-printed sheet on the sea fight, *The Dutch Armado A Mere Bravado*. But not all our ones were great. Did you hear of Captain Grove in Lowestoft Harbour? He heard the guns at sea, was ordered to sail but did not, would not. Stayed there drinking for as long he could swallow, trying to find Dutch brandy-valour at the bottom of the bottle so he could go and fight the Dutchman! Brandy-valour. But it wasn't to be found, so he will be tried for his lack of courage. And the name of his ship? The *Success*!' The Warden laughs and laughs with the Clerk.

While the Warden waves about the *Dutch Armado* ballad the Clerk pulls out his own sheet of paper, the just printed Bills of Mortality, reads, 'Hear this,

London, Bills of Mortality for 130 Parishes from the 13 to the 20 of June 1665 Buried, in all – 615; Plague – 168 Parishes clear of the Plague – 111; Parishes Infected – 19.

'Plague dead 168, parishes infected 19,' he repeats. 'Worse. Getting worse, much worse.'

The Warden has no reply to this. What can he say? He has faith the godly party will prevail; finds comfort in his past; waves a God be w'ye to the Clerk; and walks away whistling, then singing, the *Zealous Soldier*, drumming his fingers on the churchyard wall. The Clerk wonders if Frances Barrow sees the plague as an enemy that can be defeated by zealous soldiering? And he disapproves of the Warden's rapid singing – he takes it too fast. All know the correct time of a tune is to be found in the steady beat of the pulse, in the regular clock-work up and down movement of the arm for all to follow. The Warden races along with his *Zealous Soldier* as if he is Blue Cap running at Newmarket. Much too soon Philip Carter hears him sing the last verse.

> *Sing to the Lord a Psalm of thanks and praise,*
> *And to his holy Temple let us bring*
> *An Heart unspotted, let's an echo raise*
> *With our loud voices may to Nations ring*
> *Far distant from us, chaunting loudly thus,*
> *Prais'd be the Lord that hath assisted us.*

* * *

London, Friday, 23 June 1665

'The plague remedies, nephew, the remedies? Have you brought them?' Uncle Rowland, who spends much of his time in bed, has got up, with help, and has dressed in an old gown, with help, and made his cautious way downstairs. 'I don't need help, I can walk. Leave me be.' The unexpected arrival of Walter Hall at the rectory and the uproar caused by Uncle Rowland's noisy progress to the reception room has brought forth all the family and servants.

'Yes, dear uncle, I have, and they are special remedies.' Of all his kin the Reverend Walter Hall is most fond of Uncle Rowland Holmes. While Walter Hall, and the king, were in exile Uncle Rowland sends covert letters to his nephew. He writes in a cipher of his devising: numbers substituted for letters and misleading words thrown in at random to confuse any government agent who might intercept it. He also writes the same to Tom Bampfylde, a friend from Christ Church Oxford days, later become Colonel Bampfylde and a trusted aide to the king.

Proud of his cipher, Rowland Holmes continually refines and improves it, informing Walter Hall, and Colonel Bampfylde – when he remembers to do so – in old code what the new code is. Walter Hall found the arrangement confusing, often frustrating, and the intelligence Uncle Rowland sends of little value – 48 9 24 28 8 44 15 15 16/7 9 24 24 11 44 9 16/16 44 44 13 'Cromwells troopers seen'. But spending long hours trying to untangle Uncle Rowland's latest message was a welcome distraction in exile and amused others at court who would join him, bringing bottles of wine, to companionably work on the decipherment.

This time is now long past, yet some at Whitehall still ask Walter Hall after his uncle and jocularly enquire whether he has further refined his codes, brought them up to the minute? 'Thankfully no need for such things now,' they add, including those who know the king is sending urgent ciphers to France. The more considerate refrain from mentioning – it has been said so often – that Colonel Tom Bampfylde was discovered to be a Cromwell man, one of Secretary Thurloe's secret agents.

Rowland Holmes has long forgotten his codes, and only one subject is of any interest to him. 'These remedies are special you say? Special? How?'

'From the court, Uncle,' Walter Hall lowers his voice in due reverence, 'A remedy from the court.' He has a piece of fine paper, filled from edge to edge, top to bottom, with writing in the Italian style and hands it to his uncle who reads out in his reading voice.

'Take 2 quarts of Canary, if you cannot get Sack, take Claret, or any other wine. Poor People may make it of Good Beer.' Uncle Rowland pauses and scoffs, 'We do not need to know about beer and poor people.' He resumes, 'Put into it of Rue and Sage each, one good Handful. Boil these together in a Pipkin close covered, till about a Pint is boiled away, then strain it off, and set it over the Fire again, and put into it one Dram of Saffron, one Dram of Long Pepper, Half an Ounce of Ginger, and two good large Nutmegs, all well beaten together. Then let it boil a quarter of an Hour, take it off the Fire, and dissolve in it Mitridate and Venice Treacle.' Uncle Rowland beams, exclaims, 'I knew it! Venice Treacle, I know of Venice Treacle, the most efficacious and costly of medicines. If it has Venice Treacle this Court remedy will save us all.' He finds his place, 'I was here, yes, Mitridate and Venice Treacle of each a full Ounce – a full ounce – and keep it close stopt for use. Very good!' He holds up the paper for the assembled family to admire, waves it about.

'This has been a great secret,' Walter Hall confides, giving the impression of one who has long known it, 'but the king himself has ordered it be published, and has ordered that persons make use of it. A most efficacious remedy, both to prevent and to cure.'

'How good the king is!' Rowland Holmes says approvingly, 'And he even condescends to help the poor with their beer. Good beer the recipe says, good beer. For the poor. *We* shall have,' he consults the paper, 'two quarts of canary.'

'Yes, but we have more business to talk here,' Walter Hall says. 'This remedy is out and published because the city is become a dangerous place with the plague growing on, even in St Cyneswide and St Tibba. People are leaving for safer places and so should we, you. I have said this before now. You, my family, must leave London.'

'But where to?' asks Walter Hall's brother Ingram, 'where to? And you? Will you come?'

Walter Hall ignores the second question. 'To Bradford-on-Avon. It is a good safe distance from London, from the plague. And we have kin there.'

'Kin?' says Uncle Rowland Holmes with some irritation, 'Kin? I am the oldest and I know of no kin of ours at Bradvon-on-Ford.'

'Bradford-on-Avon. It is Bradford-on-Avon. There is a large, fine house and there is an ancient kinswoman of my father's–'

'Oh, your father's,' Rowland Holmes breaks in. He is an uncle on Walter Hall's mother's side. 'Well I have never heard of her, this ancient kinswoman. Of yours.'

Walter Hall is a man of dignity, and not always a patient man, but he loves his uncle. 'Yes, I have written her a letter and she will gladly receive you all.'

'You say a good safe distance from London,' asks Walter Hall's older brother Godfrey. 'How far is good and safe?'

'Yes,' echoes Elsa, Godfrey's wife, 'How far, brother?'

Walter Hall, who has seen fraught negotiations at European courts, witnessed and even played a role, a small one, in the manoeuvrings at his own king's court, both across the sea and then at Whitehall, is not thrown off his stride by loud family business.

'You need to be a good safe distance from the London plague. It is one hundred miles,' he says encouragingly, and waits for cries of shock and indignation, but these are muted while his London-born family ponder this great number of miles.

'This house of our ancient kinswoman,' asks Ingram Hall's wife Luce, 'is it of a size to hold us all in comfort? As big as this house? And who is this ancient kinswoman? Her name?'

'Yes of course a large house, even bigger than this,' says Walter Hall, who has no knowledge at all of the house at Bradford-on-Avon, 'and fine gardens for my nieces to run and play.' He gives Edith and Meriall a fond smile. 'Our kinswoman is Rachel Scudamore, a grand-daughter of William Hall. A kind old woman.'

'And you are coming with us?' Ingram Hall still wants to know.

'The court is in London and my chaplaincy duties require me to be with the court. At hand when needed. We are all servants of the king, are we not?'

This can't be gainsaid, and the argument and discussion peters out. Walter Hall sees he has the advantage and pushes forward. 'People are leaving already. Carts and coaches are in great demand and you must prepare to travel in two days. I can make sure you have carts – but only two——'

'Two! Only two carts?' Luce Hall looks daggers at her husband's brother. 'Two carts will not be sufficient.'

'A waggon if I can get one, if there is still one to be had, if not then two carts. And places on a west-bound coach. Inside places of course,' he says reassuringly to Luce, who ignores him, who is mentally arranging her family's chests and chattels in the waggon and both carts. Elsa's children are grown and gone, she will have little need of much cart space.

Uncle Rowland is unhappy and agitated, takes Walter Hall aside for private conversation. 'Nephew, nephew, thank you for this wondrous remedy, thank you. I am most interested in the causes and cures of this unwelcome and devouring guest, the plague. I need protection against the infection and now I have it, so I shall not be leaving London, not leave this house. I will stay nephew.'

'Uncle, it is not safe. This is a fierce plague and London is infected. Only parts now but soon the whole town and beyond the walls. Very soon. You must leave for your own safety. And the family needs your wise counsel. You know that.'

Uncle Rowland shakes his head in despair and calls for the servants, 'Where are you all?' to come, come now, and take him up to his bed. Now! Must Have Now! He holds the remedy on high as a sure shield against the pestilence.

Walter Hall, taking his leave, can hear his uncle, who loves music, singing mournfully:

Ask me why I do not sing to the tension of the string,
As I did, as I did not long ago when my numbers full did flow,
Grief, ah me, hath struck my lute and my tongue,
And my tongue at one time mute.

Walter Hall turns back into the rectory, says to brother Godfrey, 'Tell my uncle that Bradford-on-Avon is close to the city of Bath. Very close to Bath and its healthy waters. And tell him the distance from London is perhaps only eighty or ninety miles.' This he knows to be untrue, but it might mollify his unhappy uncle.

'Bradvon-on-Ford' – Walter Hall knows Uncle Rowland does this sort of thing wilfully. He can hear the rising voices of a growing argument. Luce is saying, 'He said a waggon and two carts.' Elsa disagrees, 'No, a waggon if he can get one, otherwise two carts. *Or.*' 'No! He said! He said! Two carts will not be enough! He said a waggon *and* two carts. How otherwise can we do this?' Walter Hall hears Luce's voice break and she weeps. 'This infection, this plague, it will kill us all! My girls. We must leave.' Walter Hall is satisfied he has done what he can to help. He hears Elsa comfort Luce. It is what women do.

* * *

London, Saturday, 24 June 1665
Midsummer Day

'A visit at the rectory yesterday, minister Walter Hall himself,' Goody Parsons comments as the three women settle down on the churchyard wall and the other two are busy setting their pipes. All know a Friday attendance by Walter Hall at the rectory is an event to be considered, discussed.

Goody Parsons is a fruitful bearer of rectory news. Her sister Sibil has a friend whose daughter, Jinny Bosvill, is under-cook there. There is general pride that small Jinny has risen in the world to under-cook. She has also risen in height and in confidence – grown into a generous soul, big, loud and laughing – but is still called Little Jinny. She is the favoured protégé of Nan the cook.

'They all must leave, fly, he has told them. Fly to a big house called Bradford at Bradford, a town to the west. So many miles by coach. Four inn stops, Little Jinny says, to get there.' Goody Parsons shakes her head disapprovingly at the whole idea of such a distance, such a place.

'Mmm. Bradford. I have never heard of Bradford,' says the Widow, who has heard of very little outside London, apart from the Warden's stories of Peterborough.

'The whole household, all of them to fly?' asks Goodwife Joan Brokefild. 'Leaving the rectory empty. Will Walter Hall want that?'

'Oh no,' Goody Parsons is gratified to be able to answer, 'Oh no. Jack the footboy and perhaps one other will stay. Although the old man Rowland Holmes says if one goes all should go.'

'Rowland Holmes,' the Goodwife is interested, 'is he the man who sings? I often hear singing but never see the singer. A fine tenor voice he has, the tenor of an older man.'

'Oh yes, he sings, Rowland Holmes. And he is a talking, demanding, complaining man, Jinny Bosvill says. Always calling for this, for that. "Must Have Now" the servants say, "Must Have Now." And he does not want to leave. Took the rector aside and whispered in his loud voice that now he had the king's remedy against the infection he needn't leave.'

'What remedy is that?' the two Searchers ask together.

Goody Parsons is smug with knowledge. 'A most costly remedy, with Mitridate and Venice Treacle and much other. Sent by the king himself to Rowland Holmes.'

'Does the king know Rowland Holmes?' the Widow wonders.

'He must,' Goody Parsons thinks this obvious, 'he must. He knows Walter Hall who is always at Whitehall, at the Chapel Royal. And Rowland Holmes is Walter Hall's uncle. He must.'

'Always there and never here, Walter Hall,' the Goodwife laughs.

'He was here yesterday,' says Goody Parsons, who finds the minister's velvet reading voice and silken walk a source of pleasure, and his standing at court a great boon to the parish of St Cyneswide and St Tibba, and its parishioners. 'Beeswax candles,' she adds, 'they have beeswax candles at the rectory.'

Knowing only rush lights and tallow tapers, they all savour the rectory's beeswax candles.

'Of course the Why-toll Palace must have beeswax candles,' Goody Parsons says with firm authority. She relishes Jinny Bosvill's stories of the treasures Walter Hall brings from the Palace, including half-done candles and stubs that are then recast in the kitchen.

'Walter Hall does well from his position at the Whitehall Palace. But is he to fly the city with his kin?' the Goodwife asks teasingly, enjoying this exchange.

'Oh no, he told his family that while the court is in London, so he is in London.'

'Mmm, good,' Widow Hazard says. 'So they should stay, the king and court. So it is not just the old poor women who have nowhere to fly to who must suffer here.'

'The poor, all of us. Old poor men and old poor women and young poor men and young poor women and young poor children and poor babes. Nowhere to fly to so we are here, and we stay here,' the Goodwife says vigorously.

Goody Parsons is jolted by this outburst, not sure how the talk has taken such a turn, and says defensively, 'It is said, Walter Hall told his kin, that they, the court, make a pretence of going away, calling for carts and waggons, but they will not go for good and all.'

'My son down at the river, Joseph the lighterman on the river, sees people flying by boat,' says the Goodwife. 'Up river and down. He says at times he can see no water for all the boats.'

'You have seen your son Joseph?' the Widow asks, surprised. The Goodwife nods but says no more. The Widow thinks she will speak more freely when Goody Parsons has gone.

'At the *Cross Keys* at Cripplegate,' says Goody Parsons, finding a welcome gap in the talk that she can fill, 'they have constant traffic of coaches and waggons all full of people going into the country.'

'All the town going out of town,' the Goodwife says drily.

'That Widow Aspiner, the one with the neck and the lame leg, has left town. Gone to Salisbury,' Goody Parsons says, cautiously steering into dangerously shoaled waters. No response. The Searchers no longer have any interest in Elizabeth Aspiner or her household.

'That other one, new-made widow Hester Shipley, she's not going anywhere. Shut in, she can't!' Goody Parsons giggles. Waits to see if the name brings a response. It does.

'Mmm, her and her guineas.'

'So she did offer money. How much? Just a guinea? Not more?'

'A guinea a head,' the Widow Margaret Hazard says, gesturing to her head and the Goodwife's, 'so two guineas in all.'

'Best bargain at the Cheapside markets,' the Goodwife laughs. 'Two fine Searchers for two guineas. Who'll buy my fine Searchers!'

'Some Searchers, not here, in other parishes of course, would have taken that,' Goody Parsons observes primly, watching them closely.

'But not here in the parish of St Cyneswide and St Tibba,' the Goodwife asserts. She has heard the gossip and rumours that one of them would have taken the bribe but the other refused. The stories vary as to which of them would, and which wouldn't. The Goodwife always strongly answers, when she gets the chance, 'Not here in St Cyneswide and St Tibba.' Widow Hazard seems oblivious of the parish rumblings.

'There is another ...' Goody Parsons begins tentatively, but quails before Goodwife Joan Brokefild's fixed stare. There is silence while the two Searchers mend their pipes. Goody Parsons decides this is a good moment to say her God be w'ye.

The two Searchers also move, but only a short distance. As the sun moves, so the two ancient women shift around the churchyard wall, following the shade. Perched prominently, they can see and be seen. Their red wands giving a clear warning, as intended, for all to stay away from these friends of death.

When Goody Susanna Parsons is well out of earshot – the Searchers watch her progress across the square – it is Widow Hazard's turn to fill the silence.

'Your son?'

'Yes. Joseph came to call then he and his father went tavern fuddling. Bad as each other. Too mean, too miserable to give me a God be w'ye as they left. Isaac crawled back at all hours, drunk as a dog. His tongue well befuddled but he could still make heavy use of his hands, and his feet.' She heaves a slow sigh, shrugs, lowers her voice, 'He would occupy me but could not, yet he could still kick.'

'You poor wretch.'

The Goodwife speaks even softer, whispers to her friend, 'I would rather his kicks than the other thing.'

The Widow nods, but she took pleasure in doing the other thing with her John Hazard, and the memory of this briefly distracts her. John Hazard now long dead. Three pigeons cooing and courting and strutting around the grave stones catch her eye. The eager lad fans his tail, dances a few steps. The Widow's thoughts turn to pigeon in broth.

'Goody Parsons has a good recipe for pigeon. She knows many good recipes.'

'Recipes! Goody Susanna Parsons,' snorts Goodwife Joan Brokefild, 'she knows a lot of everything. Knows a lot about everything and everybody. Thinks she does.'

'Mmm. Her pigeon recipe – it has wine, all her recipes have wine – you part boil a pigeon stuffed with parsley and butter, then put it in a strong broth–'

'What kind of broth?'

'Any strong meat broth, beef, lamb, any kind. I wouldn't use fish. Not fish broth. Then put in mace and pepper corns and white wine – she says half a pint, but how much does a pigeon need? When all the licor cooks down you have a good, brave gravy to serve with your bird.'

'Have you cooked it?'

'No.'

'Hot pudding pies, hot!' a vendor ambles into the square.

'Too hot for hot pudding pies,' the Goodwife says dismissively.

'Mmm. She's from St Bartholomew Little. I don't know if her pies are good. She looks hot. It is hot. Hot for her, walking along under a dish of pies.'

'Hot pudding pies, hot! Hot pudding pies, hot!'

'Her recipes for fowl, Goody Parsons. They're all much of a muchness – wine, pepper, mace, parsley in all of them,' The Goodwife grumbles.

'Mmm.'

'Fine roasting forks. Buy a fine roasting fork. Fine roasting forks,' a different voice approaches. The forks are rattled, clattered.

'Who needs a new roasting fork?' the Widow asks the Goodwife. 'A good roasting fork has a long life. Sara is a steady, patient girl at roasting. A steady hand.'

'Delicate cow cumbers to pickle. Delicate cow cumbers.' The cry is loud, high-pitched and carries far.

'Maude Wattes,' the Goodwife says. 'Her belly's bigger. Seven months? More?' She defers to the Widow's greater knowledge.

'Mmm. More like eight, near eight. She's big. She was big with her others. Seven living. Male child this one. See? Lying on her right side. Belly sprung out. She's a fruitful vine.'

'Delicate cow cumbers to pickle. Delicate cow cumbers.'

'Not so long since she heard the wedding psalm.'

'A good ten, dozen years.'

'Mmm. Not so long.'

They sing:

> *Like fruitful vines on thy house-side,*
> *so doth thy wife spring out:*
> *Thy children stand like olive-plants*
> *thy table round about.*

They fall silent and watch pregnant Maude until she turns out of the square.

'Her good fortune to have so many,' says Widow Margaret Hazard. 'Seven living and this one coming.'

The Goodwife does not think this particularly good fortune but knows the Widow admires and envies those who have brought living babes into the world, and kept them living. 'Two days ago she was calling "White radish, white young lettuce." Poor, dry withered things from this heat. She sells what she can. Money in short supply in that house.' She laughs a sharp laugh. 'Her Ned and my Isaac could be brothers. Same kind.'

Widow Hazard knows, the whole parish knows, what Ned Wattes and Isaac Brokefild are like.

The Warden, a busy, happy man, comes from the church. He waves and walks over to the ancient women.

'Much to do. I won't linger.' He does. 'I won't sit.' He doesn't, but stands and chats. 'There has been a misunderstanding. A misunderstanding, but only on the part of those shut up. Yes, the parish makes sure that they have food and drink. Naturally. We don't want them to die!' He laughs, finds the notion funny. 'If they were not shut up they would be paying for their provisions. Everyone does. They cannot go out and buy so the Keepers do this for them. But to expect the parish to pay! And they do. They do expect the parish to pay. Some of them do.'

'Widow Shipley,' says Widow Margaret Hazard, 'she would expect that. Ready to pay out guineas so we would deny it was the plague. But the parish should pay for her food. She would expect that.'

'Yes,' the Warden says, 'she would. She did. I can't linger.' He doesn't move. 'Much to do in this sickly time.' He lights his pipe.

The pigeons are still dancing their courtship on the graves. They watch them. The Goodwife turns her feet to the left, turns her feet to the right, pigeon-like. Bobs up and down. The Warden laughs.

'Provisioning for those shut up is the job for an old trooper. Military organisation: detail, discipline, and time,' the Warden says with satisfaction. 'Time is important.'

'Provisioning. You could kill us some of your pigeons for our dinner, our dinner time. Dinner is as important as time. More important,' the Goodwife half-jokes. 'Keeper Parsons has a recipe for pigeons in broth.'

'Good. That's good.' The Warden's voice turns serious, he says to them both, 'When you saw the Clerk after the searching, good you spoke to him then about those guineas. That was well done. Stops stories, rumours. It should.'

The Goodwife nods, understanding what he is telling them. The Widow is not aware of anything here that needs to be understood.

The three pigeons fly off. A children's game takes over the square. A wrestle of boys and girls shouting, laughing. They gather, a wobbling, wriggling mob facing Harry Shute, one of bufflehead Walter Shute's black-haired grandchildren. Harry feints a couple of times then tosses a small string-bound ball. From the yelling ruck and screams of 'Mine! Mine!' tough Dorothy Damport emerges brandishing the ball, shoving and kicking any who dare try and take it from her. She stands out in front. Her turn to throw. She takes her time, jeering and gesturing.

Loud cries of 'Doro-thee, Doro-theeeee, to me! To meee!' fill the square. Dorothy ignores them. Sara hangs back, hoping for a high, long lob. Dorothy has powerful arms. She and her mother and her cousins, Bridget and Em, are washerwomen. Dorothy and Em are the ones who twist and wring the linen, each holding an end, giving great grunts and growls at each other as they do so, then shrieking with laughter. This hot weather is good, the washing festooned over bushes, dangled from nails on walls, hung out of windows, dries quickly. This hot weather is bad, water is scarce, precious and dirty. Whatever the season the washing girls will chant:

> Go wash well, says Summer, with sun I shall dry,
> Go wring well, says Winter, with wind so shall I.

And Dorothy's mother, also Dorothy, on hearing them will give them her own verse of country wisdom:

> Maids, wash well and wring well, but beat ye wot how,
> If any lack beating, I fear it be yow.

Which makes the girls roar with more laughter, howling, 'Yow! Yow! Yow!'

Heading north, a train of small carts packed with boxes and chests and the old and the very young push their slow way through the square, briefly breaking up the game. The children stare at the score of people who walk with the carts. They are all strangers, none are from the parish of St Cyneswide and St Tibba. These departing Londoners are uneasy, close-bound into their small group as it makes its way out of the city.

The childrens' play is enlivened by half a dozen dogs leaping and barking and getting underfoot. The dogs are immediately on the alert at the passing caravan of strangers and are outraged by the intruders' dogs. The children, and the watching adults, are entertained by some savage fights and cheer on their local hounds. 'Get 'im Grinder, get 'im!' Gypsy the lurcher, older, well disciplined by William Northage, has found a place in the shade and is not stirred to join in. She only bites when William Northage tells her to.

When the carts have gone the St Cyneswide and St Tibba dogs tumble back into the square. Edward Richbell's small terrier Gnasher limping and bleeding. Dorothy, brushing the dogs aside, cries out, 'Here comes!' and throws the ball straight into the air, catching it herself. Laughs and mocks, 'I caught it and I caught you out!'

As well as passing carts, the game has to skirt around a pile of bonfire wood growing in fits and starts in a corner of the square.

'Midsummer fires?' the Goodwife teases the Warden. 'Are there to be midsummer fires?'

Church Warden Frances Barrow does not answer. Stares at the pile of wood, then says with mild indignation, 'I have had to put a watch on that wood. There are those who would take it for themselves. If you can believe such low behaviour of the parishioners of St Cyneswide and St Tibba. The wood thieves must come from beyond our bounds.'

He stretches and yawns, looks to his pipe. 'We had fires for the victory over the Dutchman, and fires help burn away the pestilence. That is well known. Ancient matrons surely know the virtue that a great fire has to purge the infection of the air.'

They nod. They do know. The Goodwife declaims:

> *The wholesome heat, purging the air, consumes*
> *The earth's unwholesome vapours, fogs and fumes.*

'Yes,' agrees the Warden, pleased, 'yes it does. I knew a trooper from Dunstable Downs. It's not so far from London. John Massey, that's who it was. John Massey. They keep midsummer fires at Dunstable Downs he said. Games and dancing too.'

'Singing?' asks the Widow.

'Yes. I am sure there is singing. John Massey didn't say, but there must be singing.'

'Your own voice is a fine one,' the Goodwife says.

'Just as well since you hear it often,' the Warden laughs.

'Yes, in church of course. And sometimes singing your old campaigning songs. The *Zealous Soldier*. But other times, other places, as well. The *White*

Hind.'

The Warden is surprised, 'The *White Hind*? You heard me singing there? You don't go to such places!'

'Oh no. No. I don't go in. At times out walking I hear singing and I stop and listen. Your voice in any group of singing men stands clear.'

'So you hear singing at the *White Hind*. And more?'

'More? At more taverns?'

'No no, not at more taverns. At the *White Hind*. Do you hear talking? Conversation? Discussion? Do you hear talking too at the *White Hind*?'

'Talking? I don't listen to what men talk about in such places. Only the singing.'

'Just as well! Some times men's talk in taverns is ... is ... not fit!' he laughs again, yawns. 'Mustn't linger. Much to be done. God be w'ye ancient matrons.' He leaves, the *Zealous Soldier* on his lips again.

'And God be with you Frances Barrow.'

They sit smoking and watch the bonfire grow: the children scattering and bringing back more wood.

'I heard one of their *White Hind* songs clearly,' Goodwife Joan Brokefild says. 'Quite clearly. A catch, sung in four parts.'

'Our Warden was one of those parts?'

'He was.'

'Mmm. What song?'

'A wanton one.'

'Tell me.'

The Goodwife lowers her voice and sings quietly into the Widow's ear:

Here dwells a pretty maid, whose name is Sis,
You may come in and kiss,
Her whole, her whole, her whole estate
Is seventeen pence a year,
Yet you may kiss, you may kiss, you may kiss,
You may kiss her, if you come but near.

The two ancient matrons quiver with supressed laughter, but not supressed enough.

Isabella Undnay, with anger on her face and in her voice, runs at them.

'You sit here, laughing, doing nothing, laughing. Doing nothing,' she pants. 'You found the family of some painter, some man who is nothing to this parish, and now you sit here laughing and do nothing to find Richard Undnay. You are a Searcher, both Searchers, so search, now! and find my Richard Undnay.' Her hands claw up as if she would tear out the Widow's one good eye.

The Widow looks at her steadily with this good eye. 'That was luck, good fortune, the painter Ralph Eackles of St Martin Vintry. No such luck for your husband Richard.' She does not say it is true that she has done nothing to try to find Richard Undnay. Sees no need. It is not what Searchers do. This woman will not listen to reason.

The distraught Isabella shakes her head, turns away, turns back and sneers, 'Sitting there on your beshitt'n arses, as always, when you should be out searching for Richard Undnay. If I offered you a Guinea you would find him, find him today. If I had a Guinea I would. Your ways are known. They are known.' She rubs her fingers, sneers, 'A guinea, a guinea.'

The Widow shrugs. Isabella Undnay has lost her husband and her mind has turned. She has seen it before, remembers her own state when John Hazard died.

Goodwife Joan Brokefild waves away Isabella Undnay dismissively, says to Widow Hazard, 'We,' she stresses the *we*, 'cannot help her. What she says about Guineas is wrong. Ignore what she says about Guineas.'

'I do. Her husband is dead of the plague. Buried in some pit. Somewhere. Somewhere where no-one can find him. Except God. God knows where Richard Undnay is.'

'I know a midsummer song, a midsummer fire song:

When midsummer comes with brushwood and broom they stoke the
*   bonfire flame,*
And swiftly then, the nimble young men, leap o'er it in a game.
The women and maidens together do couple their hands,

With piping sound they dance a round, no malice among them stands.

'Mmm. Then we should couple hands with Isabella Undnay so no malice inside her stands.'

As the long day starts to dim the impatient children, calling, shouting, laughing, bring brands and start the fire. Bring more wood. They chase each other with sticks, beating at legs. The wilder ones set their sticks alight, waving and slashing them at their fellows. The Widow stands up and watches closely. Sara knows her mother's mind and stands well back from the mayhem, waves to her mother to show that she is keeping out of it. Shows she is a good child. The Widow nods back and keeps watching, thinks Sara is a good child but still must be watched. Their family only has three eyes and it cannot lose another.

Standing, watching Sara, the Widow is conscious that her nether parts are close to the Goodwife's face, asks, 'Is my arse beshitt'n?'

Goodwife Joan Brokefild sniffs deeply, pauses, says, 'No more than mine.' The Widow finds this comforting, nods her thanks. The Goodwife laughs.

The children's random running is interrupted by Dorothy Damport's sharp voice. 'Join hands! Join hands!' She grabs Christopher Northage's hand. The large circle of youngsters moves slowly clockwise around the fire, then faster and faster, until Dorothy gives a great tug with her left hand and changes the direction, shouting, 'Widdershins! Widdershins!'

The dance goes on and on. Faces red with the heat, bodies sweating, voices shouting, 'Round and round and round and round!'

When the fire starts to die to embers Dorothy Damport calls, 'Thread the needle, thread the needle!' Sara has joined the dance, her mother has not stopped her, and with the others she snakes under the arch formed by the joined hands of Dorothy Damport and Christopher Northage, her feet, all their feet, skipping quickly over the dulling coals. The big ones swing the littlings safely above the embers, the small ones squealing with excited terror. The noise grows even louder when watching adults roar, 'John

Clapshaw stop that! Get that small Sam Stiles away from the fire! Do you hear?' Sheepish John Clapshaw, who has been having a fine time teasing his little cousin by swinging him down close to the coals, shows he has heard by lifting the child as high as he can.

The needle is threaded again and again and the shrieking rises as the dancers stamp out the fire. A sudden heavy downpour of rain finishes the job for them and they stand laughing, soaking and sooty. Then hurry away as the rain pelts down harder. Sara takes her mother's hand and skips along sideways singing, 'Round and round and round and round.'

Thomas Snow comes up and hands the Widow a brace of pigeons. 'From the Warden. Got two more here for Goodwife Brokefild.' The Widow, surprised, shows she's pleased. The lad sees an opening, offers, 'Pluck em for you? A farding a piece?' The Widow takes the birds and continues on home. Thomas Snow optimistically calls after her, 'Farding for both?' When she does not answer he runs off towards Goodwife Joan Brokefield's house. Thinks his mistake with the Widow was setting his opening bid too high. He'll give the Goodwife his best smile and say 'Pluck em both for you for only a farding.'

Indoors, the Widow checks Sara's hard, calloused feet. Soot blackened but not burnt. Picks off a few cinders with her nails. Gets a dipper of water and tells the child to wash her face and hands, properly, not just a few swift swipes of the wash cloth.

The rain rains on and thunder and lightning crash above St Cyneswide and St Tibba, echoing around its small square. The Widow plucks and guts the pigeons. Wonders if beer would be a possible substitute for wine but after some thought decides it wouldn't.

Sara is still singing 'Round and round and round' to herself. The Widow hands her the bible, says, 'Book of Psalms, psalm the seventy seventh. The verses on storms, seventeen and eighteen.'

Sara obediently finds the Psalm and reads:

Verse the Seventeenth: The clouds poured out water: the skies sent out a sound: thine arrows also went abroad.

Verse the Eighteenth: The voice of thy thunder was in the heaven:
the lightnings lightened the world: the earth trembled and shook.

'Mmm.' The Widow's views are confirmed: Sternhold and Hopkins word it better. She tells her daughter to turn to the metrical Psalms at the back, 'Sing the Seventeenth and Eighteenth verses.' They do:

The clouds that were both thick and black,
did rain full plenteously:
The thunder in the air did crack,
thy shafts abroad did fly.
Thy thunder in the air was heard,
thy lightnings from above,
With flashes great made men afraid,
the earth did quake and move.

The thunders and the lightnings slowly move away, the rain continues full plenteously.

Sara sleeps and Widow Margaret Hazard thinks of the fortunes that can be told, the future that can be seen, on a Midsummer night. She stares at the coals on her hearth but they only show that some pathways through the fire are open, some are not, and these keep changing. She finds nothing there for Sara or for herself.

The Widow wakes at the bell-man's cry.

Past one o'clock, and almost two,
My Masters all, Good day to you!

Troubled with a looseness, she goes out through the rain, a steady downpour, to the house of office. This late at night she has good hopes of finding it unoccupied. It is. Before she returns to bed she takes care to make sure her arse is not beshitt'n.

CHAPTER VI

London, Sunday, 25 June 1665

'Hear'st, O Lord, the poor men's plaint.'

'Boy,' says Philip Carter the Parish Clerk to Thomas Snow in tones kinder, gentler, than normal, 'go and peer towards the Rectory and see if there is a carriage arrived, or if the parson is now walking here. Go see if he's coming. Could be this rain has stayed him back.'

Time is overdue for the Sunday service to begin. Not unusual, but today it is long overdue. The rector is long overdue. The Clerk does not seem disturbed. He looks cheerful. Smiles. He catches the Church Warden's eye: nods his head at the empty pulpit; raises his hands and shrugs with a 'who knows?' gesture. The Warden responds with a shake of his head: 'I don't.' This is not true. Both think it unlikely Walter Hall will take the service today, and have a good idea why.

* * *

'Warm and dry out of the rain,' Widow Dorothy Bullen says agreeably to fellow Keeper Goody Parsons and Viewers Anne Abowen and Widow Ursula Chaukley. The Viewers and Keepers have placed themselves some distance from the Searchers so they can, should they wish to, talk freely. They make up one of the many small plots of comfortable conversation that fill the nave of St Cyneswide and St Tibba while the parishioners wait, with no sense of urgency, for Walter Hall to glide in with his beautiful walk.

'Dry and *too* warm,' says Anne Abowen, a woman of strong opinions, adds, 'Even with the rain these days are too hot. Rain doesn't cool them. Too warm in here.' She shifts from side to side, gains herself more space.

'Today is Sunday!' Bufflehead Walter Shute shouts. He has recently taken to reminding himself, and others, of where the week stands. 'Today is Sunday, Lord's day!' These latest outbursts amuse the parish, but – as Eppie Smoote tells her friend Beatrix Sutterwhit – 'It's a well done thing the way Bufflehead Walter calls the day. Tells me where I am.' Beatrix Sutterwhit always knows the day and does not need the Bufflehead's help with this, but understands that her friend Eppie does.

* * *

'Gnasher's healing better than I thought she would.' William Northage always sits with Barnard Clapshaw, the two men are fond of their dogs and swap dog stories. 'Edward Richbell should have his bitch back soon. Green Oil of Charity's doing the business. Start with Green Oil of Charity. I always start with the Green Oil. Then after three days if needs be go to Sanicle. Three days or so. Could be more, could be less. That stranger dog nearly tore a piece out of her.'

Barnard Clapshaw listens with interest; wonders if William ever uses ground moss; knows his turn will come to describe how one of his pups drags its legs; both hind legs; William will have some ideas about that; remembers how, in a moment of drunken wit, he'd thought of calling the pup Carter the Clerk, but decided best keep this to himself if he wanted to stay a parish watchman. He had taken the pup in his pocket to the *Three Tuns* and let it drag itself along the table to amuse fellow drinkers George Hillcocke and John Girling. You couldn't say anything in front of John Girling without him telling any and every.

* * *

'This doctor, this Doctor Barnett, who has shut up himself in his house because – he says – the plague is there. It is not for him to say, it is the Viewers,' an angry Widow Margaret Hazard gestures vigorously towards

Viewers Anne Abowen and Widow Ursula Chaukley. 'It is for the Viewers of his parish to see the signs, the Viewers, and to report what they find to their Parish Clerk. Do they do things differently in St Katharine Coleman? They must. In St Cyneswide and St Tibba the Viewers view the sick, the Keepers keep the sick and Searchers search the corpse. If this doctor is to die will he then report to the Clerk of St Katharine Coleman that he died of the plague? Mmm? No.'

Goodwife Joan Brokefild, like all London, has heard of the doctor who caused himself and his plague-struck household to be shut in. The goodwill this handsome act has engendered in the doctor's neighbours and friends does not extend to Searcher Widow Hazard in St Cyneswide and St Tibba. 'You are not one for doctors,' the Goodwife says.

'No doctor ever did any good for those dear to me. They all died. Parish nurses, we are the ones who know.'

* * *

'Half a dozen pigeons each the Warden gave them. Half a dozen. Each,' Widow Chaukley says confidently. 'Gave them, not sold them. Our Lord Jesus overthrew the tables of the moneychangers and the seats of them that sold doves, or pigeons. Thomas Dugdale read that from the bible. A lesson.'

'He did, Thomas Dugdale. I remember that lesson. I heard it was a dozen, a round dozen each, Frances Barrow gave them,' Goody Parsons offers. Widow Dorothy Bullen nods her support for this higher figure.

Anne Abowen says, 'Two or twelve pigeons, however many, why did he give them to those two? See the way she flung her arm out at us just now? Pointing at us? What she's saying about us to Goodwife Brokefild I'd like to know. Something unkind. She has something in her gizzard. Look at her, face as sour as spoiled milk.'

'Isabella Undnay says the Searchers will not look for her missing Richard,' Goody Susanna Parson whispers, even though it is not possible for the Searchers to hear her. 'Widow Hazard does nothing, so Isabella Undnay says. Poor creature.'

* * *

Thomas Snow, dripping wet, runs into the church and makes his report to the Clerk. 'No carriage and he's not walking here. No sign at all of the rector. At all.' The boy shakes himself like a dog – even this does not irritate the Clerk.

'Did you see anything at all, boy?'

'I saw Jack the footboy standing in the rectory porch.'

'And?'

'I gave him a wave. He gave me a wave. I called out: Have you seen the carriage? He couldn't hear me so I run over and ask him: Have you seen the carriage?'

'And? Had he?'

'No. He said he hadn't seen the carriage and he asks me: Had I seen the carriage? And I said I hadn't.' Thomas Snow does not tell the Clerk that Jack the footboy had spoken in a fruity voice, in hilarious imitation of Walter Hall, and that he, Thomas, had responded by staggering about, hunched and dragging his legs in a way not unlike the Clerk. Thomas Snow sniggers at the memory.

'Go look again.'

The Warden walks up to the Clerk, says in quiet excitement, 'He's run, hasn't he? He's run away, the dog.'

'Not yet, hasn't gone yet. Getting ready to run. But he'll be a no-show today and no curate arranged for here. Useless and feckless, as always. I'll know more Tuesday at Parish Clerks.'

Thomas Snow runs up again, panting loudly, showily, says very loudly, 'Some of the family coming!'

'Who?'

'The brother and his Goodwife. Gregory? Godfrey? Gerard, I think.'

'Godfrey Hall boy, Godfrey Hall. He's coming is he?'

Godfrey and Elsa Hall, wet, better dressed than most of St Cyneswide and St Tibba, take their places in the family's front pew. Godfrey Hall beckons the Parish Clerk, tells him, 'The Rector is on urgent business at the

Palace of Whitehall. Urgent business. We cannot expect him today.'

'A curate coming?' the Clerk asks, sure that one isn't.

Godfrey, stiff, duty-bound and responsible – the oldest of the Hall brothers – says sharply, 'There was no time to engage one. Too short notice. My brother needed urgently at the Palace. At the Whitehall Palace.' He stops, stares at the Clerk. 'You will know what to do, Parish Clerk.'

The Warden close by, his round pie-face bland, looks on, listens. Many others are straining to do the same.

'Times past, in the Protector's time, there were parishes where the clerk did the ministering, there being no minister to do it,' Robert Tomlinson tells his neighbours. 'Philip Carter could do the ministering. Been here a long time. Knows it all. Heard it often enough.'

'That was twenty years ago, when we lost all those ministers who wouldn't take the Solemn League and Covenant. Wouldn't take it,' Thomas Billington, two pews back, speaks loudly, wants all to hear him take issue with Robert Tomlinson. 'Good men forced out because they wouldn't take Oliver's Solemn League and Covenant, and not enough of that other kind of minister' – he puts a mustard touch of scorn on 'that other kind of minister' – 'not enough Sectaries, to do the job so parish clerks had to. That's why parish clerks did it. No real ministers and not enough Sectaries.' He rounds this off with a snort and sits glaring at the back of Robert Tomlinson's head.

'Nothing wrong with parish clerks. The problem is bishops! Bishops is the problem,' jeers Robert Tomlinson. 'Thieving, greedy bishops! That's all his kind cares about,' he jerks a thumb back towards Thomas Billington, 'rank and privileges. Bishops!'

'Leveller! Just what you Levellers say. Bring us all down to your level.'

The congregation stirs; shift in their seats; look around; catching the eyes of those who are like-minded, avoiding the eyes of those who are not. All know those who are for Church, bishops and the Book of Common Prayer; and those who still favour the extirpation of popery, archbishops, bishops, and the Book of Common Prayer. The comforting roll of relaxed chatter gives way to a tense, growing rumbling.

Philip Carter Parish Clerk holds up a hand, announces in his great voice, 'Parson's been called away on business—'

'Urgent business at the Palace of Whitehall,' Godfrey calls out.

'His brother says parson has business at the Why-toll Palace. We will sing psalms to the glory of God. Psalm the twenty sixth, singing of the joy in going to God's house.'

The congregation is pleased with this choice, glad to be united again in singing.

The Clerk's arm swings up, he chants the first line and the St Cyneswide and St Tibba slow mill of voices follows in familiar song:

O God, thy house I love most dear, to me it doth excell:
I have delight, and would be near whereas thy grace doth dwell.

The next psalm is a favourite, always sung with relish. 'We shall sing the one hundred and sixth psalm, to the glory of God.' The parishioners of St Cyneswide and St Tibba delight particularly in the verse:

Both we and our forefathers all have sinned ev'ry one:
We have committed wickedness, and very lewdly done.

And later lustily sing of the wicked sins of the Baal-worshipping Israelites:

Thus were they stained with the works of their own filthy way:
And with their own inventions a whoring they did stray.

Each parishioner has thoughts about who these words might fit today, the year 1665. They exchange covert looks.

The Clerk calls for the eighty first psalm which is agreeable not only to St Cyneswiders and St Tibbers who are for the Book of Common Prayer, but also to those who think of the Book as Porridge, as hatched in hell to impose popery: all are united against the papists, against Rome:

Thou shalt no god in thee reserve, of any land abroad:
Nor in no wise bow to or serve a strange or foreign god.

'We shall sing psalm the one hundred and thirty seventh to the glory of God.' The Clerk's voice is now rasping, hoarse, but the surge of song carries him on.

Widow Margaret Hazard hates psalm one hundred and thirty seven, and resents her Parish Clerk when he announces it. The cruelty of the last verse shocks and angers her.

> *Yea blessed shall that man be call'd that takes thy children young*
> *To dash their bones against hard stones, that lie the streets among.*

Blessed! She broods.

She would never tear her bible, but did have the thought that a page might not be missed. She had checked to see if Sternhold and Hopkins echoed the psalmist's words. They had. She found: 'Happy shall he be, that taketh and dasheth thy little ones against the stones.'

Happy! She broods. Holds Sara's hand so tightly the child winces but says nothing. She knows her mother and she knows she is the flowers in her mother's garden. She has sometimes, rarely, been told this.

Widow Margaret Hazard tries to ignore the words but cannot. She dreads the approach of the last verse, and when Phillip Carter lines it out anger and despair fill her. And doubt. Because if such an abomination is set down in the holy book what other – flaws? – she cannot find the right word, might be there? God the Father she understands. Jesus Christ the Son she understands. The Holy Ghost makes no sense to her. She does not understand the Holy Ghost. Wonders if it is some clerical joke imposed by learned Churchmen – bishops – on ignorant poor ancient matrons. What could the Holy Ghost be? Is it the ghost within that departs, flies away, at death?

She has seen many dying, many dead, and has never seen the Holy Ghost depart. She has only seen life stop.

Three times she *has* seen a corpse slowly sit up, whispered sounds hissing from its mouth. She had been told this is what a murdered man does: dead, yes, but still driven to name his killer. Yet for all three she saw there had been no murder, only death by meagrome, by tissick, by jaundies.

The first time it happened she had started in terror. Wanted to run, but she was a new-made Searcher and determined not to show weakness. Stiff with fear she had stayed, and saw the corpse of Gregorie Woodnet, dead of the meagrome, sink back with a long expulsion of foul air. She was sure this Holy Ghost could not be the noxious fart of a dead man. Unless it was.

In a fogged, formless way she suspects all good Christians each have their own book of belief. She has hers, but she never speaks of this. Women less cautious have confided their doubt, bemusement, sometimes even amusement, at the virgin birth. They have all seen those mothers who say they do not know what is the matter until their child is born, or who deny how they are while their bellies precede them. Single women, wives whose husbands have been absent for too long, or those women with too many infants and desperate to have no more. The virgin birth of Jesus does not bother the Widow. It is a story and the bible is full of stories. Psalm one hundred and thirty seven angers her and she will not sing it.

King David. She has no time for kings. David had six wives, then he took a seventh, the filthy whoring heathen. And there is a king in London today who, while he has but one lawful wife, has many more than seven whores, the filthy whoring heathen. Oliver Protector and his godly party knew what was best done with kings. Oliver could have been made king, but said no. No kings. The Widow has no time for kings.

The end of the cruel psalm comes, 'That lie the streets among,' and her wandering mind returns. The tautness, the anger, slowly ebbs, leaves her. She loosens her grip on Sara's hand and pats it. The child pats her in return, until the Widow becomes aware they are playing an unseemly hand-over-hand game in church and abruptly stops.

This parsonless Sunday the loud singing congregation have successfully drowned out the constant rain and, with shared relief, have come back together from division. The Parish Clerk announces, 'Psalm the tenth, to the glory of God.' And the people of the London parish of St Cyneswide and St Tibba, never flourishing, never rich, and now afflicted by the plague, sing with fervour:

Thou hear'st, O Lord, the poor men's plaint, their prayers and request:
Their hearts thou wilt confirm, until thine ears to hear be prest.
To judge the poor and fatherless, and help them to their right:
That they may be no more opprest by men of worldly might.

Philip Carter closes his Sternhold and Hopkins.

'Today is Sunday! Lord's day!' breaks the silence.

The Clerk shrugs, nods; the congregation stand, stretch, and amble out. Watchman William Hawkins, who has been waiting, and singing while he waits, brings a message to the Clerk. Thomas Snow is despatched to fetch the Searchers.

'Clerk sent me. He says come.' Thomas Snow walks with them, chats, 'More dead. More dead to search.' He looks closely at their potent red wands, looks at them, thinks with fear and excitement, 'Friends of death!'

'Corpses to search. Houses of Widow Pewe and Francis Wawin,' the Clerk rasps. 'William Hawkins says no sounds, no answers, when he knocks.' He waves them away.

Waiting for the Parish Clerk is his wife, Jane-Pym Carter, a small, plump plug who has, she tells everyone, legs thick enough, strong enough, to bear her lame husband as well as herself. And, she adds, all their children. Jane-Pym Carter is a loud, laughing woman. Waiting with her are Philip Carter's daughter Nan Carter, Jane-Pym Carter's daughter Betty Stopford, and the two children, Annie and Johanna, who Philip Carter and Jane-Pym Carter have with each other. Their Robin Carter died when two days old. There are times when, with sly delight, Widow Margaret Hazard, Goodwife Joan Brokefild and the other ancient matrons refer to fecund Jane-Pym Carter as 'Home To Bed.'

Philip Carter has buried two wives. His first died in childbirth, as did his second, but the child, Nan, survived. His third wife, Jane-Pym Carter, is very much alive. She has not buried her first husband. There was no body to bury.

* * *

In the year 59 widower Philip Carter, sitting on his churchyard wall, smoking, heard her singing cry, 'Who'll buy my sweet primroses? All in bloom! All in bloom!' He knows all the voices in St Cyneswide and St Tibba and has not heard hers before. He calls her over, looks closely at her primroses, says, 'Not from this parish?' She grins, 'Me or my flowers?' 'Both.' 'Me, I'm from Seamen's Church, my flowers from Kent.' 'Good long way from All Hallows the Great, Seamen's Church, Hay Church, Rope Church.' 'Good strong legs to carry me,' she waggles a foot at him, asks, 'your legs?' 'Falling stone. Carting a load of stones. One fell. One was enough.' She sits down beside him. 'Rest mine,' stretches out her legs with a sigh, gestures to his crutches, 'Good you can still move. How did a big stone fall on you?' 'Sliding around on the cart, not fixed surely. I stopped the cart, tried to move it to make it steady. It fell.'

'And you're not a carter now?' 'Yes and no.' 'Yes and no?' 'Not a carter, Parish Clerk in St Cyneswide and St Tibba, here,' he waves towards the church, 'but Carter is my name, so–' 'So you're still a Carter!' she laughs, looks approvingly at him. Laughs again. 'Do St Cynsa––?' 'St Cyneswide and St Tibba.' 'Your saints – strange names – Parish Clerk Carter do these saints like flowers in their church?' He smiles, 'Not now,' shrugs, 'who knows? Richard Protector gone. Who knows? Your Fifth Monarchy Men at All Hallows, they might know?' She shakes her head dismissively, has no interest in politics although her brother John Burre is a Fifth Monarchy Man. She has heard of Richard Protector but did not know he had gone ('where?' she wonders); nudges her basket of flowers and raises a questioning eyebrow.

He tries to feel in his purse unobserved but she notices, knowing such movements well. He finds one farthing, two farthings, offers them. She hands over half her flowers but shows no signs of standing up and moving on; opens her pipe case and takes out her pipe. They smoke in comfortable silence.

She muses, 'Falling stone. He fell. My husband Peter Stopford fell from high up on the mast. Ship was moored, at dock, not even at sea. Hit the side of the ship before he hit the water. Went under. I didn't get a body to bury. If it was found down river no-one brought news to me and Betty. My daughter Betty.' She offers him this information, waits for his response, if any.

He smokes, thinks, says, 'I have a child. Nan.' Wonders, then wonders some more, if he should be clearer about his state. Taps his pipe stem on his teeth. Eventually says, 'Motherless child, Nan.' She nods, understands, and after another pause says, 'Fifth Monarchy Men, my father and my brother. My father wanted his first-born to be a boy he could name after John Pym. But it was me so … Jane-Pym, my name.' 'Are you a Fifth Monarchy Woman?' he asks, half joking but wanting to know. 'I'm a Flower Selling Woman,' she replies lightly. 'I leave politics to those with nothing better to do with their day.' His turn to nod. She stands, asks, 'And is your St Cynsa and Tibbs a good parish to sell flowers?' 'Come back and see.' 'It may be I shall. Should I?' 'Yes.' She hoists her basket onto her head and moves off singing 'Who'll buy my sweet primroses? All in bloom! All in bloom!' and does not look back.

Parish Clerk Philip Carter takes great delight in wife Jane-Pym Carter, a lustful woman. Before she chose to marry him she made sure – a warm hand on his cods – that although his legs were sadly lame, his yard, and all his generative parts, were in good order. They were. The married couple share love's delight in copulation. She is a knowing woman and her bed-whispers tell him things he did not know, nor would ever have known. How *she* knows he does not bring himself to ask, but soon learns she has a good friend, midwife Hester Fenner, a woman of much learning and knowledge in the art of midwifery.

He can hear traces of Hester Fenner's hoarse, pipe-smoked voice when Jane-Pym Carter passes on, in frequent lessons, the teachings of her friend. Although sometimes phrased in words that might be heard at some great school of learning, her tuition still warms his blood. 'The clitoris,' she moves his hand there, 'makes women lustful and take delight in copulation. Were it not for this we would have no desire nor delight. So says Hester Fenner, and she is right.' He wants Jane-Pym to have both desire and delight. Under her guidance he is a quick student and becomes, like her, much given to venery. He is, they both know, cunt-struck.

It is well known that a woman's delight in the act forwards conception. Six years of marriage have given them three children, two living and Jane-Pym is carrying a fourth although, as she says, this is her fifth time with child. She delights in all her children, in those she has with Philip Carter, in Betty Stopford her first-born, and in Nan Carter, his child.

* * *

London, Monday, 26 June 1665

'Uncle Rowland! Uncle Rowland! Has anyone seen Uncle Rowland? Is he ready? Uncle Rowland! Is he still upstairs? Go look for him someone!'

The rain, not as heavy as yesterday, is still thrumming down. The waggon and carts, covered by tarpaulins, are slowly being loaded from the pile of chests, canvas bags and boxes that have been assembled in the reception room. The job is taking some time because the carter, having told the boys to load the carts and watching them do so, then shouts, 'You've done it wrong! All wrong!' and shoulders them aside to redo it himself. This means all the chests, canvas bags and boxes are dragged off the carts and left out in the rain while he shunts them around on the cobbles – talking to himself the while – and works out which should go in first as the bottom layer. 'Always the boxes first, flat tops first, all the flat top boxes first, (he gathers the boxes into their own separate company) *then* the barrel-topped chests, (also assembled into a troop) then, and only then!' he shouts at the boys, 'the soft canvas bags! Who'd put the soft canvas bags at the bottom! Who would?' He makes a pile, a small hill, of canvas bags on the wet stones.

The boys stand with Jack the footboy under the porch, out of the rain, and pretend to listen earnestly, nodding frequently, all the time nudging each other, fleering and sneering and muttering hilarious insults of their master: 'Crossgrained fool.' 'Changeling.' 'Boobee.' Jack enjoys the play but has no reason to join in. The carter is not his master.

Uncle Rowland is a man who knows rain and when it is coming and there is a song he has been singing over and over and over. The household can hear the too familiar words, sung sweetly, sadly, in his clear tenor, making their way from his room upstairs.

> *If Doves or Pigeons in the Evening come*
> *Later than usual to their Dove-house home;*
> *If Crows and Daws do oft themselves bewet,*
> *Or Ants and Pismires home apace do get;*
> *If in the Dust Hens do their Pinions shake,*
> *Or by their flocking a great number make.*

Godfrey Hall, waving his hands before his ears to try and wave away the insistent song, walks with increasing irritation to the door to see why the lading is taking so long. The carter's boys and Jack jump aside so he can see the game being played on the cobbles. The carter has meticulously slotted six of the boxes into the first cart and is looking closely at the others, now very wet, to see which will follow next to make the best fit.

'What are those boxes, those chests, those bags doing out in the rain? What the devil are you doing?' Godfrey Hall bellows at the carter, turns to the boys, 'You boys, lazy boys!' he clouts them all, Jack included, 'Go cover them up now! Better, get them on those miserable carts now! They're all soaking wet! Wet!'

The rain keeps on, Uncle Rowland's song keeps on.

> *If Swallows fly upon the Water low,*
> *Or Wood-lice seem in Armies for to go;*
> *If Flies, or Gnats, or Fleas infest and bite*
> *Or sting more than they'r wont by day or night,*
> *If Toads hie home, or Frogs do croak amain,*
> *Or Peacocks cry, soon after look for Rain.*

'Woodlice, flies, gnats. Fleas infest and bite!' Godfrey sighs in bemusement, 'Fleas. When do they not infest and bite? If flea bites were all that was needed to herald rain it would be raining, pouring, every day!' The absurdity of Uncle Rowland's song – called, Uncle Rowland has often told the family, *Infallible signs of Rainy Weather, deduced from the Observation of divers Animals* – has unexpectedly lightened Godfrey Hall's mood. That, and the fact that the cart loading is now proceeding quickly, although he still snorts and glares at the carter and the carter's boys.

'Uncle Rowland! Uncle Rowland! Has anyone seen him? Is he ready? Uncle Rowland!! Is he still upstairs? Go look for him, find him!'

It is Elsa crying out, loud and frantic. They are leaving London and she is distraught – will not stay and will not go. Her two sons are at Oxford. Her married daughter, Alice, will not leave town. But Oxford is much too close to London and the plague, and Alice says she *will* stay in London with her husband George Crofts, a merchant in the Baltic trade who is dealing a handsome business in marine supplies. He imports Baltic fir for masts, Riga hemp for ropes, Norwegian deal for cabin boards, and Stockholm pitch and tar, along with Russian oil, for caulking, sealing and waterproofing. George Crofts needs to stay in London, cannot and will not abandon his business, and Alice Crofts will stay with him, says she will not leave.

Luce Hall, Ingram's wife, has already overseen the filling of the large waggon with her family's goods, each item wrapped in waterproof and then carried singly, carefully, from the reception room to the waggon and the first cart. It is the belongings of Godfrey and Elsa Hall that have sat soaking in the rain, waiting to be arranged like puzzle-pieces in the remaining cart.

Luce Hall reassures Elsa Hall, 'Alice will see sense. She will not want to stay if this plague grows on. And a naval merchant's wife can fly easily by water, fly to, to, to the Kingdom of Sweden, the Kingdom of Denmark if she will.'

'To Sweden! To Denmark! Why would she go to such out-landish kingdoms when her family is here? Not here in London, not here *here*, but here in England at this Bradford place. And if she is here and we are there, how will she ever find us? And this house at Bradford, this country house so far away, it will surely be damp and drafty and the people, the people there will be will be–'. Elsa Hall cannot find words for what the people at Bradford-on-Avon will be.

It is not only the plague growing on that makes Elsa Hall despair for daughter Alice. Alice who is impatient, irritated by her mother's too frequent visits, by her mother's constant lament that she must leave London, escape the plague, fly with family to Bradford-on-Avon. Alice who yesterday had snapped, 'Oh leave me be! Leave me be!' Then wept and wept, crying into her mother's bosom, 'George Crofts is ruined. We are ruined.' 'Ruined? How ruined?' 'The Hamburg fleet is lost, all eight vessels. All Mr Coventry's fault. The fleet lost. Mr Crofts' cargoes lost.'

Elsa Hall knows that Hamburg, like Sweden and Denmark, is some out-landish northern place where sea trade happens. She knows nothing of this man Coventry who lost the fleet. 'What did this Coventry do,' she asks, 'to lose the fleet?' 'Eight merchant ships, five of them carrying George Crofts' naval stores, were to be escorted home from Hamburg by our ships of war. But our English escort ships sailed away from the coast, were no longer there to protect the merchantmen, and this Coventry in the Navy Office forgot, forgot to tell the Hamburg fleet that their naval escort had gone. Left the coast. This Coventry!' Mother and daughter shake angry heads at Coventry's disastrous neglect.

'The Hamburg fleet sailed, not knowing our ships of war had gone. They see a number of sail waiting off the coast of Holland and make towards them, expecting these to be their escort. But it was the Dutch! And George Crofts' merchantmen sailed into the very middle of the Dutchmen. All taken, thanks to this Coventry. This Coventry who is Admiral of the Navy Office!'

'Ruined you say, but George Crofts is a wealthy man, a trading man.'

'Was, was a wealthy man but now ruined. The goods on the Hamburg ships were valued at, at,' Alice lowers her voice,' she finds it hard to say, drops her voice even lower, 'at two hundred thousand pounds.'

Her mother does not believe this. 'Poo, two hundred thousand. Pounds.' 'Not all of it George Crofts', not all,' says Alice, 'some of it is, was, the king's.' 'His Majesty's goods. George Crofts and his Majesty? Their goods?' Elsa Hall finds this an impossible conversation. 'Yes,' says Alice, 'but the major part was George Crofts. He says one hundred and eighteen thousand, six hundred and seventy three pounds thirteen shillings and eight pence. He says. He, we, are ruined. Thanks to Coventry.'

George Crofts and his Majesty. His Majesty and George Crofts. Two hundred thousand pounds. George Crofts is a common man, a coarse man, a crude man, who speaks crudely of his Majesty, calls him 'His Royal Whore-ness.' He has extravagant whiskers, wears a grotesque wig, absurd with an over-abundance of curls. A wig he even wears, Alice has confided to Elsa, when in bed with his wife doing what a married man does with his wife. Asks her mother if it is customary for men to do such with a wig on. Elsa Hall does not know about all men, but has never experienced Godfrey Hall bewigged in bed.

George Crofts and the king and two hundred thousand pounds. But Elsa Hall does not want him ruined, does not want her daughter ruined, her grandchildren ruined. Alice Crofts will not leave George Crofts.

Elsa Hall's laments mingle with Uncle Rowland's rain song, with the rain, with the shouts of the carter.

Edith Hall, elder daughter of Ingram and Luce Hall, is a young maid who watches her family closely, her best and most interesting subjects being her mother and Uncle Rowland. Each has their own way of getting their own way, and Edith is keen to learn these skills. Her mother sets sight on her prize and, by dogged persistence – she will not be side-tracked or blocked – talks of nothing else until she gains it. The household heard for months on end of the necessity, the importance, that she have her own waiting woman. As for Uncle Rowland, Edith has seen how he jokes, diverts, entices, entrances, sings, cajoles, charms, and – should all these fail – glowers and sulks and whines that he is ancient and ill and going to die soon, very soon, and makes the household a place of uncomfortable, dark misery. 'It is all your fault, all of you!'

Uncle Rowland's victory in his campaign to seize the fine corner bedroom – and so displace Godfrey and Elsa Hall – took less time than Luce's extended siege on Ingram to engage a waiting woman. Edith, who is good at overhearing, overheard Nan the cook tell Jinny Bosvill this was because changing bedrooms did not involve an outlay of wages. Hiring a waiting woman did.

'Eight pounds a year,' cook says with considerable irritation, conscious that she herself asked for £6 but had settled, grudgingly, for £5.2.6. Jinny, who grabs at any opportunity to talk to Jack the footboy, relayed these battles to him. He jested, half-jested, that since Uncle Rowland was always lamenting he was to die very soon, he had been ceded the bedroom in the hope and expectation he would not be occupying it for long.

A sad Uncle Rowland sings his rain song. Edith and small sister Meriall are hoping he will do his grand imitations: his belly down on the ground as he scuttles about like the ants and the pismires; his waddling hen shaking her pinions; his jumping fleas; his croaking toads; his crying peacocks. It is a show, a spectacle, a play, a pageant the whole household enjoys, collapsing in laughter. Even Luce, who finds him an ancient silly man of little account, laughs.

Young Edith has seen that Uncle Rowland, when he is the ant, the toad, the hen, is an Uncle Rowland who moves more freely and easily as he crawls and waddles and leaps than Uncle Rowland the ancient, weak man who finds walking too difficult and must be helped, supported and part-carried from bed to table to house of office and back to bed.

This raining Monday in June in the year 65 there is no imitation of divers animals by Uncle Rowland as he sings. With groans and gasps and grimaces he has lowered his ancient, sad body, 'My sad, ancient body', down on the floor, but not as an ant. Rather he is an ancient, weak man, 'A sad, weak, ancient man with not long to live. Leave me be!' who will not leave London, not leave this house, not travel two hundred and fifty miles, one thousand miles, by jolting, jarring coach over bad roads to this miserable country cottage at Bradvon-on-Aford.

'I have His Majesty's remedy, the protection of His Majesty the King!' he flourishes the piece of paper with the magic words Venice Treacle. 'The King himself gave it me because he does not want me to leave! His Majesty himself.'

But the waggon has left, driven by the carter. The carts have left, a boy in charge of each. Most of the servants have left, sitting or lying under the tarpaulins of the waggon and the carts, some of them already dozing, relishing the fact that for days they have nothing to do except laze and talk and flirt and gossip and only need to get out to walk and push when they come to hills, and then find good dry sleeping straw in stables and barns when they stop for the night.

Most of the family, along with the upper servants who will tend them as they travel, have left in hackney cabs for the *Swan with Two Necks* in Lad Lane, Cheapside, where they will board their west-bound coach. Luce Hall has her eight pounds a year waiting woman, Mary James, at her side.

Uncle Rowland's cries boom through the empty house. The walls are unhung, the hangings folded into the canvas bags that are now damp mattresses for the servants in the waggon and carts.

Uncle Rowland, lying on the floor, arms held tight to his side, has done what he can to make his inert, heavy body as unwieldy as any sodden canvas bag. Says to Godfrey, 'I have a mind to stay nephew, to stay. Just a little longer.'

Godfrey thinks 'Poor wretch,' says to Jack, 'Fetch some street boys, we will carry him to the hackney if we must.' Jack's face beams at this exciting order and he runs: they will carry this great lump of ancient Rowland to the hackney! He knows good lads more than glad to do it. Wonders how much Godfrey Hall will pay them. Jack knows he will not be paid, but as the recruiter he will demand his share back from the lads.

The empty house quickly fills with the noise of the bounding and jostling bodies of shouting James Kerton, Thomas Snow, Daniel Stiles, John Clapshaw, Harry Shute and Jemmy Pooly.

Faced with grinning, excited young rogues crowding around him, looming above him, Uncle Rowland decides to stop being a heavy canvas bag and demands in harsh tones, 'Help me up! You wild boys, help me up! How dare you leave me lying here!'

Godfrey Hall has locked up everything in the house that can be locked up. Repeats to Jack the footboy that while the family is away he is to have nobody in the house. Godfrey Hall knows you must be watchful with servants, careful about who comes to see them, and that is, he tells Jack, nobody at all. Jack agrees earnestly, his head nodding and nodding. 'Nobody in sir. Yes Master Godfrey, nobody in at all. I'll see to it.' Nobody does not mean that he cannot entertain friends in the kitchen, where no-one will see if he has anybody in.

The hackney cab is brought as close as possible to the porch so Uncle Rowland can be loaded in by Jack and the street lads, who are still hoping that Godfrey Hall will find a coin or two for them. He does not. But Uncle Rowland, struck by sudden magnanimity, casts before them some Horatian pearls: 'Vale fumum et opes, strepitumque Londinii!'

He is ignored.

'Going to the *Swan with Two Necks*,' snickers Thomas Snow. He holds out an empty hand to Godfrey Hall in the departing hackney, calls out, not too loudly, 'Thanks for nothing sirrah. The *Swan with Two Necks*,' he says knowingly to his fellows, 'is called that because it is a whoring house.' The others look dubious. This is the first they have heard that the respectable coaching inn in Lad Lane is a whoring house.

'All the world knows that when two swans are fucking and reach their pleasure they arch up and screech and coil neck around neck. I've seen it. They do. That's why the *Swan with Two Necks* is a place of whoring. Its name tells the world that.' He snickers again.

Jack the footboy has heard otherwise from Uncle Rowland: the inn is named for the Company of Vintners' swans, the Company's ownership of the swans signified by two nicks on the birds' beaks. The inn is the *Swan with Two Nicks*. But the boys dismiss this as a nonsense. The *Swan with Two Necks* must be a place of whoring because of the fucking swans – who has not seen fucking swans? Jack is swayed by the majority opinion. Fucking swans are much more likely than some fat drunken vintner taking the trouble and risk of putting two nicks in the vicious beaks of snapping swans. A silly fancy the ancient man has invented to amuse himself and gull others. The boys take pleasure in loudly repeating 'fucking swans.'

The cab makes it to the *Swan with Two Necks* in time for Godfrey Hall and his uncle to board the Bradford and Bath coach, but to the very last Uncle Rowland, now fallen silent, lingers on the street, showing unwilling to go, until he loses his place inside and must ride outside, at the back in the waggon section.

The coachman whips up the horses, the coach gathers itself and jolts forward as the straps take the strain. Uncle Rowland strikes up the rain song, which delights the other outside passengers. They quickly pick up the words and tune, join in, and call for more. When the coach stops for the first change of horses an inside place becomes free and Godfrey beckons him to come in. Uncle Rowland sees himself cavalierly – a favourite word – turning this down (a hand held up, an heroic shake of the head), his self-denial admired, applauded, by his new friends outside. But the rain has not stopped and the hard bench has dug red welts into his soft flesh. He farewells his new friends, who join in as he reprises:

> *If Toads hie home, or Frogs do croak amain,*
> *Or Peacocks cry, soon after look for Rain.*

A drawn-out 'R-a-a-a-i-n-n' and cheers follow him as he climbs inside. He sleeps, his head finding refuge on Mary James' unwilling, flinching shoulder.

CHAPTER VII

London, Tuesday morning, 27 June 1665

'To fart before a Justice, to kiss like a clown.'

'This child is not dead,' the Widow announces.

'What's that? What's she saying? What did she say?'

'I can't hear. What did the Searcher say? Dead?'

'Course she said dead. She's a Searcher, she searches the dead.'

'Look at the blood on his head. Dashed his brains out. He's dead. No question.'

'That's just a cut on his head, only a cut. It's his thigh. Crushed to the marrow. Look.'

'You get a child's limb under the great wheel of a cart – broken as easy as crack a nut.'

'Not just a child's. A grown man'd be crushed the same. I've seen it.'

The Widow can feel the soft pulse of the bloodied child she has lifted from the street stones. 'Not dead,' she says again. 'Not dead.'

The Goodwife bends down to peer at the blood on the cart wheel, the blood on the cobbles. She is jostled by the gawking loud crowd gathered around the cart. Cradle Alley is narrow and is blocked.

'Who saw what happened?' the Goodwife asks. 'You, first finder, John Farren. You saw the child go under the cart? The cart go over the child? How?'

'It was the child!' Carman Robert Bethel breaks in before first finder John Farren can find an answer. 'The child. Ran himself under the wheel before I could stop the horse. I heard the noise, the cries. I stopped the horse.'

'Children. They were playing a running game,' another voice, a loud, confident woman's voice. A hot codlin seller who is happy to be both information-giver and trader, making the most of the crowd to sell her roast apples.

Heads nod, voices agree: children playing a running game. 'She's right. What she said. That's what it was, a running game.'

'Today is Tuesday! Tuesday! Today is Tuesday!' booms bufflehead Walter, just arrived. He is met with mirth by some, irritation by others. 'Away with you! Here is a hurt child. We know the day.'

'The little lad was laughing, looking back, not looking where he was going. Laughing little goodfellow one minute and under the cart the next. Carman here was up the front leading the horse. He stopped when he heard the cries.'

'This small boy's cry?' the Widow asks.

'He made a noise but not so much of a noise. It was the ones chasing him that set up a cry. Calling out. Calling his name. Jan. Jan they said.'

'The child is not dead,' the Widow says again, loudly, unconscious small Sam Stiles in her arms. 'Not dead,' she gazes around to make sure this is known, understood. 'To his mother. The child to his mother,' she announces, walks away.

The Goodwife stays. She is told many stories. The child was running alone. The child was playing a joyful chasing game with other children. The child was running away in fear from the other children. The other children were older, younger, the same age. They were all boys. There were some girls. They were all local St Cyneswide and St Tibba children. Yes, heads nod in agreement, all local children.

'I've seen passengers fall off coaches. Coachmen flung off by a sudden jolt. A wheel hits a rock, hits a fallen baulk of timber. Coachman flies off.' Edward Richbell makes a swooping, tumbling sweep with his right arm, 'Coachman flies off.'

'Or the coach turns short, people flung off under the wheels. Seen that one,' William Sutterwhit offers.

'Yes, yes,' heads nod.

'Seen crushed between two coaches. Or some poor soul who can't get out of the way in time, man with a limp and stick, caught right up against a wall. Life squeezed out of him. No escape there. None.'

'Wheel goes into a ditch, whole coach goes over. Crash. Smash. All on it spilled out and broken on the road like a tray of eggs dropped by an egg seller. A tray of eggs. All over the road.'

'Barrel falls off a brewer's dray. You don't want to be under that. No.'

Heads shake. Heads nod.

'Clerk Philip Carter, stone fell off a cart, crushed his legs.'

'This carter here, you saying a stone fell on him?'

'Not this carter. No, not this one. Philip Carter the Clerk, the one with the legs. Stone fell on his legs, fell off his cart.'

'Carter the carter.'

'Not any more the carter, not after that stone. It crushed his legs. Vestry made him Clerk.'

'That Searcher, the one with the eye, where's she gone with that child?'

'Child's not dead. Taking him to his mother she said.'

'A strange one with that eye she is. Hard ancient woman. Fixes you with her look.'

Shoulders shrug. The Widow's strangeness is not news in St Cyneswide and St Tibba.

The children have run off, gone, but the Goodwife has seen glimpses through the throng of one lurking close by. She waits for the crowd to thin, for the talk of wheels falling off, of coach floors falling out, of the great hooves of shire horses plodding heads to mash, she waits for this talk to move away to the *Three Tuns* where it can be savoured with beer.

Goodwife Joan Brokefild beckons Nell Girling, who tightens her mouth and clenches her hands, but slowly comes. She will come for the Goodwife but would never have come for the Widow, would have run and hidden from Widow Margaret Hazard.

'Tell me,' says the Goodwife, 'what made this?'

'It was a game, a game, only a game. A chasing game. Small Sam always wants to be the one we chase. He begs us, "Me! Me! Let's play rabbit and hounds" he says. He's the rabbit and we're the hounds. "I want to be the rabbit," he says. He always says. That's what he wants.' She sticks out her lower lip, looks defiant, then weeps and weeps. 'Now he's dead, small Sam. He's the rabbit and while he runs he puts his hands up beside his head for rabbit ears and sticks out his top teeth.' Through her tears she shows the Goodwife what she means, puts her hands to her head, waggles them, shows her top teeth.

'Not dead,' the Goodwife says, 'no, not dead. Hurt but not dead. His mother will care for him, look after him. Widow Hazard is taking him to his house, to his mother. And his father,' she adds, an afterthought. The fathers the Goodwife has seen are little use when it comes to stopping blood and mending broken bones. Most are of little use for anything, other than drinking and hitting and swearing and fighting. And spending money they don't have. But perhaps Samuel Stiles is not so bad. She knows him, the parish of St Cyneswide and St Tibba knows him, as a bricklayer of mostly sober comportment, sober habits. Except for the fortnight of Bartholomew Fair when many parishioners of this and other parishes are not of sober comportment. Yet if Samuel Stiles does worse than this the parish pump in water square has not heard it.

'The rabbit always gets away. Doesn't get caught. And when Sam does get caught we tickle him. The rabbit doesn't get killed.' The child follows the Goodwife down to the channels, walks beside her, talking to her, to herself. 'The rabbit laughs when he gets caught. It's a game.'

The Goodwife nods. Agrees it was a game. A game comes to mind. She sings the verse inside her head, then sings it out loud. Holds up her red wand and mimes bending a bow.

> *All a row, a bendy bow,*
> *Shoot at a pigeon and kill a crow.*
> *Shoot at another and kill his brother.*
> *Shoot again and kill a wren,*
> *And that'll do for gentlemen.*

'All a row, that's a marching game for little children,' Nell Girling says scornfully. 'Not a game for grown children.' But she sings along with the Goodwife. Knows the song well. Goodwife Joan Brokefild has seen and heard Nell Girling leading the very small children, all marching and singing. 'All a row, a bendy bow.'

'Angus McManus sang it to his children,' the Goodwife says, half to Nell, half to herself. 'Sang it in his Scots voice.' The parish liked the song, liked singing it and imitating the exotic Scotch sounds. But they didn't like McManus, and their singing in mock Scotch always had some jeer in it.

'Poor little Sam,' Nell Girling weeps afresh, 'dead like the crow, killed like the wren.'

Goodwife Joan Brokefild has little time for tearful children, has had enough of this crying child. She likes children laughing, thinks of Sara's joy at the Italian puppets. She says impatiently, sharply. 'He is not dead, I told you.'

The child sniffles back her tears.

'What is your best psalm? Tell me. Your best?' The Goodwife asks, a distraction.

Nell Girling sucks in a last sob. Pauses to think. Their slow progress takes them past houses marked with the red cross, houses asking 'Lord have mercy upon us.' The Barrett house still has its cross but is empty, its dead all gone, all buried. In the Gipps house not all those left have died, only father Henry and son Giles. Inside young Helen Gipps, still free of the signs, cares for her mother Agnes and sister Margery. William Hawkins, the watchman at the door, half raises a hand, blinks his eyes in his own odd way, and gives a short nod to the Goodwife. She replies with a lift of her red wand.

'My best psalm is clap hands, "Ye people all with one accord clap hands and eke rejoice." And I like the starry sky, "make my songs extoll thy Name above the starry sky". I like the starry sky.' She stops walking to think, eventually says, 'When I make the fire and light the candle I sing this one, my best:

And as the fire doth melt the wax, and wind blows smoke away:
So in the presence of the Lord the wicked shall decay.

'Good psalms,' Goodwife Joan Brokefild says absently. She is thinking of the Widow carrying off the bloodied boy.

'Let us sing to the praise and glory of God,' Nell Girling announces, 'this is my best one too, the bird one:

The sparrows find a room to rest, and save themselves from wrong:
Also the swallow hath a nest wherein to keep her young.

She stops, startled, her voice breaks in distress, 'The sparrows and the swallows are in their nests, not dead like the crow, like the wren, like poor Sam.' She weeps anew.

The Goodwife shrugs and trudges on. She shoos Nell Girling home when they reach church square, glad to be rid of her. She goes to her own home to get a pail. Isaac Brokefild is at the table, staring at the door.

'Here you come, finally, at last. What have you for me to eat? For my dinner?' He fixes his glare on her. He is foxed, as usual, the drink heavy upon him.

She points resignedly to the bread, to the cheese, there on the table in front of him, to the soup pot by the fire.

He shakes his head dismissively. Waves away her offerings. 'I can see woman, nothing wrong with my eyes. I can see. I've got two eyes, not like your ugly fellow. I want pickled oysters. With all your searching, always away searching, even at night, away searching, you get your pence. Your death pence. Enough pence from the dead to buy my pickled oysters.'

The Goodwife has no energy or time to argue, moves past him. 'I have more work to do, more searching. There is food here if you want to eat.' She is thinking of blood. Picks up a pail.

'Go first and buy my oysters.'

She throws twopence on the table. 'I have work I must do. You buy your oysters.'

He sweeps the coins into his left hand. Flexes his fist on them. Stares hard at her. 'What do you need pails for?' She has picked up a second one.

'Blood.'

'Blood pudding,' he nods. 'Good. I will have blood pudding then. But go buy my oysters first.'

'I have work to do,' she hefts the pails.

'Oysters!' He lashes a foot out, kicks as hard as he can, lands on her thigh. She falls against the wall. Rights herself and limps outside. Denies him the pleasure of crying out in pain.

'Mind you don't take a fall!' he calls after her. Laughs.

The pain slows her walk to water square. She distracts herself by seeing her hands push his head into a bucket of blood and hold it there; seeing him slowly trampled from toe to head by the great hooves of a shire horse, herself on the horse, urging it forward. She hates him. Then, shocked, begs the Lord for forgiveness for such sinful thoughts, thoughts which must have come from the devil. She must bear her pain as our Lord, who suffered so much more, bore his pain to save us all.

'Where is Richard Undnay?' Isabella Undnay shouts at her. 'Where is he? Why are you fetching water when you should be looking for him?' The distraught Isabella runs at her, looms at her, thrusts her face at the Goodwife. This is unwise. It is not the right time for this.

Goodwife Joan Brokefild jabs her red wand hard into Isabella Undnay's ribs, pushes her away. 'Leave me be, mad woman,' advances angrily on the shocked and retreating Isabella. No longer pondering the Lord's suffering, Goodwife Joan Brokefild wants to shout at Isabella Undnay what a fortunate woman she is that her husband is gone, gone forever, dead. Still in pain, in anger, she wants to dash Isabella Undnay in the face with her pail, but this passes and she feels a little pity for the deluded creature.

This clash has been watched with interest by those on water business in the square. A ragged ring has gathered around the two. The Goodwife becomes a Moses woman, lifts up her wand, stretches out her hand, and divides them, crosses the damp cobbles to seize pride of place at the deserted water spout and fills her buckets.

Her thigh aches in waves of pain on her way to the Widow's house. She stops to balance the pails, to hold the water steady. A child's rhyme comes to mind. It is her day to remember childish rhymes.

Draw a pail of water
For a lady's daughter.
Her father's a king and her mother's a queen,
Her two little sisters are dressed all in green.
Stamping grass and parsleys,
Marigold leaves and daisies.
One and a hush, two and a rush,
Pray thee, fine lady, pop under a bush.

She sings it slowly to herself, her limping walk taking on the pace of the rhyme. The third time through she stops at marigold leaves. The juice of marigold leaves, mixed with vinegar, will ease the throbbing pain in her thigh. She will ask the Widow.

Widow Margaret Hazard opens the door, looks at the pails of water, the Goodwife's tense face. Nods her inside.

'Fair water to wash the blood from your dress.'

'I have water. My Sara fetches water.'

The Goodwife puts the pails down. Sets herself down on the bench. Heaves a deep, broken breath. Does not speak. She is broken.

'The water. Thank you for it. Kind, you are good to think of it. Mmm.' The Widow pauses, ponders, then looks pleased, says cheerfully, 'Still some blood on my underskirt. That's good. Your water will be good for my underskirt. When I've finished these,' she goes back to her own pail, squats, takes up again the work of scrubbing her knuckley hands against the stains on her soaking bodice. Grunts as she scrubs, her eye focused on the stain. Says without looking up, 'Little Sam Stiles at his mother's. Purging and physick. A comfrey syrup.'

'Will he live?'

'If God wills it.'

'God often does not.'

The Widow nods, 'Often not.' She thinks of the dead. Dead infants. How life is. Then it isn't. The abandoned infants she has found dead in the street, dead from cold, from hunger, from cruelty. Not her Sara, she saved Sara. And some few others.

'Comfrey,' Goodwife Joan Brokefild says, 'comfrey or marigolds. My Isaac did this.' She moves closer to the Widow, lifts her skirts up her leg. Shows her swollen, discoloured thigh.

Widow Margaret Hazard has comfrey, makes a poultice. The Goodwife sighs, sits in gratitude.

'When Sara returned from her school I sent her for water,' the Widow lays on the poultice with more care than usual. For most, her nursing is brisk and abrupt, not of the gentle kind, but she does not want to cause her friend more discomfort.

'Sara was at Widow Packe's school today?' Goodwife Brokefild speaks through a wince – the Widow's hands are hard and cold.

'Of course. Not running the streets with the wild children. Not there when they ran Sam Stiles into the cart. Chased him under the carter's wheels. Not the carter's fault. Ungodly games, these children. Ungodly. Why are they not at petty school?'

'Nell Girling is not ungodly. They were children playing a game. They did not mean for it to happen, but it did.' Pain and tiredness of spirit goad the Goodwife to speak her mind with harshness.

'Mmm. Well,' the Widow spreads the poultice wider, to cover all the bruise.

Goodwife Brokefild sighs, flinches, says bleakly,'Most of the time it is all turd. For me it is mostly all turd. You have your Sara.'

The Widow nods, 'Yes, she is honey for me. Most of the time she is honey. A good scholar. Very good. Her reading delights. She reads when I comb her hair for the lice. The school is a breeding farm for lice. Her teacher is French but a Christian and a good woman for all that. Reformed Christian, married Christopher Packe an Englishman. Now a widow. I put her to the test, Sara, I put her to the test on her day's learning, and to check she does not read with a Frenchified voice. I did not search his corpse. Not of this parish Christopher Packe, a St Benet Fynck man. A weaver. Searchers of bad repute out there in St Benet Fynck. Sarah Collymor. Corruption and false reporting. Not sober. Not discreet. They had a name for her.'

'Silent Sarah, bribe coins in her mouth.'

'Mmm. Other parishes this happens, but not in St Cyneswide and St Tibba. Not here.'

The Goodwife considers how best to speak of bribery, says, 'There are still viperous tales in this parish that … we, we were paid by John Sly to come late to his house. That it was a notion born of corruption–'

'My notion,' the Widow interrupts, 'And a notion born not from corruption and false reporting but because John Sly's house is close by Thomas Dorbridge's house. What do the vipers say to that? Mmm?'

'Your notion then. They say it was to give him time to remove the corpse of Doll Matthews so we could not search it. They say we proposed to him that, for money, we would delay our search so he could get rid of the corpse, the infected corpse.'

'And how are we, I, supposed to have made this offer to John Sly? How do these viper tongues explain that?'

'That we sent a messenger to him. They say.'

The Widow scoffs, 'What messenger? Who?'

'A child perhaps.'

'One of the messenger boys? Bah.'

'No. Not a boy.'

Widow Margaret Hazard, ponders this, says, 'What? If not a boy then who? A girl? My Sara?' she asks scornfully. 'A nonsense.'

The Goodwife nods. 'They will say anything.'

'That will be Viewer Anne Abowen who does not know what to look for on the sick body, and when I show her what to look for she resents *me* and despises *me* for *her* ignorance. She is making these tales, spreading these falsehoods, lies.'

'I have not heard it from her, not her, only from gossips at water square. Where everyone knows everything, but when you ask them can't say how they know. They just know.'

'Wicked fools,' the Widow, back at her washing, scrubs harder at the blood stains. 'The idle fool is whipped at school. That is the letter F in the book of letters. F in the reading book Sara learns from. Her teacher, although French, has a good way of teaching. She says it is the way she learned to read English. She takes a scripture all the children know, the Lord's Prayer. They say it then she writes the words, one by one, for them to copy. To learn. A good method. Sara tells me what she has learned, and how, and so I learned my letters. I learned to read. There are pictures with each letter. In the book. Have I told you this?'

Goodwife Brokefild nods. She has heard this story many times, but listens, half listens, because it gives the Widow pleasure.

'The letter D,' the Widow says. 'A Dog will bite a thief at night. A good picture of a dog leaping to bite the thief's hinder parts. The letter H is My Book and Heart shall never part.' The Widow stops talking, pauses to squint closer at her soaking dress.

The Goodwife's mind wanders to a merriment called the *Figure of Nine* in a penny chapbook. A merriment which boasts of its Mirth, Wit and Pleasure. She asks lightly, 'Do you know nine sorts of foolish things that are unseemly?'

The Widow does not but is willing to hear.

'To eat pottage with a ladle, to blow one's nose at supper, to fart before a Justice, to slabber in eating, to laugh at prayer, to kiss like a clown, to stand like a fool, to jeer continually, and to laugh at a dog's tail wagging.'

Widow Margaret Hazard laughs in shock and delight, 'To fart before a Justice!'

'Isaac Brokefild kisses like a clown, stands like a fool, jeers continually. At me. He is nine sorts of fool.' Cheered, the Goodwife helps the Widow hang her wet clothes before the fire.

'Does he fart before the Justice?' the Widow asks.

'He certainly farts before me. He farts before everyone.'

The Widow finds this mighty witty. More laughter. They are glad to be in each other's company.

CHAPTER VIII

London, Tuesday, 27 June 1665
Parish Clerks' Hall, Vintry Lane

'Brethren together fast to hold the band of amity.'

'Let us sing to the praise and glory of God psalm the thirty fourth,' says young John Bell, Clerk of the Worshipful Company of Parish Clerks.

> *I do delight to laud the Lord in soul, in heart, and voice:*
> *That humble men and mortifi'd may hear, and so rejoice.*

With rejoicing solemn stateliness, sixty three assembled parish clerks make their way, note by slow note, through twenty two verses to the comforting last:

> *But they that fear the living Lord, are ever safe and sound:*
> *And as for those that trust in him, nothing shall them confound.*

They are all loud men, and proud to test themselves in loudness against their fellows. Their Hall in Vintners Lane of a Tuesday afternoon is full of worshipful noise. There is no need for lining out, these men know their psalms well, but the practice is an essential, natural, part of their parish lives and it would be unthinkable to abandon it here.

'Confound' is held as long as lungs will permit. Singing parish clerks have strong, practised lungs. Although the plague grows on daily, here in their Hall the clerks are ever safe and sound.

Parish Clerk of St Cyneswide and St Tibba Philip Carter looks with comfort at his fellow clerks sharing the bench – their bench, third row back, right hand side. These are not always smiling men, but in the right circumstances can give a nod of content to companions of the same mind.

Philip Carter sits, naturally he sits, with those clerks who still believe in full root and branch Reformation. Who favour congregations. Who do not favour bishops at all. He sits on the aisle end, the place kept for him. The easiest spot for a man on crutches to swing into, to swing out of. To his right: William Orrell, St Martin Vintry; Henry Sharrow, St Benet Fynck; Alexander Muzzard, All Hallows the Great; John Vigor, St Bennet Sherehog; Job Royce, St Michael Crooked Lane; Joad Godscall, St Gabriel Fenchurch. All men for full Reform.

These seven, and more before and behind them on the right side of the Hall, take particular pleasure in this day's singing. There is no organ playing to intrude upon their song of praise.

'Master's new organ not working,' sniggers John Vigor. The clerk of St Bennet Sherehog is a coarse man whose particular humour makes him see the bodily parts of generation in every place, likely and unlikely, and who can posit the act of copulation on to any circumstance. According to their own humours, his fellows benched beside him snort, grin, or raise wry eyebrows – it is only John Vigor being John Vigor. Philip Carter, who has his own strong interest in matters of copulation, wonders if John Vigor only knows the subject from book, jest and song, or whether his cock really is as active as he makes out. Philip Carter cannot tell. Men brag.

'New organ no better than the old one,' Alexander Muzzard joins in. They remember, with undiminished resentment, the old one. Brought in, along with the king, in 1660. Cobbled together from parts hidden away. 'All organs – *music instruments* – are unnecessary noise: noise that strives hard against our voices lauding the Lord, the living Lord. None should ever be set up.' Alexander Muzzard can quote, does so often, Parliamentary orders of May 1644: 'An Ordinance for the further demolishing of Instruments of Idolatry and Superstition – all Organs, and the Frames or Cases wherein they stand in all Churches or Chapels aforesaid, shall be taken away, and utterly defaced, and none other hereafter set up in their places.'

'John Bedford lends money – twenty pounds he says. Twenty. Pounds. – to this new one,' William Orrell flicks his chin at the current Master of the Worshipful Company of Parish Clerks, fidgety, anxious, ancient John

Bedford, who is in close conversation at the front of the Hall with the Clerk of the Clerks, young John Bell, and one other. John Bedford who has only been Master for a month – elected, as set out in the Charter, on Ascension Day – and who must constantly consult young John Bell.

William Orrell, Clerk of the parish of St Martin Vintry, his church just across the lane, knows all that happens within the bounds of his parish and well beyond – certainly as far as St Dionis Backchurch. 'Man's got a servant! What parish clerk has a servant? Tell me that! Have I got a servant? No! Have you got a servant?' He elbows Henry Sharrow, 'Have you?'

'Course not,' Henry Sharrow says testily. 'Who has money for a servant?'

'John the man who knows his money, John Bedford is who.'

'Wealthy parish St Dionis Backchurch. Wealthy. How many Masters of City Companies live there? Five! How many Aldermen? Five again. There's money in that parish. And John Bedford gets gifts, John Bedford does – gifts! – from some Lady. Lady Harpy.'

'And from Nicholas Abed. Nicholas Abbey? Money begets money.'

'Money begets high office in the Worshipful Company of Parish Clerks. John Bedford, first in as Assistant, one of the chosen seventeen, then Under Warden, then Upper Warden, and now this year, the year 65, what is he? I'll tell you what he is, he's Master. Bah.'

'First time Master. Won't be the last. Francis Grey twice, Henry Smith twice, William Snelling twice.'

'William Williams four times. Four!'

'No. Not four. William Williams only twice. In 51 and again in 57.'

'And the rest! 53 and 54.'

'That was –– 53 and 54 was William Snelling not William Williams.'

'Too many Williams.'

They talk, they watch the Master, who continues in agitated conversation with young John Bell and a newcomer they have not seen before, a stolid, slow man who bobs at the Master. 'Up and down like a pump handle,' Philip Carter says.

'Master looks like he's lost a silver crown and found a token.'

'He always looks like that.'

'Sure to be something to do with money.'

'Debts owed him, debts he owes. You'd think he'd collect the one and pay off the other, then he'd be back to taws.'

'And after that he could do it all over again.'

'He would! He will!' To general mirth.

'Who's the new one?' points to the stolid, bobbing man.

'One of them. Another drop of porridge for the wrong side of the aisle.'

'Too much porridge over there. Too many over there with their Book of Common Porridge. Their numbers going up.'

'Ours down.' Glum agreement. Righteous men all, they know that the righteous sitteth on the right hand. But, the other side still grows on.

'New one's for St Mary Aldermary, name of Robert Foster.'

'Hope he sings better than the one before.'

'Edward Dades. Most jesticulous way of singing. Thought he was in a cathedral.'

'Here's another one of them. St Mildred Poultry.'

'He's got almost as far to come as you Philip Carter, and he's got two good legs. You're not late. Never.'

Philip Carter acknowledges this. He has two bad legs so he makes a point of not being late.

'And you William Orrell, live so close and never early.'

'Never late either,' responds William Orrell.

'All of them over there. We're down now. Once they were up, then we were up. Now they're up. Why shouldn't we be up again? We shall be. We shall.' Alexander Muzzard bursts out confidently, too confidently.

Little reaction from his fellows. Alexander Muzzard, parish clerk of All Hallows the Great, Seamen's Church, Hay Church, Rope Church, is a known Fifth Monarchy Man. This is what they say. Job Royce shushes him. This is not the place for insurgent talk, loud insurgent talk.

A loud crash at the back of the hall. 'Bedlam!'

'What's that?' Joad Godscall and all turn to see what has crashed. Joad Godscall must always be the first to know. 'I know that voice.'

Two latecomers, pressing to put their weekly Bills of Mortality into the box (all can see they have missed the two o'clock deadline) have collided and knocked the box over.

'One of us, one of them,' Alexander Muzzard says. His voice is never quiet.

Thomas Mounck, parish clerk of St Botolph Bishopsgate, an always running man, a man with a port-wine marked face, won the charge to the Bill box but knocked it over and cried out 'Bedlam!'

Victorious, he picks up the box, nodding to himself, and moves to the right side of the Hall.

The other party, Henry Wyldgoose of St Anne and St Agnes, goes left, ignoring the commotion. Nothing to do with him.

'Order!' young John Bell calls. 'Order.'

'Bit of disorder there, Thomas Mounck,' Job Royce calls to him. 'Bit of Bedlam disorder Thomas?'

'Yes. Yes. Beat him to it,' nods Thomas Mounck. 'Yes.'

'Dressed in your St Botolph Bishopsgate best eh? Dressed up for the meeting?'

Thomas Mounck looks down at his worn clothes. Holds up a well patched sleeve. 'St Botolph Bishopsgate best. Not so many clothiers, not new clothiers, to be found in our bounds. Lots of slops though. Not so many merchants and aldermen. And when I think on it, in fact none to be found. Do with what we can. What we have. Yes, wearing St Botolph Bishopsgate best, yes.' He looks at his sleeve again, nods with satisfaction. Sits with his righteous friends.

'Order! Call to order,' young John Bell's voice carries through the Hall. The Hall can see that Master John Bedford has finished his long talk to the new man and is slowly adjusting his Crown of office. Not satisfied with the way it sits, he adjusts it, and adjusts it again.

'The Worshipful Company of the Parish Clerks of the City of London and the Liberties thereof, and of the Parish Clerks of the Out Parishes to the said City of London adjoining, and of the City of Westminster, be you called to order.' Young John Bell is in good voice.

'Old John Bell,' Joad Godscall speaks over the call to order. 'Remember how old John Bell, he'd go through all 130 parishes! All 130. St Albans Woodstreet, St Allhallows Barking ––'

'Yes, yes, we all remember. Be quiet,' Henry Sharrow breaks in.

'Right through to St Mary Savoy and St Margaret Westminster,' Joad Godscall ignores Henry Sharrow.

Master John Bedford still has problems with his Crown. He sends John Bell for a glass and examines closely, critically, how the Crown sits. More adjustments until he is satisfied. This is good mirthful sport for those on both the right and the left hand sides of the Hall. They have seen this dumb play before.

The Master begins. 'Wardens, Assistants, Brethren of the Worshipful Company of Parish Clerks. Here is a new Clerk to join us. Robert Foster of St Mary Aldermary.

'The office Robert Foster is joining is truly valuable, and of such high account with persons of the highest rank and quality that we Parish Clerks have had the honour of being a Guild or Fraternity for four hundred years and upward––'

Familiar words.

'Bald. Old William Williams,' William Orrell says to his companions. 'Bald. Crown kept trying to slip down over his eyes and he kept pushing it back. Good bass voice.' William Orrell takes pride in his own deep bass, and admires, and envies, those who can go deeper. 'Voice coming from the bottom of a great tun.'

'Held a note. Could hold a note longer than any,' Job Royce agrees.

'Man didn't need to breathe,' John Vigor offers.

'He doesn't any more,' says Alexander Muzzard.

'Died, when? In 59, 60?' Henry Sharrow asks.

No one is sure, not even William Orrell. 'It has slipped out of my mind.' He sings, not loudly:

> *Give thanks to God for all his gifts, shew not thyself unkind:*
> *And suffer not his benefits to slip out of thy mind.*

Dropping his voice to deepest depths on 'unkind' and 'mind'. 'William Williams went still lower,' he concedes.

John Bedford reaches that part of his address where he speaks warmly of 'that pattern of true piety King Charles the First, of ever blessed memory, who renewed our Parish Clerks Charter.'

Warm approval from the left hand side of the Hall, dismissive frowns from the right.

'William Williams,' says Joad Godscall, 'Of course! Of course! He died in 59, days after leaving office. Course he did. Didn't live to see the great shame and disgrace the year 60 brought.'

'One of us,' Alexander Muzzard says, 'a good and godly man, William Williams. Gone to God.'

'Gone to our Lord and Saviour. Gone to Jesus Christ,' adds Phillip Carter. 'The good man.' Loud Amens to this, one of the loudest from nodding Thomas Mounck four rows back.

'And by which Charter,' continues John Bedford, 'we Clerks enjoy certain privileges peculiar to us. In respect of the great and continual attendance and charge we do undergo, we are free from all other offices. Again, we Parish Clerks are privileged to have a printing press here in our common Hall, for the printing of our weekly and general Bills of Mortality.'

'Printing press,' Alexander Muzzard tries to whisper. 'A printing press is a powerful engine to have. In the right hands. In the hands of the righteous.' His bench mates agree, but show no outward sign of this. Alexander Muzzard has no discretion.

'Clerks,' Master John Bedford tells Robert Foster, 'are enjoined by our Charter to make written report of all the christenings and burials, etcetera, which happen in their parishes, on every Tuesday weekly, by six o'clock in the afternoon at the farthest, but – according to the By-Laws,' he turns to certain clerks present, 'but according to our By-Laws, John Lavimer, St Mildred Poultry, Henry Wyldgoose, St Anne and St Agnes, Thomas Mounck, St Botolph Bishopsgate, by two of the afternoon. Two.'

Such admonitions are a weekly occurrence, the list of latecomers a source of mild interest. The clerks listen for the familiar names of repeat offenders – greeted with laughter and jeers – and the more surprising entries of those normally punctual.

'Such punctuality is necessary so that the King's Majesty may have a true account of the full and complete Bills of Mortality upon the Wednesday from a Book drawn up by the Clerk of the Company,' he gestures graciously to young John Bell.

'Robert Foster you have produced a Certificate under the hand of the Minister of St Mary Aldermary, Robert Gell, of your election to the place of Parish Clerk for St Mary Aldermary, which gives a sufficient warrant to this Company for your admission. Yet to be fully satisfied, the Company seeks proof of abilities to sing, of your competent skill in singing.'

This is a matter of great interest to all.

'Singing is the peculiar province of the Parish Clerk. Our church music is of divine origin, and truly primitive and Christian in its institution, pious in its use, and most heavenly in its end, and consequently, most commendable and praise-worthy.'

Cries of solid agreement roll throughout the Hall. 'Hear him! Hear him!'

'For the sake of those in the congregation that are illiterate I do advise you to read the psalm line by line, for the most unlearned are to bear a part in singing God's praises, and some of them are considerable proficients in learning tunes by ear and keeping time when the psalm is read to them from the Clerk's desk. So now shall you prove to this Company your singing skills by leading those who would be your Brethren in psalm the one hundred and thirty third.'

Robert Foster, well prepared by young John Bell who has given him due notice of the chosen psalm, confidently lines out:

> How happy a thing it is, and joyful for to see,
> Brethren together fast to hold the band of amity!

Which is returned in full measure by men who sing gladly through to the righteous end:

Ev'n so the Lord doth pour on them his blessings manifold,
Whose hearts and minds without all guile this knot doth keep and
hold.

'A good voice,' says William Orrell, 'a good tunable voice.'

'Gives the line well, in a fine singing tone,' agrees Joad Godscall.

'Bah. One of them,' Alexander Muzzard growls.

'One of them, one of us, one of them,' Philip Carter is annoyed. 'What does that matter with singing? He can sing.'

The Hall agrees. There is stamping of feet and slapping of knees from both sides.

At the front the Master, the Clerk of the Clerks, and the new man, all are pleased.

'Brethren,' says the Master, 'no men living have more fair opportunities of being happy and good men than we Clerks, who are always conversant in holy places, in holy things. Yea, and in the most serious things too, such as the visitation of the sick, where we do often attend, and at the burial of the dead, in which, if at any time people are serious, it is at such times.'

Solemn, serious, voices call through the Hall, 'Hear him. Hear him.'

'The Oath,' announces the Master. 'By our Charter we are empowered to administer an Oath to the Members of this Corporation upon their first admission.'

'Ah, here we shall have the "you shalls,"' says John Vigor.

'You shall swear,' intones John Bedford, making his way through loyal and true, through obedient in all lawful things and causes. 'You shall at all times come to all assemblies for the necessary use, commodity and profit of the said Company and Fellowship, and bear your part in charges belonging to the said Company.'

Both sides of the Hall know what comes next, and the left looks with knowing suspicion, with scorn, at the right as the Master says, 'You shall know no Conventicles or assemblies, nor any deed done, that may be prejudicial to the estate or harmful to the said Company, but you shall give warning to the Master and Wardens thereof.'

Some of those on the right side of the Hall have attended, do still attend, Conventicles and assemblies of Independent churchmen, gatherings of those who still hold to the Good Old Cause. And yet they have given no warning thereof, neither to the Master nor to the Lower or Upper Wardens.

'In your own person you shall do the best always that in you lieth, and that you lawfully may do, for the benefit and profit of this Company.' The Master repeats at this point, as he does, 'for the benefit and profit of this Company.' Ends, 'All this you shall do and observe. Do you so swear, so God you help and Jesus Christ?'

'I do so swear, so God me help and Jesus Christ,' swears Robert Foster.

The Company stamps its feet again in approval. Young John Bell hands the Master a copy of the Company's Orders and Rules. The Master with formal ceremony bestows it on their newly sworn brother, Robert Foster.

'These Orders and Rules, ten Orders and Rules, are to be observed and kept by all and every Parish Clerk. You see them here on the wall, hung there in their frame. I will not rehearse them all now,' says the Master.

'That is a relief,' Henry Sharrow mutters, 'else we be here 'til midnight.'

'But I will make note of the two last. Rule Nine orders "That no Parish Clerk shall by himself, his Deputy, Servants—"'

'Only Parish Clerk I know with servants is you, John Bedford,' William Orrell mutters to Henry Sharrow.

'— deliver or disperse any weekly or general Bills of Mortality to the inhabitants of any other parish of which he is not Clerk, neither shall he deliver any to the inhabitants of the parish of which he is Clerk, until the Thursday morning of each respective week. Lastly, no Parish Clerk shall cause to be sold any of the weekly or general Bills of Mortality to any Bookseller, Gazette, Hawker, or other person whatsoever who shall again offer the same for sale, unless it be by the knowledge and consent of the Master and the Wardens of the Company for the time being, and for the common profit and benefit of the Company of Parish Clerks.' He pauses, repeats, 'for the common profit and benefit of the Company.'

'Guards our purse well,' Joad Godscall says.

'Guards his own better,' says William Orrell.

'That Robert Foster will have to pay his first penny.' They watch as young John Bell passes a blank Bill to the Master, who hands it to the new Clerk in exchange for a penny.

'Think we could make a gift of the first one,' Alexander Muzzard says, 'a good welcoming gesture to a new man.'

'We all paid our first penny,' Henry Sharrow replies, 'why shouldn't he?'

They re-light pipes, stand, move about. The business of the meeting stops while John Bedford takes Robert Foster aside and goes through, thoroughly goes through, all ten Orders and Rules of the Company.

'Sad, half empty Hall today,' says Philip Carter, rolling his shoulders, flexing his arms.

'Pestilence. Who's fled, who's dead?' asks William Orrell, answers himself. 'Too many fled. Too many dead.'

'Some ailing, some failing,' Thomas Mounck suggests, joining his companions. 'I know some too ill to come.'

John Vigor chants, looking pleased with himself, 'Some might have fled, or so they said, when instead, they're home in bed, on top of the maid.'

'Do not disperse,' young John Bell calls out. 'More business to come. New and important business to come.'

'You have suffered the worst, Thomas Mounck? Your parish?'

'Not the worst. This week eleven burials and only three of plague. North and west they're finding it much worse. William Bromskin at St Sepulchre, my neighbour, forty five burials and eighteen of them plague. Eighteen.'

'Very bad to the west,' John Cakebread of St Bartholomew Little wanders over, joins in. He is one of them on the other side, but also a man who will talk kindly to anyone. 'St Giles in the Fields, one hundred and forty three plague dead. This week alone, one hundred and forty three, and one hundred and eighty five burials in all.'

This shocks. 'Two burials, only one of plague, in my St Michael Crooked Lane,' Job Royce says.

'Nothing in St Bennet Sherehog,' says John Vigor. 'No deaths, no burials, no plague.'

'Nobody dies in St Bennet Sherehog,' scoffs Henry Sharrow. 'Nobody and no bodies. Your last burial was when? Mid May?'

John Vigor shrugs. 'Healthy parish.'

'Small parish,' nods Thomas Mounck. St Botolph Bishopsgate is large. He thinks but does not say, that John Vigor is thought to be a clerk who will adjust his weekly Bill if the right sized purse is offered. It is said that in St Bennet Sherehog with sufficient money you can pay not to die at all.

'Twelve burials, eight of plague in St Cyneswide and St Tibba,' Philip Carter says sombrely.

'So your Searchers searched eight plague corpses? Did not miss any?' William Orrell asks.

'Is that an innocent question?' Alexander Muzzard wants to know.

'As innocent as the Searchers at St Cyneswide and St Tibba?' John Vigor knows his own reputation has been talked of and is happy to throw suspicion elsewhere. 'There is talk, Philip Carter.'

'Talk, there is always talk, John Vigor. People talk. Often talk of matters that are not true. Frequently of matters not true.'

'Not true of the Searchers of St Cyneswide and St Tibba? Not true that they sought a bribe from a widow? Took food and drink from the Shipley widow then sought a bribe to say death was, was fever, flox, flux or frightened? Delayed the search of John Sly's house so the corpse of the maid could be carried away? Not true?'

'There is always talk, John Vigor. Talk does not make it true. These are good and respected ancient matrons.'

'One with a face that would scare a robber's dog and the gentle manner of a builder's hammer, the other a flighty old trout who spouts poetry. An ancient matron poet!'

Both sides of the Hall find this exchange of interest, gather around.

Out the front the watchful young John Bell can see that no good will come of this. 'Order. Order! There is important business still to come here. The Master has important business for us all. Orders from the Lord Mayor and Aldermen concerning the infection of the Plague.'

'You are an honest man,' John Cakebread says comfortingly to Philip Carter. 'You are honest and so will your Searchers be honest.' John Cakebread goes back to his bench on the left side of the Hall.

'What did he say?' Thomas Mounck asks Philip Carter.

'Only good words.'

'Good clerks on both sides,' nods Thomas Mounck.

Alexander Muzzard shakes his head, 'No.'

'There are new Orders issued, these to take place upon the first of July. This Saturday coming, the first day of July,' the Master announces. 'There are——' he turns to young John Bell, asks, 'how many Headings are there?'

'Twenty seven.'

'There are twenty seven Headings in these new Orders conceived and published by the Lord Mayor. I will rehearse here the major——' he leafs through the large document, 'the major Headings.' Pauses. 'There are copies for all. Copies for all to take to your Vestries and, and tell your Vestrymen. Tell them. Ready for the first day of July. Two watchmen, one for the day one for the night, outside infected houses.'

'Nothing new there,' William Orrell says.

'Searchers,' the Master looks suspiciously at both sides of the Hall. 'Searchers. There shall be special care to appoint women Searchers in every parish, such as are of honest reputation, and of the best sort as can be got in this kind. Of honest reputation,' he repeats.

John Vigor snorts.

'Physicians who shall be appointed for cure and prevention of the Infection, do call before them the said Searchers who are or shall be appointed to the end they may consider whether they are fitly qualified for that employment. And no Searcher during this time shall be permitted to use any public employment, or keep a shop or stall, or be employed as a laundress, or any other common employment whatsoever.'

'Who would want a Searcher as a laundress?' comes a voice from the other side of the Hall, greeted by general laughter.

'Surgeons. For better assistance of the Searchers, for as much as there has been heretofore great abuse in misrepresenting the disease, to the further spreading of the infection.' More suspicious frowns from the Master at the assembled clerks. 'Because of heretofore great abuse in misrepresenting, it is therefore ordered that able and discreet Surgeons join with the Searchers for the view of the body, to this end that there may be a true report made of the disease.'

'Physicians to examine the Searchers to see if they are fitly qualified? And surgeons? To do viewing with the Searchers? The physicians and surgeons in my parish have left town already or are intending to. There will be no physicians or surgeons,' Joad Godscall says to agreement from both sides of the Hall. 'There are none, or the few that remain not enough.'

'Searchers, Searchers, Surgeons … and, and––' the Master loses his place in the Orders, young John Bell guides his finger back to the right spot, 'and Buriers are not to pass the streets without holding a red rod or wand of three foot in length in their hands, open and evident to be seen.'

'Again, not new,' William Orrell mutters. 'But hard to bury a body and hold a red wand at the same time. Did he mean bearers? Same problem: carry a corpse and a red wand? Stick the wand in your belt?'

'Sequestration of the Sick,' the Master looks annoyed, confused, says with irritation to young John Bell. 'This Order, these Orders, under some Headings it says sequestration of a plague house for a month, shut up for a month, but elsewhere the period is twenty eight days. Which is it to be?'

'If one Heading says a month, then whatever applies under that Heading it shall be a month. And if another Heading says twenty eight days, then whatever applies under that other Heading, then it shall be twenty eight days,' young John Bell explains. This is already clear to the clerks. They are used to dealing with Orders that do not always agree the one with the other.

The Master brushes this away, hurries on. 'Burial of the dead. Always either before sun-rising or after sun-setting. All graves at least six foot deep. No neighbours or friends to accompany the corpse to church, upon pain of having his house shut up. No children at time of burial in any church, churchyard or burying place.

'Every house visited by the pestilence to be marked with a red cross a foot long and the decreed words "Lord have mercy upon us." This is not new,' grumbles the Master, turns more pages. 'Streets to be kept clean; the filth of houses to be carried away daily by the Rakers; the Raker shall give notice of his coming by the blowing of a horn, as heretofore has been done. Orders concerning Beggars, Plays, Feasting Prohibited,' the Master sighs, stops. 'There are copies of these Orders for all.'

He beckons young John Bell forward. 'I have important business, matters I must attend to, so I give the management of this meeting into the hands of our Clerk. Copies for all,' he repeats unnecessarily. Young John Bell, his father's son, needs no instruction on how to carry out his duties.

'Important business,' Alexander Muzzard laughs. 'Off on his own business. Wine merchant business. It's to the good fortune of the Master that our Hall is here in the Vintry.'

'We shall close with psalm the twenty seventh, the first part.' With skill and ease young John Bell, Clerk of the Clerks, leads the assembled Brethren back to harmony.

> *Therefore within his house will I give sacrifice of praise:*
> *With psalms and songs I will apply to laud the Lord always.*

'New man still needs to sing with book in hand.'

'Not surprising, he's a new clerk, a new Brother. And some others still sing with book.'

'Not I. I learned my psalms from singing, from when a small child. The book came later, when I knew my letters, but I already knew my psalms from singing.'

Agreement.

Young John Bell issues fresh printed copies of the new Orders. 'Printed here. Special permission from the bishop, the Mayor, and the Stationers' Company to have them printed here. Time's short, I said, we need these in the hands of all our clerks at Tuesday assembly, twenty seventh June, I said. Come into force first July. Stationers didn't like it, but Mayor Sir John

Lawrence over-rode all, "It has to be" he said, and it was. And it is.' Young John Bell is pleased.

'Good a Clerk as his father was.'

'Better. Old John Bell turned very sour in his last years.'

Alexander Muzzard sneers, 'Young John Bell! One of them. Became one of them. Turned into one of them.'

'Yes, and a good Clerk of Clerks even so,' answers William Orrell.

'Organs,' says Alexander Muzzard, scratching at another grievance. 'We don't need organs. We sang well, better than ever today, without an organ. Hear this: the other side made this verse to scorn us so we took it and made it our own:

> What'er the Popish hands have built
> Our hammers shall undo;
> We'll break their pipes and burn their copes
> And pull down churches too.

'And we did. And we should still.'

His fellows are used to Alexander Muzzard, the always angry man, and pay no attention.

'Now, business done, us to the *Three Cranes*, and them over there to the *Vintage*. As always, as always,' says Job Royce. Down Broad Lane to the wharves he leads those from the right side of the Hall.

'Those to the *Vintage* be filthy, and he which is filthy let him be filthy still, and he that is righteous, let him be righteous still,' says Alexander Muzzard, suddenly cheerful. 'And we the righteous are to the *Three Cranes*.'

'You Fifth Monarchy Men, always great for the Book of Revelation,' says William Orrell.

'Of course we are! A Book of mighty prophecy. Shows the way to salvation, to eternity. Shines a light on the path for all saints to follow. And we do.'

'Be in God's keeping!' John Cakebread, headed to the *Vintage* with Robert Foster, John Lavimer and Henry Wyldgoose, calls cheerfully.

John Lavimer says, 'They will need all of God's keeping to stay safe in that narrow dog hole the *Three Cranes* calls its best room. The food there would poison a street cur.'

'Off to their pots of stale porridge at the *Vintage*,' Alexander Muzzard jeers in turn. 'That John Lavimer, turd in his teeth.'

Job Royce sings their way into the Three Cranes, sings to the tavern keeper:

> *Show a room, show a room, show a room,*
> *Here's a knot of good fellows are come*
> *That mean for to be merry,*
> *With claret and sherry.*
> *Each man to mirth himself disposes,*
> *And for the reck'ning tell the noses.*
> *Give the red nose some white,*
> *And the pale nose some claret,*
> *But the nose that looks blue,*
> *Give him a cup of sack, 'twill mend his hue.*

All know the catch and amble in, singing. All in good humour.

'A nose that looks blue? That's your face as marked Thomas Mounck,' John Vigor laughs. 'A cup of sack won't mend it. A tun of sack won't mend it. A shipload from Sackland won't mend it!'

'Needs no mending, this is the face God gave me.'

Henry Sharrow takes Philip Carter aside, says urgently, 'Your Searcher Widow Hazel——'

'Hazard. Widow Margaret Hazard.'

'Your Widow Hazard, is she like my Silent Sarah? As was my Silent Sarah. No longer a Searcher in St Benet Fynck.'

'Do you mean does she keeps coins in her mouth? No. She does not.'

'Philip Carter!' Exasperated Henry Sharrow. 'You know my meaning! Is there corruption? False reporting by Widow Margaret Hazard?'

'No. No. I don't think so.'

'Don't think so. There are tales told Philip Carter.'

'I know the tales.'

'You heard the talk in the Hall. These tales pass from mouth to mouth.'

'Like coins?'

'Philip Carter! Listen seriously. John Vigor is a great man for unkind gossip. There are those in your parish who are no friends of the Widow nor the Goodwife poetess. They are keeping these tales alive, feeding the fire of scandal.'

'There is always gossip. My Searchers are not corrupt or false reporters. No matter how they look or, or how they spout poetry. No matter how. Thomas Mounck has his face marked from birth and is a good man. The Widow Hazard has her face marked from fire. This does not make her corrupt. It makes her a woman with a burnt and twisted face, and no more than that.'

'You do not have to convince me, Philip Carter. You say the Widow and the Goodwife are honest, and I, who am your friend, am satisfied. But watch out for John Vigor. And some others. Have you talked to your Vestrymen, or they to you? Raise it first yourself at the next Vestry meeting. Call for evidence. If there is none, that'll be the end of the matter.'

'Perhaps. I will think on it.'

'Do think on it. Then do it.'

'Come sit and drink you two,' John Vigor calls to them. 'What mischief are you plotting in your corner?'

'Plotting? Mischief? We leave that to Alexander Muzzard and his Fifth Monarchy Men,' Henry Sharrow answers lightly.

Alexander Muzzard waves his can, happy to acknowledge the charge.

'This new Order,' says Thomas Mounck, 'pages of printing, pages of reading.' Throws it down on the tavern table, where it soaks up spilt beer.

'How many Headings?' asks Job Royce in good imitation of the Master's querulous voice. 'Twenty seven,' he answers, now as young John Bell, 'and if you had taken the time to read it yourself I would not have to do all your business for you. As I always do.'

'The Master's doing his own business now, this very minute, down at the Vintners' Hall. Twenty years ago he had a tavern in Londonderry, traded in wine and tobacco. But he can't manage money, can't manage debts, his big debts, comes back, as clerk to St Dionis Backchurch. Down at the Vintners' Hall now with his friend Daniel Rawlinson. Buying, selling, who knows?' Alexander Muzzard asks, expecting no answer.

'Some of his business very small,' says Henry Sharrow. 'If a new Clerk has not brought his penny to buy his first blank Bill, the Master, all kindness, says "No matter, here take it now and bring me a penny farthing next week." A usurious rate!'

'Every farthing adds up,' says John Vigor.

'Who is this Lady Harpy who gives him money?' Philip Carter asks Joad Godscall.

'Not Harpy!' breaks in John Vigor, full pregnant to give birth to a scurrilous tale. 'Not Lady Harpy, Harvey, Lady Harvey. The King's whore——'

'Is this Lady Harpy, Harvey, one of the Scotchman's whores?'

'Let me tell the tale. Castlemaine, the Scotchman's whore——'

'He's a scarlet whore himself, the Scotchman,' Alexander Muzzard says.

'Do you want to hear this?' John Vigor asks, annoyed. 'Castlemaine the whore hates this Lady Harvey, a friend of the Scotchman's Portuguese wife. Hates any friend of the Queen. So, in some play in the playhouse Castlemaine tells the player Doll Common, surely paid her to do so, pays this Doll Common who was playing an old doxy, to move and speak the way this Lady Harvey moves and speaks.' Here John Vigor waves his arms and does his best to sound like a court lady. 'The Castlemaine whore thought this a great joke on the Queen and her court ladies!'

John Vigor's enthusiasm for court gossip and scurrilous broadsheets is regarded as bemusing and suspect.

'So is this why Lady Harvey gives money to Master John Bedford?' Henry Sharrow asks innocently. 'I don't understand, because of some play? And haven't the playhouses been closed now. For weeks?' He points to the new Orders, reads out, '"All plays, bear-baitings, games, singing of ballads, buckler-play, or such like causes of assemblies of people be utterly prohibited and the parties offending severely punished by every Alderman in his Ward."'

'It has nothing to with the money to John Bedford!' John Vigor finds his fellow Clerks slow and obtuse.

Baiting John Vigor, unlike bear-baiting, has not been prohibited, and is widely held to be good sport.

Alexander Muzzard takes up Thomas Mounck's copy of the Orders, now beer and grease stained. 'A good print. Our Hall's press does a good print. A printing press is a powerful engine for good, for righteousness, in godly hands. What cannot be done with a good, righteously written, well printed pamphlet? To rouse the people from their sorrowful slumber?'

'You won't print any such pamphlets on that press,' Philip Carter gestures back towards the Clerks' Hall. 'Only three keys to the printing room. One with the Master, one with the Upper Warden, one with the Lower.'

'Mistress Ellinor Coates, our printer, she will have a key?' Alexander Muzzard asks hopefully. 'Her house in Aldersgate, not so far from you Philip Carter?'

'Orders say only three keys, Master and the Wardens,' Philip Carter replies.

'Think what we saints could do, can do, with a printing press,' Alexander Muzzard yearns. 'Become masters of ourselves again. No bishops. No Lord bishops. We once had our own church, our own minister, worshipped our way. Not Rome's way, not the Porridge way. Worshipped the peoples' way, the congregation's way. All equal before God in the next life, and equal in this life too. Under Oliver Protector we were. Then Oliver dies and then Charles the Bastard, the scarlet whoreson whore, comes back and they dig him up, our Protector, and put his sad dead head high on a stake.

'In 61 just fifty of us, we could have done it, taken the City, almost did. We would rescue the poor remains of our dead Protector, martyred when even dead. Our cry was "King Jesus, and the heads upon the gates!" Thomas Venner told it was time to fight for King Jesus. Not to fear that our numbers were small, for one should chase ten and ten should chase a thousand. Swords not to be sheathed until Babylon, the whoreson Charles, had become a hissing and a curse with nothing left, neither remnant, son nor nephew.' He pauses, exhausted, dispirited, says quietly, 'King Jesus and the heads upon the gates.'

Silence. Some agree as much, some much less.

'Hanged drawn and quartered, Thomas Venner and Roger Hodgkin,' says John Vigor who saw it. 'Done in Coleman Street. Them dying, crying down the wrath and vengeance of King Jesus on Charles the false king, on wicked and corrupt judges, and on the whole filthy city of London. He was a wine cooper, Thomas Venner, must have done business down here in the Vintry.' Turns to Alexander Muzzard, 'And you, not so hot Alexander Muzzard. We want to go to our houses tonight, not to be locked up by a Constable for sedition, for treason, in some filthy gaol.'

Alexander Muzzard, angry and ready for brawling, stands abruptly, jolting the bench. 'The heads at Westminster Hall! Shaming us all, looking down on us and seeing our shame.'

Job Royce, all for peace, points to the last page of the new Orders and laughs, 'Hear this: "Disorderly tippling in taverns, alehouses, coffee-houses and cellars be severely looked unto as a common sin of this time, and greatest occasion of dispersing the plague. No company or person be suffered to remain or come into any tavern, alehouse, or coffee-house after nine of the clock in the evening."' He throws the Orders down. 'Here's a catch for those who would commit a common sin by tippling in a tavern, or an alehouse, at any time of day or night. Come in when ready:

The pot, the pipe, the quart, the can
Hath spoiled many an honest man,
The hare and horn, the hawk and whore,
Hath quite undone, quite undone, as many more.

They sing it through five times.

Alexander Muzzard roars, 'Here's a jest for you! That catch, William Lawes, a king's man, he made it, and we shot him dead at the Rowton Heath fight in 45! There's a good laugh!'

The cheerful singers stuff the Orders in pockets and leave in good humour.

'This new Order,' Philip Carter grumbles to Henry Sharrow. 'I have just had the old one printed fresh and posted on the wall in St Cyneswide and St Tibba. Now here is this new one,' he shakes his head.

Henry Sharrow claps him on the back. 'God be w'ye, Philip Carter.'

'And God be w'ye, Henry Sharrow.'

London, Bills of Mortality for 130 Parishes
from the 20 of June to the 27 of June 1665
Buried, in all – 684; Plague – 267
Parishes clear of the Plague – 110; Parishes Infected – 20

CHAPTER IX

London, Wednesday, 28 June 1665

'Care to be had of stinking Fish, unwholesome Flesh,
and musty Corn.'

'The child is dead?'

'Died in the night. Daniel Stiles, Philip Carter's running boy, came early this morning to say the Clerk wants us to come. "Clerk says come!" he shouts at the door. I told him to shush, I didn't want him to wake Isaac. Although with a night's drink in him he's hard enough to wake. But you can never know.'

'Daniel Stiles told you?' Widow Margaret Hazard asks.

The Goodwife nods, continues, '"When should I come?" I asked him. "Soon!" he says. "How is your small brother? Is he any better?" I asked. "Not good, not better"' he said. "Poor Sam is dead. Died in the night. Our mother and father wept. We all did. All the house weeping. He was a small lad who liked play."'

'Did his mother give him the physick, the purging? A good comfrey syrup?' the Widow asks crossly.

'Daniel Stiles did not say but she must have. His mother, she would do all she could do,' the Goodwife pauses, draws deeply on her pipe. 'He was a little, pretty child.'

'God's will,' the Widow says, still annoyed. 'Mmm.' Thinks once more that life is, then it isn't. Her own pipe has gone out and she inspects the bowl for any remains of tobacco. None, only ash. 'It was running boy James Kerton called me. Said we're to come because the Clerk has more news. News of the infection.'

They sit on the churchyard wall. The vestry door is still closed, and no sign yet of Philip Carter.

'I don't understand,' Widow Margaret Hazard says in a tone of voice the Goodwife knows well and does not want to hear this morning. She offers no encouragement, draws on her pipe and stares out into the square at the hackney-coach stand.

Not put off, the Widow continues single-mindedly. 'I do not know what to make of Abraham and Isaac.' This is not so, she knows clearly what she thinks about Abraham's willingness to kill his son. It is wicked and inexcusable. 'The death of children.' She shakes her head.

'Sam Stiles was run over by a cart wheel. He was a small boy. Small body, small bones. There was little chance for him, or none,' the Goodwife says. She wants to change the subject. She could point, draw the Widow's attention to the busyness of the hackney coachmen setting up, a skittish horse, but does not do this for fear it will set off a grievance about the false charges Isabella Undnay is still making against the Searchers, how they have neglected their duty.

A distraction arrives, a button seller comes into the square crying: 'Buttons and thread, the best to be had! Buy my Buttons! Butt-onnnns!'

The Goodwife sings:

> Betsy Blue came all in black,
> Silver buttons down her back.
> Every button cost a crown,
> Every lady turn around.
> Alligoshee, alligoshee,
> Turn the bridle over my knee.

Although she does not want to be distracted from her misery, the Widow joins in, links arms behind with the Goodwife, skips her legs forward, back.

'Hard to dance seated,' she says, cheered despite herself. Then recalls the children playing and singing this game in the square, small Sam Stiles doing his best to join in. Her mood falls again.

'Having trouble with his bridle,' The Goodwife points to John Pooly, whose nag is skittish.

'The Clerk must have sent out all his running boys.' The Goodwife can see the Keepers and the Viewers gathering near the lychgate. 'A meeting on the pestilence for us all. Must be pressing news. Constable coming too.' Samuel Snow walks with slow importance across the square.

Widow Hazard stares bleakly at the gathering numbers the Clerk has summoned. 'Mmm.'

'Samuel Snow is a man pleased to be Constable,' the Goodwife says lightly.

'And why shouldn't he be?' the Widow is scratchy. 'Why shouldn't he be pleased? It is an important office and any man would be pleased to hold it.'

The Goodwife allows herself a gentle sigh, settles quietly.

Surprising both Widow and Goodwife, Goody Parsons starts across the churchyard to join them.

'What does she want?' Widow Margaret Hazard grumbles. 'We don't want her with us. We don't need her.'

Goodwife Joan Brokefild replies briskly, 'She must want our company. A change of company from those others. We must be a better sort of person.' The Goodwife laughs at this.

'Viper. Carrying tales. Saying unfriendly things. That's why she sits with us, to burrow into our confidence and then make up more lies. Tells lies about us to that Anne Abowen. Urges her on.'

'Goody Susannah Parsons has only shown us goodwill. If there are tales——'

'There *are* tales!'

'If there are tales, why should it be Goody Parsons who spreads them? Or Anne Abowen? More like Isabella Undnay who says – wrongly, says wrongly – that we do not do our work.' The Goodwife stops talking, makes welcome space on the wall for Goody Parsons to sit beside her.

'We all wait for the Clerk,' Goody Parsons says brightly.

'Mmm!' the Widow makes it clear this is not news.

'Yes, we are all here now. Or are there more to come? Do you know?' the Goodwife's voice is kind, making up for the Widow's surliness.

'Well ...' Goody Parsons thinks. 'The Church Warden? Surely the Church Warden will be coming.'

'Do you know that?' the Widow asks, still crossgrained.

'He's coming now,' Goody Parsons says with satisfaction, 'See? And other parishes are to have their Wardens present. And their Viewers, Keepers, Searchers and Constables. All one hundred and thirty parishes are to be told. One hundred and thirty! There is a great deal of new matter in these Orders that must be told before the first day of July, when the Orders begin.'

'How do you know all this?' the Widow asks, outraged.

'My aunt Joanes, her son, Iwan Joanes, my cousin, is sexton at St Bartholomew Little. The clerk there, a kind man, John Cakebread, has summoned his church officers to tell them today of these new Orders from the Mayor.'

'Mmm. Then I suppose your aunt Joanes' son – a sexton – already knows what is in these Orders? Has he been summoned to hear these new Orders? At St Bartholomew Little?' the Widow asks snidely.

'Oh no, he is only a sexton and they have not been summoned. And he only told me some of what is in the Orders. Not all of course. He had it from clerk John Cakebread. Of course the new rules about burial of the dead are things a sexton must know, must be told.'

'And are there new Orders for Searchers?' the Goodwife breaks in.

'There are. Something about Searchers being under physicians and surgeons. Something of that. My kinsman Iwan Joanes––'

'The sexton?'

'Yes, the sexton, my kinsman, he heard some scraps of these Orders when John Cakebread returned from the Clerks' meeting. They sing there, at their meetings of a Tuesday. All the clerks of all the London parishes singing together.' Goody Parsons smiles at this picture.

Goodwife Joan Brokefild can feel the Widow stirring angrily, hear her muttering 'Physicians and surgeons, who know nothing of the dead and little of the living.' The Goodwife turns to the Widow, says firmly, 'We will listen carefully to what Philip Carter has to say of these new Orders. He will tell us all there is to be told.'

They see the vestry door open and Frances Barrow beckons them all in. The three ancient matrons stand, and Goody Susanna Parsons adds as they walk, 'There is also concern about great abuse in misreporting the infection, so surgeons are to join with Searchers to view corpses and make a true report of the disease. And there are to be more red wands.'

Goody Parsons goes ahead, joining Widow Dorothy Bullen, Anne Abowen and Widow Ursula Chaukley.

'Mmm. Mmm,' the Widow snorts, ready for battle.

'We will listen to what Philip Carter has to say,' the Goodwife repeats. 'He has Orders from the Mayor, the Lord Mayor of London,' she says as they enter the vestry, repeats quietly, 'and we will listen.'

'The first were St Giles in the Fields,' the Clerk, propped on his stool against the wall and talking to the Warden, reaches into his chest and pulls out a bundle of Bills. 'Here, the Bill for the week 18 April to the 25, at the bottom here, in the parishes without the walls: St Giles in the Fields, thirty burials, two of them plague. St Giles Fields, John Shingler their clerk – he wasn't at Hall yesterday – told us at the time in April it was only two poor beggars, not like the rest of his parish, all dukes and duchesses. So he says.'

'Nothing at all at the Pesthouse then. No plague, no burials,' Frances Barrow, seated at the vestry table, peers at the Bill, grunts, 'All the popishness and superstition put back at St Giles Fields in 1660. Before, in the good days, the congregation rid itself of statues and hangings and relics and all such. Comes back the Scotchman, comes back all the coloured glass in the windows.'

'These saints,' Philip Carter says, shaking his head, 'St Giles and his red deer and the arrow. A piece of popish nonsense in one of their coloured windows. John Shingler goes on and on about that. How the light comes in through it and spreads its colours over the pews and the floor and the walls.'

There is a stirring among the Viewers, Keepers and Searchers sitting around the vestry table. Some keen to hear more of this story of St Giles and the red deer, others – Widow Margaret Hazard included – impatient to hear the new Orders.

'The papists have many strange and magical tales,' Widow Dorothy Bullen says placidly. Quickly adds, not wishing to be misunderstood, 'Fantastic and unbelievable they all are.'

'A bitmaker over against St Clements shut up from the plague two days ago,' Constable Samuel Snow says. 'Plague growing on and we need these new Orders or we shall all go to ruin. Shall we hear them now, Philip Carter?'

'Orders for you, Samuel Snow,' Philip Carter reads, 'Watchmen. Two for each infected house, one for day and the other for night. Day watchman to attend until ten of the clock at night, and watchman by night until six in the morning. Watchmen to have a special care that no person go in or out of infected houses, upon pain of severe punishment.'

Samuel Snow is pleased, repeats, 'Severe punishment. Yes.'

'Watchman to do such duties as the sick house requires, and if the watchman is sent upon any business he is to lock up the house and take the key with him.'

Satisfaction is heard around the vestry table. These are good Orders. So far.

'Watchmen to minister necessaries to those shut up at their own charges, if they are able.' The Parish Clerk looks up from the Orders, 'Meaning, Samuel Snow, at the charges of those shut up, not the watchmen.'

The Constable is relieved to hear this. 'Good. Our watchmen could not afford to do that. Pay for the necessaries of those infected.' He shakes his head at the thought.

'And if those shut up are unable to pay, this shall be at the common charge.'

Noises of assent. This is seen as only fair and reasonable. All those sitting in the vestry are poor men and women living at the common charge of the parish, and they do not begrudge others who have a call on parish help. Provided it is a rightful and just call.

'Those watchmen we have now, Samuel Snow, no trouble between

Robert Tomlinson and Thomas Billington as they do not watch the same house?'

'Not between them, no,' Samuel Snow says with meaning. 'Not them.'

All pay close attention to this, hoping to hear more.

'Between others then?' asks the Church Warden?' expressing the interest of all.

Samuel Snow rubs his chin, sighs. 'We already need many watchmen and will need even more as the infection spreads. It's not that easy to find good, reliable men. Not as easy as it sounds. Francis Neale complains that Roger Geoffrayes is always late in coming at night. And you can see his point, Francis Neale's point. He does a long watch during the heat of the day – although he does have passers-by to talk to – and comes late night he wants to get home to a drink and to bed.'

The Constable stops to attend to his pipe, resumes, 'And Roger Geoffrayes, who's already had more than one drink himself, comes late more often than not. In no good state to watch well and closely, and even to stay awake. Roger Geoffrayes has been told. I have told him, more than once.' Samuel Snow frowns at the slackness of those who have been entrusted with an important job of work but fail to do it. 'And that's only one case. Now—'

The Parish Clerk waves him to silence. 'That is for you to deal with as parish Constable.'

'I know that,' Samuel Snow says with some irritation. 'I know that. And I do and will.'

'These physicians and surgeons,' Goodwife Joan Brokefild has a back broad enough to ask what all the ancient matrons wish to know. 'What do the Orders say of them Philip Carter?'

'I am coming to that,' he replies shortly, 'if all are ready to hear. It comes under the fourth heading, namely Searchers.'

The Viewers and Keepers share brief looks.

'Special care to be taken to appoint Women Searchers in every parish, such as are of honest reputation and of the best sort as can be got.'

Widow Margaret Hazard, Goodwife Joan Brokefild and Frances Barrow nod approvingly, endorsing these words. Vindicated. There is no reaction from the Viewers and Keepers. Constable Snow is busy with his pipe and does not hear.

'And for as much as there has been heretofore great abuse in misreporting the disease, to the further spreading of the infection,' he stops, addresses the Goodwife and the Widow, 'I am reading what is set down here. These are not my words. To continue: Physicians appointed for the cure and prevention of the infection shall call before them said Searchers to consider whether they are fitly qualified for that employment, and charge them from time to time if they appear defective in their duties.'

A slight rustle of suppressed satisfaction is heard.

'And the surgeons,' the Widow breaks in, her voice thick. 'What do these Orders say of them?'

'Surgeons. The fifth heading. The City and Liberties are to be quartered, and one surgeon appointed to each quarter, and the said surgeons to join with the Searchers to view the body, to the end there may be a true report made of the disease.'

This is met with open cries of disbelief and mockery.

The Warden is quick at calculating. 'Let us say each of these quartered surgeons has 32 parishes in his care. He is to view every new corpse in his quarter? Bah. And how many surgeons have fled the town already? Off to Oxford or some outlandish place. Same with the physicians. Searchers know their work. They do not need physicians or surgeons to tell them. Our Searchers here in St Cyneswide and St Tibba know their work.'

'I am only reading out what is in these Orders. And here it says that these surgeons shall have twelve pence for each body searched by them. To be paid out of the goods of the party searched, if able, otherwise by the parish.'

'Twelve pence a body!' the vestry meeting is united in outrage at this enormous fee.

'Three times your fee,' the Church Warden says to the Searchers.

'If they haven't yet fled to Oxford, then after a week of plague they will be able buy a train of coaches to take them and all their family there!' Anne Abowen says indignantly.

'It is a lot of money for one corpse,' Goody Susanna Parsons agrees.

'What of Keepers,' Widow Dorothy Bullen asks. 'Do the new Orders have anything of Keepers?'

'Expecting twelve pence too?' the Warden asks lightly.

'No,' Widow Bullen replies. 'No. I would like to know if these new Orders have anything in them for Keepers. Anything to say about Keepers.'

'There are to be Nurse-Keepers for those infected,' the Clerk answers. 'Keepers who will stay in infected houses – not you,' he says to Widow Bullen and Goody Parsons, 'you will continue to do as you do.'

'Ah, yes,' Widow Dorothy Bullen says, pleased with this sensible and desirable arrangement. She and Goody Parsons are relieved that they are not to be made Nurse-Keepers shut up in infected houses.

'And,' the Parish Clerk continues reading, '"if any Nurse-Keeper shall remove herself out of any infected house before twenty eight days after the decease of any person dying of the Infection, the House to which the said Nurse-Keeper doth so remove herself shall be shut up until the said twenty eight days be expired."'

'Or the Nurse-Keeper herself be expired,' the Church Warden suggests.

This unseemly frivolity is met with a passing smile only from Goodwife Joan Brokefild, always susceptible to levity.

'No Nurse-Keeper would do such a thing, remove herself,' says Goody Parsons on behalf of all Keepers.

Widow Dorothy Bullen agrees, adds a caution, 'It might not prove easy to recruit for such.'

'Our Master,' Philip Carter says to Frances Barrow, 'was all aflame that under the Nurse-Keeper heading the Orders say "to be shut up twenty eight days," and yet here, under Sequestration of the Sick, they say "any man sick of the Plague though he die not, the house shall be shut up for a month after the use of due preservatives taken by the rest." Our Master John Bedford worried himself at the difference between twenty eight days and a month.'

The Warden can see that several around the vestry table share the Master's confusion.

'Then why *is* there three days' difference? Why?' Widow Hazard asks, speaking for herself and the puzzled faces of Widow Ursula Chaukley, Goody Susanna Parsons and Widow Dorothy Bullen.

'There is three days' difference because that is what the Lord Mayor and the Aldermen of the City of London have written in their Orders,' the exasperated Clerk says.

'These due preservatives that are to be taken by the rest of the house, which preservatives are they?' Widow Dorothy Bullen worries aloud. 'There are many preservatives and cures, but does the Lord Mayor say which are to be used?'

'Smoking!' 'Tobacco!' Clashing voices call.

'No tobacconist has ever died of the plague. None has ever,' Goody Parsons states.

'Fume to vapour the house, I have always heard,' Widow Margaret Hazard offers.

'Plague Water,' Widow Ursula Chaukley is in no doubt. 'Plague Water.'

'There are many recipes for Plague Water,' Anne Abowen says, 'but which–'

'Only one good recipe,' Widow Chaukley knows, 'only one. Mugwort, rue, sage, celandine, sorrel, rosemary, pimpernel and balm. A pound of each. Yes, a whole pound of each, all in a pot and cover the lot with white wine. Some say let it stand for four days. Not enough. I let mine steep for at least six days, at least six.'

'And angelica and agrimony,' Widow Margaret Hazard says firmly. 'Do not forget the angelica and agrimony. Agrimony is in flower now.'

'I have no use for them,' Widow Chaukley dismisses angelica and agrimony.

'Venice Treacle,' Widow Dorothy Bullen says.

'Ha, Venice Treacle,' the Warden is scornful, 'a preservative only for those in Why-toll Palace. Or in our rectory,' he adds.

'The very best recipe for Venice Treacle is––'

'Back to the Orders,' Philip Carter taps the sheaf of Orders on the table, 'the Orders. More for you, Samuel Snow. "Constables do take special care that no wandering beggar be suffered in the streets of this City, in any fashion or manner whatsoever upon the penalty provided by the law to be duly and severely executed upon them."'

'A good Order that one,' Samuel Snow is satisfied.

'Yes, yes, but here is another that will cause a deal of trouble in this and all the parishes.'

Samuel Snow frowns. A deal of trouble.

'This Heading is, where is it?' the Clerk says, turning pages. 'This Heading, here it is: "Care to be had of stinking Fish, unwholesome Flesh, and of musty Corn." In full: "No hogs, dogs, cats, or tame pigeons, or conies be suffered to be kept within any part of the City, or any swine to be, or stray, in the streets or lanes, but that such swine be impounded by the Beadle or any other Officer, and the owner punished, and that dogs be killed by the Dog-killers appointed for that purpose." This animal Order,' the Parish Clerk pauses, 'this Order will cause a deal of trouble. Dog-killers.'

'Dog-killers appointed to kill dogs,' the Constable is unhappy, repeats, 'To kill dogs. As you say, Philip Carter, this will cause a deal of trouble. A deal.'

'And pigeons, tame pigeons,' Goodwife Joan Brokefild impetuously intervenes on the Church Warden's behalf, looking at him. The Warden's small house, which sits above the passage into Bird-in-hand Court, has a dovecote built into the gable. The comings and goings of the Warden's pigeons can be seen by ancient matrons enjoying their pipes on the churchyard wall.

'No matter,' the Warden looks put out by this attention drawn to him, to his pigeons, and waves away the Goodwife's concern.

'Pigeons,' the Constable says dismissively, 'It's the dog killing that will cause a deal of trouble. Not so easy to, to tell people their dogs must be killed. William Northage, Bernard Clapshaw, Edward Richbell, many more, all got dogs. People have dogs for good reasons. Guard dogs, ratters, some have them for warmth in winter. So these Orders say we must appoint Dog-killers. Who would do that, be a Dog-killer?'

'Anyone the parish pays to do it,' the Warden says confidently. 'There will be no problem finding Dog-killers.'

'The Orders say we must do it and so we will. For the good reason that the Orders are all against the spread of the infection,' Philip Carter wants a halt brought to this pointless chat. 'These Orders are,' he turns back to the first page, 'they are "very expedient for preventing and avoiding of infection, if it shall so please Almighty God, and these Orders hereafter shall be duly observed."'

'If it shall so please Almighty God,' the Viewers and Keepers and Searchers of St Cyneswide and St Tibba repeat the familiar, comforting words with satisfaction. The Warden and Constable nod agreement.

'William Northage and his Gypsy,' the Constable cannot help adding, shaking his head.

'So, we have heard all these new Orders?' Frances Barrow asks. 'From Watchmen to Physicians to Dog-killers?'

'Yes, the main part of them, and they will be posted on the porch wall, replacing the old Orders. Recently newly printed,' he adds with a sigh of irritation. 'But first there is this matter of,' he turns pages, 'of "great abuse in misreporting the Disease." Clerks' meeting had a deal to say of errors, and worse. The old Orders, the good old Orders, have this to say of ancient women going about parish duties in time of infection, women sworn to their duty,' the Parish Clerk knows the words by heart. '"Every woman so sworn, for any corruption or other false reporting, shall stand upon the pillory, and bear corporal pain by the Judgements of the Lord Mayor and Court of Aldermen."' He looks slowly in turn at the ancient matrons around the vestry table. 'And it writes "every woman refusing or failing to do that service shall not have any pension out of the parish."'

There is a heavy silence. No heads nod or shake. All is still in the vestry of St Cyneswide and St Tibba.

'Talk among the clerks – we met yesterday – talk of corruption, of money-taking, of bribes in this time of infection. General matters spoken of at our meeting by the Master, he spoke in general terms. No names mentioned.' Philip Carter Parish Clerk is heavily serious. 'In tavern-talk after the meeting there were words said to me about this parish, about searches being delayed so an infected body could be removed, about bribes being sought to make a false report. Gossip that was not new to me, but others were happy to repeat it, spread it.'

Silence.

'The Vestry will meet. If there is information, evidence, of corruption, of bribes, of false reporting, the Vestrymen will hear it and judge accordingly. And if no information, or if deceitful information, is brought forward, then Vestry, this parish, and all parishes will know these rumours of St Cyneswide and St Tibba are nothing but wicked gossip. Lying tales.'

Heads gaze at the table, faces set.

'One final item in these new Orders. "Searchers, Surgeons, Keepers and Buriers are not to pass the streets without holding a red Rod or Wand of three foot in length in their hands, open and evident to be seen."'

'More red wands at two-pence each,' the Warden says.

'Searchers, Surgeons, Keepers and Buriers, and what of the Viewers?' Anne Abowen asks indignantly. 'What of the Viewers? What do these new Orders say of red wands for the Viewers?'

'The Viewers,' Widow Ursula Chaukley repeats, 'What of us?'

'The Orders say nothing,' Philip Carter shrugs away this quibble, waves his arm towards the door, dismissing them.

The six women leave, most disgruntled, angry, except for Keepers Goody Susanna Parsons and Widow Dorothy Bullen who are gratified they are to have red wands.

'Corpses to search?' Widow Hazard turns back, asks the Clerk loudly.

'No, no corpses to search. Small Sam Stiles, his death is known, its cause known to you two. No other deaths today, so far,' the Clerk replies.

Constable Samuel Snow leaves quickly, with a brief nod at Clerk and Warden. They hear him say to himself in anguished tones, 'And Gnasher. Gypsy and Grinder.' His fading voice slowly reciting the names of all the dogs of St Cyneswide and St Tibba.

'He's off to tell William Northage and the others of the Dog-killers,' the Warden says, stretching his arms. 'The plague set to kill us all, and our

Constable is worried about dogs.'

'Why not? This sickness puts all out of order. And what of your pigeons?'

'What of them? I will deal with my pigeons. Anne Abowen has country family who send her live conies to sell. What of her and her conies? And more money will be needed for clubs and bludgeons for these new Dog-killers. More charges to the parish. As for swine,' he shakes his head. 'Swine. Filth. Noise. Barging through the lanes. Impound the lot. The lot.'

'Clubs no good for pigeons,' the Clerk says, 'Hard to club a pigeon.'

'They'll use nets and lime-sticks. Not on my pigeons they won't. Pigeons are Bible birds. There are many pigeons in the scriptures. Offerings made of two young pigeons.'

'Physicians and surgeons!' the Clerk laughs. 'St Thomas's Hospital, their two physicians have already left town. Gone into the country.'

'The parish won't have to find many twelve-pences for each corpse searched by a surgeon,' the Warden says. 'No surgeons, no twelve-pences, money saved. As for Nurse-Keepers in these new Orders, Nurse-keepers who are to stay inside infected houses! That is a nonsense. No-one will be a Nurse-Keeper. We must not bother ourselves with that. A nonsense.'

They reach again for pipes and tobacco. The Warden sees the Clerk's pouch dangles slim and offers his own. They thumb tobacco into their pipes, share a light, and sit in silence smoking.

'A song, I have heard a good song. Tobacco and snuff song,' says the Warden.

'Tavern song?'

'Yes, a good song to sing in a tavern.'

'The vestry is not a tavern.'

'It will not harm the vestry to hear it.' Frances Barrow the Church Warden sings:

> *Some write in praise of tobacco,*
> *Tobacco, tobacco, and wine,*
> *Whilst others praise women,*
> *but snuff shall be mine!*
> *For help as ye sneeze, and Chee-ho,*

Chee-ho, Chee-ho, do cry:
God bless ye, God bless ye!'
The people reply.
Snuff causes this blessing,
Then tell me, God bless ye tell me,
Which think ye, is't best to cry so?
Or cry 'Damn ye and sink ye!'

The Clerk waves his pipe in time, observes complacently, 'More of a tavern song than a vestry one.'

The Warden smiles, shrugs. 'Some say snuff is greater against the sickness than pipe tobacco. Promotes a virtuous, salubrious sneeze to do brave combat with wicked, deadly ones. A snuff sneeze is the only sneeze I want to hear in these sad, sickly times.'

'The "some" who say that, do they have purses heavy enough to take snuff?'

'No! They say it, sing it, but don't take it. A pipe for them, like the rest of us.'

'Your *White Hind* companions? Fellow singers?'

The Warden shrugs again.

'No hogs running astray in the streets and lanes of St Cyneswide and St Tibba,' Philip Carter says, turning pages of the new Orders.

'The French sow has run back to France,' the Warden offers.

'The Scotsman's mother?' asks the Clerk.

'Yes, Henry Jermyn's whore. Mother of Charles the bastard. Alexander Muzzard and his Fifth Monarchists give her the name the Great Whore of Babylon,' he laughs.

The Clerk is not comfortable with these words, says, 'Fifth Monarchy Men call many the Whore of Babylon,' but he does not want to be drawn into Fifth Monarchy talk. To his worry, his marriage connections leave him vulnerable should there be a great round-up of those thought to be fanatiques.

The Warden agrees, 'True, there are many Babylon Whores for the Fifth Monarchy Men.'

'Alexander Muzzard can be a prating man. Do you see him at the *White Hind*?' the Clerk asks. Alexander Muzzard is also known as a man who shits rage.

'Sometimes. Yes, he is a talking man.'

'And at the *Three Cranes*?'

'Yes, there too.' Now the Warden is uneasy. Stands, picks up his tobacco pouch, says in farewell, 'We must hunt down some Dog-killers. But not pigeon hunters. God be w'ye!'

He sees the Goodwife and the Widow sitting where they always sit on the churchyard wall, but does not linger to talk.

'Hurrying off to save his pigeons,' the Goodwife says.

'That goes against the Orders,' Widow Margaret Hazard says firmly, righteously. 'No hogs, dogs, cats, conies or tame pigeons to be kept within any part of the City. The Orders say that.'

'No more pigeon presents from the Warden then. At least, no more after the first day of July, in three days.'

'Widow Ursula Chaukley, she knows nothing of plague water. How does she think we, you and me, have kept free from plague all these years? Our plague water always has angelica and agrimony. And tops of red brambles, and wild dragons. She said nothing of the tops of red brambles nor of wild dragons.' Widow Margaret Hazard pauses. The Goodwife draws on her pipe, says nothing.

'Care is needed with wild dragons, the Widow ruminates. 'The wild one can be too strong, too much promotes venery. Never use it alone, the fumes can go into the head.'

Goodwife Joan Brokefild remembers something she meant to tell the Widow. 'It is being said,' she likes the sound of this, repeats, 'It is being said that the Doctor Barnett who had himself shut in because his servant died of plague——'

'Doctors. Physicians. Surgeons,' the Widow breaks in, 'What do they know, of plague, of anything.'

The Goodwife continues, 'It is being said that his servant did not die of the infection but was killed, murdered, by his master the doctor. That is why he shut himself up, to hide his crime, to falsely claim it was plague that killed his servant. To hide himself away.'

The Widow nods at this news. 'Mmm. Hiding himself away.' Then lets out a great sigh. 'Small Sam Stiles. Dead, poor child.'

The Widow in misery wants to gnaw at every dry bone. Goodwife Brokefild will console her friend. 'We see many deaths. Some are harder.'

'Delicate cow cumbers. Delicate cow cumbers to pickle.' Maude Wattes comes slowly into the square, her belly big before her.

'She'll be brought to bed soon,' the Goodwife says to her friend.

But Widow Hazard will not let new birth distract her from mournful thoughts of children dead. 'That cruel psalm. Why sing of such cruelty? Sing praise of such cruelty?'

'It's a song, just a song, like the blue button song,' the Goodwife tells her, encourages her.

'It's a sacred song, a psalm!'

'Yes, but all songs are songs. You sing them because, because singing is a delight. That's why you sing. Not to hear of death and cruelty. Unless it is a maiden dying for love. But that is different.'

'Just a song. You wouldn't say that to Walter Hall. Even to Thomas Dugdale you wouldn't say that a psalm is just a song.'

'No. I wouldn't say it to anybody but you. And you won't say it to anyone else, so I can say it to you. And I would not say to anyone that you think psalm number the one hundred and thirty seventh to be an abomination, and King David a filthy, adulterous whoremaster. Which he was.'

'Mmm,' the Widow nods, thinks, laughs. 'And we don't sing in church Betsy Blue came all in black, silver buttons down her back!'

'And we don't dance in church. But my feet move sometimes to the singing,' the Goodwife says, tapping her feet.

'So do mine,' says the Widow in happy agreement, 'So do my feet move! But is it possible that Bible kings have, have holy permission to do wicked things? Are they different?'

'Not different to our kings. Not at all different. They are all the same.'

'Mmm, the Widow nods.

'This Vestry meeting,' the Goodwife begins slowly.

'I will not talk of it,' Widow Hazard snaps. 'There is nothing to be found against me, against you, against us. Nothing. We are honest in our office of Searchers. We do not take bribes, seek bribes, nor give advance warning of our coming. I will not talk of it.'

'Then I will talk of Jack the footboy. He spends more time out of the rectory than in.' She points to Jack, lounging with Thomas Snow by the laundry. 'A sharp, scheming boy, is Jack. Cheerful and obliging, but scheming. Yet very clean. A very washing lad, Jack. Always at the water house with a bucket to wash himself.'

'Mmm.' But the Widow will not be drawn to talk of Jack, his scheming and his washing. Still gnawing at bones, she lights upon more aggravation, explodes, 'Keepers! Red wands for Keepers!'

CHAPTER X

London, Thursday, 29 June 1665

'The more you stir a turd the worse it stinks.'

It is Jack the footboy who brings the news.

Jack has no keys to the cupboards, chests and boxes left locked in the rectory. He is trusted by Walter Hall, trusted by Walter Hall's brothers Godfrey and Ingram, and trusted by Uncle Rowland – who prides himself on his good judgement of character – to take close care of the rectory, its little remaining furniture and furnishings, its locked cupboards, chests and boxes. But not trusted with keys.

The day after the family's departure Jack satisfies himself that Walter Hall is unlikely to make an unexpected return to the rectory. John Clapshaw, a knowing lad who has learned much about doors and locks from Barnard Clapshaw, his father the watchman, sold Jack a useful picklock. So Jack has peered with his sharp eyes, and sifted with his experienced fingers, his curious way through all the now unlocked cupboards, chests and boxes. Then carefully restored the contents. His trusting employers have left in the rectory no jewels, watches, coin or plate. No rings, precious cloth or finery. He approves of this caution. It is sensible of them. In their position he would do the same. After all, he is a reliable footboy who can be trusted, but not too far. A footboy the family have known for five years and who is always an obliging, cheerful, obedient and useful servant. Give him a chore, any chore, and he does it, uncomplaining and promptly. An invaluable boy.

Five years before younger Jack had overheard Walter Hall lamenting the loss of just such an invaluable boy. Walter Hall newly back in London in 1660, bivouacking in cramped, temporary quarters near Whitehall Palace. Walter Hall whose French footboy, his bon garçon Jean-Claude, has disappeared, returned to France.

'And so reliable a boy,' Walter Hall despairs.

'Not so reliable,' his wife Margery snaps. She has had more than enough of this carry-on about nothing more than a decamping footboy. Has had more than enough of bad housing, of wet English weather, of English dining where the courses are promiscuously piled on the table all at once. 'He has left. You. Our household. So he is not so reliable. Not reliable at all.'

But, strongly feeling his loss, Walter Hall will say more. 'Even so, I do need – must have – a clever, reliable boy to do all those necessary small things that, though small, make my day proceed smoothly, easily. That is what a good footboy does. Smooths the way, smooths the day. Does the too tedious tasks.' He stops, then adds quietly, with grievance born of his great deprivation, 'That is the truth of it.'

'Well get an English one. An English bon garçon, a good boy,' she says these words with a sharp edge. 'One who knows London and its ways. How many will there be of such? Good boys eager to serve one of His Majesty's Chaplains?'

Jack Micoe, the gong farmer's boy down in the cesspit quietly filling a dung pot, listens with interest to this exchange. The oddities of the old building's walls and floors and cavities have carried the voices of Walter and Margery Hall, even his soft whingeing, down into the pit.

'And these damned candles are tallow,' Walter Hall has more grievances.

'Yes,' Margery Hall agrees, 'they are. They certainly are.'

'And these damned candles are tallow,' Jack repeats, very quietly. Then tries again to get the voice, the tone, the sound, of Walter Hall, 'End these demmed cendls ah talloh.'

Jack is a hard-working, clever boy. All at the very same time he can fill his dung-pot, practise and perfect his mimicry of any voice he hears, and – most importantly – run his fingers carefully through the waste, soft and hard, to find those objects he is so good at finding.

Jewels will fall from rings into the privy – Jack is happy for those jewellers who use cheap glue – and, sometimes, rings themselves will plop down into the muck. And coins. There is always a chance, a good one, of coins, small and large. Keys too. Although with keys the distraught housewife will often pay to have a dung-pot boy search for them (after her own efforts with fishing line and hook have failed) on the very day they dropped. This is no good to Jack Micoe, for the unhappy key-holder always asks his father, the gong farmer Thomas Micoe himself, to recover the lost keys. It is Jack who sifts the cesspit and Thomas who gets the reward.

His years of night work cleaning out cesspits have yielded up to young Jack combs, chains, scissors, tweezers, pipes, pots, cans, cups, broken Dutch plates, and even – twice – watches. Very young Jack always hands over such finds to his father. And receives praise for doing so, but nothing else. Somewhat older Jack finds that while praise is ever pleasing – and his father is a kind, cheerful man who rarely beats him and encourages him to wash well when they get back to Blackfriars, to Dung Wharf – yet praise is not as rewarding, as useful, as negotiable, as chains, coins, combs, rings, ear pendants, purses heavy and purses empty, jewels. Jack begins to keep some of these for himself. He works in the dark, he is covered in shit, so there is no great difficulty in concealing his finds, carrying them away, washing them in the river when he washes himself. His treasures are easily kept hidden and safe in the pungent surrounds of Dung Wharf. It is a place for nightsoil men, and dung-pot boys, not a place where nightwatchmen, or anyone not in the dung business might be found.

'Worth a fortune,' his father laughs, pointing to the mountains of ordure at Dung Wharf, held in laystalls waiting for dung barges to ferry it to farms and market gardens, 'but who'd steal it eh?' Yet Thomas Micoe keeps three dogs on guard: Dog, Maydog, and Third. 'My St Malo dogs! Need dogs against hogs. Rootling hogs make a fine mess of a dung heap. Especially ones as big as these.' The dogs are happy in their work, barking from the top of the pile. 'Dogs love it!' Thomas says fondly, 'My dung dogs do.' The dung dogs roll in it. Thomas Micoe says with pride, 'Lay dung up in heaps, good profit it reaps. That's wisdom Jack.'

Young Jack, a thoughtful and careful boy, does not abruptly stop passing found treasures to his father. At first he keeps for himself only a few particular items: he favours the groat, liking the sound of the word and the heft of the coin in his hand; and red jewels remind him of raspberries. He also likes things coloured green, silver, gold. They are all his favourites. He thinks he favours red because his mother had red hair, like him. He does not remember his mother's hair, but sometimes, when he is river-washed and the sun is bright on him, his father will look at him and say, 'Elinor Micoe had red hair,' and shrug.

Thomas Micoe's shrug does not mean he is unfeeling about his dead wife, a sharp, outspoken woman – he thinks of her as the bright quivering splinters of light seen in a fire. She had taken exception to William Gouge, Minister at St Anne Blackfriars, because the old man's book, *Of Domesticall Duties*, written long before she and Thomas were born, held that wives must always be subservient to husbands. She would read out:

> *What if a man of lewd and beastly conditions, as a drunkard, a glutton, a profane swaggerer, an impious swearer, and blasphemer, be married to a wife, sober, religious Matron, must she account him her superior, and worthy of a husband's honour?*

'No!' Elinor would spit, 'No! She must not because he is not.' Then reads out William Gouge's answer to his own question, interspersed with her own high commentary:

> *Surely she must. (Bah.) For the evil quality and disposition of his heart and life, (Yes, he is evil) doth not deprive a man of that civil honour (he has no honour) which God hath given unto him. Though a husband in regard of evil qualities may carry the image of the devil (may carry? Does carry!), yet in regard of his place and office he beareth the image of God: (Bah!) so do Magistrates in the commonwealth, Ministers in the Church, parents and masters in the family. (Bah again!)*

In her family, and others, she had seen lewd and beastly men: drunkards, gluttons and profane swaggerers, her own father the worst. She attended William Gouge's church under sufferance, was pleased with his death, and until her own death in the year 57 she and Thomas Micoe found peaceful refuge in the teachings of John Reeve and of Lodowick Muggleton. Elinor Micoe dies holding tight the Muggleton doctrine that does not blame or revile Eve. As the Muggletonians sing in one of their Divine Songs, it was Lucifer who her innocence did beguile. Eve was innocent, is innocent.

The year 51 is revered by Thomas Micoe and his family. It was the year when Jesus spoke aloud to tailors John Reeve and Lodowick Muggleton, calling them forth as the two witnesses in the Book of Revelation with the high powers of prophecy, blessing, and cursing. ('The Book of Revelation, Chapter the Eleventh–' says John Reeve. 'Verse the Third,' breaks in Lodowick Muggleton.) For all his conversion to Muggletonianism, Thomas Micoe does not totally abandon attendance at St Anne's. The excited, denouncing pulpit men of Blackfriars provide rich theatre. Too rich. St Anne's regular lecturer, Christopher Feake, calls Oliver Protector 'a man of sin and an old dragon,' which sets Thomas Micoe back on his stumps.

Apart from groats and small jewels and shiny coins, Jack will hold back, occasionally, from his father some small object whose shape or feel appeals. He has a comb of ivory, a chain that spins and shines after he has washed it and held it up in the slotted sunlight under the neighbouring wharf. Thomas Micoe does not notice any falling-off in the cesspit finds made by his small, diligent son – a willing boy the perfect size to climb into a pit and fill a dung pot.

Jack has a younger brother, Oliver, born of the same red-haired Elinor, although Oliver is dark like his father. And there was almost a sister, but child-bed killed mother and daughter both. Thomas' second wife Joan has given him a son Richard, born in the first year of Richard Protector, and then daughter Margaret. Infant Elizabeth died. New-born twins Rupert and James died.

Dead infants are not new to nightsoil men and dung pot boys. When Walter Hall and Charles Stuart arrive back in London in 1660, Jack Micoe has already found, over his years of night work, three small human corpses (and countless pups and kittens) down in the cesspits he empties. He has, of course, seen dead dogs and cats and beasts, and twice a corpse, carried by the tide past Dung Wharf. Tiny bodies in dung are a sorry sight, but little more. 'The real trouble,' Thomas Micoe says with exasperation to Jack, back at Dung Wharf after the constable has been called, again. 'The real trouble with the dead in our business is the law, the inquest, the coroner, the jury. All done at a time that takes no heed of those who must sleep by day and work by night.'

But Thomas Micoe can easily restore his own good humour with a saw or a song. 'The rich wisdom of the heap,' he tells Jack. 'Hear now the rich wisdom of the heap:

> *The better the muck,*
> *the better good luck!*

Jack has thought of one of his own, slowly devised, refined, over three nights' work:

> *Poor house or rich house, when down in the pit,*
> *The dung-pot boy still smells the same shit.*

He eagerly offers this when, washed and clothes shifted, he and Thomas and Eliezar Smith, who carries away the full dung tubs with Thomas, share an early morning draught.

Thomas Micoe is proud of his clever, sharp son and gets him to repeat the verse until he has it down pat. 'Joan Micoe will get a good laugh from that,' he tells Eliezar after he has had the boy twice test his recitation. Joan Micoe is a sober, serious person, not given to mirth, but if others laugh she will join in with a mild smile. What wife would not want to see her husband happy? She has been as good a mother to Jack and Oliver as she is capable, but keenly feels the loss of her dead children, Elizabeth in particular, and would keep Margaret still swaddled if she could. Joan Micoe is tired and sickly, always tired and sickly, and can feel the great mounds of dung draining, decaying, her vital powers. She longs to get away, but Thomas Micoe is a good man, a good husband. And the dung midden has the opposite effect on him, makes him grow stronger, happier, wealthier.

Thomas Micoe rewards, and jovially competes with, his versifying son by chanting in turn a country saw, once heard from someone, somewhere, but cannot recall who and where or when. 'Listen to this, boy, a country man's song:

> *Foul privies are now to be cleansed and fide,*
> *Let night be appointed such baggage to hide.*
> *Which buried in garden, in trenches alow,*
> *Shall make very many things better to grow.*

Jack asks for one repetition, then has it by rote. 'But I do not know this word fide.'

'Aha!' says Thomas Micoe, 'Nor did I, and I asked the very same question, the very same, when I first heard it. Now I remember him! Now I remember! He was an old country man, very old. White hair. Yes. Saw our dung barge and walked beside the river, talking. Told us this one. Near Maidenhead. Yes, the old country man, farmer, near Maidenhead.'

'What does fide mean?' asks patient Jack, used to his father's rambling ways.

'Fide? Why it means to rake, to brush away with a stick, that's what fide means. That's what the old country man said.'

Jack nods and will remember it.

'He said he had many more songs like such, but the river carried us past him and we never saw him again. I looked for him when we came back down river, shipping bricks back. Many more he said.' Thomas Micoe adds on reflection, 'Brick dust is a very noisome thing. Very.' He clears the memory of brick dust from his throat with a deep drink.

'You're fortunate to be in a good business like dung my son,' he laughs at the jest coming. 'Dung will never go out of fashion!'

All join in the great joke.

'Yes, more fortunate than some. Eliezar do you remember the poor fisher boy – he was like a drowned rat – who we dragged from the river?'

He corrects himself, 'Like a half-drowned rat. Pissing rain, tide running out hard, his skiff overturned. Saved him and his skiff. Pulled them on board and took him down by the fire in the cuddy, made him a bed of sorts. When he would talk at last, and he didn't talk much, he said, the poor fisher boy he said – listen closely to this Jack – he said he had not been in a bed in the whole seven years since he came to be a prentice. Seven years.' Thomas Micoe takes another drink. 'And, hear this, he still had two or three years more to serve. See how fortunate you are Jack, as we all are, to be in dung.'

Down in the cesspits Jack often hears the padding and scratching of rats and other vermin, but there are also times when human voices from the houses above echo with great clarity through the dung pit. Jack once heard a riotous game in play among the ladies and gentlemen in the great house above. 'Oh,' cries out a lady's voice, 'Oh how I love my love with an I, because he is so Impertinent, Insipid and Ill-tempered!' To Jack's surprise these harsh words give rise to great mirth among the company. A man's voice quickly comes back with, 'And I love my love with a V because she is so Vapouring, Vicious and so,' there is a drawn-out pause then he declares, 'And sooo Virginal!' There is an explosion of laughter at this sally. Young Jack finds it a puzzling, an odd game.

'Vapouring, Vicious and sooo Virginal.' Jack repeats until he has it voice perfect. Then – his hands still busily filling his dung pot – his mind turns to the letter V and he sees the picture in the reading book for U & V. It is of naked Bathsheba in her large bath, set beside the verse:

> *Uriah's beauteous wife*
> *Made David seek his life.*

Jack knows this story from Samuel, his second book, where David walks upon the roof of his house and sees a woman washing herself, a woman who is very beautiful, and very naked, to look upon, as the picture in Jack's reading book shows. For Jack the story – like the game the ladies and gentlemen are playing – is confusing because David the king has a child with Bathsheba, and then has her husband, Uriah the Hittite, killed in battle. To Jack these do not sound like good and proper things for anyone to do, let alone a king. He asks his father, who tells him: 'Ah! That is just what kings do! Kings do that. That is why we must have no kings.'

Livery. On a cold, wet day in September the year 60 Jack Micoe in the cesspit hears Walter Hall bemoaning his absconded footboy, Jean-Claude. Jack thinks Livery as he fills his dung-pot. Repeats under his breath, 'Jean-Claude' just as Walter Hall said it. 'Jean-Claude.' A footboy wears Livery. Finery in the colours of his Master. What more could a boy want? Black and gold. Blue and silver. Red and black. He has seen footboys in their Livery. Stared and stared.

In the mire Jack says softly in the very voice of Walter Hall, 'A clever, reliable boy to do all those necessary small things that, though small, make my day proceed smoothly, easily. That is what a good footboy does. Smooths the way. Smooths the day.'

Jack is sure he can wear Livery and smooth the way for Walter Hall. But how to? How to present himself, a clever, reliable boy, to Walter Hall? His hands sift and load the pot, and he thinks, seeking a way, but mostly his thoughts run on Livery.

His is night work, and although for his father and for Eliezar day is for sleeping, Jack goes well with small sleeps during the day, leaving him time to sport by the river with the boys. To call jokes and challenges and insults to passing barge boys, to ships' boys. He has an endless store of dung to fling if he wishes. Sometimes he does. He has strong arms from his work. The huge mounds at Dung Wharf are both mocked and envied. His cheerful mimicry, and his good judgement when to fight and when to fly, give him a good place in the wild boys' world by the river. But no-one wears Livery here.

Thursday, Friday, Saturday, Jack digs out gong. Thinks of Livery. Says in good French, 'Jean-Claude.' Says over and over in good Whitehall Court English, 'A clever, reliable boy to do all those necessary things. A good footboy.'

He has his store of treasure, perhaps he can buy the position from Walter Hall? Monday, he has decided, must be the day he is to present himself, offer himself. Saturday morning he spends his groats on a doublet and breeches in sober black from the Cheapside slops market, and buys Castle soap, cried up as coming only last week from Spain. Guaranteed used by King Philip IV of Spain himself, his Queen Maria Anna, and their many princes and princesses. Saturday night he is in the cesspits. Sunday, Lord's Day, is not a day of work. There is no cesspit cleaning of a Sunday night. He washes, and washes again, cleans his finger nails with a nail, and washes again, scouring his skin until it is raw and bleeds.

Early Monday he presents himself at Walter Hall's door, a sweet-smelling, clever, reliable boy with angry-looking skin. In fine voice he tells the footman he wishes to speak to the Master, to be his new footboy. Before the door can be closed on him, as it is about to be, he discreetly holds out a gold crown, says, 'Pour vous Monsieur une douceur, s'il vous plait.' And wisely adds in English, for it is clear that the footman understands what the coin means but not the language it is offered in, 'A gift, a small present for you.' Jack waits. Confidently.

'Master's in bed, asleep,' the footman pockets the coin, shows Jack in, says confidingly, 'Sleeps Mondays after church Sundays. You can wait. Down in the kitchen.' Jack's eyes are fixed on the footman's Livery, green lined with red. Green and red. He will wear it.

Jack, given a morning draught, is all politeness when subjected to close questioning by Nan the cook. Jinny, the maid of all-work, a little girl, listens with interest.

'Where have you worked before?' Nan asks.

'For a gentleman from Maidenhead,' Jack answers glibly, 'A country gentleman.'

'So you was mostly in the country, as his footboy?'

'Yes,' he replies, thinking: this is going well.

'So why did you leave him?'

'He died.'

'What of?'

Jack pauses, but finds an answer. 'He was old, old and white haired and he, he couldn't remember things and he died.'

'Did he forget how to live?' the little girl asks, and Jack is not sure if she is joking or serious.

'Course he didn't forget how to live!' the cook laughs. 'The very idea! The boy said he was old, that's why he died. You're Jack. Jack what?'

'Jack what?' he asks in confusion.

'Jack what! Your last name boy, your family's name.'

He does not want to be Jack Micoe, the nightsoil man's boy, the dung-pot boy. He wants to be Jack the footboy, in a Livery of green and red. 'Jack Green,' he says, sure that Green must be a name, there are all kinds of names that people have.

Passing by outside, a street seller calls, 'Four pair for a shilling Holland socks! Socks four pair for a shilling!'

Jack catches the high-pitched cry and squeaks to perfection, 'Four pair for a shilling Holland socks! Socks four pair a shilling!'

'Hear him!' Nan the cook cries in amazement, 'Hear him!' Roars laughing, and looks at him expectantly.

Jack obliges in voices low and high, rough and smooth: 'Rosemary and bays! Come glasses, glasses, fine glasses! Old shoes or boots! Come buy my brooms! Ends of gold or silver! Buy a hair-line or a jack-line! Wainfleet oysters!' Ends with the booming cadence of a bell-man, 'Maids in your smocks, look to your locks!'

If it were in their gift, Nan and Jinny would immediately make him footboy.

'Wainfleet oysters! Look to your locks!' Nan turns knowingly to Jinny. 'That is fine sport!'

'Master is awake,' the footman returns, 'having his draught.' Beckons Jack to follow, says to him in quiet advice, 'Ask him for three pounds. You won't get it but ask anyway, it'll do you no harm to ask high.'

Walter Hall sits at table, slowly packing tobacco in his pipe. 'You know there is a position here?' he asks.

'I heard that your boy Jean-Claude,' Jack takes great care with his pronunciation, repeats, 'Jean-Claude has left.'

'How do you know that?'

'Boys hear things. London boys. That the French boy has left this house. Gone back to France.'

'You are a London boy? You know London well?'

'Yes sir. Born in London. I was lately in the service of a country gentleman of Maidenhead. An old country gentleman, now dead. I know London well, and Maidenhead well.'

'We will not concern ourselves with Maidenhead, or maidenheads,' Walter Hall permits himself a smile.

'No sir.' Jack stands still, upright, doing all he can to look clever and reliable. 'I know London's streets and alleys and lanes and closes and squares by day and by night sir. All of them. I can guide you well by link at night, if needs.'

'Are you strong boy? In arms and legs?'

'Yes sir, I am that boy.'

'Pick up that chest.'

Jack does so, easily. Holds it up high.

'What is that boy doing with the chest?' Margery Hall enters, looking displeased. 'What?'

'Showing his strong arms,' Walter Hall replies.

'Do you speak well boy? Do you?' she asks.

'I trust Mistress, I hope, that I can speak as well as any boy of a good house in London.' Jack uses the polished voice, the words and phrases, he has heard while digging in the cesspits of the rich, lifting the shit of merchants and Aldermen.

Encouraged, Margery Hall asks, 'Do you speak French, boy?'

Jack has learned some French from barge boys and ships' boys, mostly low, salty French. He is not strong in higher discourse. He is safer with songs, and knows many. But knows enough to rule out his favourite, about the country lad, his pig, and his girl Alix crossing the wide plain, and how she asks him to commit a sin with her. Not that song, Jack thinks, instead he adopts the stance of a fine singer and sings a love song. The French boys sang this one, and acted it out, with much hilarity and obscenity, humping each other and pouting out big round, lewd lips, to the great amusement of all. Jack sings, but omits the coarse gestures, confident that sort of performance would not be fitting in present company.

L'amour, la mort et la vie
Me tourmentent a toute heure.

The first lines visibly move Margery Hall, her eyes tear. She blinks, nods approvingly to her husband, waves a hand in time with the song.

Walter Hall is used to his wife and her ways – thinks once again she has been too long in France, has become much more of a French lady, much less of an English one. Yet if she approves this well-spoken boy, who seems clever and reliable, and since the boy has pleased him, then this Jack can be his new footboy. He is a clean-smelling boy, and as for his red, angry skin, Walter Hall has seen worse in France.

'I can try you as my footboy. Bartholomew Bigmore my footman will show you further.'

'My wages,' Jack asks politely. 'What will be my wages be?'

'What were your wages before? With the old country gentleman?'

'Three pounds, and food and lodging all found.'

'Three pounds per annum? Three pounds for a footboy? I doubt it. I very much doubt it. Unless he was a very foolish country gentleman.'

Jack silently raises his eyebrows to show this could well have been true: Yes, he could well have been very foolish, the white haired old country gentleman, Master Maidenhead, now sadly dead.

'Cook gets three pounds. A chaplain, even to the King himself, does not pay three pounds for a footboy.' Walter Hall pauses, is going to say two pounds, but feels a twinge of warmth, of kindness, to the small boy standing before him and says, 'Two pounds and eighteen pence. And food and lodging all found. Two pounds and eighteen.' Walter Hall is satisfied that this is good, generous, but not excessive, and is pleased with himself. Pleased that he has gone beyond the two pounds one shilling he had also been toying with, and so shown himself a good Master to this new, most junior member of his household.

Jack nods his agreement, his thanks. But asks, 'All found means a

Livery, Master?'

'Of course a Livery. But enough, enough, go now with Bartholomew Bigmore. Go.' The conversation is over.

Jack Green is to be Walter Hall's footman – is Walter Hall's footboy – in Livery of green lined with red.

Back in the kitchen, in high spirits, he grins and gives out the knife sharpener's high-pitched cry, 'Ha' y'any knives to grind! Grin-ding! Sharp-ning!' and finishes with the ear-splitting, painful screech of a blade on the spinning whetstone. To great applause.

There is his father. Also his step-mother, his brothers and sister, but first and foremost his father, to be told.

Tuesday morning, after the night's work in dung pits under London's privies, Jack waits until Eliezar has finished his draught and loped with his long strides off to find his bed, before saying, 'I wish to buy out my apprenticeship. My apprenticeship in the gong business.'

Thomas Micoe receives this surprising information calmly, wondering what his son is saying. Waits patiently for the boy to say more.

'I am to be footboy to a chaplain.' It is best not to say to his father, a chaplain to the king.

His father drinks slowly from his can. Says nothing. Waits.

Jack does not know what his father is thinking. He pauses and they look at each other. Thomas Micoe waits.

'Here,' Jack produces a bag of his treasures. 'To buy out my apprenticeship.'

His father raises a large hand and the boy stiffens, expecting a blow. But Thomas Micoe's hand falls on the bag. He opens it, looks inside. Rummages. Says thoughtfully, 'Bog finds, Jack Micoe.' It is a statement, not a question.

The boy nods, 'Yes.'

His father raises an eyebrow.

'I kept them, chose these ones, because I like them. The colours,' Jack explains. 'Not kept them for myself. Not kept them for ever.'

'Gold and silver colours,' Thomas Micoe pulls out coins of gold and silver.

'And red and green,' Jack points to the gem stones.

'And what will I do without a clever, hardworking boy like you?' his father asks. 'To go down into the cesspits?'

'Oliver is fit to do so,' Jack replies. He knows his brother can do so, wants to do so. Has done so.

'Yes, he can. But with two strong small boys working I can clear more pits.'

'So these,' Jack points to the bag of treasures, 'these will pay you for the work I will not be doing.'

'You will not, will you?' his father asks.

The boy shakes his head, says, 'No. I will buy out my indenture.' He pauses, adds for good measure, 'And I am no longer so small. I am becoming too big to climb down easily into the pits.' It is true that Jack, like his father, has waxed large, grown well, from the dung.

Thomas Micoe, holding the heavy bag, is tickled at the thought of a dung-pot boy being apprenticed. 'A footboy?' he asks. 'Footboys do not find themselves valuables like this. Not honest footboys. Honest dung-pot boys do not keep such treasures from their father.'

'No,' Jack agrees, 'they do not. Not for ever. And here I am handing them to you.'

'Handing over to me things that are rightfully mine?'

This is a puzzler. Jack does not know how to answer. Sits quietly. Thinks: they rightfully belong to those who sat on their privies and lost their valuables by accident, but this is not the time to say this to his father.

His father shrugs, says, 'Riches are like muck, which stink in a heap, but spread abroad make the earth fruitful.' Shrugs again, says to Jack, 'The rich wisdom of the heap that is. So these riches here,' he squeezes the bag, 'are spread from careless, feckless people to the cesspit, to you, now to me. And you will still be a footboy?'

Jack nods, 'I will. And wear a Livery. And carry a sword.'

'Will you still know your family? Your father? Your brothers? You a footboy in livery and carrying a sword?'

'Why would I not?' Jack asks, thinking this a strange question. 'And Eliezar and Joan Micoe. I will know you all.'

'Well,' says his father. 'Well. This is a good heavy bag you've given me. Saved for me. It seems you have bought out your indenture, and you will still know your family. Drink your draught and we will tell Oliver he is to take your place. As dung-pot boy. What colours are to be your livery?'

It is true that Jack has turned over all his bogpit finds to Thomas Micoe, excepting the groats he spent on fresh clothes and soap. And the ivory comb with its handle shaped like an otter. But not the bag fat with coins and table silver he found lodged in the cavity of a privy wall. These were no valuables lost by accident, dropped through the privy hole. Jack ponders on them: a householder's prized store hidden away for fear of theft? Or, more likely, a thief's horde, stolen by a servant who used the house of office to conceal his spoils. Jack considers that different rules apply to ill-gotten loot such as this: the rule of Finders Keepers. Jack keeps the fat bag but has no immediate use for the contents. The bag is his bank, to draw on, when needed.

For now, in Walter Hall's household, he is well satisfied with: his food – Nan the cook is a good cook and favours him (a healthy boy who likes his meat); his lodging, a trestle bed in the kitchen, warm at night; his two pounds and eighteen pence per annum, paid at the rate of ten shillings fourpence halfpenny each quarter day; his Livery of green lined with red which pleases him beyond measure; his sword, small and mostly for display, but, even so, sharp; and his easy acceptance into the household.

He pleases his Master with his knowledge of London's streets, by day and by night. He shows initiative: forgotten by his Master at St Mary Overie when told to wait his return, after staying a good interval Jack makes his way home – to the relief of Walter Hall and the rest of the household who have not gone to bed, anxious and troubled, waiting up for him. He is agile: climbs into the house through a window when Walter Hall has been abroad late, beyond 11 o'clock at night, and finds the door locked against him, and the household sound asleep. He is trusted: carries important papers, and even money, on messages for his Master. He is cared for: the household fearing for his life when he falls sick, and rejoicing on his recovery.

In short, Jack Green is a clever, reliable footboy. Not without faults: he carelessly drops a can of beer upon Walter Hall's papers and has his ear boxed. There are times when he stays out late at night, vexing his Master, and is beaten for it. Some of these nights – not wearing his Livery – he goes to meet his father, brother Oliver, and Eliezar where they are working. Some nights he drinks with other footboys at the *Leg*, or *Angels*, or *Lamb's*.

Walter Hall and his footboy Jack impress each other with their courage when, together, they fight off street thieves who would waylay and rob them. Walter Hall grabs the boy's link and lunges at the thieves with the flaming torch while Jack, shouting, charges at them with his sword.

'Good! Good! Well done!' Walter Hall takes the boy to the *Bell* in King Street where Widow Walker hears the stirring story many times, it growing each time, while they drink two bottles of her Rhenish wine.

So satisfied with the happy end of this failed robbery, and with himself and with his boy, Walter Hall as a regular practice now takes Jack along with him when he has his morning draught. Walter Hall drinks with fellow courtiers from Whitehall and Jack listens closely, unobtrusively, to their talk, and also shares the company and gossip of the other footboys who attend their masters. Jack, like Walter Hall, is ever with child to hear or see any strange thing. His reputation as a handy boy with a sword is well known. He does not need to tell it himself, Walter Hall is ready to do so, and does, unintentionally bestowing on Jack the further virtue of reticent modesty.

And there was the time, Walter Hall tells: 'Alighting a coach at Martin the Booksellers my little boy Jack slips and falls, and were he not a most nimble boy he would have been run over by the coach. I saw how he did it and was mightily pleased with him for it.'

But for all his acknowledged virtues, it is the fact that he is a droll boy that endears him most to the household, with his voices, his mimicry. He can do cook, can do Jinny the small girl, do Bartholomew Bigmore (who is enraptured, in stitches), do Master and Mistress – when they are not present. He gets his greatest applause, greatest laughter. when he ventures into his own native Blackfriars voice, Thomas Micoe's voice. He feels uneasy doing this, but a laugh is a laugh, applause is applause.

Margery Hall says, 'Yes, that is the way they talk there. Just so.' Unaware Jack is one of they.

'There are rich and poor both in Blackfriars,' says Walter Hall, who likes to know things.

Jack is liked, trusted. Walter Hall now spends his days and nights at Whitehall Palace and when, due to the plague, he removes his family from London in the year 65, it is trusted Jack – an almost ideal servant, with only one or two faults – who is left in charge of the rectory. It is also Jack who sifts through all the rectory's cupboards, chests and boxes.

It is Jack who takes sharp-eyed interest in the doings of the parish, and beyond, from windows close under the gables at the top of the tall, narrow rectory. One window at the front looking south, over church square; one at the back looking north, with a good prospect of St Cyneswide and St Tibba's lower churchyard, and beyond, in the distance, the City Wall.

Jack, in his seventeenth year, is ambitious. Torn between being as wealthy as Sir Thomas Vyner, lately dead, or as cunning, as powerful, as full of secret knowledge, as John Thurloe, Oliver Protector's chief of spydom who is still living and still doing much the same service for his latest master in Whitehall Palace.

Friends Jack the footboy made as a servant at Whitehall are friends he keeps close, in good standing. Friends he meets and talks to, exchanges chat of this and that. He is also in good standing with the St Cyneswide and St Tibba street boys, known as a jolly, droll companion.

He knows, knows well, one of Thomas Micoe's pieces of wisdom of the heap: he that wrestles with a turd is sure to be beshit. Fearing his son's entanglement in the affairs of the great – the princes, dukes, bishops, prelates – Thomas Micoe, with growing concern cautions his son that this piece of heap wisdom is not just about turds as turds, it is about the dangers of getting caught up in the dirty dealings of besmirched, wicked men. Offers one more piece of wisdom, 'The more you stir a turd the worse it stinks. That wisdom means,' Thomas says, unnecessarily, 'don't get yourself caught in unwise plots, unwise deeds. Don't go sticking your oar in,' he adds, changing metaphors mid-stream.

Jack knows these saws of his father, has heard them often, and knows better.

It is Jack the footboy who brings the news to the parish of St Cyneswide and St Tibba.

CHAPTER XI

London, Thursday morning, 29 June 1665

'Now, where's Beloved*? Why,* Beloved*'s gone.'*

'Take care! Take care!' Viewer Anne Abowen cries out to Widow Ursula Chaukley. She grabs her slow friend, pulls her back from the chaos barrelling through the street. They find slight refuge up against a wall. Widow Chaukley breathes heavily, staring wide-eyed, blankly.

It is the second great rout of hogs rumbling in an overflowing river of swine through the streets and squares of St Cyneswide and St Tibba. Some charge on, battering their panicked way forward. Some stop and root enthusiastically in the foul, odour-strong mess down in the channels.

'We should not be here!' Anne Abowen says fearfully, indignantly. 'This is not work for Viewers.'

Widow Ursula Chaukley gathers herself, says, 'Constable told us to. Told us.'

'Told us,' says Anne Abowen, 'Yes, he did, but this is not our work.' She throws out an arm – not too far – at the rioting hogs. 'I have viewed nuisance smoke, and neighbours at odds over encroaching buildings. I have never been sent to view the nuisance of hogs in the streets.'

'He is busy with matters of the infection, the Constable,' Widow Chaukley says placatingly. 'Otherwise he would have come himself.'

Anne Abowen is not convinced, frowns. Constable Samuel Snow was at his most irritating when he ordered them to go and view the damage caused by a passel of hogs. 'It could also be,' Samuel Snow, country bred, says thoughtfully, helpfully, 'a sounder of swine or a drift of pigs. But … from what I have been told, these are hogs. So you are to look to the damage caused by a passel of hogs running riotously through the parish.'

Widow Chaukley nods in earnest agreement, 'Yes.' Anne Abowen does not.

'This passel of hogs, passel,' Constable Snow repeats, 'came from south of us, up through Bazinghall Street – eight houses there already shut up of the plague – up through Bazinghall Street and into the bounds of St Cyneswide and St Tibba.'

'How will we find them? Hogs?' Anne Abowen asks sharply. 'Where they are now, where they have been?'

'Find them?' Samuel Snow laughs a comfortable, knowing laugh. 'Follow the fresh dung! Buckets of it.' Laughs again. 'Follow where they have toppled posts with rootling, turned up cobblestones, eaten whatever they can. Hogs do all that. You'll find them. Nothing easier.'

He is right. The signs are easy to find, to follow: a broken, gutted sack of grain outside Edward Richbell's bakery; tallow tubs smashed and plundered at John Girling the chandler; similar with the oil barrels at Harry Bosvill the soap-maker; Widow Alice Damport the washerwoman, her washing blundered into, trampled, dragged, fouled and torn; Christopher Northage the stable boy standing guard at Robin Kerton's stables with a pitchfork, keeping the swine away. Their smell and shit everywhere.

Constable Samuel Snow is right.

Anne Abowen and Widow Chaukley move cautiously away from the shelter of the wall and edge their way around a corner. They see still more hogs on the run, hogs crashing into two terrified street sellers, dashing them hard onto the cobbles. Betty Bethel's toppled basket of hot pudding pies gobbled down with hungry squeals, Abigail Joanes' load of cotton wicks for the chandler's are not eaten but trampled and enmired in filth on the ground.

Viewer Anne Abowen runs to help the two bruised, bleeding women. Widow Ursula Chaukley pants, wheezes painfully, 'I cannot run. Cannot. You see to them, I will see to the, to the baker and the chandler, and the, the …' her voice trails away and she turns and moves slowly, carefully, back the way they came, grimacing, one hand rubbing her ribs the other against the wall, back towards the square and the shops and the manufactories.

Betty Bethel is closer, sprawled on the stones, her underskirt muddied and bloodied, riding high on her gashed shins. Her hands badly grazed. Viewer Abowen asks, 'Can you stand?' Wants to help her away from the tangle of hogs. Gets behind her and takes her under the armpits, hoisting her up.

'The Lord be thanked I am not dead! The Lord be thanked. Thanked,' Betty Bethel sobs. 'I am not dead.'

They stumble to the door of Widow Lankester who is calling out, 'Bring her here. Bring her in.' They help Betty Bethel sink onto a stool.

'The Lord be thanked.'

'Filthy hogs,' says Widow Lankester, 'fouling our streets.' With a wet rag and ungentle hands she briskly wipes mud and hog muck from Betty Bethel's shins and hands. 'On your face too. Close your eyes. Close them!'

'The swine are possessed with devils!' Betty Bethel cries. 'The unclean devils whose name is Legion, who are many. You saw how many there were! Devils our Lord cast out of men into the swine. You saw them running so violently! It says so in the Bible.'

Widow Lankester keeps scrubbing at her.

'As a jewel of gold in a swine's snout, so is a fair woman which is without discretion,' Betty Bethel says distraughtly.

'I am sure you do not mean me, my duck,' Widow Lankester says with a laugh. 'Who do you mean? Do tell me.'

'Not me,' Anne Abowen says indignantly. 'She does not mean me!' Agitated, glad to get away, she goes outside and looks for Widow Chaukley, hoping she might have come back to help Abigail Joanes. She has not.

'The wicks are ruined. All of them. Look!' Abigail Joanes sits on the cobbles, she holds up a dirty tangle of what looks like cotton waste used for cleaning. 'Those hogs! Whose are they? Who owns those hogs?' She asks angrily.

'Get up,' Anne Abowen says. She too needs to know who is responsible for the hog rampage, but getting Abigail Joanes on her feet and out of the way is more pressing. On her first attempt to help Anne Abowen stumbles and falls, cutting her knees on the cobbles. She tries again.

Muttering to herself, sounding like she is arguing with someone, Abigail Joanes stands up, shakes off Anne Abowen's helping hand.

'The wicks are for tallow chandler John Girling. It's not my fault,' she says accusingly to Viewer Abowen.

'No. It's not. I didn't say it was,' Anne Abowen replies tersely.

'Well someone will. He will. And it's not my fault.'

There is no point in answering this. But Anne Abowen says anyway, 'Cotton can be washed clean. Dried. Still useful as wicks. I would think.'

Abigail Joanes gives a deep, irritated sigh. Shakes her head at Anne Abowen's, and the world's, enormous ignorance of candle-making and its particular, crucial branch, wicking. Still talking to herself she makes her way to John Girling's chandlery.

Cautiously skirting the cobble stones grubbed up by the hogs, Anne Abowen keeps an eye out for Widow Ursula Chaukley. Asks after her. Several people have seen her pass by, offer suggestions as to where she might be found. 'Try Edward Richbell the baker.'

Another voice says dismissively. 'The baker? Widow Chaukley's been there. She's viewed all the damage – baker's, chandler's, soap-boiler's, stables, Widow Damport's washing. And very filthily the washing was torn. Disgusting. Widow Chaukley's viewed it all. Where were you Viewer Abowen? Aren't you to view together with Widow Chaukley?'

'Two sellers bowled over by the hogs! Where was I? I was going to the aid of Betty Bethel the hot pies and Abigail Joanes the wicking woman. Where were you?'

'Not my job, nothing to do with me. I'm not a Viewer.' The door is abruptly closed in Anne Abowen's face. Which is wise, as she is ready spit at Jane Chetam and do her a heavy mischief.

Warden Frances Barrow, coming from the church square, waves to her and hurries through the clusters of angry parish folk who all want him to do something about the despoilment. 'Soon, soon, I will talk to you soon. Someone will talk to you soon. The Constable will come. He will talk to you, listen to you. The Viewers are here already. They have seen the damage. Viewed it.'

'A deal of damage by the hogs,' he says to Anne Abowen, his large pie face looking around with interest.

She is tempted to make a tart reply, she has had enough of hogs and their obvious damage, but Frances Barrow is the Church Warden. She nods, 'Yes. A great deal.'

'All running violently through the streets of St Cyneswide and St Tibba. And through other parishes as well. The Book of Matthew and the Book of Luke both say a herd of many swine, Mark says there were about two thousand. Were there that many? Here in St Cyneswide and St Tibba? Two thousand hogs possessed by devils?'

Viewer Abowen is not sure if this is a serious question. People are behaving strangely in these sad, afflicted days. She answers as best she can.

'Widow Chaukley and I did not see the first herd. I do not know how many were in that. There were two herds. Perhaps more than two. We saw the breaking and damage caused by the first rampage but they had gone on by the time we arrived. We were sent here by the Constable.' She says this in a critical way, suggesting that the Constable was clearly at fault to do so. The Warden gives his smile, but no more.

'I should not say herd. Constable Samuel Snow calls it a passel.' Her sarcasm is lightly put, but the Warden is left in no doubt that, as far as Anne Abowen is concerned, there is no benefit to be gained in this situation from knowing the correct word.

'We were caught by the second rout. Two women sellers were knocked over. Harmed. One was street seller, Betty Bethel——'

'Betty Bethel, hot pudding pies?'

'Yes. Her. The other, Abigail Joanes, was bringing wicking to John Girling. I looked to both of them.'

'Good. Good. And Widow Ursula Chaukley? She was here too? Of course she was?'

'Yes. She took herself to view the damage at the shops and manufactories.'

Frances Barrow nods approvingly. Surveys Anne Abowen's muddied and bloodied clothes.

'You were not hurt? Or were you?' He points to the blood.

'Not all mine. Mostly Betty Bethel, her blood. Widow Lankester took her in. Only some of the blood is mine. My——' she gestures down towards her lower extremities. 'On the cobbles.'

The Warden looks concerned but does nothing. Says cheerfully, 'So let us hope the two thousand, or however many there were, have by now run down a steep place into the sea and choked.'

She cannot help herself, says tartly, 'It is a long way from St Cyneswide and St Tibba to the sea.'

'Yes. But we can hope. And here is Jack Green the rectory boy! Jack! We need something to sit down on, something to rest our arms on, and something to drink. Dry, dirty work today. So, a draught for us all at the *Leg*? Good!'

Dirty work? Anne Abowen sees no signs that the church warden or Jack the footboy have done any dry, dirty work today.

The *Leg* is a quiet, respectable ale-house (too dull, the Warden thinks) and not one enjoyed by him and his singing fellows. Even so, he wonders if stiff-necked Anne Abowen will enter its doors.

She won't. A woman of strong opinions and fervent for Reform, she will not enter a tavern.

'I have earned a draught this morning, but not in there.'

'Then we will go to the vestry. Jack, have ale fetched for us.'

'Small beer for me,' says Anne Abowen.

'Swine. Hogs,' the Warden says cheerfully. 'Havoc, smell, noise. Know the saying: He that loves noise must love a pig.'

'I have no love for hogs this morning,' Anne Abowen says. 'Most mornings.'

'It is this new Order,' the Warden says. 'From memory: "No hogs, dogs, or cats, or conies be suffered to be kept within any part of the City, or any Swine to be, or stray in the streets or lanes, but that such swine be impounded by the Beadle or any other Officer, and the owner punished according to Act of Common-Council." Two days before the Orders come in the hog keepers are wanting to move their hogs out of the City. And they are doing so.'

This is met with silence. Jack notices that Frances Barrow left 'tame pigeons' out of the Order. Anne Abowen shows no interest in the Orders. She is thinking of her grazed knees and the filthy cobbles. Wonders what Widow Ursula Chaukley has found at the baker's and all.

Jack already knows all the Warden is telling them and ponders on a suitable comment to make about the Orders. But before he can find the right note the Warden has more to say.

'It's the doing of the Butchers' Company because of all this heat. The Butchers have declared a closed season for the slaughter of swine. No one wants measled pork. So your hog-keeper can't slaughter, but they've still got hogs to feed, and no money coming in. And the Mayor's Order says what it says. So keepers are removing their hogs.'

Jack nods, showing close interest.

'So, what do you know, young Jack?' the Warden asks kindly.

It is Jack's moment. It is Jack the footboy who brings the news to St Cyneswide and St Tibba.

He clears his throat to a deep, manly tone, 'The Why-toll Palace yard is full of waggons and carts and coaches and people ready to go out of town.' Although from Blackfriars, Jack the footboy says Whitehall as some folk in St Cyneswide and St Tibba say it: Why-toll.

'Did Walter Hall tell you this by messenger? Is Walter Hall leaving with the court? Did he say that at Why-toll they are ready to be leaving?' Frances Barrow wants to know. This is news, and more. 'All of them leaving? All?' All meaning particularly Charles the black Scotchman, the false king.

'Yes,' Jack lies easily. 'Yes, a message from the rector himself.' Jack is being Secretary Thurloe, as was. A knowing man, with spider webs of spies, informants. There is no need for Frances Barrow, for St Cyneswide and St Tibba, to know that footboys and footmen and cook-maids and waiting-women and maids and coachmen and hackney coach-men and housekeepers and laundry maids and porters, see everything, hear everything, and how they all talk, all talk to each other, to Jack Thurloe, the attentive, obliging footboy.

This is what Jack would want it to be. In truth, this past year he has seen less and less of his fellow footboys and footmen. Demanding Uncle Rowland at the rectory has demanded, commanded, much of Jack's time. Efficient, reliable, trustworthy Jack has become Uncle Rowland's walking stick, waiter and jester, and fellow songster: 'Jack! Jack boy! Come sing with a sad ancient man.' Jack's voice – improved since he first sang *L'amour, la mort, et la vie* to Walter and Margery Hall, but mostly to Margery – has become even better under Uncle Rowland's abrupt, domineering supervision. 'Come Jack, it's *Haste thee O Lord* for a sorrowful old man:

> *Haste thee O Lord, make haste with speed*
> *And help me in this time of need.*
> *My soul doth sink, my forces fail,*
> *My wearied arms cannot prevail;*
> *The waters flow so fast that I can scarcely cry:*
> *Help me O Lord, help me O Lord, or else I drown and die.*

Uncle Rowland does wonderful things with 'or else I drown and die.' His voice quavering, rising then falling falling falling on 'die.' Jack can imitate this perfectly, although does not do so in front of Uncle Rowland (but does with his street friends, where he exaggerates and burlesques the dying trill, to great applause).

Up until the family fled London, four days previously, Jack has been busied in the rectory at all hours with little time to see old friends from Whitehall Palace days. Walter Hall's footman Bartholomew Bigmore, who still fondly recalls Jack introducing himself with a gold crown, has become Jack's only regular provider of court news, of court gossip.

But the genial Bartholomew Bigmore is not the bearer of the momentous news. It comes from two different sources.

The return voyages to Dung Wharf of Thomas Micoe's dung barge are rarely empty ('What would be the point of that?' Thomas asks reasonably). Some return journeys carry bricks, and some carry wood for the many hearths of London, great stacks of wood loaded at forest wharves up river.

Thomas Micoe is on good terms with the Worshipful Company of the Woodmongers and the Coal Trade of London, particularly with wood merchant John Sled, his friend and his business connection in the Company. When the barge carries a load of wood John Sled makes the voyage back to London with it, after hard bargaining with farmers, foresters and woodcutters. ('Here's the barge waiting to be loaded and ready to go. Will you sell or will you no? Makes no odds to me, there's always more wood to be had.' A careless wave of the arm at the endless woods.)

'The Carmen,' says John Sled with deep disgust, 'Have I told you how in the year 5 we took them into our Company?' (Yes, thinks Thomas Micoe, you have told me.) 'Kindly took them in. Because they were a failed, folded, collapsed livery company, the Worshipful Company of Carmen. Worshipful! Their plate all gone, stolen, some say, by their Master but however it went, it went. Could not pay the rent on their Hall. Three, three! Quarter Days behind. Their Company fell to the ground, all of it. They could not meet even the common charges incurred in the normal course of business. Charges which they were obliged to pay, but did not. They did not pay. So we, the Worshipful Company of the Woodmongers and the Coal Trade of London, took them in. Similar trade, same trade, you might say. We did say. Made them part of us. And earned for doing this a degree of ingratitude you cannot imagine Thomas Micoe.'

Thomas Micoe nods, there are many stories of ingratitude, far fewer of gratitude. He settles himself into a more comfortable position on the barge, lightly dozing, comfortably breathing in the familiar heavy smell of dung and the novel crispness of freshly sawn timber.

'And now, now, these Carmen, never satisfied, are all of an agitation to re-form their own Company. Can you believe it Thomas Micoe? The ingratitude. We always had more carts than them. Do you know your barge does smell monstrous strong of dung Thomas Micoe? Very strong, yet you live with it eh?'

Thomas Micoe ignores, as he always does, what is said of his barge's smell, will talk of something else, 'Do you know John Sled that days before the death of Oliver Protector a great whale came into the river and was taken at Greenwich. Days before his death. What do you say to that? Don't often see great whales in our river. I have seen one, no two, small ones not great ones, in all my days on the river.' Their talk turns to fish and strange creatures seen in or by the river.

And it is from John Sled, as relayed by Thomas Micoe, that Jack Micoe hears how the ungrateful Carmen have, 'of their own motion! cunningly connived and secretly contracted, Thomas Micoe, without due and proper consultation!' to provide so many carts and waggons and coaches to the Royal Court at Whitehall Palace to remove the Court out of town, this being settled on for Thursday the twenty ninth day of June. 'Hoping to curry royal favour, Thomas Micoe, curry favour so they can re-establish the Company of Carmen. I will not say, not say, the Worshipful Company! No!'

So Jack Micoe, since become Jack Green, and hoping to be Jack Thurloe in nature if not in name, asks his friend Jemmy Pooly, son of Master Hackney Coachman John Pooly – one of London's two hundred such Masters – if his father has any intelligence of carts and waggons and coaches preparing to remove the Court? 'Yes there is such intelligence,' John Pooly tells Jemmy Pooly, who tells Jack, 'Yes.' John Pooly knows this great mustering of carts and waggons to be so, even though Master Hackney Coachmen have no truck with carmen and woodmongers, low trades. But hackney coachmen hear things, many things. They do.

You can trust a hackney coachman, their profession being a sound one, regulated as far back as June 1654, a good eleven years previous, through an Ordinance issued by the Lord Protector himself, with the consent of his High Council. Was not John Pooly trained to the trade by John Saltmarsh, one of the original Thirteen Masters? Yes. Was not John Pooly nominated by John Saltmarsh to be one of the further one hundred and eighty seven persons admitted as Master Hackney Coachmen? He was. Did not John Saltmarsh assist John Pooly in paying his admission fee of forty shillings? He did. And did not John Pooly repay this forty shillings, along with a handsome bounty, at the end of his first year of hackney coach driving? He did.

'Yes,' Jack lies easily. 'Yes, I heard of this from Walter Hall, a message from the rector himself. They are leaving, the whole Court is leaving, for Syon House. Up river.'

'The whole Court,' Frances Barrow says with relish. The whole Court. All of them.'

'Yes.'

Anne Abowen is restored by her small beer. In good humour she tells them of Betty Bethel at Widow Lankester's. 'As a jewel of gold in a swine's snout, so is a fair woman which is without discretion. This Betty Bethel said to the Widow!'

Book of Proverbs thinks Jack.

'Book of Proverbs,' says the Warden. 'She said that, in the swine's snout, to Widow Lankester?'

'She certainly did not say it to me.'

'Or did she just say it? Not to anyone? Just say it?'

Anne Abowen shrugs, 'She said it.'

'Leaving today. For Syon House. So, what else do you know, young Jack?'

Jack rubs his chin. Looks thoughtful but does not find anything else to say.

'Think on it. Well, a good draught, heh? The Orders also say that Tipling-houses are to be looked into for musty and unwholesome casks. No fear of that from the *Leg*, a very respectable house.' The Warden stands.

'While you are thinking young Jack we shall go and find Philip Carter, tell him the news,' Frances Barrow is in high good humour.

Anne Abowen goes to look for Widow Ursula Chaukley.

Frances Barrow lays a friendly hand on Jack's shoulder, says, 'Come and tell Philip Carter what you told me.' But stops, looks genially at Jack, says, 'You're still young, young Jack. Do you know your year of birth?'

Jack finds the question insulting but does not show it. 'In the year 49.'

'And what does a young lad born in 49 know of the Good Old cause? Eh? The Good Old Cause?'

'I know I have a brother named Oliver, born in the year 51,' Jack replies, 'Named by my father.'

'Oliver. Good, good. Your father is a good man.'

'Yes.' Jack does not mention his other brothers, born after 1660, dead Rupert and James. Frances Barrow does not need to know this (Jack Thurloe knows when to speak, when to keep silent). Frances Barrow's sympathies for the Good Old Cause are known in the parish of St Cyneswide and St Tibba. He is not one of those, although they are a slowly growing number, who take the easier path of accommodation – bowing to the way things are and will be – with the bishops' church and its Book of Common Prayer.

This morning Philip Carter is still at home, his legs causing him pain, as they frequently do.

'Philip Carter, hear what young Jack has to say! What he has heard from Walter Hall, hear him!'

'In the Why-toll Palace yard there are waggons and carts and coaches making ready to go out of town.' Jack repeats. But he is worried that he has not heard from Walter Hall about this or anything else. True, he received his Quarter Day pay of ten shillings fourpence halfpenny on Midsummer Day just passed, but what of the next Quarter Day? What of his Michaelmas payment due in three months' time? How will absent Walter Hall pay that? How?

'Are all going from the Palace?' Philip Carter asks, 'All?'

'Yes! All!' Frances Barrow has made Jack's news his own and will answer any questions about it.

'So,' says Philip Carter slowly, 'so the––' and cannot say more. A lump of anger fills him, blocking speech: there is the foreigner usurper who pretends to rule England, the whoremaster Scotchman; there is his foreign wife, with the stench of all the wickedness of Rome, of rank popery; there are the prattling fop-fool courtiers – Fuck Lord Rochester! Oppressive bishops in their Romish finery, their mitres and crooks. Shepherds! More wolves, more foxes. Chasubles and incense. The Book of filthy Common Prayer. Porridge and more porridge.

The glorious Reformation gave England true independent worship: made men masters of their own parish; choosing their minister; and rule in the hands of the congregation, the saints. As it should be. As it was. As it is no longer.

As it could be again?

And all those who tore this down: the king and his whores, his queen, all the great ones who dance and prance around them, are to run. Are running from this wretched city struck by pestilence. Leaving the poor, the weak, the lame. His aching, wasted legs are wrapped in brown paper greasy with Jane-Pym Carter's family salve of black soap, salt and honey.

Frances Barrow has often spoken of troopers, common soldiers, gathering to decide their claims, their demands. Choosing representatives to press their claims, their demands. As it should be. As it was. As it is no longer.

As it might be again?

And now there is hope it might be, some hope, and Philip Carter finds his tongue, 'Jack, good news. Thankee.'

'Philip Carter!' Frances Barrow enthuses. 'What a chance, what a chance! What a door has opened for us, for all the saints. We will bind them all in chains!

> *Sing ye unto the Lord our God, a new rejoicing song:*
> *And let the praise of him be heard his holy Saints among.*
> *And with glory and with honour now let all his Saints rejoice:*
> *And now aloud upon their beds advance their singing voice.*
> *And in their mouths let be the acts of God the mighty Lord:*
> *And in their hands eke let them bear a double edged sword.*
> *To plague the heathen, and correct the people with their hands:*
> *To bind their stately Kings in chains their Lords in iron bands.*
> *To execute on them the doom that written is before:*
> *This honour all his Saints shall have, praise ye the Lord therefore!*

Philip Carter, and Jack and four passers-by must join in. Who could fail to do so, Jack thinks.

'Sung,' says a triumphant Frances Barrow, 'the one hundred and forty ninth, sung at the charge, at the fights of Edgehill in 42, Newbury in 43,

Marston Moor in 44 and Naseby – a victory, as Oliver said, thanks to none other than the hand of God! – Naseby in 45. Sung at them all. Before the fight. During the fight. After the fight. To bind their kings in chains, their lords in iron bands!'

Frances Barrow stops, catches his breath. 'Yes, excellent news. Excellent news young Jack. Now,' he smiles his genial smile, 'the Clerk and I have parish matters to discuss.'

Jack, dismissed, says his God be w'ye and leaves. He is uplifted by singing the stirring psalm, but wonders if it is right, if it is wise, to be so uplifted? What would John Thurloe do?

Frances Barrow says of the departing boy, 'With Walter Hall gone we shall see more of Jack Green out in the parish. A good boy.'

Philip Carter nods, still warmed, exalted, by the psalm. Despair sung up to hope.

'They are going, Frances Barrow. They are gone. Our time has come again. Walter Hall is gone. Thomas Dugdale, we will get him back. Here in St Cyneswide and St Tibba. Our minister again. Our chosen minister. Ours. I have heard,' he says slowly, 'heard that pulpits, many pulpits not just ours, are emptying, emptying like ... like piss pots into the channels. That is the word among the clerks.' Like piss pots are Alexander Muzard's words.

'Yes! Yes,' exclaims the Warden. 'The court is leaving, Walter Hall is leaving, and with black Charles gone, his chaplains gone, how many pastors will stay with their sheep in London? How many? Not many at all. Perhaps none. Leaving their sheep to be devoured by the wolfish pestilence. Good shepherds all!'

'So many pulpits vacant, waiting to be filled,' the Clerk muses, 'properly filled.'

'Have you seen this, Philip Carter?' Frances Barrow has a new pamphlet. 'It is called *A pulpit to let*. Listen!' he reads drolly, but at times has to stop and repeat himself, so great is his laughter at the lines and at his own mock parson's voice:

Beloved; and he sweetly thus goes on,
Now, where's Beloved? Why, Beloved's gone.
No morning Matins now, nor Evening Song:
Alas! The Parson cannot stay so long.
With Clerkenwell it fares as most in town,
The light-heel'd Levit's broke, and the Spark flown;
Broke did I say? They ne're had quit the place,
Had they but set up with a spark or grace!
They did the Pulpit as a Coffin greet,
And took the Surplice for a Winding-sheet.

Philip Carter is delighted, laughs until he is overcome with a coughing fit, then echoes, 'Where's Beloved? Why, Beloved's gone! Our Beloved *has* gone.'

'Dearly Beloved, for as much as,' the Warden tries to catch – not as successfully as young Jack – Walter Hall's voice at the beginning of a service. But it is faithful enough to make them both rock with laughter again. 'We are gathered here: Yes, *we* are gathered here, *you* are not. You, dearly beloved, are not gathered here at all!' More laughter.

Returning to the rectory Jack is waylaid by neighbour Edward Richbell the baker, who hands him a letter, the baker's floury finger marks dusting Walter Hall's seal (a two-tiered hall structured as a large H, and floored with zig-zagging paving in the form of a W).

In his spy-room at the top of the rectory Jack slips his knife under the seal, opens the letter, reads:

> *TO – Jack Green Footboy at the rectory in the church square of St Cyneswide and St Tibba, London.*
> *This Twenty Ninth day of June, Year of Our Lord 1665*
> *I shall this day go out of town. The King's business takes myself and his Court from London. The day of the King's return, and thus mine, is as yet unknown.*
> *I have composed here some Items for you to attend in my absence:*
> *Item: In the rectory leave no window open, nor door unbolted.*

Item: Give admission to no-one unless on my business and sent by me, or unless they be those whose presence be required to effect necessary repairs to damage to the rectory that might be brought about by the ravages of time and weather.

Item: While most of your days and nights will necessarily be spent within the rectory, you must from time to time take fresh air. Naturally avoiding those places where the air is plaguey and unwholesome.

Item: Your Mistress Margery Hall has kindly writ out an excellent receipt that she recommends to you should you have the misfortune to fall ill of the pestilence. It is come herewith, in her own hand.

Item: Should there be matters you wish to convey to my attention (only important matters mind, concerning for example monies), then those remaining at Whitehall Palace will know whither to direct your post.

Item: At night before retiring go down on your knees and heartily pray to GOD for the safe-keeping of the King and his Court, for the safe-keeping of all, and for your safe-keeping in these sickly times in London. Pray as we were used to pray when a family assembled in the rectory.

Item: You should make it known that the King and his Court depart not out of fear or faintness of heart due to the troublesome infection. The stability of the Kingdom, so recently won back after those sad and disruptive times that brought great ruin with them, demands the safety of the King.

God bless you and keep you safe in these sickly times.
Walter Hall
One of his Majesty's Chaplains
& Rector of the Parish of St Cyneswide and St Tibba

Jack does not recall many nights when Walter Hall led family prayers at the rectory, he was rarely present to do so. It was left to Godfrey Hall, whose prayers are abrupt and brief, or Uncle Rowland, who – despite his public aversion to the metrical psalms – will enthusiastically lead the rectory household in singing them. The thirtieth is one of his many favourites.

All laud and praise with heart and voice, O Lord, I give to thee:
Which didst not make my foes rejoice, but has exalted me:
O Lord, my God, to thee I cry'd in all my pain and grief:
Thou gav'st an ear, and didst provide to ease me with relief.

With Walter Hall's letter Jack finds a smaller piece of paper with the pretty, Round script of Margery Hall:

For Jack Green. For the pestilence.
Take yarrow, tansy, featherfew, of each a handful, and bruise them
well together, then let the sick party make water into the herbs, then
strain them, and give it to the sick to drink.
Be in God's keeping.
Mgry Hall

Jack reads it carefully. Reads it again. Wonders if he were to fall sick of the plague – God forbid it – whether he would drink his own water. But if this is to be the cure, then he would do so.

He is comforted that Margery Hall, now leaving London, has paused to put quill to paper and send him this. As a new boy in the household he had enthusiastically admired her cursive hand – she writes daily notes 'Orders for Walter Hall, his Household.' She tells him it is the French Ronde hand, learned when she was over there with the King. 'Ronde means round in English,' she tells him. He knows that, but does not say so. He does say, as if in pleased discovery, 'Ah! Like the round dance song under Avignon bridge: L'on y danse tous en rond. I see, Rond!' (More obscene capering by French barge boys singing this.) 'Yes! Just so,' exclaims Margery Hall, delighted with the quick-witted child.

In neither letter is there mention of Quarter Days, of ten and fourpence halfpenny, but Jack is an optimistic lad and takes heart from Walter Hall's mention of matters 'only important matters mind, concerning for example monies' that can be raised via 'those remaining at Whitehall Palace.' Surely this means ten and fourpence halfpenny?

Jack wishes he has more intelligence to give the Church Warden, but what? That John Sled is a talking man who has no time for carmen?

That pudding pies Betty Bethel is niece to carman Robert Bethel? That John Pooly was aided to become a Master Hackney Coachman by John Saltmarsh, one of the original Thirteen Masters? Would the Church Warden care to know this? That Margery Hall writes with a Round French hand? Jack Green, even as Jack Thurloe, cannot be sure.

CHAPTER XII

London, Thursday afternoon, 29 June 1665

'Slitherum, slatherum, take her.'

'Come. Come!' Viewer Anne Abowen calls cheerfully, even encouragingly, to Widow Margaret Hazard and Goodwife Joan Brokefild. 'Come to our ancient women's room.' She waves vigorously for them to come. 'All the ancient women!'

'What does she want with us?' the Widow grumbles to her friend. 'Why should we go with her? Her of all people? Mmm?'

'If we go we will find out. I want to know what she wants of us and surely you do too?' The Goodwife can hear in her voice the coaxing tones that some mothers, the gentle ones, use with sulky reluctant children. But the Widow is no child and Goodwife Brokefild adds briskly. 'I am going and you may come or no, as it pleases you. I will tell you all that is said. I want to know.'

'I will come, of course I will,' the Widow says firmly as if this has never been in any doubt.

The room the parish has put in the service of the ancient women – where they are all meant to live for as long as they continue as Searchers, Viewers, Keepers – is a small and nasty one, found on the first floor of an old building buttressed over many years by props added piecemeal as its walls take turns to bow and sag.

Willed to the parish – when? long long ago is all anybody now knows in the year 65: 'it has always been ours' – by Sir William Tongue to buy masses for the repose of his soul. The squat half-timbered house was seen as a dubious gift even in his day ('at best worth four very short masses,' whispered aside at his meagre burial).

As for the state of Sir William Tongue's soul, the parish of St Cyneswide and St Tibba, his parish, today does not know of it, or of him. And if it did it would know that a papist soul, such as Sir William's, is burning eternally in hell fire. The great monument he intended to dominate the chapel of St Tibba dwindled to a stone slab, shallowly incised, set in the church floor. One hundred and fifty years of parish feet have scuffed to illegibility his plea: 'Of your charytie pray for the Sowle of William Tonge, Knyght, who decessed thys transitorie Wourld the XXIII of Aprile in the yere of owre Lord God M.D.XIIII, upon whose Sowle and all Christen Sowles Jesu have mercy. Aetatis XLVII.' All that can be seen now is a declivity intended by the stone mason to represent a tongue, but known by generations of parish boys to be a hand hole which might lift the slab and so reveal a hoard of gold beneath. It is not, and there is not.

The stairs up to the room rock under foot, the door does not close properly, the room is meanly furnished, the fire place never draws well, the one window is small, leaving the room ill-lit by day. All know this, none more so than the ancient women, who will not live here.

In the year 12 this shabby unwholesome place was deemed by the Vestry as best suited for the ancient women. The then Parish Clerk, Tobias Bludworth, enumerated on his fingers the reasons why this was so: 'Item One, St Cyneswide and St Tibba is obliged to provide such a room for its ancient women, as are all parishes within the Bills of Mortality. Item Two, no other use can be found for this room. No one will have it, try as we might. And we, I, have tried. Item Three, there are other, better, rooms but we have more profitable uses for those.' The Vestry unanimously declared the shabby room to be best suited for the ancient women.

The parish, having done its duty in providing the room, made little effort to insist those ancient women responsible for sickness and death should live there. The women would not do so and nothing better would be offered them. Vestry gave no further thought to the matter.

Walter Hall, on his appointment as rector in the year 60, examines with mild interest his Parish Clerk as to why 'these Searchers and Viewers and, and the other ancient women, you know who they are, all of them, why do they do not all reside in the room the parish has rightly appointed for them?'

Like Tobias Bludworth, his distant predecessor, Philip Carter counts off reasons. 'The room is too small for six ancient women; it is ill-equipped for any habitation, being in a state of decay; and the women each have good causes of their own why they will not remove to the room.'

'Causes?' the new Rector probes, 'What are these good causes?'

'Of our Searchers, both good, long serving, experienced Searchers, Widow Margaret Hazard will not move as she will not be separated from the, from her child Sara. Goodwife Joan Brokefild, her husband Isaac tells her if she leaves his house he will slit her nose so the world will know her for, these are his words, for the whore she is. His words, she is no whore. Viewer Ursula Chaukley, she is a prop to a large family who manage poorly without her. Viewer Anne Abowen flatly says she will not move, says she will not view the sick, the dying, if the parish means her to live in a, in a – she likened the room to a house of office.'

'Is this a fair comparison?' the Rector asks.

Philip Carter considers, answers, 'It is not an unfair one. The room has a most unpleasant smell. Of urine, and worse.'

'And the other two, the, the, other two? What are they? They also have good causes?'

'The Keepers, yes. Keeper Goody Susanna Parsons, misfortunes leave her with family she must keep close. A good woman, Goody Parsons. Keeper Widow Dorothy Bullen is a very ancient woman much set in her ways of doing. She says, often says, she will not and she can not change. That is them all.'

Walter Hall nods dismissively, has heard too much of these small people and their threadbare lives. It is sufficient that the parish has provided a room for its ancient women.

The ancient women, five of them, make cautious progress up the unsteady stairs to what they have long dismissed as 'our room.' All have seen it once, on their appointment, but have had no occasion, until now, to be there again.

'Today is Thursday! Thursday! Today is Thursday!' the voice from the street carries up the stairs.

'That bufflehead should be for Bedlam,' Anne Abowen says sharply. Widow Margaret Hazard and Goody Susanna Parsons nod agreement. Goodwife Joan Brokefild sees no harm in Walter Shute. Widow Dorothy Bullen must concentrate on not being overturned by these wicked stairs and thinks about nothing but her next step.

Pushing open the begrudging door Anne Abowen sniffs, announces, 'It still smells, but not so bad as before.' She gestures with mock joy to bales of cloth that half fill the room. 'Look! Some kind neighbour has decided we are a store room.'

'That will be William Lacie, his upholstery,' the Goodwife says. 'So we can sit on a bundle of his–' she pokes curious fingers, pulls at various bales, 'we can sit on his serge, or his baize, or his dornix. All his very cheapest cloths.' She chooses a comfortable bale of serge by the window.

It is a gloomy room, black with soot. Goodwife Brokefild and Widow Bullen each reach within their pockets for candles and get them quickly lit.

'Why have you called us here?' Widow Hazard cuts in, her voice as sharp as Anne Abowen's. 'And where is Widow Chaukley? If we Searchers and Keepers are here so should all the Viewers.'

'Because these are bad times for us all, for all of us here,' Anne Abowen snaps back. 'Yes, Widow Ursula Chaukley should be here. Where is she? Where is she? Do I know? Still hiding somewhere from rushing hogs.'

'She is old and not firm in her legs. And she has no skill with hogs,' Widow Bullen protests.

It is some time since Anne Abowen was cheered by her draught of small beer and she is now less certain why she has summoned the ancient women. But the rushing, stinking hogs come to mind.

'This morning we were sent, Widow Ursula Chaukley and I were sent to view hog damage, which is no job for Viewers. And–' She is encouraged by the unanimous agreement that this brings. Repeats, 'no job for Viewers.'

'I would not have gone,' Widow Margaret Hazard says unhelpfully.

'We did go. I did. And got dashed to the ground and cut on filthy cobbles trying to help sellers overturned by the hogs and only got abuse for it. That is what happens to Viewers who would do their duty, would help.' Anne Abowen hopes for vindication, for support, finds little.

Goody Susanna Parsons suddenly erupts, 'The plague comes on worse and even more worse! Everywhere people dying, dead. Houses shut up, marked with the red cross. Death all about. Those who can will fly from town. The king and his court, Walter Hall, all flying today, gone, leaving all of us, the poor, the ancient, all who have no means to fly, leaving us to die from the infection. Hogs? Hogs are nothing!'

Agitated, Goodwife Joan Brokefild must stand up, says, 'When the house, Robert Holt's house fell down, even as it was falling the vermin, the mice and rats and the things that live under the floor, they all fled to keep themselves safe,' she pauses, leaves a small gap filled by Widow Dorothy Bullen.

'What of us who have everything to do with the infection? What of we Keepers and Viewers and Searchers? And why hogs? We have nothing to do with hogs!'

'We do what we have taken our oath to do,' Goodwife Joan Brokefild says, hoping to bring this aimless gathering to an end. 'We view the ill, we keep them, we search their corpse. As we are sworn to do,' said soothingly, mollifyingly.

'As we are sworn to do,' Widow Hazard echoes self-righteously. Thinks, and she is not the only one, that Anne Abowen is in a strange passion about hogs.

Goody Parsons wants to remove herself as soon as she can, says placatingly, 'You should not have been sent to view hog damage. That is not for Viewers. Not for any of us to view hogs.' She stands, ready to leave.

'Everything is in disorder,' Widow Bullen ventures. 'The infection. Widow Chaukley has her receipt for plague water and claims everything good for it and only it. I say Venice Treacle is another, but I have now also heard – only this yesterday – also heard of this excellent preservative against the infection.' All said very slowly.

'This was told me by midwife Hester Fenner. Or was it the day before yesterday? Perhaps it was. Rise a quart of old ale on the fire, scum it, and add half handfuls each of angelica and celadine, then boil all. Six spoonfuls of dragon water then cork-seal all in a close glass. Before breaking fast each morning drink five spoonfuls. Yes. Five. And wear the dried root of angelica as a nosegay. Yes. A sure preservative against infection. Midwife Hester Fenner always wears her angelica nosegay and I am to get one. Yes.'

She is heard out in attentive silence. Such preservatives and remedies are always worth hearing. 'The good Lord will preserve us,' Widow Bullen adds.

Widow Margaret Hazard looks about her with disapproval, 'This room is much too small as a room for six ancient women to live in, and its smell is bad.'

Anne Abowen reluctantly abandons her hogs, 'We do what we are sworn to do. We do. And for it are insulted and called a jewel of gold in a swine's snout, are grazed, cut, cast down on the cobbles, the hog filthy cobbles. And worse,' she stops to catch breath, but holds her audience's attention. They wait to hear worse.

'Worse, these new Orders, we are to be examined by some physician to see if we are fitly qualified. And to be charged by this physician if he should think us defective in our duties. Defective!' The ancient women agree this is certainly worse than being called a jewel in a swine's snout or being cut on hog fouled cobbles.

'And,' Widow Bullen adds, unaware of treading on dangerous ground, 'there are accusations of false reports being made, of bribes being taken to wrongfully report a cause of death, when all know Searchers are sworn not to make report of the cause of any death better or worse than the nature of the disease. Sworn not to.'

A brief silence before Goodwife Joan Brokefild breaks in loudly over her expostulating friend Widow Hazard. 'An Item, the first, for the Vestry meeting this Sunday: the Searchers of St Cyneswide and St Tibba took money to delay a search so an infected corpse, that of John Sly's maid Doll Matthews, could be removed; Item the second, that these same Searchers sought a bribe to make a false report, sought a gold Guinea, each, from Widow Shipley to go away, to not see the body of James Shipley, dead of the plague. We did none of these but these false accusations have been made and Philip Carter, rightly, will have the Vestry consider them.'

Widow Margaret Hazard, quickly to her feet, shouts, 'And who is spreading these false accusations? Who?' she glares at Anne Abowen, and then for good measure at Widow Dorothy Bullen, who is surprised, confused; growls at Goody Susanna Parsons, 'And why?' Cowering her.

Not so Anne Abowen. 'I have done no such thing! You are a stiff-necked, hard woman Widow Hazard.'

'But not a dishonest one,' the Widow snaps back. 'Never a bribe. Never a bribe taken. Offered by some, but never taken. Never. And the same for Goodwife Joan Brokefild.'

'No high words. We want no high words here.' Goody Parsons will make peace but only gets heavy frowns and scowls from Anne Abowen and Widow Hazard.

'Well, Vestry will decide,' Widow Dorothy Bullen says complacently, unhelpfully. 'On Sunday.'

Widow Margaret Hazard turns to leave.

Anne Abowen ignores this, says angrily, 'These new Orders. Physicians to oversee. Surgeons to have twelve pence a body searched. Find me a physician, a surgeon in London today! They have fled the infection! All of them fled like Tom Sydem, physician, parish of St Augustine Watling Street. Fled. All of them cullies.'

Widow Hazard stops, agrees, must add, 'President of the Physicians' College, Edward Alston, he has fled, and where the head goes the body will follow. There will be none left in town to collect their twelve pence a corpse.'

Goodwife Joan Brokefild laughs. 'They say they know more of the plague than any ancient woman, more than women who have years of searching corpses. They will get their quills and write it, but how do they know the plague? How do they know what to write? By fleeing from it!'

Widow Hazard sits back down, bangs her wand on the floor in

approval.

'Alston, he took into his College all the physicians from Oliver Protector's time, and took their fees,' the Goodwife tells. 'All that money the College had, but does not have now. With no-one there to guard it, all fled, the thieves have it!'

'How do you know this?' Goody Susanna Parsons asks, mystified.

'Jack the footboy,' says Goodwife Brokefild. 'The boy often has news.'

'A very clean boy, Jack,' Widow Dorothy Bullen says. 'His smell is not noisome at all.'

Yes,' agrees Goody Parsons. 'He has always been that way. Some boys, most, have an odious stink.'

The Goodwife whispers to her friend, 'I will tell you of young Jack. Not here, later.'

Widow Dorothy Bullen chews slowly on something Widow Hazard said, turns to her, 'Yes, this room is much too small for all we ancient women. And it does have a rank stench.' She pauses, sniffs. 'Hogs. I have a wholesome receipt for blood pudding.'

'Yes?' Anne Abowen asks.

Widow Margaret Hazard has her thoughts, and lets them run free. 'So. You are to be an information against us at the Vestry?' She asks them all but stares hard with her one eye at Anne Abowen.

Who answers, 'No! How would we? We know only what we have heard. We have all heard the rumours, the gossip. You have heard them. We know nothing of what happened.' Adds, 'Or what did not happen. How would we know anything of that? None of us were there.'

'So. None of you to be informations at the Vestry?' Widow Hazard presses.

'No,' says Goody Parsons. 'None,' then looks around uncertainly to check if she has spoken well, but no one dissents.

'We will see,' says Widow Hazard. 'We will see.'

'Enough,' says Anne Abowen, who has had enough. She stands and takes Widow Bullen's arm. 'Tell me your blood pudding receipt. I hope you need the blood of many dead hogs.'

'I wonder, I do wonder where Widow Chaukley is,' Widow Bullen says, moving carefully down the stairs, holding on to Anne Abowen. 'These broken steps would kill her. I hope she is safe.'

'*She* was not bowled over by a troop of gruntling hogs. She is safe.' Anne Abowen is sure of that.

'I hope she is. Take the warm blood of a hog, only one hog, but more if you wish, and steep it in oatmeal grits–'

Goody Parsons turns back to Widow Hazard and Goodwife Brokefild, says quietly, 'This Vestry business, may God give a good end to it. You are both honest women. That is known. The parish knows.'

The Goodwife is touched, thanks her. Widow Hazard greets this kindness blankly. Who is Goody Parsons to accuse her of high words? She has little regard for Goody Susanna Parsons.

'–take mother of thyme, parsley, spinach, succory, endive, sorrel, and strawberry leaves and mix–'

Out in the street, away from the others, tapping their red wands as they walk beside the channel, the Goodwife says encouragingly to her companion, 'Good news then. None of them to be against us, God be praised.'

'If you believe them.'

'Why say one thing to us today, then another to the Vestry on Sunday?'

The Widow shrugs, 'Fear of my evil eye. Or, if they are liars, then they will lie today and then lie to the Vestry on Sunday. Just tell different lies.'

'I do not believe they will,' the Goodwife says sternly. 'Goody Parsons said rightly that we are honest women, and so they are too.'

The Widow will not let go. 'If not them, then there will be others to bear false witness against us. The scriptures say that there are false witnesses to be found.'

The Goodwife, exasperated, gives a great gust of a sigh. She kicks a stone that freakishly skips five times down the street. Delighted, she chants:

> *A duck and a drake,*
> *And a halfpenny cake,*

And a penny to pay the old baker,
A hop and a scotch's another notch,
Slitherum, slatherum, take her.

The Widow bats a pebble with her wand and it too skims across the cobbles. She says with her lop-sided grin:

Hen-pen,
Duck and mallard,
Amen.

They laugh their way back to their comfortable friendship.

'That very clean boy Jack the footboy,' the Goodwife says with her wide smile. 'Now I will tell you. This is not for those other ears in that small room. A room which does have a noisome stink, not like young Jack. Not at all like.'

'I must piss,' the Widow says. 'Too long in that stinking room and no pot. It smelled like the whole room was one big pot.'

The Goodwife laughs. 'That room, and not a pot to piss in! Here, the Wawin house. Empty. Use their house of office.'

They know no-one now lives there, the house is empty. Here, four days before, they searched the corpse of Mary Wawin. No sign of Francis Wawin, or of any family. All fled, neighbour Daniel Maxfilde said. Fled the night of Saturday last. He had heard noises from next door. Not the usual noises of chairs scraping, plates clattering, talking. Just hurrying noises, urgent noises. He looked out of his door, saw them leaving quickly, called to them, but they hurried off without answering, without looking back. Gone. Sunday morning he had told William Hawkins, watchman at the Gipps house. 'You know William Hawkins, the one who blinks in that way.'

The searched corpse of Mary Wawin showed no signs of plague. 'Measles,' the Searchers can see immediately. 'Not plague,' the Goodwife tells Daniel Maxfilde. 'Measles, not plague. No red cross on the Wawin door.' He stares back, blank, absent. A look they have seen before. A look that, in this time of sickness, takes in some, but not all, of what's said.

'If he does not think of it, then he believes it will not happen to him, the infection,' the Goodwife says to her friend. For her part Widow Hazard thinks Daniel Maxfilde's empty stare shows him to be simple-minded.

Red wand Searchers may go where they will, without challenge, and for their easement they can piss in Francis Wawin's house of office, and do.

In water square, resting against their shaded wall, they fill their pipes and smoke. After an easy pause the Goodwife says, 'Jack the footboy and Jemmy Pooly. You know there are some nights when I will walk, because–'

'Yes I know,' the Widow nods.

'There are times when I am out that I have seen Jack Green and Jemmy Pooly, and seen them go to a hot-house. Not just once. They go often. Three times I have seen them do so this year, and perhaps they went other times when I did not see them. But I saw them twice to the Longacre hot-house and once to the Queen Elizabeth bath at Charing Cross.'

'They bath? They would go to a hot-house bath that often?' The Widow is shocked, finds this odd, hard to believe, but certainly her friend would not lie about such a thing. 'Three times this year you say? And it is now only mid-year.'

'Yes. Three times. A strange thing.'

'Washing the body? The whole body? Do they do that at a hot-house?'

'Yes, the whole body. In hot water. At the hot-house.'

They ponder this, fascinated and appalled.

'I have read in the Almanack,' the Widow says cautiously, searching memory. 'The Almanack says–' She thinks on it. 'The Almanack says – and I always thought it a nonsense, put there only to fill the book – it says,' she slowly summons the words. 'It says: "If any will enter the bath for cleanness, let the moon be in Libra or Pisces." But even that is only two times in the year. Not more.' And hear this, the Almanack says: "The time of tarrying in the bath is commonly one hour." One hour!'

They laugh at the absurdity of it, repeating, 'One hour!'

'Why put such stuff in the Almanack?' the Goodwife wonders, 'Why?'

'And,' says the Widow, 'there is also this: "Be wary and circumspect in resorting to a hot-house immediately after or with such persons as be unclean." I can–' She is at a loss for words.

'Yes!' exclaims the Goodwife. 'Yes. I can see what is meant here. There are those who would piss, or even shit, in the bath water. Sharing a bath with such!'

The thought of washing in someone's shit leaves them shaking their heads.

'Yet Jack looks clean, very clean, and he does not smell of shit,' the Widow says.

'The coach stand is empty,' the Goodwife points across the square.

'I hope crazed Isabella Undnay is elsewhere, running shouting mad at some other Searcher who has done nothing wrong and knows nothing of missing Richard Undnay, who is surely dead of the plague in another parish,' the Widow grumbles. 'Hackney coachmen go all over the city. He could have died anywhere.'

'I have had pain of the colic, taking cold from washing my feet,' the Goodwife says. 'I once washed my legs and feet with warm water, mainly to show an example to Isaac, but only got a great deal of cold from it. The colic badly.'

'Did he wash at all?' the Widow asks, knowing the answer.

The Goodwife shakes her head. 'Ha! No, he did not.'

'I remember your bad colic.'

'So many farts great and small to shift the wind griping my belly,' she frowns at the memory.

The Widow nods, 'An abundance of wind behind eases the pain. Washing with warm water brings the colic in its wake. I use good cold water to wash face and hands, and make Sara do so,' the Widow says. 'But just face and hands, not more.'

'Not the whole body,' the Goodwife laughs.

'Oh no.'

'Rosemary water?'

'Yes, rosemary.'

They refill their pipes, reluctant to stand and move on. Glad to stay in the shade. The heat is harsh.

'I heard a street preacher in Oliver's time,' the Widow begins slowly. 'A Christian but not an Oliver man, or a Rome man. A Christian man but one who had strange, different sermons. Thomas Dugdale would not have him in the parish. Drove him away. Said he preached evil lessons.'

The Goodwife waits. Wonders what is to come.

'Richard Prigmore his name, the preacher. He preached of a Pelagus – not an English name, but this Prigmore said,' she pauses. 'Richard Prigmore said this Pelagus was English. Born an English woman she went to the Bible land, lived in a cave as a man and preached that ...' the Widow pauses again.

'As a man?' the Goodwife says, then realises she has interupted something – what? – important to her friend. She urges the Widow to continue, 'Yes? This Pelagus preached what?'

'Pelagus, and this Richard Prigmore, they preached that we are not damned by the sin of Adam. That Adam's sin was his, his alone. That babes are not born with Adam's sin in them.' She stops and grimaces. 'But Thomas Dugdale said I was not to listen to Richard Prigmore and drove him away. Said he spoke nonsense.'

The Goodwife knows that her friend thinks and worries greatly about the innocence of babes. And as for a woman who chose to live as a man, the Goodwife finds this too puzzling. She has no good opinion of men, says firmly, 'I have no good opinion of men.'

The Widow shrugs, 'He or she, this Pelagus was English and has the right of it on the innocence of babes.'

'Delicate cow cumbers to pickle. Delicate cow cumbers,' Maude Wattes cries her way into the square.

'Maude Wattes,' the Goodwife says. 'She looks as heat-wilted as her cow cumbers. And her belly's even bigger.'

They do not want delicate cow cumbers, but look up encouragingly at Maude Wattes, who needs encouragement. Maude Wattes knows them well enough to understand they are not signalling that she approach to sell. No-one buys and she drags herself out past the tallow chandler and the stables.

'No business for her there. John Girling will not,' the Goodwife says.

'Robin Kerton might, his goodwife might. Many mouths to feed there. Babes,' the Widow ruminates. 'The getting of babes ...'

'Yes?' prompts the Goodwife.

'I have this from Jane-Pym Carter who has it from Hester Fenner midwife. For a man to get a child with his wife Hester Fenner has ten items of good advice. Item the first he should not hug his wife too hard nor too much. Item the second eat no late suppers. Item the third drink juice of sage. Item the fourth take red wine and toast. Item the fifth wear cool Holland-drawers. Item the sixth keep the stomach warm and the back cool. Item the seventh it does not matter whether it is done at night or morn, but best done when both have a mind to it. Item the eighth drink spiced ale and sugar–'

'Red wine and toast, and now spiced ale and sugar. All this for the husband? I hope the goodwife also has her wine and her toast and her spiced ale,' Goodwife Joan Brokefild says. 'Strong spiced ale. I prefer strong spiced ale.'

'Yes, strong, of course strong. Now Item the ninth, the wife not to go too straight-laced. That is a good one. I have never gone too straight-laced. Item the tenth, and the most important Hester Fenner midwife says, make the bed high at feet and low at head. I would not like that!'

'Philip Carter and Jane-Pym Carter, her big belly. They must follow these items very closely!' the Goodwife laughs.

'Yes,' agrees the Widow earnestly, 'they must. I knew none of this, of these items, when I got children. I listened to the goodwives. They told me that work stirs up natural heat and this breeds strong children. They said country people work hard, digest what they eat, and their children are usually strong and long-lived. I worked hard. But all my children, my babes, they died. I wish I had known of these ten items of Hester Fenner,' she pauses. Thinks. Adds in a different tone, 'Whether they be true or no, at least I would have had red wine and toast and strong spiced ale with sugar,' and she laughs a small laugh.

'An angelica nosegay,' the Goodwife is half listening, her mind returns to the plague. 'It is a good protective to have, Widow Bullen has the right of it. Jane-Pym Carter will know where they can be found.' She smiles at the thought of Jane-Pym Carter, who – unlike Widow Margaret Hazard – knows very well how to conceive and to breed strong children.

* * *

London, Thursday evening, 29 June 1665

Dusk settling in, but still too early for the bell-man, Goodwife Joan Brokefild smokes out her pipe in the church square, spits. She has fed Isaac Brokefild: feeding a dog – he wolfs down food like a starved street cur. Then he goes to get drunk at the *Black Bull*, calling, as he always does, to neighbour William Malaber the drayman, 'Going to pluck a hair from the same wolf as last night,' and raises an imaginary pot to his lips. 'Will you?'

This first said on a day three years before when sour, pinched Isaac Brokefild takes real pleasure in William Malaber's new arrival as neighbour. 'William Malaber! We were together, fought together for the City in winter 42. Dug ditches, put barricades beyond the walls, we were there to fight, won a great victory!' he tells his Goodwife. 'Militia men both of us. William Malaber the drayman!' This cheerful, even light-hearted, Isaac Brokefild is a surprise to his Goodwife. She has not seen him as such for – she cannot remember. A long time, a livelong time.

'William Malaber a drayman, you and him together for Parliament, for Oliver,' she says with matching cheer. 'Then William Malaber must know Colonel Thomas Pride the drayman?'

Isaac Brokefild's good humour turns rancid in a blink. 'How would William Malaber know Colonel Pride you fool woman?' he rages. 'Know someone like Colonel Pride? How would he? How would we? We were militia men, trained band men, fighting for the City, for Parliament! We were together in the Orange Regiment. We didn't drink with colonels!' He barges out to go and fight, once more, the battle of Turnham Green with William Malaber, this time at *Ringstead's Star*. Shouting over his shoulder, 'London would have been lost to the king if not for us! Think on that you stupid woman!' She does not say that it is no longer the year 42 and London *is* lost to a king, and has been so for the last five years.

Why he should be so raging, she does not know, but that is the man, that is Isaac Brokefild. Again she tells herself she must never ask him anything, never talk to him civilly. It is useless. He is useless. She does not mind mild William Malaber, a quiet, modest man, but there is no point in saying this to Isaac Brokefild, he will take it in any wrong way. When frowning, begrudging Isaac Brokefild is elsewhere William the drayman will give her a small neighbourly smile.

Lightened by his absence, the Goodwife ponders another pipe, taps a tune with her wand, *Cuckolds all a-row*. Two or three years ago was it? It was at Christmas time, perhaps in 62, or 63, yes 63, when Walter Hall told Gilbert Swaile of a great Ball at Whitehall. The king himself called for a country dance, a particular dance, and this was *Cuckolds all a-row*. Gilbert Swaile listened in silence, only later unbuttoning himself to Ingram Hall – Ingram a Hall, but, unlike his brothers, never a man for the king.

'This Charles,' Gilbert Swaile had said to Ingram Hall with heat, 'This Charles, he chose this song at his ball to mock us all. This song his men sang during the late wars, a favourite to jeer Parliament London. Cuckolds they called us. Us cuckolds! Us! This Charles he has a court of cuckolds, a cuckoo's nest of a court, and the cuckoo wears the crown. All those cuckolds at court, were they so without shame, so without honour, that would they stand up and dance this dance? Roger Palmer, the greatest cuckold of them all, Edward Greene, Francis Boyle, Robert Carnegie? They are the cuckolds all a row!'

The Goodwife unobtrusively eavesdropping, knowing old women are invisible, paid close attention. Repeated it all later to the Widow, who grimly shook head and hand at the court's wickedness: Gilbert Swaile had the right of it. The Goodwife agrees, but now, in the year 65, sitting at rest, tapping the tune with her wand, she cannot stop the silly, merry words taking temporary lodging in her head:

> *And when they come to Cuckolds Point they make a gallant show,*
> *Their wives bid the Musick play Cuckolds all a-row.*

Her feet join in.

She stretches her legs, sees Jack the footboy come from the lane behind the rectory. No Jemmy Pooly with him, but perhaps they will meet near one of the hot-houses: red-bricked Queen Elizabeth bath, or blue-tiled Longacre? She will find out. It is neither.

It is a night for noise. And singing. The Goodwife follows Jack past the *Three Cups*, the *Mermaid*, the *Cock*, each a growing burst of loud cheer and merriment that peaks then fades until replaced by the next, but Jack does not stop at them. He makes his careful way to the *White Hind*. This pleases the Goodwife, who knows a comfortable niche where she can settle and listen to the singing.

'Here's Jack! Young Jack, welcome, young Jack!' Frances Barrow says in a voice already cheered and bleared by ale. 'Come to join the ancient men, the old troopers gathering at a time of good news! To drink to it! Great news!'

Jack says something but the Goodwife cannot make out what, his words lost in the hubbub of drinking talking men.

She can hear herself relating all this to the Widow tomorrow, and also hears the Widow's unexpected questions: What cooking smells came from the *White Hind*? Were those men all wearing the Blue of reform? Did the old troopers come from London or beyond? (She can already answer the last: some from beyond, and some from London, in which case the Widow will ask Which parts of London?)

'A drink for young Jack!' the Warden calls. There is an inflamed, almost frenzied sound in his voice. The Goodwife would propose the juice of beets squirted up his nostrils, excellent for purging and cleansing the head. Followed by a drink of posset ale boiled with lettuce to bring him back to a temperate mildness. But she can hear that he is already doing vigorous work on the ale.

'Jack is footboy to Dearly Beloved–' this greeted with cheers and laughter, '–footboy to Dearly Beloved, but a boy that knows and stands with the Good Old Cause though footboy to Walter Hall our dear brother here departed.'

Jack's allegiance is news to the Goodwife and she wonders if it is also news to Jack. She has seen no sign that he is a political lad. She cannot hear any words, any response from Jack and wishes she could see his face, see them all.

'A toast to our dearly beloved brother here departed. To Walter Hall!' calls Frances Barrow.

'To dearly departed Walter Hall!' many voices shout.

'Jack! Here are some old troopers, some of my dearly beloved brothers, and not departed at all but still with us,' this cheered loudly. 'Name, names of Anthony Erlam, Thomas Trew, Erasmus Bacockie – many Bacockies in the Eastern Association Army!'

'Too many!' says a new voice, to laughter.

'Zachery Waite of Colonel Fleetwood's regiment of horse.'

'Present!' says a loud voice with the sound of Frances Barrow, likely a countryman of his.

'And Nathaniel Hale a trooper with the Protector's own regiment. And here is a good London man – there are some! – John Barriffe, a militia man volunteer of the Private and Loving Society of Cripplegate.'

The Goodwife hears a loud rumbling of old man voices greet Jack.

'Jack these are new faces to you. Here is a familiar face, one you know well.'

The name that belongs to the familiar face, if it was said, is lost in tavern noise. The Goodwife strains to hear but does not catch it. She urges this familiar one to talk so she can match the voice to a name.

'What a time this is!' says one of the new voices. A London voice, John Barriffe? 'What a time! What a day, what a time! The papist whoremaster Charles the Bastard fled. His Roman queen fled with him. His scoundrel court gone too. Your dearly beloved, Frances Barrow, your Walter Hall, him too. We, we saints, we will have the city again. Our England again!'

This must be Cripplegate John Barriffe of the Private and Loving Society. Goodwife Joan Brokefild wonders about a Society with such a name, such a fine name.

'Remember,' says John Barriffe, 'remember the statue at the Great

Exchange, remember what was written there when this statue of Charles Stuart the tyrant was torn down? The head knocked off? I remember the writing: Exit tyrannus, regum ultimus, anno libertatis Angliae, anno Domini 1649, Januarie xxx!'

There is a tipsy chant of 'Libertatis Angliae! Libertatis Angliae!'

Over the drinking noise the Goodwife can suddenly hear the voices of Frances Barrow and Jack the footboy, as if they have found a quiet corner to speak near where she is concealed.

'Philip Carter the Parish Clerk,' says Warden Barrow. 'Did you tell him there would be a gathering of friends here at the *Hind* tonight?'

'Yes I did and he wished all well but said he would not be here,' Jack replies.

'Rather be at home, at night, with his Jane-Pym Carter. A wife-bound man our Clerk. Has his own Private and Loving Society,' Frances Barrow says, and roars at his own wit.

If Jack replies Goodwife Brokefild cannot hear it.

'A song! A song! The *Zealous Soldier*! All of us here, all of us, zealous soldiers in the Good Old Cause!

> *For God, and for his cause, I'll count it gain*
> *To lose my life. Oh can one happier die*
> *Than for to fall in battle to maintain*
> *God's worship, truth, extirpate Popery?*
> *I fight not for to venge my self, nor yet*
> *For coin, but God's true worship up to set.*

The company shouts its way through verse upon verse. Loud, triumphant.

'Let me, let me say by rote–'

'Hear Erasmus Bacockie, hear him!' other voices say.

'Let me say by rote what was printed of us in the year 43, printed in, it was printed in the – it will come to me. It said: "Colonel Cromwell has 2,000 brave men, well disciplined. No man swears but he pays his twelve pence–"'

'So many twelve pence paid!' someone says to great laughter.

'Yes! Many pence! The *Special Passages Gazette*, that is it. It was printed in the *Special Passages Gazette*. "He pays his twelve pence; if he be drunk he is set in the stocks, or worse," more cheers. "If one calls the other Roundhead he is cashiered." I can recall it all perfectly by rote!'

The company is helpless with mirth, the word Roundhead flung back and forth. There is a loud crash of a table, a bench, overturned, pots clattering to the floor, and still more laughter.

'The stocks for you Anthony Erlam!'

'Or worse!'

'Yes worse for Anthony Erlam, who himself is worse for drink. Can't stand upright and even the table won't hold him up, won't support him. Put the table in the stocks too!'

'Or worse!'

'Stash,' Anthony Erlam slurs, tries again. 'Statues. Another one of him – how many damned statues are there of that damned king? How many? There was a statue, bronze statue – I know metal, I know bronze, of course I know bronze! – on a horse. King on a horse. Parliament, *our* Parliament, ordered it broke. Good! But some metalsmith had his hands on it, has it – I know all the metalsmiths in London – it is Holborn man John River. Rivet. He has it. Liar Rivet! Told Parliament he'd done their orders, destroyed it. And here's the joke! Showed Parliament some broken pieces of brass, brass! And that Parliament knew bugger all of metal, nothing. It believed him! Brass is copper and zinc. Bronze is copper and tin. Any fool knows that.' Anthony Erlam pauses, peers at the floor looking for his pot.

'I heard–'

'Let me finish. I haven't finished!' Anthony Erlam says sharply. 'This Rivet, he dodn't, didn't break the statue. Well, he did, but he buried the pieces, now he's dug them up and will sell the thing to the highest bidder. King's party wants to set it up in the city. Charing Cross. Wants to bring it back!'

'What I want to bring back, and now we can, now this tyrant has exited,' says Frances Barrow loudly, firmly, 'is bring back all our good men, our saints who went out in the Great Ejection. Bring them all back. Thomas Dugdale to St Cyneswide and St Tibba, we petitioned that he be kept. He wasn't. Same for Robert Bragge at all Hallows the Great – congregation asked he be kept. He wasn't. And at St Giles Cripplegate, John Barriffe, your Samuel Annesley, a preacher supported by Oliver himself, ejected–'

'And John Dolbin, royalist *Major* John Dolbin brought in,' says John Barriffe in bitterness.

'Every good man, every saint, who was driven out, will come in again!' exults Frances Barrow.

'That brother of yours,' says Zachery Waite, 'Colonel Robert Barrow. Anything heard of him? Will he come in to England? Come back? Any news of him? A good Fleetwood man, your brother. After the arrest warrants went out for him – so many warrants in 63! For him, Captain Elton, Colonel Danvers, James Hill, William Pryor, who else? Nathaniel Strange, and the Quartermaster-General himself, John Vernon. So many warrants! Got away to the Low Country did he, did Colonel Barrow? It's said he did, with many others.'

A brother to the Church Warden is interesting news to Goodwife Joan Brokefild. This is the first she has heard of it. If Charles Barrow answers Zachery Waite his words are drowned out by the *White Hind's* loud hubbub.

There are calls for more ale, 'Pot boy! Pot boy here!' More furniture is moved roughly, scraped across the floor, there is the sound of men copiously easing themselves into chamber pots. One stands at the door, pisses into the street. The Goodwife can see that this is not Frances Barrow, nor Jack the footboy.

Instead, she clearly hears the Warden's voice close by once again. And with him another voice she knows. Now she realises this is the one who, Frances Barrow said, Jack will know well. It is William Sutterwhit, neighbour of the family Barrett, now all dead. William Sutterwhit, who has a short right leg. Jane-Pym Carter, confident in sailor talk, says he has a list to Starboard, calls him Starboard Sutterwhit.

'Tell me, William Sutterwhit,' says Frances Barrow, his voice loose with drink. 'Tell me, in St Cyneswide and St Tibba, how many for us, how many against us?'

William Sutterwhit says quietly, confidently, not sounding much affected by ale, 'As I see it now, today, it is half by half.'

'Yes,' says Frances Barrow, 'I see it the same.'

'But our half,' adds William Sutterwhit, 'our half are thinning as time passes. In the year 60, even year 61, we were well more than half, much more – almost all the parish for reform then.'

'Who do you say are ours? I can list who, but I wonder if you see it the same. Who do you think? Those who would have Thomas Dugdale back?'

They lay out names and the Goodwife does the same in her head.

'Gilbert Swaile is still with us,' says Frances Barrow. 'Samuel Snow goes with whoever sits in Why-toll Palace, with whoever wears the Lord Mayor's chain in Guildhall.'

'Constables,' William Sutterwhit says, 'they do. Robin Kerton is one of us. John Girling one of them.'

'Yes, yes. William Pickhering, still with us. Edward Richbell, I'm not sure. Harry Bosvill never one of us. I never trusted him.'

They work they way through the parish of St Cyneswide and St Tibba. But not all the parish. The Goodwife listens closely. She hears no woman mentioned, no names of women are listed. None. The support, or not, of women is not worth considering or saying.

'You the cabal in the corner, you two plotters! Come back with us! Your pots are empty!' John Barriffe shouts.

'This plague, the new Bills say, they say this plague–'

'No talk of plague here! We won't have such talk here!' Erasmus Bacockie is shouted down.

But this brings a great cloudburst of weeping from Erasmus Bacockie, 'I must draw my Will! So must we all! The town has grown so unhealthy a man cannot depend upon living two days to an end!'

'A song! What we all must have is another song!'

'Erasmus! Sing first, then make your Will, but sing first!'

There is a loud agreement. 'Sing first! Thomas Trew, name us a song!'

'There is only one song, for such as we on such a night. Only one. *The trooper watering his nag!'*

More lound cries, 'Yes! *The trooper waters his nag!* You know this one Erasmus Bacockie! Sing!'

'Jack!' calls Frances Barrow, '*You* won't know this one but come in on the chorus, an easy chorus.'

The Goodwife listens closely to the verses. They are not hard to hear, they are sung very loudly. It is a song of trooper who comes to an old woman's inn for drink and lodging. She has a daughter named Siss, and the trooper drinks off his pot, calls for another, and kisses Siss in front of her mother. The Goodwife can hear Jack doing well with the chorus.

> *And when night came on, to bed they went.*
> *Sing tolley, lolly, lolly, lolly, lo!*
> *It was with the mother's own consent.*
> *Ho, ho! Was it so? Was it so? Was it so?*
> *Quoth she: What is this so stiff and warm?*
> *Sing tolley, lolly, lolly, lolly, lo!*
> *'Tis Ball, my nag! He will do you no harm!*
> *Ho, ho! Won't he so? Won't he so? Won't he so?*
> *But what is this that hangs under his chin?*
> *Sing tolley, lolly, lolly, lolly, lo!*
> *'Tis the bag he puts his provender in!*
> *Ho, ho! Is it so? Is it so? Is it so?*
> *Quoth he: What is this? Quoth she: 'Tis a well,*
> *Sing tolley, lolly, lolly, lolly, lo!*
> *Where Ball your nag may drink his fill!*
> *Ho, ho! May he so? May he so? May he so?*
> *But what if my nag should chance to slip in?*
> *Sing tolley, lolly, lolly, lolly, lo!*
> *Then catch hold of the grass that grows on the brim!*
> *Ho, ho! Must I so? Must I so? Must I so?*
> *But what if the grass should chance to fail?*
> *Sing tolley, lolly, lolly, lolly, lo!*
> *Shove him in by the head! Pull him out by the tail!*
> *Ho, ho! Must I so? Must I so? Must I so?*

CHAPTER XIII

London, Saturday morning, 1 July 1665

'Sit and sing, and call a spring!
O-U-T spells out! Out! Out! Out!'

'Soon there will be no-one left to flee from our red wands,' Widow Margaret Hazard gestures with her wand at the unpeopled street.

'Listen! Can you hear that?' Goodwife Joan Brokefild asks.

'What? Hear what?' Widow Hazard swivels her head, her good ear searching for a strange sound. 'Hear what? What am I listening for? I can't hear it, what is it?'

'There is no sound. Just quiet. No noise.' Somewhere, off in the distance, a dog barks. 'Almost no noise.'

'Mmm. So,' the Widow is annoyed, 'so I am listening to hear nothing? Is this what you are telling me to listen for? Nothing?'

The Goodwife shrugs, delves into her pocket. 'Here. I don't mean listen, I mean *here* is an angelica nosegay, and one for Sara. Jane-Pym Carter has angelica. She gets such things from her midwife friend Hester Fenner. One for you, one for Sara, one for me.' She laughs. 'I did not get one for Isaac Brokefild. Take off your hat.' She lifts the leather-strung angelica root over the Widow's close cropped head. 'There.'

'No. No you would not get one for Isaac Brokefild. Nor would I.' The Widow feels for her purse. 'How much?'

'To pay for them? You to pay me for them? Is that what you mean?'

'Yes. How much.'

'Nothing.'

'Nothing? They cost you nothing? Jane-Pym Carter charged you nothing for the nosegays?'

Goodwife Joan Brokefild replies slowly, with oppressive firmness. 'They. Did. Not. Cost. Nothing. I bought them, paid for them. Not a great deal. These two are a gift. To you and Sara.' She pauses, breaths deeply, says in measured tones, 'A gift because of the friendship between us.'

'Yes, of course we are friends. How much did they cost?' Still feeling in her pocket.

The Widow looks up expectantly for an answer. She does not get one. The Goodwife's face is closed. Blank.

'Mmm. Good strong stink,' the Widow says, holding the nosegays close under her good nostril. Good. An excellent preservative, such a stench.' Adds uncomfortably. 'Mmm, my thanks, and my thanks for Sara too. She will thank you herself of course. She will thank you. She will take close note of this leather cord. She has a skill with strings and ribbons.'

Goodwife Joan Brokefild relaxes, smiles. Accepts that this is the best her friend can do. 'Jane-Pym Carter wishes you, wishes Sara, wishes me, wishes us all health. "Hale and hearty!" she said. "Safe and sound!" she said. That is Jane-Pym Carter for you.'

The Widow nods. 'Yes. She would say that. A loud, cheerful woman Jane-Pym Carter. Not like her Philip Carter who can be loud angry but not often loud cheerful. Although they fit well together.'

'Yes, fit well together, both Home-To-Bed together,' the Goodwife laughs.

'I can hear noises now,' Widow Hazard says.

There is shouting and banging from Ram Alley to their right, and then a familiar voice behind them announces the coming of the Constable. 'Constable here! All to know the Constable is here!'

It is Samuel Snow himself heralding his approach. The ancient women turn to see the Constable moving at a good trot accompanied by outliers of parish messenger boys brandishing their black rods and greatly enjoying themselves, baying like hunting hounds.

'Constable! Constable! Here in Ram Alley! Here! We saw them here!' the boys' voices call back. The hunting party wheels into Ram Alley.

The Searchers, down where they are meant to be, by the channel, are ignored. They follow the party to the mouth of Ram Alley and see two men, half on the cobbles, half on the steps to a door, pummelling each other. Thomas Billington, the bigger man, pounds his fist into Robert Tomlinson's chest, his face, punctuating his blows with abuse.

'You filthy windfucker! Always slandering me, you slanderer. Man of lies! I never was wed to Jennet Bladwell, never promised to wed her, never bedded her – who would want to bed her! – so Stop. Your. Lies!' Each word accompanied by a blow. 'You Sectary!'

'Fight! Fight!' the messenger boys cry and a small crowd is conjured up from vacant streets and lanes, fills narrow Ram Alley.

Robert Tomlinson stretches an arm, his fingers scrabbling for any loose cobble he can smash into Thomas Billington. Constable Samuel Snow stomps a heavy foot on his grasping hand.

'Stop! And you Thomas Billington, you stop!' Shouts the Constable. 'Both stop! Watchmen brawling like – like–' not waiting for a suitable comparison to come to mind, Constable Samuel Snow uses his staff to try to wrench the two apart. When this fails he shoves the staff end into those privities of Thomas Billington that, he says, are unknown to Jennet Bladwell's. Thomas Billington cries out and falls back, nursing his pain and cursing Samuel Snow and Robert Tomlinson.

'Like sailors on shore who've, who've taken too many a cup. Like sailors.' Samuel Snow is pleased to have found words that suit. 'Sailors. The pillory for both of you. Watchmen fighting in the street like sailors.' He pauses to think, rolls his staff between his hands. 'The pillory. This sickness. It would be the pillory, of course it would be, should be, but with this sickness what good would you be in the pillory, two of you, when we need plague houses watched? No good plague service can be done in the pillory.' He sounds uncertain.

He pauses once more, says, 'Vestry. Vestry meeting tomorrow. Vestry shall decide what is best done.'

'Then Vestry will hear of you Samuel Snow and you Robert Tomlinson as, as oath-breakers and Sectaries, and all those others in St Cyneswide and

St Tibba who are oath-breakers and Sectaries, who said the oath in 63 but did not *take* the oath. Not take it truthfully. Spoke empty words,' Thomas Billington shouts.

There is an unsettled rumbling in the crowd. Such things should not be said out loud. Strong views, differing views, should be kept out of the streets, out of the squares, only aired behind doors in like-minded company. How else can they live together? There are those who willingly conform to the Liturgy of the Church of England as it is now by Law established, and those who do not. And both parties live close in St Cyneswide and St Tibba, in the city of London, and beyond.

Samuel Snow is outraged. He remembers well the Good Old Cause and, if it had not become the Old, would still be part of it. But it *is* now the Old Cause and he has accepted the new order, which – as he thinks and sometimes says to his family – is just another old order made new again in the year 60. Samuel Snow has taken the Oath and will not have it challenged. He does not want to lose his position, or worse. He will not have his, his dutifulness, that is the word, his dutifulness put to question. This time of sickness unsettles all.

'Beggars! Samuel Snow, beggars!' the Widow shouts down Ram Alley. This startles all. Goodwife Joan Brokefild, who will not watch faces and bodies being bruised and battered, finds her mind turned to Home-To-Bed Philip Carter and Home-To-Bed Jane-Pym Carter. Why? Perhaps Thomas Billington speaking of not bedding Jennet Bladwell? She thinks of a small, lewd verse in her salvaged book:

> *Julia and I did lately sit*
> *Playing for sport, at Cherry-pit:*
> *She threw; I cast; and having thrown,*
> *I got the Pit, and she the Stone.*

Her quiet amusement at this word-cleverness is broken into by the Widow's loud cries.

'Beggars! Samuel Snow, beggars!'

Having closed, for the present, the disturbance of Thomas Billington and Robert Tomlinson – he vigorously shakes his staff at them and repeats 'Vestry tomorrow!' – the Constable turns and runs. The Widow is pointing down Rose Street. The Constable and the boys are glad to be on the chase again. They can see just the coat ends of a man and a woman and hear the excited barking of beggar dogs. Their escaping quarry turn down an alley off Rose Street.

'That was well done,' the Goodwife says. 'A good diversion to distract them from all that foolish talk of Sectaries and oath-breaking. To stop all that. It was well done.'

'No,' says the Widow, bemused by her friend's comment, 'I did not do it for that. That was not my purpose. The new Orders, from the Lord Mayor, order that Constables do take special care that no wandering beggar be suffered in the streets of this City, being a great cause of the spreading of the infection. The Orders say that. These two, just gone now out of Rose Street, are wandering beggars. That is why I called to Constable Samuel Snow.'

'That is why you did it. I see that now,' the Goodwife says neutrally. She would not do such a thing, but the Widow sees matters differently.

They leave the channel to make way for a passing cart carrying a small load of chests, two ancient women with blank, stony faces, a mother with a sucking infant, and a train of men, women and children following beside and behind. The children chatter and skip and ask if they are still in London. They are the only ones who look at the Searchers and their red wands until their parents growl, 'You stay away from them. Don't go near them.'

The cart passed, the Searchers walk back to the channel. 'Not many carts on the streets now,' the Goodwife says.

'I must smoke a pipe and sit,' Widow Margaret Hazard grimaces. 'And water. I need water, or something.'

'To take water in or let it out?' asks the Goodwife.

'Both.'

'And somewhere quiet, and shaded,' says the Widow almost petulantly. The heat is oppressive.

'I know the place. Quiet, dark, cool. It is close by. You ease yourself and I will find some small beer and we will go there.'

The Widow is more than ready to be annoyed when the Goodwife leads them up stairs to the ancient women's room, but it is quiet, cool, restful. They sit on the bales of cloth, drink their beer, smoke their pipes. And the Goodwife has bespoke half a roast fowl, brought to them by a boy who stops uneasily at the door of the ancient women's room and will not enter.

'More surgeons and physicians fleeing,' the Goodwife says, leaning back comfortably. 'Not just from St Thomas' Hospital, now four more have gone, these from St Bartholomews. But – hear this – the Matron there, Matron Blague, *she* has stayed. And some surgeon I don't know who, only one, all the others have fled.'

The Widow snorts in disgust. 'All fleeing, physicians and surgeons. King's doctors, Timothy Clarke, John Knight, fled the town with all the other cowards at Court. Now what does *she* want?'

'You are here? You are here.' Goody Susanna Parsons, who has also found her way to the ancient women's room, is puzzled.

The Goodwife answers quickly before the Widow can make some harsh response. 'Yes, seeking and finding a place to sit. A cool place. We are here.'

'Yes,' says Goody Parsons, 'so am I.' She still stands, silent, with a worried, furrowed brow.

'Sit down, rest,' the Goodwife invites. 'Smoke.'

There is an uncomfortable silence. The Widow glaring resentfully at Goody Susanna Parsons' red wand.

'Clerk Carter.' Goody Parsons stops. Starts again. 'Parish Clerk Philip Carter sent me to find you. To tell you, to ask you. This is the last place I have looked.'

'To tell us what?' asks Widow Margaret Hazard.

'To ask us what?' says Goodwife Joan Brokefild.

'Widow Ursula Chaukley.' Goody Parsons stops once more.

'Yes?' prompts the Goodwife. 'Yes? What of Widow Chaukley?'

'Widow Chaukley has shut herself in! Her and her whole family. Shut herself in. The infection, the plague has taken them. They have the signs and she has shut herself in. There is the red cross and the God Have Mercy on the door.'

The Searchers are shocked. 'She, they, are in God's hands now,' the Widow says. 'May He have mercy and protect them and bring them safe.'

'We have not seen her since the hogs.'

'Two days ago.'

'Yes,' sobs Goody Parsons. 'She told me through the door, just now she told me – she would not let me in, and I am a Keeper! – she told me that it was on that day she saw some signs, she was not sure, but today she is sure. At first light this morning she passed word to the Clerk and so had herself, her family, her large family, shut in with the red cross.'

'In God's keeping,' the Goodwife echoes the Widow.

'What is it Philip Carter is asking of us?' the Widow wants to know.

'He wants to know who you, we, who we would want made Viewer to take Widow Ursula Chaukley's place. The Vestry, of course Vestry will decide. But who do you–?'

'Beatrix Sutterwhit,' the Goodwife says.

'Mmm. Viewer? Too low a job for her,' the Widow says.

Goody Parson looks taken aback that anyone might think a Viewer, or a Keeper, or even a corpse-searching Searcher, a low occupation.

'She has a quick eye, a sharp mind,' the Goodwife defends her choice.

'A sharp tongue too. Cutting' the Widow returns. 'Widow Lankester will make a good Viewer.'

'Another even sharper tongue. A hard woman, Widow Lankester,' Goody Parsons says, and wonders about Anne Abowen and Widow Lankester yoked together as Viewers. Two stubborn, head-strong oxen pulling in different directions.

'Who is not? And why should we not be hard?' Widow Margaret Hazard asks belligerently.

Only a little cowed, Goody Parsons offers, 'Mabell Billington. Perhaps?'

This meets with shrugs, and no more names are put forward. They sit and smoke.

'We should go,' Goody Parsons finally says, but makes no move to do so. 'Philip Carter wants to hear what we, all of us, have to say about a new Viewer. A new Viewer for Vestry to decide on.' Goody Parsons fills herself a fresh pipe.

They sit and smoke.

'The Vestry, at the Vestry tomorrow,' Goody Susanna Parsons begins slowly. 'You know we, Anne Abowen, Widow Bullen, me, have been told we must be at the Vestry to say what we know of – of what is being said about the guineas.'

Goodwife Joan Brokefild nods, Widow Margaret Hazard glares.

'I know nothing of it,' Goody Parsons says. 'And I will say – whether asked or not – that I believe, know, you both are of honest reputation. And have always been of honest reputation.'

Goodwife Brokefild smiles, thanks her, 'That is a fine thing.'

The Widow stops glaring. Gives a surprised dip of the head, but still asks, 'Will the others say the same? Even Anne Abowen?'

'None of us has reason to tell lies about you Searchers. And you do not – none of us do – show signs of any extra shillings, extra guineas, to make our houses richer, our clothes finer, our diet more voluptuous. We none of us take bribes.'

'No,' says Widow Hazard, 'We. Do. Not.'

Goody Parsons weeps again, 'Widow Chaukley – poor Widow Chaukley! – she would say the same if she were not shut in.'

'Yes,' Widow Hazard says, 'she would.'

'There is a story,' Goody Parsons says after a long pause.

'Tell it.'

'I heard this of Alderman Bence. At night in the street he fell over a plague corpse–'

'How is that possible?' the Widow is outraged. 'Fell over a corpse? He did not see it? Where was his link boy? How could he not see a corpse? And he an Alderman!'

Goody Parsons and Goodwife Brokefild wait patiently for this to pass.

'I do not know where his link boy was. The story does not mention a link boy. But the story continues that when Alderman Bence goes home and tells his wife of the corpse – his wife who is with child – takes fright, falls sick, and dies of the plague. Falls sick and dies of the plague. That is the story.'

The Widow says, 'There are many ways the infection will take hold. What became of the child? Was it removed from her? Does it live?'

Goody Parsons sees her story escaping from her. 'I don't know what became of the child. That was not part of the story I heard. But Alderman Bence, his wife, she died from fright of the plague! That is the thing!' Goody Parsons sobs, 'It was those hogs! For poor Widow Chaukley it was those hogs that made her take fright and caused the plague to come into her.'

The plague.

The Goodwife adjusts her angelica nosegay, turning it into a more prominent, protective position. The Widow follows suit.

'Ah! Angelica nosegays!' exclaims Goody Parsons. 'That is what I can smell.'

'From Goodwife Brokefild, from Jane-Pym Carter, from midwife Hester Fenner,' the Widow generously answers Goody Parsons' unspoken question.

Goody Parsons nods her thanks. 'From Jane-Pym Carter.' She counts on her fingers how many nosegays she will need for her family.

'This new Viewer,' Goodwife Brokefild must return to the subject.

'Isabella Undnay,' the Widow states.

'Do you mean it? Isabella Undnay?' Goody Parsons asks. 'Do you mean it?'

'No,' Widow Hazard answers.

At this there is a pleasant community of mirth, of scorn, for Isabella Undnay who has no understanding of what Searchers do, Keepers do, Viewers do.

They file down the treacherous steps and are met in the street by an unruly game of Hot Cockles. Jemmy Pooly is bent forward with his head against the wall, eyes closed. The street boys take turns to slap his buttocks as hard as they can, crying Hot Cockles with great hilarity.

'Thomas Snow!' calls Jemmy Pooly.

'No!'

'Jack Green!'

'No!'

'Dan Stiles!'

'No!'

'Harry Shute!'

'Yes!'

Jemmy Pooly breaks away, chases the fleeing, roaring, Harry Shute. The boys' chant goes up.

> *The wind blows east, the wind blows west,*
> *The wind blows o'er the cuckoo's nest.*
> *Where is this poor man to go?*
> *Over yonder cuckoo's hill Hi Ho!*

The ancient women stay, watching.

'Stupid boys.' 'Foolish boys.' Widow Margaret Hazard and Goody Susanna Parsons agree.

Goodwife Joan Brokefild laughs.

The boys take no notice. Harry Shute is caught:

> *Elder belder, limber lock,*
> *Three wives in a clock! [laughter, pointing at the three ancient*
> *   women]*
> *Sit and sing, and call a spring!*
> *O-U-T spells out! Out! Out! Out!*

To her companions' surprise, Goody Parsons says mildly, 'That game is a Yorkshire funeral game. Played at funerals.'

'Slapping boys on the arse at funerals?' the Widow asks in disbelief. 'I have never seen that!'

'Were you ever in Yorkshire?' Goody Parsons asks in apparent innocence.

'Yorkshire? Never! Never beyond London.'

'I would like to see that. At a funeral,' the Goodwife says.

'Women may not go to funerals in Yorkshire,' says Goody Parsons.

'Women may not go? May not go?' the Widow does not believe it. 'I would go, Yorkshire or anywhere.'

Goodwife Joan Brokefild wonders if mild Goody Parsons might not be deliberately teasing, provoking the Widow.

'Now, today in London, you cannot go. The new Orders start today, and you can not. The new Orders say that no Neighbours nor Friends be suffered to accompany the Corpse to Church,' Goody Parsons quotes. (She *is* doing it deliberately, the Goodwife thinks.)

'Yes,' replies the Widow argumentatively. 'Yes, but at the burial, the burial itself, no *children* – the Order only says no *children* – be suffered at the time of burial to come near the Corpse. I am no child.'

The others do not respond. This game has run its course. If the Widow wants to be present at a burial the Orders do not prevent her.

Tomorrow's looming Vestry meeting has her, them all, unsettled.

'Three wives in a clock!' the Goodwife laughs. 'Funerals and a clock. Listen–'

'Goodwife Brokefild has good verses,' the Widow says proudly to Goody Parsons, 'Listen. Hear her!'

> *Whatever comes, let's be content withall:*
> *Among Gods Blessings, there is no one small.*

While the Goodwife versifies a dark headed boy, broad chest, strong arms, comes to talk to Jack Green.

'Not of this parish,' the Goodwife says, gesturing as the two lads walk away.

'Mmm. No, that boy, he is not from here.'

Jack turns to his friends, who are still slapping arses, and calls in Walter Hall's voice, 'Dearly Beloved, urgent business t'day et the Wheat Horll summons me hence. I end this young man air t' go thither end dine on a mess, a great mess, a noble mess, ef Porridge.'

This is greeted with loud cries and laughter from the boys, 'Porridge! Porridge!' Even the ancient women smile.

Then Goody Parsons, her mind fixed on 'three wives in a clock. Out! Out! Out!' laments, 'Poor poor Widow Chaukley! This plague is stopping many watches long before their time is out.'

Verses run through the Goodwife's head, join hands, link up: 'His watch is down; His pipe is out.'

The Widow carefully spells O-U-T to herself: sees the reading book's pictures as she does so: O is the Oak; U is Uriah's beauteous wife; T is Time cutting down all with its scythe.

The only watch Goody Parsons has seen is that of brewer Gilbert Swaile. It is a neat Puritan watch that sits handsomely in a silver case. When new bought, she and the parish caught many glimpses of it as Gilbert Swaile often consulted it, held it high in church to see what o'clock it was.

* * *

London, Saturday night, 1 July 1665

In bed Jane-Pym Carter says to her husband, 'Tell it again.' She scissors her legs around Philip Carter's right thigh, settling both her pregnant belly and his inert legs until he and she lie comfortably. 'This Robert Thomson Billington and who else? Tell me more.'

'Robert Thomson Billington?' he sighs, mock cross. 'You know,' pinches her, 'you *know* it is Thomas Billington and Robert Tomlinson.'

'I do, do I?' She asks, all innocence. 'I know of these strange men of this strange parish do I?'

'I told you, the Constable caught them fighting like street boys.' He shakes his head, 'The street boys were there, cheering them on. It is all about – it is *still* all about – Jennet Bladwell. Years later. Still.'

'And what did Thomas Billington call Robert Tomlinson? Tell me again.'

'Ah, you remember their names now. Thomas Billington called Robert

Tomlinson a windfucker. He called him a windfucker.'

Jane-Pym Carter laughs in delight. 'There are so many windfuckers in St Cyneswide and St Tibba, but Robert Tomlinson is not the chief one.'

'No, Walter Hall is Master of that guild.'

'A *guild* of windfuckers? What is their livery?' She makes him laugh. 'You are not a member of that guild, not a windfucker, Philip Carter.'

'No, I am a Jane-Pym Carter fucker.'

'As you should be, Parish Clerk of St Cynsa and Tibbs. Your pipe in my pipe case.'

Philip Carter does not mind that she says this every time. He would miss it if she didn't.

She climbs on top of him. He has long been used to her mirth during copulation, although at first, six years ago, it had made him shrivel. Dismayed at the effect on him, she had tried, ineffectually, to stifle her giggles until, in time, and with much reassurance, he had understood that it was pleasure not mockery that made her laugh.

She knows much of venery from her good friend the midwife Hester Fenner.

She is a pupil of sorts of Hester Fenner. Jane-Pym often laughs that if she did not have so many children and expect more she would have time to be a midwife herself. 'When I am as old as Hester Fenner,' she tells Philip Carter.'

As she learns she passes on her latest knowledge to Philip Carter in bed. Each lesson to him is brief as it is always interrupted by what she now describes as 'copulation.'

'I was used to say cunt, cock, or cockerel, balls, fuck – Peter Stopford was a sailor and our room was by the docks – but Hester Fenner says these are low words and will have me say privy passage, yard, stones, and copulation.' She remembers Hester Fenner's mild reproof: 'I have heard everything, every word of all kinds, from women in childbirth. A midwife must know such words but not use them herself – or only rarely.'

Jane-Pym has told Philip Carter, taught him – 'All from Hester Fenner' she assures him – 'If the lips of a women's privy parts have much hair when they are very young then she is much given to venery.'

In answer to his unspoken question she tells him, 'As a maid I was very hairy down there. And the wings inside the lips, these give women great pleasure in copulation.' She demonstrates.

Jane-Pym's lessons with Hester Fenner have continued, and as for passing this new-gained knowledge on to Philip Carter, he is too easily diverted from theory to practice.

Tonight, as every night, Jane-Pym Carter finds her pleasure quickly, and smiling sinks down beside him. Handling her breasts he thinks that they are the finest breasts that ever he saw in his life. Says to her, 'These are the finest breasts that ever I saw in my life. That is the truth of it.'

'The right one is more swollen than the left. Feel. No, the *right* one. Hester Fenner says if it be a boy the right breast will swell more, for males lie most on the right side. And my belly – feel – especially on the right side lies rounder and more tumefied for a boy.'

'Tumefied? What sort of a word is tumefied?' He asks.

'Hester Fenner's word. One of her midwife words. Swollen in English.'

As he knows she likes him to do, he slips his finger in. Into what he had once called her thing. 'My thing? This,' – she had demonstrated – 'this is no thing.'

His finger fiddling away in finger play, he asks ruminatively, 'Tumefied? Can a privy passage be tumefied?' She is occupied, and too occupied to answer.

Her second pleasure still tingling, Jane-Pym shifts and moves again to find an easy place for her big belly. 'Hester Fenner,' she says thoughtfully, hands on her belly, 'can explain why women desire copulation even when they have already conceived.'

'Why?'

Jane-Pym frowns, 'That it is because, she says, Hester Fenner says, Adam's first sin lies heavily upon us, bringing the curse of God upon us, and inordinate lust is a great part of this curse, and the propagation of many children is an effect of this intemperance. Hester Fenner says that Hippocrate forbids a woman to use copulation after conception, but Hester

Fenner and other midwives say this would do us all, man and woman, too much wrong.'

Philip Carter nods his agreement, dismisses Hippocrate. He hears more of Hester Fenner.

'She married – her second marriage – into a family who think much of themselves and very little of her, and of most others. A Porridge family. They are fleeing the city. Have fled. His family, Thomas Fenner's family, said – Thomas Fenner he is dead a year now – they said that she was ignorant and ill-bred and they despised her because she wears her hat! Yet she knows more of generation and childbirth than anyone! She is an excellent midwife.

'Ignorant and ill-bred! They would despise me, you, everyone in St Cyneswide and St Tibba as ignorant and ill-bred. Thomas Fenner was not like that. It was only his family, his connections, who think too highly of themselves says Hester Fenner. She has four children from cordwainer William Ayres, none from Thomas Fenner, but her big daughter will not be a midwife. From Thomas Fenner, his death, Hester Fenner had £300.'

With tomorrow's Vestry looming Philp Carter's thoughts have drifted. 'For wearing a hat? A hat? My Searchers wear hats. Hats. This Vestry tomorrow. All of a muddle now.'

'What is all of a muddle? What is?'

'Tomorrow's Vestry meeting. It was to be an easy matter of hearing these false accusations against my Searchers – no-one with information in support. Discussed and dismissed for no evidence, just rumours. Then turn to the serious matter of getting Thomas Dugdale back now Dearly Beloved has fled. That was how I thought it would run.'

'And it won't?'

'No, it won't. Now we have these brawling Watchmen and there is to be a new Viewer.'

'I heard of poor Widow Ursula Chaukley. Shut herself and her family in. What a good woman to do so!'

'It is hard enough to get a Vestry to meet in these times. People sick, dead, fleeing. Who knows when the next will be? I want all this business done and now there is more business to do.'

'Will your Thomas Dugdale come in?'

'God willing he will. If Vestry will call him back. I pray they will. And now a new Viewer needed.' He snorts, 'I asked for some names. Some promising names I was given, I don't think. Beatrix Sutterwhit, Mabell Billington–'

'Wife of Thomas the brawler.'

Yes. Widow Lankester, even Isabella Undnay!'

She yawns, 'It is a deal of do. You must not have Isabella Undnay. What you must do is consult your pillow.'

'Then my pillow will have to work hard tonight. Not just a new Viewer. What will be if the worst happens and Vestry finds against one, or both, of my Searchers? How will I get new Searchers in a time of plague? Who would be a Searcher, having to search plague corpses? Plague houses? Infected corpse after infected corpse? It is getting worse. How many ancient women are there in the parish willing to do that?'

Jane-Pym Carter hears none of this lament. She has, as she does, fallen abruptly into a deep sleep. Lying on her back, she snores. Philip Carter lies awake.

CHAPTER XIV

'Be of good courage, all ye just.'

'Today is Sunday, Lord's day! Lord's day!'

Within the parish church of St Cyneswide and St Tibba this Lord's day is an ill-tempered, ragged, restless day.

'Things are not going well with them,' Church Warden Frances Barrow remarks to Parish Clerk Philip Carter, waving an embracing arm over the congregation. 'Full of discontent.'

'Many things to ail them,' the Clerk replies.

'He has not left! Our sovereign King has not fled! He would not flee! Brave as a lion!' David Smoote argues stridently with George Hillcocke.

'Ha! Of course he has. Fled with all his wives and whores and lords. Carried our Dearly Beloved with him. Fled the plague, fled London, fled Londoners. All the coaches and carts and waggons are gone from Why-toll. Gone David Smoote. There's your lion. Where's your lion? Gone. A brave beast? Ha! A belly crawling cur!'

'They are always in disagreement, always,' says a peeved Eppie Smoote who sits with her friend Beatrix Sutterwhit a good distance from husband David Smoote. 'About anything. If bufflehead Walter Shute were to make a mistake and say today is Monday, or even Tuesday – do you notice he never does make a mistake? He always gets the day right even if everything else is wrong in his head – if the bufflehead were to say today is Tuesday and David Smoote were to set him right and say, "No, today is Sunday, Lord's day," then George Hillcocke would cry back "Wrong! Today *is* Tuesday!" He would! I have heard him say it. Not say that as such, but something very like. Very like.'

'That is men arguing, that is what they do,' Beatrix Sutterwhit declares.

Her friend Eppie Smoote nods, 'Yes, they do.' Nods again. She also thinks, but does not say – she would not, could not, say this to Beatrix Sutterwhit – that the Sutterwhits, all of them, man and woman, are themselves quick to take up an argument and reluctant to let it drop.

'That Charles the Scotchman *has* gone. This is now well known to all, to all London. Fled.' Beatrix Sutterwhit says with a hard, challenging look at her friend. She knows, the parish knows, Eppie Smoote has a sneaking fondness for the restored king – the handsome black man that she says he is – although she is never public in this, unlike David Smoote, her loud nokes of a husband.

'Jane-Pym Carter is doing a deal of business in nosegays of angelica,' Eppie Smoote says, sidling to safer ground.

'Yes, she is. I have known that for several days now,' Beatrix Sutterwhit says dismissively. She will not have anyone, especially not her friend Eppie Smoote, know more of the doings of St Cyneswide and St Tibba than she does. 'Her angelica is from midwife Hester Fenner. Hester Fenner is a woman *not* of this parish. A woman from All Hallows on the Wall.' Beatrix Sutterwhit pulls a face in distaste. 'A poor, miserable parish. They will need great buckets of angelica there if they are to preserve themselves against the infection!'

* * *

'Thomas Billington, he is an angry ball of spite,' Robert Tomlinson tells Francis Neale.

Francis Neale is tired, the parish is tired, of the never-ending warfare between Thomas Billington and Robert Tomlinson.

'You do not have to share a watch with Thomas Billington. Your good fortune,' Francis Neale says shortly. 'My problem, mine, is this sot Roger Geoffrayes. Even today, Lord's day, church day, he comes late for the exchange. Foxed and fumbling and falling about after a night's drinking.

Him a watchman! That is my problem.'

Robert Tomlinson has no interest in this. 'That fight. I bested him. Broke his hand. Kicked him in the cods. Still bent double. He only caught me in the face by chance. Oath breaker. I bested him.' He gently fingers his bruised face. 'Now because of him I am before the Vestry. He started it. Not me. He should be in the pillory. He will be.'

* * *

'No parson today. So far no parson today.' Philip Carter, propped up against his Clerk's desk, announces to the congregation in his Clerk's voice.

'So far no parson today,' leaves the divided parish confirmed in its division. Those for the Book of Common Prayer have told themselves and each other that Walter Hall has not deserted them, will not desert them, and although they acknowledge coaches and carts and waggons have left Why-toll Palace, they know Walter Hall will make every effort, every exertion, to come back to St Cyneswide and St Tibba. Almost certainly today – although this is looking less likely – but if not today then next Sunday. Or the one after.

Those for Reform – and they are still strong – have heard the glorious news that Thomas Dugdale will come in and they keep eager eyes on the door. Surely Philip Carter – a man whose sympathies, they know, lie with them – surely he means that Thomas Dugdale is expected today, any minute? 'So far no parson today.' But soon.

Philip Carter bellows, 'Let us sing to the praise and glory of God, psalm the eighty second. He gives the lines and the congregation follow at their stately rate:

> *Amid the press of men of might the Lord himself doth stand,*
> *To plead the cause of truth and right with Judges of the land.*
> *How long, said he, will ye proceed false judgment to award?*
> *Why have you partially agreed the wicked to reward?*
> *Whereas of due you should defend the fatherless and weak:*
> *And when the poor man doth contend in judgment justly speak.*

'*Not* the fifty eighth, not that psalm,' says Parish Clerk Philip Carter to Church Warden Frances Barrow early this morning before church. 'I thought that might be the one to set the Vestry thinking in their right minds about this low slandering of our Searchers. I was seeking psalms that speak loudly to partial judges – and there are some of those in our Vestry. Verse the first of psalm the fifty eighth I thought, that is what is wanted. The verse sings: *Ye rulers that are put in trust to judge of wrong and right* – and that's the Vestrymen as will gather after church today; *Be all your judgements true and just, regarding no man's might.*'

I know what it sings, Frances Barrow thinks.

'A good start you might say and I do, did, but – but Frances Barrow, but – the second verse does not serve my purpose: *Nay, in your hearts ye mark and muse in mischief to consent; And where ye should true justice use, your hands to bribes are bent.* Well that–'

'I see, I see,' Frances Barrow (who also knows the second verse, knows the whole psalm) breaks in, Philip Carter is being very long-winded. 'I see. No good for the congregation to be singing *your hands to bribes are bent* before the Vestry meeting. Yes I see. Minds would turn in the wrong direction. You are right, the eighty second will do the business.'

'I think and hope so. Now, the Vestry, you are primed and ready to speak?'

'Yes, yes,' Frances Barrow understands that Philip Carter places great store on this meeting – as does he – but he will not be catechised about what he is going to say. 'Philip Carter I have spoken, as you asked, to young John Bell at the Parish Clerks. And as you said he is a sensible and good-thinking man. So thanks to him I now have many good points to make.'

'Good, good. Tell me what he said.'

Frances Barrow smiles his flat smiling pie smile. He will *not* be put under questioning by Philip Carter. His mind is particularly taken up with the return of Thomas Dugdale now Walter Hall has gone. He asks, 'What other psalms will we sing Philip Carter? Have you something to help bring in Thomas Dugdale? To bring him back? Sing him back? Vestry needs encouragement in that too.'

The ancient women – Searchers, Keepers and Viewer, all five – sit together. This surprises some of them as much as it surprises the rest of the congregation. More. It surprises Widow Margaret Hazard. It surprises Widow Dorothy Bullen. It does not surprise Goodwife Joan Brokefild, who is responsible.

Yesterday, in private words with Goody Susanna Parsons outside the ancient women's room, Goodwife Joan Brokefild has said she hopes the Widow, and herself, can be sure that the Keepers and the now sole Viewer, Anne Abowen, will say only good words if asked at the Vestry. Can she vouch for Anne Abowen? Goody Susanna Parsons says that Anne Abowen is a strong-minded, hard-voiced woman – as is, it is only fair to say, Widow Margaret Hazard – but whatever Anne Abowen says of the Widow (and there are things she does say) she does not call her dishonest, or scandalous.

What, then, of Widow Dorothy Bullen? the Goodwife wants to know. Goody Susanna Parsons says in her own good-natured way that Widow Dorothy Bullen is a mild, ancient woman who does not seek out strife, does her best to avoid it. So, the Goodwife asks, then Widow Dorothy Bullen will not speak against the Searchers? If she did, Goody Parsons replies, what could she say? But even so she will herself speak earnestly to Widow Bullen. She thinks this is what the Goodwife would like her to do? Yes, and also for all the ancient women to sit together in church. To show.

Now, in the parish church of St Cyneswide and St Tibba, Searchers, Keepers and Viewer sit together. Even more surprising they sit: Anne Abowen, Widow Hazard, Goodwife Brokefild, Goody Parsons, Widow Bullen. Who has ever seen Widow Hazard and Anne Abowen sit side by side?

Goody Parsons says with feeling, 'I am sure it is because of that Dr Burnett–'

'Barnett! Dr Barnett!' the Widow snorts.

The Goodwife, who has made sure she sits beside her friend, gives her a brisk poke in the ribs, 'Shush.' The Goodwife knows that it is Burnett, and also that her friend Widow Hazard has imperfect hearing.

But the Widow will continue: 'This Dr Barnett he had no right to do so, to shut himself in.'

'Yes, that doctor,' Goody Parsons, not fazed, continues, 'that doctor who shut himself in. I am sure that good Widow Chaukley did the same on his example, and out of the greatness of her heart. Of her own accord she shut herself, her whole family, shut them all in. It was very handsome of her.'

'Yes, she is a Viewer so of course she knows the signs,' the Goodwife says quickly, and is relieved to hear Widow Hazard say: 'An ancient woman knows the signs better than any doctor, better than this Dr Barnett. It is for Viewers,' she looks with approval and nods at Anne Abowen, 'for Viewers to say if the plague is present. Or not. Widow Chaukley did well to shut herself in, and now she is in God's hands. But this Dr Barnett, he murdered his servant and has locked himself away to escape discovery.'

Anne Abowen finds Widow Margaret Hazard's words unexpected, and gratifying. She responds in turn with her own gracious nod, 'You are right Widow Hazard. As you say, a Viewer, Widow Chaukley, can discover the signs herself. It is what Viewers do.'

* * *

Parish Clerk Philip Carter, propped at his desk, announces in the customary way the next psalm. The psalm that – in the depths of his soul – he wishes to be a fiery beacon to the Vestry, to the congregation, to London, to all the land, to light the way for the return of Thomas Dugdale. A return in glory to his welcoming saints, to his eager parish of St Cyneswide and St Tibba. The Parish Clerk feels the blood of enthusiasm, of passion, rush to his face, turning it beacon red.

'Let us sing to the praise and glory of God, psalm the forty fourth.'

> *Our ears have heard our fathers tell, and reverently record,*
> *The wondrous works that thou hast done in older time, O Lord.*
> *How thou didst cast the Gentiles out with a most pow'rful hand:*
> *Planting our fathers in their place, and gav'st to them their land.*

The congregation of St Cyneswide and St Tibba slow marches its way through to the last verse, verse the six and twentieth, and booms:

Rise up therefore for our defence, and help us Lord, at need:
We thee beseech for thy goodness, to rescue us with speed.

To those for Reform the psalm sings of the near approach of Thomas Dugdale. Yet the whole congregation can hear, as well, a heartfelt plea for rescue – rescue us with speed, O Lord – from this plague that is upon us.

* * *

'There you see,' says John Girling, who speaks as if his companions are not sharp enough to notice what is in front of them all. 'There you have them, sitting together, all six ancient women, and–'

'Five,' corrects William Northage, 'five ancient women. Only five of them now. Widow Chaukley has–'

'Yes, yes, five, I know that,' John Girling says testily. 'Five. Viewer Widow Chaukley has shut herself in. Everyone knows that by now. My point is that they do not sit together. There is always ill-feeling from Widow Margaret Hazard – sour old sow – towards the Viewers and Keepers. Always. She and Goodwife Brokefild always sit separate from the others. You must have seen that?'

'Yes John Girling, yes, of course we have seen that,' Edward Richbell the baker will not take condescension from John Girling the chandler, who carries the stink of tallow with him. 'And now we can see, this Lord's day, that they are all sitting together.'

'The Vestry meeting. To do with the Vestry meeting. Must be,' Barnard Clapshaw says. 'Must be.'

'I saw just then,' William Northage says heavily, 'that Widow Hazard looked well upon Viewer Anne Abowen.'

'All friends, I do not think!' John Girling is scornful. 'More likely all conspiring together to hide their own wicked deeds. Bribes and false reporting.'

'Do you know this?' William Northage is shocked. 'I've seen no such thing, and a bell-man sees things. We see things.'

'And I hear things,' John Girling says with his all-knowing air.

Barnard Clapshaw does not like this talk. Knows that watchmen can also be accused of taking a purse. Bribed to turn a blind eye, to take a lengthy absence in the house of office, so those shut up can escape, flee. 'New Viewer needed now,' he says. 'Place to fill. Vestry will have that as an item.'

'A Viewer is a Viewer and nothing more,' Edward Richbell says. 'The big matter is who, now Walter Hall has gone–'

'Now, where's *Beloved*? Why, *Beloved's* gone,' Barnard Clapshaw snickers in a low voice.

Edward Richbell knows and likes the verse but ignores the interruption. 'Who will stand in the pulpit here in St Cyneswide and St Tibba?'

'Many empty pulpits to be filled,' John Girling says. 'Who will you have come in?'

But John Girling is not a man to be trusted with a confidence – the parish has learned that he will trade a secret for a drink, a laugh, a sense of mastery.

His question is greeted with shrugs, bland smiles, grunts.

'Thomas Dugdale?' he pushes. 'Would you have Thomas Dugdale back in? Many will. You, Barnard Clapshaw? You sounded pleased just now about Walter Hall, *Beloved* you called him, being gone.'

Barnard Clapshaw is uncomfortable. 'Beloved, that's just an amusement, a street pamphlet for a bit of merriment.'

'Is it? But do you want Thomas Dugdale?'

'Same question for you John Girling,' Edward Richbell breaks in. 'Who do you want to come in? Do you want Thomas Dugdale back? Are you one of the many who will?'

John Girling smiles his knowing smile, 'Not for me to say.'

'No? You will be at Vestry, we both will. We might have to say there. Soon.'

'Then I will say there. If I have to.'

William Northage, who has no say in who will come in, and who knows that such questions will be resolved by his betters, for good or for ill, has more important business in mind. 'Dogs,' he says. 'This sad business about dogs. A bell-man must have a dog and I have Gypsy and I don't like this business. Killing dogs. I have it by memory: "No Dogs be suffered to be kept within any part of the City, and the Dogs be killed by the Dog-killers appointed for that purpose." These new Orders, from the Lord Mayor himself.'

'Parish Clerk doesn't like it. Constable doesn't like it. Say it will cause a deal of trouble. And it will. I don't like it.' Edward Richbell is of the same mind as the Clerk, the Constable, and the bell-man. 'My Gnasher healing well thanks to you William Northage. Healed back to health and then killed? No, I won't have it. I need a good ratter in the bakery.'

'Green Oil of Charity was the one to do the healing, I didn't need Sanicle. What about your Grinder Barnard Clapshaw? You wouldn't want your Grinder killed.'

'I would not!'

* * *

'Last psalm before Vestry,' Clerk says aside to the Warden. 'A good one to set their minds the right way about this bribery nonsense.' He draws a deep breath and declares in his church voice, 'Let us sing to the praise and glory of God, psalm the thirty first.'

> *O Lord, I put my trust in thee, let nothing work me shame:*
> *As thou art just, deliver me, and set me free from blame.*
> *Hear me, O Lord, and that anon, to help me make good speed:*
> *Be thou my rock and house of stone, my fence in time of need.*

The fourth verse is one the ancient women can sing lustily and with good courage:

> *Pluck thou my feet out of the snare which they for me have laid:*
> *Thou art my strength, and all my care is for thy mighty aid.*

They take heart from the rousing roar the congregation brings to the last verse:

> *Be of good courage, all ye just, on God your strength depend:*
> *For those in him that put their trust, he ever will defend.*

They gladly put their trust in God, knowing he will defend them.

* * *

London, Sunday, 2 July 1665
Vestry Meeting

'Parish Clerk leads us in prayer,' Gilbert Swaile announces.

Parish Clerk does: calls on God to look kindly on this Vestry meeting of the parish of St Cyneswide and St Tibba; to grant wisdom to these Vestrymen here assembled; and to bless their deliberations, that they might make good of the business here before them.

'Amen,' the Vestrymen say.

'Parish Clerk,' says Gilbert Swaile in the President's chair. 'Vestry Clerk William Harbie has left the parish, the city. Fled. I have always said that a separate Vestry Clerk for a parish of this size and means was an extravagance but our minister would have one. Now he, both, are gone. Minister and Vestry Clerk both gone.' This said with some satisfaction.

This is not news, the departure of Walter Hall and William Harbie are talked of throughout St Cyneswide and St Tibba.

'I am gratified that we can muster sufficient Vestrymen here today, before there are any more flights. Many of us still here. Are there to be more flights?' Gilbert Swaile asks as if this is a question of no great import. 'No? Well then perhaps there will be more Vestry meetings in these sickly times. But for today and for our future meetings we still need entries made in the Minute Book. Parish Clerk Philip Carter will do this Vestry Clerk work for an increase, a slight increase, in his salary. The parish will save money by not having to pay for two Clerks.' He smiles.

This has been arranged and agreed in advance with Philip Carter and Church Warden Frances Barrow. Gilbert Swaile sees no need to pay anything extra to Philip Carter for Vestry work. Philip Carter, supported by Frances Barrow, says the extra work has to be paid for. Frances Barrow says the parish can afford it. Not the full Vestry Clerk's salary says Gilbert Swaile. No, not the full salary, but two-thirds, Frances Barrow replies on his friend's behalf. One third, counters Gilbert Swaile. They settle on half.

'How much?' Emmanuel Bird asks. 'What is the increase in the Parish Clerk's salary?'

'One pound per annum,' the Church Warden replies. 'Provided Vestry approves this expenditure.'

'So now three pounds per annum in all to our Parish Clerk?' William Pickhering asks it as a question but knows his calculation is correct.

The Church Warden nods. Gilbert Swaile looks impatient, is about to speak but is over-ridden by John Girling.

'Pro tem? These double duties for our Clerk pro tem until Walter Hall, or who so might be minister, wants a proper Vestry Clerk?'

'For as long as needs,' Gilbert Swaile says heavily. 'This arrangement is for as long as needs be. The Clerk will make an entry in the Minutes of his new duties and salary and that is that – all agree? Yes? Good, agreed, then that is it – and we have more important matters before us.' He sighs, 'Yet there is still one other item before we turn to this matter of the Searchers. Are they waiting outside?' He asks Philip Carter.

'Yes, all the ancient women. Waiting.'

This is met with severe nods of approval.

'There is an item Walter Hall left with me. It is this. He expressly instructed that the Oath from the Act for Regulating Selected Vestries be fresh lettered and put prominently in this room whenever we meet. Church Warden.'

Charles Barrow, with no sign of his shame at having sworn this Oath in 63 – shame still strong – places a large-lettered page on the Vestry table.

'So that is done and its doing will be entered in the Minutes,' Gilbert Swaile says. The Oath lies flat on the table, overlooked.

'To real business now. Item: the accusations made against the

Searchers, the Widow and the Goodwife.'

This brings a rumble of stern, righteous anticipation from some of the eleven Vestrymen present. Not from the Parish Clerk and the Church Warden. Their faces blank, revealing nothing.

'Bring them in! All these ancient women. Bribe-takers. Making false reports. Bring them in.' George Lumme has bitter memories of these Searchers from the day Robert Holt's house fell. He has not forgotten how the two corpses, crushed by the toppling building, were brought into his house. A disgrace. These Searchers showed no concern for him, no concern for his household's dire peril of more collapses. He does not know which one is worse: the evil-looking one, or the smiling flighty one.

'No high words,' Gilbert Swaile warns. 'We will hear what is said against them, and what they have to say for themselves.'

Frances Barrow opens the door, beckons to the five ancient women who wait, smoking, and perched like pigeons on the churchyard wall. Goodwife Joan Brokefild gives Widow Margaret Hazard a lucky touch on the back.

The small vestry room is already crowded, the Vestrymen jammed up against each other. The ancient women find tight standing space inside the door.

'The new Orders from the Lord Mayor and Aldermen of the City of London,' Gilbert Swaile begins. 'I will read: "That there be special care to appoint Women-Searchers in every Parish, such as are of honest reputation—"'

'Of honest reputation!' Emmanuel Bird, who sits slumped, eyes heavy, bursts out indignantly. 'Of honest reputation! Do ye hear that!'

Gilbert Swaile impatiently waves him down. 'No high words. Listen to the Orders, "—of honest reputation, and of the best sort as can be got in this kind." So the Order says.'

'Well, the best sort as can be got. Perhaps they are,' John Girling scoffs. 'Ancient women!'

'I will finish reading this,' Gilbert Swaile says ominously. 'I will.'

There is silence. It is accepted that a wealthy brewer, though he smells of beer, will not give way to a middling man of a tallow chandler who smells of mutton fat.

'To continue: "And these to be sworn to make due search and true report–" he looks around the table to see if any will offer a sarcastic commentary on "true report." None do. "–to the utmost of their knowledge, whether the Persons, whose bodies they are appointed to Search, do die of the Infection, or of what other diseases, as near as they can." That is what these new Orders say. Parish Clerk, are our two Searchers for St Cyneswide and St Tibba duly sworn?'

'They are,' Philip Carter replies.

Emmanuel Bird, now roused, cannot hold back, spits, 'Sworn! It is the pillory for false reports! Loss of pension! Old Orders, good old Orders, have it that for any corruption or other respect of falsely reporting, they shall stand upon the Pillory, and bear corporal pain by the Judgement of the Lord Mayor and Court of Alderman.' He looks around triumphantly. Glares at the ancient women.

'No. High. Words.' Gilbert Swaile says, with no hope this will stop Emmanuel Bird.

'The Oath,' Harry Bosvill says with earnest irrelevance, pointing to the document, 'Minister Walter Hall wants it prominent here to remind all that in his absence, and in His Majesty's absence, to remind all that it is unlawful to take up arms against the king, and that to do so is to hold a traitorous position.' Harry Bosvill speaks with determination, even allows himself to pick up the paper, holds it up for all to see, says, 'Traitorous position.' Shakes his head in admonition.

'Thank you for that Harry Bosvill,' Gilbert Swaile replies. 'The Vestry, and beyond, will keep that in mind. The presence of the Oath here with us at this meeting, and at subsequent ones, is recorded in the Minutes Vestry Clerk?'

Philip Carter nods, 'Yes. In the Minutes. It is in.' He gestures with his quill, nods encouragingly at Harry Bosvill. Harry Bosvill is proud that a girl with his name – his niece Jinny, daughter of his brother Richard Bosvill – has a position as under-cook with Walter Hall, which makes him, he considers, something of an agent for the rector and so able to speak on his behalf.

'My father was an Attorney,' Emmanuel Bird will not be stopped. 'An Attorney who has, had, the full Order from the year 92,' he pauses, glares, '1592. That is the Order – I have my father's copy, it is somewhere in my chest of papers – that Order says every woman Searcher shall stand upon the Pillory and bear corporal pain–'

'Not every woman Searcher shall be pilloried!' William Sutterwhit scoffs, 'Not every woman Searcher, only those, Emmanuel Bird, where there is corruption or false reporting.'

'That is what I said! Corporal pain!'

Frances Barrow looks to Philip Carter. They had discussed what volatile William Sutterwhit might do in these proceedings. That he is taking against Emmanuel Bird is a good thing.

'These ancient women Searchers, they said – this one, she said! the one with the eye – she said I had the plague! I do not have the plague, have never had the plague, and never will have the plague!' Emmanuel Bird picks up the Vestry Oath. 'I take my oath here that I do not have the plague and never will!'

'That is noted,' says Gilbert Swaile, 'but not, I think, necessary to go in the Minutes. That is a personal matter for Emmanuel Bird concerning the plague rather than a decision of this Vestry, and it would be – excessive – to have to record all here in St Cyneswide and St Tibba who do not have the plague. Where they do have the plague, die of the plague, the Parish Clerk's weekly Bill of Mortality will record that. But not those who don't. I am in the right of it Parish Clerk?'

'You are.'

'Excessive! I do *not* have the plague,' Emmanuel Bird lapses into somnolent mumbling. 'A respected Attorney of great repute, respected and of *great* repute. Excessive! Attorney of great ... chest of papers ...'

The five ancient women by the door stand impassively, listening, observing, while these matters are played through. It is not for them to intervene, to comment. Their comments – there will be several – on the way the men of the parish of St Cyneswide and St Tibba go about their business will come later, when they are in the ancient women's room. In the meantime they wait – they can only wait – for the accusations against the Searchers to be aired and addressed.

'These charges against, against – them – let's hear them!' Emmanuel Bird demands, sitting up abruptly.

'Accusations,' Gilbert Swaile says. 'We are a Vestry, not a court of the law. No charges have been laid.'

'Don't tell me about the law! I know the law! What are the charges?'

'There are two charges, accusations, two accusations against the Searchers of this parish, against Widow Margaret Hazard and against Goodwife Joan Brokefild. Who you know and see here.' He points out the two Searchers, who meet the stares of the Vestrymen with stony, unmoving faces.

'The accusations are that Widow Margaret Hazard altered the order of searches, the order in which the searches were to be made, so she could send word to John Sly of this parish, so he had good time to remove the corpse of his maid Doll Matthews, so her corpse could not be searched for the plague.'

'So, so, so. Too many of these so's,' Emmanuel Bird says. He is ignored.

'This first accusation is against Widow Hazard, and it is accused she did this corruptly, for money. Whether or no Goodwife Joan Brokefild was a party to this, some say yes, some say no. That is the first accusation. The second is that at the house of John Shipley, his corpse showing the signs that he was dead of the plague, the two Searchers, both of them, sought bribes of a guinea, or guineas, from Widow Hester Shipley to make a false report and say the death was due to spotted fever.'

This is heard in silence.

Gilbert Swaile proceeds calmly, sombrely. 'We are not a court of the law. We cannot make orders of standing in the pillory, of suffering corporal pain. Yet in this time of plague we must not, cannot have false reports being made by Searchers, by Viewers, by Keepers. We cannot have bribes taken so corpses cannot be searched. Corpses that might have the infection but cannot be searched to see if this is so. So if – if – this Vestry finds that these ancient women have been taking bribes, making false reports, we cannot have them as Searchers. We need honest ancient women. Women of honest reputation and of the best sort in this kind as can be got, as the new Order says. So we must consider these accusations with great care. Because for those of us who cannot flee, who *will not* flee.' Gilbert Swaile does not add 'like some' but drums his fingers on the Oath. 'For those of us who stay, the lives of this parish, the lives of London, all our lives, depend on – on honest reporting.'

Fists are banged on the table until it shakes. Loud cries of 'Hear him! Hear him!' bounce around the small room. The Oath flutters off to the floor. Harry Bosvil picks it up, smooths it, and puts it back on the table.

The ancient women are despondent. They agree with all Gilbert Swaile's words, but the result of these words is that the mood in the room runs strongly against them.

'So,' says Gilbert Swaile, 'we will turn to the first accusation first.'

'We know,' shouts Emmanuel Bird that she,' he jabs a finger at Widow Margaret Hazard, 'she took bribes from the Widow Shipley to give a false report. Ten guineas, ten guineas to each Searcher. Or twenty guineas to each.'

'That is the second accusation,' Gilbert Swaile says flatly. 'We are talking about the first.'

'A question,' asks Harry Bosvill. 'If the Searchers are dismissed who will be a Searcher in these sickly times? Search plague corpses?'

'There will always be those who will, ancient women who will,' says Gilbert Swaile confidently.

'Well I would not,' Harry Bosvill says.

'I did not know you were in the running Harry Bosvill, but you say you will yield to the other ancient women?' Robin Kerton asks.

Gilbert Swaile waves down the laughter. 'We are talking about the first accusation,' he reminds them.

'It is known,' John Girling says, 'that the Searcher Widow Hazard changed, altered, the order of searching on a day of many deaths so that John Sly who should have been searched first was searched last. The Widow told him this so he had time to remove the corpse of his maid. So the maid's corpse could not be searched. That is all well known.'

'Philip Carter, now speaking as Parish Clerk, what can you tell of this?' Gilbert Swaile asks.

'Gilbert Swaile does this well,' Edward Richbell says aside to Robin Kerton.

'The names I gave to the Searchers – this was Monday, a fortnight past tomorrow – the names were Robert Sedgwicke, John Sly, Francis Woodhouse, Henry Gipps, Thomas Dorbridge, Frances Aspiner, John Shipley, the Widow Barrett.' Philip Carter stares at the ceiling as he recites the names.

'But,' George Lumme pounces, 'they did not do the searches in this order!'

'So what order did you do them in, and why?' Gilbert Swaile asks the Searchers.

'This was not an instruction from the Parish Clerk,' Goodwife Joan Brokefild speaks easily. 'No instruction that Searchers must follow a set order. Corpses will always wait, and there were many to be searched that day.'

'Yes, but the order of searching was changed. Why?' Gilbert Swaile presses.

'I changed the ordering of the searches,' Widow Hazard's voice is loud, challenging. 'Changed it to search Widow Barrett's house first. This was a known plague house, Will Barrett and his two sons already dead of the infection – as searched by Goodwife Brokefild and me – his Widow and daughter shut in but no answer given the Keepers.'

Keeper Goody Susanna Parsons nods her agreement, says, 'No answer given.'

'A known plague house put first,' Widow Hazard says, 'to be searched first.' Her good eye travels around the room to see if any dare challenge this. She sees neither agreement nor disagreement so continues, 'The order of searching of John Sly's house changed because his house is close by Thomas Dorbridge, his house.'

'A sensible way of taking the houses in turn,' the Goodwife adds. 'For convenience.'

'You changed the order of searching?' William Sutterwhit asks Widow Hazard.

'Yes. To make it an easier way to do the searching.'

'An easier way! Oh yes, an easy way!' John Girling shoots out his lips, shakes his head.

'How did you get word to John Sly of the changed searching so he had time to remove the corpse? Word sent with that small girl Sara Potts who you call your daughter?' John Girling presses.

Widow Margaret Hazard is enraged, clenches her hands tightly. Before she can say anything that can be understood, Goodwife Joan Brokefild intervenes.

'The small girl Sara Potts was at her school with a French woman, she has nothing to do with this business.'

'The small girl Sara named for that Sarah Collymore in St Benet Fynck, a Searcher who took bribes? Silent Sarah, coins in her mouth? Corrupt. False report maker. Not sober. Dismissed.' John Girling is enjoying himself. '*Who* has nothing to do with this business? The small girl or the French woman?'

'Did you send the small girl to John Sly?' Gilbert Swaile asks.

'No! And—'

'Enough.' Gilbert Swaile holds up his hand, asks, 'Did anyone see the small girl Sara take a message at this time from the Widow? See the small girl run to John Sly? Did anyone see?'

'Just because it wasn't seen doesn't mean it didn't happen,' George Lumme says, sounding reasonable to his fellow Vestrymen.

'Agreed,' says Gilbert Swaile, 'but we cannot say it *did* happen.'

'Must have,' John Girling says.

'What does John Sly himself say?' William Pickhering asks. 'He is a Vestryman. He should be here at this meeting to answer this. If these

Searchers are bribe-takers then John Sly is a bribe-giver. What does he say?'

'Yes,' says Gilbert Swaile, 'he should be here as a Vestryman and to answer for himself. As you see he is not here.'

'Fled,' Frances Barrow says. 'Fled, it is said he fled due to the increase in the infection. Fled the day after the search – the day after the Searchers came.'

'If he were here,' Gilbert Swaile asks smoothly, 'if he were to be here and this Vestry asked him "Did you pay a bribe to the Searchers to delay the searching of your house?" what would he answer?' He leaves the question hanging, then says, 'I think he would answer "No! certainly not!" That is what I think. But he is not here, so what do we have on this first accusation?'

'It is well known! The truth of this scandal is well known!' An angry Emmanuel Bird says.

Gilbert Swaile sighs, 'No proof of this first accusation. The Searchers deny it. No-one saw the small girl Sara, or anyone else, run to John Sly. And John Sly, like so many others,' again he taps the Oath, 'like so many others we know of, has fled. Any more to say on this accusation?' He looks around, sees some Vestrymen still dissatisfied, some nodding acceptance.

Beavis Piggot stands, 'A piss,' he says to Gilbert Swaile, and walks outside, past the ancient women, giving them a nod. He is followed by Robert Holt and Robin Kerton, going outside on the same business.

'Who I call my daughter! Is my daughter!' Widow Hazard says loudly to the Goodwife, to the other ancient women. 'And *not* named after the Collymore!'

'Later,' says the Goodwife, 'this is talk for later. Not now.'

John Girling hears and smiles, pleased his blow has struck home.

Goodwife Joan Brokefild and Goody Susanna Parsons would also go and piss but know no such latitude will be granted to ancient women.

The pissing men return, and Gilbert Swaile resumes. 'The second accusation against the two Searchers. Bribes sought from Widow Shipley to make false report of John Shipley, his death. Before we have more on this, I now ask the Keepers and the Viewers if they have anything to say on these accusations. If they know anything of them?'

'Only that there are accusations, of course we know that,' Anne Abowen says, 'we have all heard them. But I know nothing of corruption, of false reporting, by Widow Margaret Hazard, by Goodwife Joan Brokefild. I know them for honest, upright ancient women Searchers.'

'As do I,' says Goody Susanna Parsons, glad Anne Abowen has said it so well, so clearly. 'As do I.'

Widow Dorothy Bullen stands there dumb, overwhelmed by the majesty of the Vestry meeting. Looks about herself terrified.

'What does Keeper Widow Bullen have to say,' presses William Sutterwhit. 'Anything? For or against?'

Widow Dorothy Bullen shakes, looks faint, manages to say, 'As I do.'

'As you do what?' John Girling asks, 'What are you saying you do?'

'I do what they say, what Goody Susanna Abowen and what Anne Parsons say. I say the same. I do,' says Widow Bullen in confusion.

This met with a heave of discontent, of amusement, from the Vestrymen.

'They all say the same,' says George Lumme, 'of course they all say the same. Ancient women all standing by each other. What you would expect? They would say that, wouldn't they? All the same!'

'So what is known of the bribery at Widow Shipley's house? We cannot ask her. She has not fled but is shut in. Shut in. And, like John Sly, if we could ask, would she admit to bribery? So what is known?' Gilbert Swaile asks. This is taking longer, is more tedious, than he had anticipated. He slowly takes out his magnificent watch, stares at it, slowly puts it away.

'They both, both Searchers, sought bribes from Widow Shipley for a false report,' Emmanuel Bird says.

'It is said that one would take it and the other wouldn't,' Robert Holt says.

'I heard the Widow would but not the Goodwife,' says Robin Kerton, to some murmurs of agreement. Others have heard the same.

'I heard the other way around,' says Edward Richbell, 'The Goodwife would but not the Widow.' There is little support for this.

'Both!' says Emmanuel Bird, echoed by George Lumme, 'Both!'

'Philip Carter as Parish Clerk, what can you say?' Gilbert Swaile asks.

'On that Monday tomorrow fortnight past, the Searchers returned from searching the many corpses and told me, told me that day, that Widow Shipley offered them each a gold guinea to say that it was not the plague. Told me that very day, as Parish Clerk.'

'What is your story?' Gilbert Swaile asks the Searchers. 'A short story, we do not have all day even though it might seem like it to some.'

Widow Hazard gestures to the Goodwife to answer for them.

'The short of it is Widow Shipley would not have us inside, we saw the coffin waiting outside. She said the corpse had been taken–'

'Another corpse taken?' John Girling asks. 'Another one?'

'We went in. It was Widow Hazard who got us inside. We found the corpse. The signs were there, dead of the plague. Widow Shipley offered us a guinea each, took them from her purse before us, to say it was spotted fever, not plague. We took no bribe. That is the short tale. We reported it to the Parish Clerk, as he himself just said, on our return. Reported it ourselves. Reported the death as plague and reported the bribe. The end. Finis,' she says lightly, which mightily annoys Emmanuel Bird and George Lumme. Beavis Piggot and Edward Richbell are amused.

'Is there any information about more spending by the Searchers? Information that would show bribes were received, spent?' Gilbert Swaile asks.

There is none.

'There is the cherry tarts and the small beer,' John Girling says triumphantly, playing his trump card. 'They took cherry tarts and small beer from Widow Shipley! More, Widow Margaret Hazard even took tarts for the small girl Sara Potts! Was seen outside here, sitting on the churchyard wall, feeding the child bribe tarts.'

Gilbert Swaile wonders when this will all end. Looks at his watch again. 'Did you take cherry tarts and small beer from Widow Shipley?' He asks the Searchers.

'Yes,' they reply.

'There! You hear! They did!'

'Did you take guineas? Guineas as well?'

'No.'

'Did you report John Sly's death to Philip Carter, as Parish Clerk, to be the plague, the infection?'

'Yes.'

'I do not think,' says Gilbert Swaile, hoping to end the matter, 'that cherry tarts and small beer will do the business here. So, is that not so?'

'More of his so and so and so's,' Emmanuel Bird says. 'Of course they do the business. Bribes offered and taken. Bribes!'

'Can I speak? Yes? Hospitable, we took it as hospitable, however it was meant,' the Widow says in a hoarse voice. 'Searching corpses is hungry work, thirsty work, although some have no appetite while they do. I, we, have done it long enough to keep our appetite. Widow Shipley's was the seventh, no eighth house, eighth house we searched that day, and the last. Seven before her. We had not yet found plague there in the Shipley house. Not yet. The corpse concealed from us. She, Widow Shipley, offered a bit to eat and drink. Gave us cherry tarts and small beer, as John Girling says, cherry tarts and small beer. Then we found the plague corpse. Then guineas offered, pressed upon us, but not taken.'

'Guilty of eating cherry tarts, drinking small beer,' Goodwife Joan Brokefild says. 'But if we was to search your house John Girling for plague and you offered us cherry tarts and small beer we would have them and thank you for them, as we thanked Widow Shipley.'

'Wicked insolence!' John Girling rises to his feet, pushing the bench violently back, to the discomfort and danger of others sitting on it. 'Masters beat their insolent servants! These women are servants of the parish and should be beaten for their insolence! Beaten!'

Frances Barrow, the reassuring old trooper, soothes like a salve, 'The Searchers have rough, hard work to do. It is not work for gentle folk, not work for masters–'

'Of course it is not work for the better sort of person!' George Lumme says scathingly.

'No. No, no it is not. And it may be that words are chosen, things are said, that come out harsher, rougher, than some might like. But I am sure no harm is meant?' The Warden looks to the Searchers.

'No. Not at all. No harm meant,' Goodwife Joan Brokefild says cheerfully.

John Girling sits down, glaring. Thumps the table with an angry fist.

'Is there any more to be said of these cherry tarts and the small beer?' Gilbert Swaile asks in a weary voice.

'Yes,' says the Widow. 'After we eat the tarts and drink the beer, we find John Shipley's plaguey corpse, and when we go into the kitchen we see the cook has the signs,' the Widow laughs. 'The *cook* has the signs. But here you see us. No signs.' She pushes her face at them.

The Vestry shrinks back as far as it can from the rough and peculiar ancient women by the door.

'Still bribes, bribes,' Emmanuel Bird persists.

He does not carry the Vestry room with him. Most grudgingly accept that the case is not made.

'What about the rumours? All the rumours? No smoke without fire, no fire without smoke. That's well known. I have heard,' John Girling glares at Philip Carter, 'from a man of great vigour, great vigour,' he repeats with meaning, 'that these rumours are true. Too many rumours for them not to be true.'

Philip Carter knows John Vigor is a keen pedlar of rumours, but was unaware that the troublesome noise of the St Bennet Sherehog Clerk has reached John Girling in St Cyneswide and St Tibba.

'Rumours,' says Frances Barrow easily, 'rumours. There are rumours about many things, about many people. I'm sure there are rumours about me. Even rumours about you, John Girling.'

This is met with general laughter, smiles, nods. There are rumours about John Girling.

The man is outraged. Again. 'What are the rumours about me? What are they?'

This produces even more laughter. The ancient women exchange unobtrusive knowing looks. There are rumours about John Girling.

Ann Abowen, fond of her bible and knowing it well, says softly to the Searchers, not too softly, '"An hypocrite with his mouth destroyeth his neighbours, but through knowledge shall the just be delivered," and so you are.'

'Frances Barrow, you have spoken, but you have something more to say?' Gilbert Swaile asks.

He does. 'This matter of honest Searchers, as presiding Vestryman Gilbert Swaile said, this matter is always important, but never more so than in time of plague. I have spoken to John Bell, Clerk of the Guild of Parish Clerks, whose work gives us, gives London, the weekly Bills of Mortality for the 130 parishes.'

'Frances Barrow sent by Parish Clerk Philip Carter to this John Bell!' John Girling sneers.

This is true, but the Vestry wants to hear what John Bell, Clerk of the Clerks, has to say.

'John Bell says that the Bills of Mortality have been said by some – ignorant people – said to be of little worth by reason that the Searchers, all London's Searchers, are generally old and simple women who are not able to judge of and distinguish between diseases and therefore cannot make a true report to their Parish Clerk.'

'Yes, just so,' says George Lumme.

'Or,' continues Frances Barrow, 'that some Searchers are not honest, but corrupt and will take bribes to make a false report.'

'Just so,' repeats George Lumme.

Frances Barrow continues, 'John Bell answers this, and now I read his words, words he makes public to all:

> True and undeniable it is, that the Searchers are generally ancient women, and I think are therefore most fit for that Office. But sure I am they are chosen by some of the eminentest men of the Parish to which they stand related; and if any of their Choosers should speak against their abilities, they would much disparage their

own Judgements. And after such Choice the ancient women are examined touching their sufficiency, and sworn to that Office.

Frances Barrow looks guilelessly about the room. 'This Vestry, London's Vestries, have chosen ancient women as Searchers, and John Bell, the Clerk of Clerks, speaks highly of the honesty and judgement of the Vestrymen choosers, and thus of those chosen as Searchers. The Bills of Mortality are built on that honesty. The honesty of those who choose, and of those chosen who search.' Frances Barrow's smooth pie face asks the Vestrymen whether they endorse, or deny, their own judgement and honesty, knowing – as does young John Bell, Clerk of the Parish Clerks – how they must answer.

There is some puzzled thought, then the Vestrymen's faces show they are satisfied with their own judgement and honesty. It is undeniable.

Gilbert Swaile makes ready to close this matter but cannot do so yet, for Isabella Undnay will come in, bursts in.

'These ancient women! They do not do their duty! They take bribes! They do not search for my husband Richard Undnay, now missing a fortnight.'

'This is not right,' Gilbert Swaile declares. 'No high words!'

'It is right! It is a fact that my husband is missing and they do not search for him.'

'A fact it may be, but I will not, this Vestry will not,' Gilbert Swaile booms magisterially, 'will not be swayed by facts unrelated. Will not hear facts unrelated.'

'I am an information against them!' Isabella Undnay is roughly jostled out the door by Anne Abowen, Widow Hazard, Goody Parsons and Goodwife Brokefild. Widow Dorothy Bullen looks on, at a loss.

'Bedlam woman!' Anne Abowen calls out after her. Whispers to her companions, 'That one is a Bedlam bitch.'

Gilbert Swaile approves the removal of Isabella Undnay. 'So this second accusation is concluded, with no alteration in the Searchers of St Cyneside and St Tibba. Let the Minutes, Vestry Clerk Carter, so record.

We still have the ancient women here, so now I am going to change today's order of business, turn some items about for convenience – it seems from what we have heard it can be easily and properly done – so we will hear of a new Viewer to replace Widow Ursula Chaukley, now shut in. Then the ancient women will leave us.'

He turns to Philip Carter. 'The brawling watchmen are waiting outside?'

'Yes. Outside.'

'Then let them wait longer. Not again, Beavis Piggot?'

'When the cockerel calls, whatever the time of day, I must get up.' He shrugs and makes for the door.

'Early morning, and every hour on the hour his cockerel calls! He's a water clock! A water cock! Let the Minutes record, Philip Carter Vestry Clerk, that Vestryman Beavis Piggot pissed away this item, whatever number it has become,' Robin Kerton calls out.

Beavis Piggot laughs.

'Boy,' says Robert Holt in a schoolmaster's harsh voice. 'Boy, did you ask leave to go forth?' then he whines like a child, 'Please Dominus, please, please, I need to go forth!'

Beavis Piggot laughs again, glad to see Robert Holt, sombre and sullen since the collapse of his house, jesting, making light.

'The new Viewer,' Gilbert Swaile says, 'Even in this sickly time there will be names proposed, Philip Carter as Parish Clerk.'

'Yes, names proposed. Two who will do it. Their names–'

'Slower, Philip Carter as whatever Clerk you at this moment, slower,' John Girling says. 'What about Widow Ursula Chaukley? What of her? What if she recovers? And she may well, then she must come back as Viewer.'

There is strong support for this from Edward Richbell, Robin Kerton, Harry Bosvill.

'We would not want to see the poor woman put in difficulties and we hope and pray for her full recovery,' says Robin Kerton.

The Vestry taps the table to make known its support. The ancient women standing at the door are surprised and gratified at this show of concern for their fellow, the shut in Widow Chaukley. It is an unexpected side of the Vestry.

'So do we all,' Gilbert Swaile agrees, 'but for now we must have a Viewer, must have two Viewers in the parish. So we can make an appointment pro tem—'

'As Philip Carter is Vestry Clerk pro tem?' George Lumme asks.

The patient Gilbert Swaile says, 'Yes, for the moment, pro tem.'

George Lumme is satisfied, repeats 'Pro tem' as if he has just explained the term to his fellow Vestrymen.

'These names you have, Philip Carter, have you asked the parish for names? Of course you have,' Robin Kerton says.

'I have. Some suggested but not agreeable, or not suitable. But two likely names, two likely ancient women of good repute: Mabell Billington and Widow Lankester.'

'Mabell Billington?' Beavis Piggot says as he re-enters the room, 'Mabell Billington? The wife of the brawler waiting outside?'

'A brawling husband does not make a Goodwife less honest, less suitable,' Gilbert Swaile observes. He looks at the ancient women standing by the door. 'You Searchers, Keepers and Viewer, you know these women, do you have anything to say, knowing what you do of the work, who might do it best? Viewer Anne Abowen?'

'Widow Lankester,' Anne Abowen answers without hesitation.

'Will she take the oath?' Harry Bosvill asks.

'We can ask her that, she herself can answer that. It is for Vestry to put that question,' Gilbert Swaile says.

'Were there other names proposed Philip Carter?' William Pickhering asks.

The Clerk shrugs. He will not mention Beatrix Sutterwhit who would be insulted to know that her name had been put forward, and husband William Sutterwhit sitting across the table would be even more insulted.

'Isabella Undnay,' Widow Margaret Hazard mutters.

Those nearby laugh, then pass the joke on to those who did not hear.

Widow Hazard shows unexpected wit.

'So it is the view of Vestry that for Viewer,' Gilbert Swaile chuckles at his small joke, repeats, 'view, Viewer, that Widow Lankester will–'

'Always provided she takes the Oath,' Harry Bosvill will persist.

'And pro tem?' John Girling also persists.

'Yes, both. Is Widow Lankester close by, Philip Clerk? That is to say Philip Carter.'

'Vestry Clerk, Parish Clerk, but you are right Gilbert Swaile, Philip Clerk serves both,' Robert Holt is still in humorous mood.

Philip Carter gestures to the ancient women, but Anne Abowen has already gone to fetch Widow Lankester and brings her to the door.

Widow Lankester reins in her sardonic smile, looks as mild and compliant as she can, but looks neither very mild nor very compliant.

'Widow Lankester, you know of the sad circumstances of Widow Ursula Chaukley?'

'I do know. Very well,' she replies loud and confident.

'Who may yet recover,' John Girling says. 'Shut up for a month but may still recover.'

'Who may yet recover. But the parish needs a Viewer now,' Gilbert Swaile will not be thrown off course. 'The position will be pro tem until Widow Chaukley's, until her fate is clear. Known. And there is the Oath? You will take it?'

'Oh yes,' the Widow says in a voice that can be read one way – she is very willing – or read another – she has no choice but to do so. 'Oh yes.'

'This item is successfully completed. Let the Minutes record, Philip Clerk, that Widow Lankester has been appointed Viewer, pro tem.'

Gilbert Swaile dismisses Widow Lankester and all the ancient women with a flick of his hand, calling to them as they go, 'Send in the two watchmen.'

He turns to Philip Carter, 'There is still more to be done. This is taking an age. Can we move quickly now?' He takes out his watch once more, places it on the table in clear sight of all.

'As quickly as Vestry will,' Philip Carter replies. 'This item, the watchmen, and one more after that.'

The bruised, hang-dog watchmen are stood at the door.

'This is simple,' Gilbert Swaile tells them. 'You are watchmen. If you were not you could beat each other to blood and gristle in some side street, some lane, some court. People might even pay to see you do so, wager on the outcome. But in these pestilential times the parish needs watchmen. Good, observant, wide awake, sober watchmen. It is your duty to protect us, the parish. Beaten and maimed you cannot do so. Fined a day's pay for dereliction of duty. All agree?' Vestry agrees. 'And, Parish Clerk, these men are always to be so scheduled on watch so that one is by day, the other by night, so they never see each other, meet each other. You two men, go.'

Thomas Billington and Robert Tomlinson slouch out. Once outside the slouch becomes a swagger. They go their separate ways.

Gilbert Swaile is one of the people there are rumours about, and Thomas Billington sings in bravado.

> *Oh the brewer, the lusty, lusty brewer,*
> *The brewer that brews both ale and beer.*
> *He never heats his liquor hot*
> *But he takes, but he takes,*
> *But he takes his maid by the gear.*

The song can faintly be heard by those just come outside. Anne Abowen raises shocked eyebrows at Goody Susanna Parsons and Widow Dorothy Bullen. Goody Parsons' eyebrows do not move. Widow Bullen looks away.

'I hastened that business,' Gilbert Swaile explains. 'Did anyone have other views on it?'

'Does it matter now if we did?' Emmanuel Bird asks.

'Well did you? Have other views?' Gilbert Swaile replies. 'Did anyone?'

They are all exasperated, tired. It is a long meeting and no-one wants to make it longer.

'Let the Minutes record the decision then,' says Gilbert Swaile.

'Wait,' William Sutterwhit calls out. 'No Constable here today. Why no Constable Snow who caught these watchmen fighting? He should be here to tell us what he can tell us.'

An irritated Gilbert Swaile points to the Clerk to give an answer.

'Vagabonds,' Philip Carter says. 'It was vagabonds, rogues and wandering beggars that the Constable was on the chase for that day and by chance came on these two fighting. Didn't catch the vagabonds because of the need to deal with these two. Today again – these new Orders – today again Constable Samuel Snow is on the chase for beggars seen in the parish, to whip them on. Orders say no wandering beggar be suffered in the streets of this city. Constable Snow is not here because he is in the streets on the Orders.'

Gilbert Swaile looks challenging at the Vestrymen. Repeats, 'Let the Minutes record the decision made on the watchmen.'

'Last item,' Philip Carter announces. 'The minister gone–'

'King's Chaplain, Walter Hall, with the king, who is no longer in London,' Harry Bosvill says.

'Yes, Walter Hall gone, there is the matter of who is to come in.' Philip Carter speaks eagerly, earnestly. 'This parish has had, knows it has had, good, excellent ministering from Thomas–'

Gilbert Swaile holds up a hand, his face unreadable. 'Wait Philip Carter. No more. Here is a letter from Walter Hall, endorsed by the Bishop of London himself, that Reverend Jenkin Williams will come in to St Cyneswide and St Tibba. Will take his first service here in church Sunday next, and thereafter. Until Walter Hall returns. For the Minutes, Philip Carter.'

'Pro tem!' a voice, Gilbert Swaile is not sure who, calls out. It could be one of several.

Shocked looks, rebellious looks, satisfied looks, pleased looks.

'Endorsed by His Grace himself, Humphrey Henchman, Bishop of London,' says John Girling, one of the pleased.

More mutterings, those for Reform are not fond of the bishop of London, of any bishop, and particularly dislike this one who helped Charles the Bastard escape in 51 after the Worcester fight.

'Humphrey Henchman, a heavy, ruinous landlord to the booksellers of Paternoster Row,' mutters Robert Holt, whose wife's cousin is a bookseller of Paternoster Row.

'There it is. There is no more to be said,' Gilbert Swaile announces and takes up his watch, but Harry Bosvill must say his piece.

'Walter Hall is particular, very particular that this parish, his parish, should remain loyal to the King's Church.'

'Which church is that Harry Bosvill?' William Sutterwhit is in a fury. 'The Church of England? The Church of Rome? One? The other? Both? Which? Church of the Great Whore of Babylon? Or more likely the Church of King Charles' Yard Long Tarse. His favoured instrument of rule, his idol of worship!'

'Enough!' roars Gilbert Swaile. 'This Vestry meeting is concluded! Ended!'

'Finis.' Frances Barrow shakes his head.

St Cyneswide & St Tibba, July the 2nd, 1665

Vestry Present
P Carter, Parish Clerk
F Barrow, Church Warden
G Swaile, presides
B Piggot
E Bird
J Girling
R Kerton
E Richbell
W Sutterwhit
H Bosvil
W Pickhering
R Holt
G Lumme
Ancient women Searchers, Keepers, Viewer, present as required
Item – P Carter Vestry Clerk pro tem, £1 p.a.
Item – Vestry Oath tabled this meeting & meetings hereafter
Item – accusation the 1st & accusation the 2nd against Searchers

dismissed, Searchers remain

Item – Widow Lankester Viewer pro tem

Item – Watchmen T Billington, R Tomlinson fined days pay fighting; one to watch day, other night

Item – J Williams comes in minister, pro tem, in place of W Hall

CHAPTER XV

'All we young children, we are sure to die.'

'Oh! These stairs. Oh! These stairs.' Widow Dorothy Bullen's voice is frail, agitated. 'This wand, my red wand, what will I do with it? I can't hold it. What will I do?'

Goody Susanna Parsons, standing backwards on the stairs to the ancient women's room, holds Widow Bullen's hands in hers, says soothingly, 'One at a time, one at a time,' as she walks her up, a step at a time. 'Half way already.'

'Why? Why do I go up these stairs? Where is my daughter? What will I do with my red wand?'

'I can take it for you, I know red wands well,' Widow Hazard says, coming up behind the slow procession. 'Give it to me. I will hold it until you are there.'

Widow Bullen looks around, totters, is held firmly by Goody Parsons and is butressed by Widow Margaret Hazard's shoulder.

Goody Parsons has put her own red wand under her belt. Widow Bullen awkwardly clutches hers in her right hand, making it harder for Goody Parsons to help her.

Widow Hazard reaches around and takes the wand.

'My wand! Who is that there? Who took it?'

'Your friend, a Searcher friend, Widow Hazard. I will hold it for you. You will sit down soon and hold your red wand again.'

'Soon! I want to sit down now. Not on these stairs. Oh these stairs.'

Widow Bullen is hauled and pushed into the room and plonked down on the nearest bale of cloth.

'She is not in good health,' Goody Parsons says. 'Has been in a decline since the Vestry meeting.'

'I can see that,' and declining well before the meeting the Widow thinks. 'Here is your red wand, Widow Bullen.'

The red wand comforts Widow Bullen. She holds it close, heaves a great sigh.

'That Vestry meeting,' Widow Hazard snorts in derision through her one good nostril, finds her own cloth bale to sit on.

'The Vestrymen!' Goodwife Brokefild laughs, coming in with Anne Abowen. 'We have had good sport on our way here talking of the Vestrymen!'

'Tallow chandler John Girling saying my Sara was named for Sarah Collymore. It is he, John Girling, who should be beaten for wicked insolence. A ranting, wicked man, John Girling.'

'So he showed himself to be,' Anne Abowen agrees.

'I have never been at a Vestry meeting before,' Goodwife Brokefild muses, 'a play up upon the stage must be like that. Men shouting, taking a position, pointing accusing fingers. I am pleased I have now seen a play.'

'A comedy made by fools,' Anne Abowen says, 'With a sudden entry by that Bedlam woman Isabella Undnay.'

'Gilbert Swaile, he was a bear leader with a string of badly behaved, angry bears,' Widow Hazard says.

'Leading stupid bears who cannot dance, do not know how to,' once more Anne Abowen agrees with the Widow.

'When Gilbert Swaile first spoke of these, these accusations, I feared from what he said that things would go badly, go very badly,' Goody Susanna Parsons says.

Heads nod, 'So did I. So did I.'

'But not so,' beams Goodwife Joan Brokefild, 'Not so, thanks to the good words from the Clerk's Clerk, John Bell. And God bless Philip Carter and Frances Barrow for finding them.'

'If I understood,' Widow Hazard says slowly, 'Clerk John Bell says that because it is the responsibility of Vestrymen to appoint Searchers–'

'And Keepers and Viewers,' Anne Abowne corrects, but does so mildly.

'Yes, Searchers and Keepers and Viewers they appoint, the Vestrymen. And because Vestrymen will only make wise, honest appointments of wise, honest, ancient women, then Searchers, and Keepers and Viewers,' the Widow nods obligingly at Anne Abowen, 'then–' the Widow has lost her thread.

'Then,' the Goodwife helps out, holds her arms wide towards her fellows, 'we must all be wise, honest, ancient women. And so we are.'

'And the Vestrymen must agree, and they did,' Goody Parsons says cheerfully.

'We do,' Widow Dorothy Bullen chimes in, 'we do agree. I agree.'

'That song Thomas Billington sang. Did you hear it. Scandalous! A song about, well, it is a song about a brewer.'

'It could well be a song about Gilbert Swaile, a lusty man when his drink is on him,' the Goodwife says. 'Those are the rumours.'

'More than rumours,' Goody Parsons confides in her quiet voice. Nods knowingly.

'John Girling!' Widow Hazard explodes in laughter. 'John Girling! See how he jumped when Frances Barrow said there are rumours about him! There *are* rumours. Talk. Mmm.'

'I have heard several,' says Anne Abowen, 'several rumours of John Girling. A spy in the parish for the bishops. A man who says some of his candles are finest beeswax but they are more mutton than bee. And it is known he does not clean his grease from the cobbles. A penny-pinching mean man, and that is not rumour but fact.'

'Fact. This Vestry will not be swayed by facts unrelated!' Widow Hazard says in a voice approximating Gilbert Swaile's.

'Yes,' laughs Goody Parsons, 'and Emmanuel Bird will take an oath that he does not have the plague and never will!'

'And the talk of Beavis Piggot pissing! These are Vestrymen!' Anne Abown says.

'He was fortunate, he could go forth, I would have done the same, wanted to, but dared not leave,' Goodwife Joan Brokefild laughs her laugh.

'Yes, I wanted to,' Goody Parsons says.

'And I would piss too,' Widow Bullen's voice comes as a surprise.

'Now?' Widow Hazard asks,'You would piss now?'

'No! At the meeting, at the Vestry! Not now,' Widow Bullen says indignantly.

'Shall we have Harry Bosvill come here as an ancient woman? Will he suit this room?' Anne Abowen is enjoying herself.

'Who should be here is Widow Lankester, Viewer as appointed,' Widow Hazard says.

'Taking the Oath today. She will come here when she has taken the Oath,' Anne Abowen speaks proprietorially of her new companion, Viewer Widow Lankester.

'Thomas Dugdale not coming in,' Goodwife Brokefild sighs. 'This new man Williams, Book of Common Prayer. There was hope it would be Thomas Dugdale.'

'He that lives upon hope shall die fasting,' is Widow Bullen's surprising intervention.

This observation stills the room.

'This room is small, dark and smells!' Widow Lankester makes a rough entrance. Crashes in like a passel of hogs, is Anne Abowen's first thought.

'Here are cherry tarts,' the new Viewer flourishes a small basket, offers cherry tarts. Widow Bullen takes three. 'Smells,' repeats the new Viewer, 'but cooler here than out in the street.'

The room grows even cooler.

Anne Abowen takes responsibility for the reception of Widow Lankester, her preference – supported by Widow Margaret Hazard – as fellow Viewer. 'We were talking of the Vestry meeting,' Anne Abowen says to her, to bring her in.

'Not talking of the other news?' Widow Lankester asks with offensive incredulity.

'What other news?' Goodwife Joan Brokefild speaks sharply. Widow Lankester was not her preference for Viewer, she favoured down-trodden

Mabell Billington, yoked to a brutish husband.

'She was seen fleeing! The whole family with her! Fleeing by night! You haven't heard?' Widow Lankester shakes her head in exaggerated disbelief.

'We have been busy all this day about our work, our duties,' Goody Parsons says defensively, almost angrily. 'All of us, keeping, viewing, searching. Our parish duties.'

'Widow Ursula Chaukley,' Widow Lankester explains with satisfaction. 'Fled by night, all of them. All gone from her house. All her large family, gone.'

'It is a plague house!' Widow Margaret Hazard exclaims. 'Widow Chaukley with the plague has fled her plague house? It has the cross on the door!'

Widow Lankester manoeuvres a cloth bale to make a comfortable and prominent seat for herself, takes a bite of cherry tart, takes another bite. Looks around, 'Never had the plague. She did not. Wicked woman. A trick! She stole, they all stole. Her big family. Thieves.' She looks to see the effect this has.

The effect is silence.

'Well tell more,' says Widow Dorothy Bullen impatiently. 'We will hear more.'

'More,' Widow Lankester claps her hands on her thighs. 'More. She, Widow Ursula Chaukley, stole from the sick, thieved from the dead, knew her way about houses where she viewed, took what she wanted to take. What she could not take herself she had her family, her large family – sons, daughters, grandsons, grand-daughters – had them take. Told them what to take. A wicked, thieving woman, Widow Chaukley.'

'No,' says Widow Bullen, 'No, I know her.' Anne Abowen, Widow Margaret Hazard, Goodwife Joan Brokefild, Goody Susanna Parsons, all nod, they know her.

Widow Lankester shrugs, laughs, 'One of the grand-daughters was taken as she ran from the house. The watchman at least got one of them, after he woke from his sleep! Caught the smallest one. Small child by name of Libby. She had coins with her, even some gold coins. Watchman beat her until she told all. The house breaking – small children in through a window, told what to look for and where to find it.'

'But the plague,' Anne Abowen persists. 'She had the signs, she herself said so.'

'Yes, of course she said so.' Widow Lankester is enjoying herself. 'So *she* said. Did any Viewer, or Keeper see these signs?'

'She is a Viewer!' Anne Abowen protests, 'She knows the signs well!'

'She knows cunning and deceit even better. That doctor, that doctor Burnett–'

'Barnett,' Widow Hazard corrects her.

'That doctor whatever his name who shut himself in, Widow Chaukley knew of that, used that, did the same.'

'Why not just flee? Why such a trick?' Goodwife Brokefild asks.

'The child said she, they, the whole big family were about to flee with their loot, flee plaguey London, but for the hog man Philip Kilsby.'

'What has that hog man to do with all this?' Anne Abowen thinks it all sounds like some silly tale peddled on cheap paper. 'When Philip Kilsby's hogs ran wild Widow Ursula Chaukley was most busy in viewing the damage. Philip Kilsby, did he make threats to the Widow?'

'Bribes,' Widow Lankester is growing tired of this questioning. She flourishes a cherry tart. 'She took bribes, Viewer Chaukley did, from anyone for anything. Took moneys from Philip Kilsby – told him there would be no claims on him for the damage done by his running hogs. Promised him she would protect him from claims, for a price. Which he paid.'

This met with dejected sighs.

'Hogs,' says Widow Dorothy Bullen, 'All a-siden as hogs fighten.'

Widow Lankester ignores her. 'Here in the parish she cheated and gulled even more. She viewed the hogs' damage and mess, the damage at Edward Richbell the baker, John Girling, tallow chandler–'

'Yes, yes,' says Anne Abowen, 'she went to view the damage as a Viewer. I know she did. I saw her go.'

'Harry Bosvill, soap boiler, Widow Damport, laundry, Robin Kerton, stables,' Widow Lankester proceeds, unstoppable.

'Yes! Yes! And so?'

'And so she took money, bribes, from Edward Richbell, John Girling, Harry Bosvill, Widow Damport, Robin Kerton. Promised them all, if they paid her, she promised Philip Kilsby would shell out large make-amends for all damage done by his hogs.' Widow Lankester laughs, 'Wicked woman.'

'How do you know this, all this?' Widow Hazard asks suspiciously.

'After the Oath,' Widow Lankester shrugs away the Oath, 'I was sent to the Clerk, to the Warden, told them I had taken it, the Oath. But they were all aflame about this news of Widow Chaukley. Talked and talked of it, told it again and again, all they had heard, had learned. I listened as best as I could. The parish talks of nothing else.'

'Those men, those Vestrymen,' Goody Parsons says indignantly. 'Their concern for Widow Chaukley shut up. It was concern for the money – the bribes! – they had paid her. That was their concern!'

Widow Lankester laughs again. 'The thieving, she preferred those houses where people had fled or were dead. Empty houses, easy to plunder. Always something worth taking. Only a few cherry tarts left. Who will have one? Not you Widow Bullen, had more than your share.'

The remaining tarts are taken, the last by Widow Lankester, who also has had more than her share.

'It is hard to hear this,' Anne Abowen says, 'She is a good Christian woman.'

Widow Lankester scoffs, 'Baptised with pump-water!' She holds up a small morsel of tart, 'Bribes? That good Christian woman Widow Ursula Chaukley? It was she who stoked the fire about you Widow Hazard and you Goodwife Brokefild, about you taking bribes. Fanned the fire alight, fed it with rumours and gossip and all manner of flaming fuel, she did. Did it because if the parish was looking at you two burning, then no-one would look towards her and her large family. And no-one did. Fire. Who has tobacco? My pipe is empty.'

Anne Abowen is the first to offer.

'Mine too,' Widow Bullen says. 'My pipe is empty too.'

They sit in peace, draw until their pipes are in a glow.

'I do want to piss,' Widow Bullen says in surprise, looking for the chamber pot.

'Been about your duties. What duties today have you been about?' Widow Lankester asks. 'I am with child to learn.' She is also a known sponge for gossip.

'Back to Francis Woodhouse, his house,' Widow Hazard says promptly, eager to teach. 'Francis Woodhouse, dead of the plague. Wife and son dead of it three Mondays past. Searched today and Francis Woodhouse found dead of the plague.'

The Goodwife nods, 'Edward Woodhouse his son, still alive, still no signs. None.'

'Shut up for two more weeks, and if no signs then Edward Woodhouse, his door is opened,' the Widow rocks her hand back and forth, perhaps his door will be opened, perhaps it won't.

As they talk Widow Lankester takes the full chamber pot from Widow Bullen, goes to the small window and calls, 'Heads below! Heads!' Then pours out the window. 'Some,' she says critically, 'some do not wait after they call Heads but empty their pot without waiting. How can you turn quickly aside if you are not given time to do so? I always wait.' She looks for a challenge to this but none comes.

'Philip Kilsby is kin to Widow Chaukley!' Susanna Parsons says, 'I remember now. Yes.'

'A large family!' Goodwife Joan Brokefild says and laughs.

'Widow Chaukley gained great goodwill among her neighbours for shutting herself in,' Widow Bullen protests. 'Great goodwill. Shut herself up of her own accord. Why would she flee? Great goodwill.'

'Hester Shipley, Widow Shipley, she has no signs,' says Viewer Goody Parsons, tapping her red wand on the floor.

'Where is my red wand? Who has it? Taken it?' Widow Bullen asks.

'In your hand, where I put it,' Widow Hazard says sharply. 'In your hand. Find it there.'

'John Chaukley, who died,' Goodwife Brokefild says reflectively, thinking out loud, 'his sister Agnes, her husband is Timothy Middleton and Timothy Middleton is cousin to Philip Kilsby. Timothy Middleton's mother Ellen sister to Johanna who wed Samuel Kilsby, their son Philip. Yes.'

'Ellen Middleton would not flee,' Widow Bullen says.

'No. She is dead,' Anne Abowen says.

'Yes, she is dead. She would never flee.'

Widow Margaret Hazard is angry, brooding. 'Widow Chaukley always said I should not have kept Sara, that she was not mine to keep. Always said it but never to me. Never to me but I knew she said it. Viper.'

'That song,' the Goodwife says, 'Thomas Billington sang—'

'William Bullen would sing that, or something like,' Widow Dorothy Bullen says.

'I have heard it sung,' Goodwife Joan Brokefild continues.

'When would you have heard a song like that sung?' Widow Lankester asks.

The Goodwife shrugs, 'When I walk at night, out at night, there is tavern singing.'

Widow Margaret Hazard glowers at Widow Lankester should she be challenging why Goodwife Brokefild walks out at night. But Widow Lankester says no more, understands why the Goodwife would stay away from her house.

'There are ten verses for ten trades,' Widow Bullen says. Counts off on her fingers, 'Miller, baker, brewer – the brewer is the third – butcher, weaver, barber, blacksmith – no, tailor then blacksmith – tanner and tinker. Ten. William Bullen sang it.'

'Yes,' says the Goodwife, pleased, 'there are ten. All of the same thing. All about wenching men and their yards, and – you know what else.'

They know.

'Yes, *we* know,' Widow Lankester will emphasise.

'Most verses I would not sing, but the tanner, except the tanner perhaps.'

'Oh yes, the tanner, you could sing that. Do,' says Widow Bullen.

Goodwife Joan Brokefild does.

Oh the tanner, the merry, merry tanner,
The tanner, that draws good hides into leather.
He never strips himself to work
But his maid, but his maid,
But his maid and he's together.

'Yes, you can sing that one,' says Widow Bullen. She laughs, 'It is one of those songs, the many songs that William Bullen would sing. That verse, only nakedness there and no more, the tanner and the maid. Naked with your husband is no bad thing. We have all been that.'

Goodwife Brokefild's Issac has no time for stripping to nakedness on those occasions they are together. A harsh fumble up her skirts and he is done. She does not wish to see him naked, nor him her. She says wryly to Widow Bullen, 'That verse is not of the tanner's wife but his maid.'

Widow Bullen shrugs this off, continues, 'The first verse is of the miller and *his* maid and that is the most lewd of all. The worst. Oh yes,' she laughs, stands. 'Who will walk me down these devil-made stairs? Made to kill ancient women. This room does smell, but the cherry tarts, I like the cherry tarts. We will have more next time.'

Anne Abowen and Widow Lankester will walk her down. Walk with her, slowly, to her house.

'The Searchers, Goodwife Brokefild is the good-humoured one, laughs easily,' Widow Lankester says.

'She would laugh at the wagging of a straw,' Widow Bullen herself laughs.

Goody Susanna Parsons, Widow Margaret Hazard and Goodwife Joan Brokefild walk together back to the church square of St Cyneswide and St Tibba.

'Widow Lankester speaks her mind,' says Goody Parsons.

'She certainly does that well, may she be as good a Viewer as she is speaker,' the Widow replies.

There is a girls' game filling the square. Sara is there. Libby Chaukley playing enthusiastically, is there, some bruising starting to mark her face.

'She will be with some of the large family who have not fled. Not all will have fled. Agnes Middleton, her aunt, great aunt, is not a thief. The girl Libby Chaukley could well live with her,' the Goodwife says.

'Mmm, until her mother or her grandmother send for her,' says Widow Hazard. 'Wherever they are. Have fled to.'

The girls dance in a ring, sing:

Wallflowers, wallflowers,
Growing up so high,
All we young children,
We are sure to die.
Excepting little Annie Carter,
She is best of all,
She can skip, and she can dance,
And she can turn the candlestick.
Oh my, fie for shame,
Turn your back to the wall again!

'The youngest one, it is always excepting the youngest one. That would have been little Mary Barrett who would be in the game, this wallflower game, but has died,' the Goodwife says.

'Mmm.' Widow Margaret Hazard stares at little Libby Chaukley. Unaware of the scrutiny, the child plays on, full of excited, shouting joy. She is a small child.

Widow Hazard breaks through the circle, stopping the game, goes up to the child and takes her roughly by the chin, stares closely. Libby Chaukley stands still, unflinching, although her legs stiffen to hold her up. She stares back at the Widow's fire-twisted face. The Widow releases her and waves her back into the stalled game for it to resume from where it was interrupted.

'She is a fair child, fair enough. Does not have thief's eyes, no thief's eyes there,' Widow Hazard says to the other ancient women.

'Little Libby Chaukley will not be sent for,' Goody Parsons says. 'She will be left here in this sickly city.'

'She could be the one excepted who is best of all,' the Goodwife says cheerfully.

Widow Hazard agrees. 'She is the best one of that Chaukley family, and not all the young children are sure to die,' she says confidently. 'Not all.'

* * *

London, Bills of Mortality for 130 Parishes
from the 27 of June to the 4 of July 1665
Buried, in all – 1006; Plague – 470
Parishes clear of the Plague – 97; Parishes Infected – 33

CHAPTER XVI

London, Thursday, 6 July 1665

'The Lord is my defence and strength, my joy,
my mirth, and song.'

'Watchmen!' the Parish Clerk explodes. 'To watch, to stay awake to watch! Not hard, it does not require an apprenticeship of years under a harsh master to learn what a watchman must do.'

'Stay awake,' the Church Warden agrees.

'Stay awake, keep his eyes open. Stand up. Move about. Look about. Matters go to turd as soon as he leans against the wall. Go even worse when he sits down to lean against the wall. He falls asleep. They all fall asleep.'

'And many find themselves a cup or two.'

'For Roger Geoffrayes it is a cup or ten, or twenty, twenty tens. They all crept past him. Widow Chaukley and her family. Crept? They might have walked, marched past him, drums beating, trumpets sounding. Just opened the door and, and went out, past the sleeping watchman.' Parish Clerk Philip Carter sighs a sigh of deep discontent.

'He says Widow Chaukley's cousin Thomas, or was it her uncle Abraham, or her nephew Kenrick? Roger Geoffrayes says one of them, or all of them, brought him drink. A kindness he says. They brought him drink to thank him for keeping such good watch on Widow Chaukley's house!' The Warden laughs, shakes his head. 'For keeping her and her large family safe.'

'And she stealing all the time. From the houses of people she viewed. Her sons and her daughters, her grandsons and daughters – thieving magpies the lot – creeping into the houses of the dead. Thieving. If that small girl had not tripped over his great sleeping log of a leg they would all be gone and no-one knowing the better. The house would be quiet. Eventually, yes eventually the Searchers would be sent for, to search what? An empty house!' If Philip Carter could prowl around the vestry he would. He bangs a crutch on the floor in frustration.

'I have buriers who say sixpence a grave means sixpence a corpse buried,' the Warden has his own grievances to air. 'I say sixpence a grave is sixpence a grave no matter how many corpses might go in it. How can you do business with uncouth men, filthy with earth and worse, whose only answer is to glare at you, lay their spades on the ground, glare at you though a fog of pipe smoke? And they will have tobacco, or money to buy it.'

The Parish Clerk grunts, winces, his legs are giving him grief. He looks to his pipe. Talk of plague corpses makes him set about having his own pipe alight and glowing.

'The buriers are pressing for all they can get. The new Order and its "allgravesshallbeatleastsixfootdeep." All they do is scoff and ask where can they find a patch of unburied ground six foot deep. "Can't be done," they say, "can't be done." Ask me to find an undug plot!'

'Can you?' The Clerk knows the answer.

'Smoking all the time, pipes never leave their mouths, clenched there. So many pipes bitten through! Ground and graves littered with broken stems. They will have pipe-money.'

Philip Carter does not want to hear that the buriers will have pipe-money, has had enough of this talk of buriers. Money business, payments, are the Warden's concern, not his. 'At least William Northage is a man content. Ringing his bell, crying out the names of the dead.'

'And will *he* have more money? For doing the work it is his duty to do?' Frances Barrow asks.

'No, he is content. The only payment demanded is listening to him talk of it. Endlessly. He likes clanging his bell and crying the names of the dead.' Philip Carter frowns, 'This business with Widow Chaukley, it is now well known, widely known.' He thumps his crutch down. 'At Parish Clerks' this week John Vigor, St Bennet Sherehog, was making a great noise about it. "Your Viewers and your Searchers," he says, "What things go on in St Cyneswide and St Tibba," he says. "Not the Searchers," I say, "and only one Viewer." But still a laughing stock.'

'Your young John Bell, his words helped the Searchers at Vestry.'

'Yes, I told him and it pleased him. He is a porridge man, young John Bell, through and through. But a good Clerk of the Clerks. Obliging, helpful. He was a good help to us in this business.'

'Are you softening towards the porridge men?' The Warden asks, only half in jest.

Philip Carter shakes his head, 'No softening on either side. None. With Charles the Scotchman fled everything has become harder, sharper, between our saints' side and their bishops' side. They fear that because he has run this will work to our gain, and on our side we hope and pray that it will be.'

'It will,' the Warden says with complete assurance. 'It will.'

'One of the psalms sung at Parish Clerks, psalm the second, when we sang this verse:

> *And thou shalt break them mightily as with an iron rod:*
> *And as a Potter's vessel thou shalt dash them all abroad.*

'Those porridge men on the left side of the Hall, their faces told clearly that for them it meant *us* being broken mightily, and on our side of the Hall we knew it was *them* being smashed with an iron rod like a potter's vessel. So, no softening there. We call ourselves saints, godly, God's elect. They call us ungodly, unregenerate, disaffected fanatics. Sectaries. We call them courtiers, apostates.'

'The new one coming in here, Jenkin Williams, he must be the same as Walter Hall. That was clear at the Vestry meeting. Book of Common?' the Warden asks.

The Clerk rocks his hand, smiles wryly. 'Not the same as Dearly Beloved, no. Now Jenkin Williams is for bishops and the porridge Book, but not always so. I found this out at Parish Clerks, always gossip and rumour to be had there. If Jenkin Williams were a clerk, a parish clerk, he would have made his way back and forth across the aisle at our Hall. First on the other side, then over to ours, and now back to theirs.'

Jenkin Williams is not the only one who has done this. There is nothing to say.

But Philip Carter will add, 'Young John Bell says St Cyneswide and St Tibba is fortunate to have the new man, this Jenkin Williams. Fortunate because there are so many empty pulpits, with no chance of them being filled, and also fortunate because this Williams is "A kind, friendly, gentle man, an adaptable man," says young John Bell.'

Frances Barrow laughs, 'Very adaptable it seems. Will he adapt to a saints' parish in the time of plague?'

'Work for him in this, just issued,' the Clerk produces from his chest new-printed sheets. Reads:

> *By the King. A Proclamation for a General Fast Throughout this Realm of England.*
>
>   *Whereas it hath pleased Almighty God, after many years of Health, and many great and miraculous Mercies afforded to this Kingdom, to visit the Cities of London and Westminster, and places adjacent with the Plague and Pestilence, which by the spreading thereof into several Parishes, & other the more remote parts of this Kingdom, seems to threaten a general and most dreadful Visitation: To the end therefore that Prayers and Supplications may every where be offered up unto Almighty God for the removal of this heavy Judgement, and that some Solemn Days and Times may be set apart for the performance of these and other Religious Duties.*
>
>   *His Majesty is pleased, by the Advice of His Privy Council, to Declare, and doth hereby publish and declare his Royal Will and Pleasure, That Wednesday next being the Twelfth day of this instant July, shall be observed and kept within the Cities of London and Westminster, and places adjacent, as a Day of Fasting and Humiliation; And Wednesday three Weeks after being the Second day of August, shall be observed and kept in like manner in all parts of this Realm; and so from thence forward every First Wednesday of*

every Month successively, until it shall please God to withdraw this
Plague and grievous Sickness.

'There's more, there's always more, let me see: form of prayers to be published to be used in all churches; collection of alms and charitable benevolence upon these Fast days; which collections be paid to the bishops – ha! to the bishops! – and the bishops shall take care (bah) that the moneys be applied to the relief of such places as shall be visited with the plague; and the overplus, if any, to be paid to the bishop of London to be applied to the poor who are sick and visited with the plague in London or Westminster – good, *if* there is any overplus that hasn't been pocketed by some bishop, good that it should come to London; preachers on the said Fast days to exhort the people to a free and cheerful contribution towards the relief of their Christian brethren whom it hath pleased God to visit with the sickness. Hear this! – "Given at St James this sixth day of July!" Not St James London, more likely St James at Syon House where he keeps court.'

'Already packing to remove to Hampton Court. Wednesday next will be first in church for this Williams, for the Fast day?'

'No, he'll come to take the service this Sunday. Coming today. Or tomorrow. Or Saturday, coaches and roads allowing.'

'Dogs,' the Church Warden says, 'William Northage, his Gypsy. A bell-man needs his dog. Barnard Clapshaw, his Grinder, and a watchman needs his dog. Edward Richbell, his Gnasher–'

'Yes, yes, a baker needs a dog, a good ratter, for the vermin. I know, they all need their dogs. No Dog Killers have been appointed in St Cyneswide and St Tibba. Who knows? Perhaps this plague will soon end and there will be no need.'

Neither Clerk nor Warden believe this.

* * *

London, Friday, 7 July 1665

'So, what do you bring to the table?' Gilbert Swaile asks.

Jack has not thought to bring drink, or food, or a present to Gilbert Swaile's brewery. And who brings ale to a brewery? The table is a barrel and on it a list of accounts held down by a brick. There is little space for anything else even if Jack had brought something. He is not invited to sit.

Jack has come to Gilbert Swaile's brewery with a speech prepared, and when asked by a curious Gilbert Swaile why he has come delivers the speech as rehearsed in his garret room. Item the first: he acknowledges that these are sad times, bad times, but business must still be done. Item the second: indeed there are particular pieces of business, particular trades, that are already more in demand due to these sickly times. Item the third: this demand will only grow as the sickness grows on. Item the fourth: men of enterprise who can see where the growing demand lies and who are prepared to move quickly, to spend wisely, will do well for themselves. Item the fifth and the last: also they will be benefactors in a time of need to a suffering people, to a city and nation in distress.

Jack stops, looks for signs on Gilbert Swaile's face that he is impressed, convinced. He sees none.

'So what particular trades, business, do you mean? What do you propose?' Gilbert Swaile asks.

'I know the parish well. I speak to many in St Cyneswide and St Tibba. To gentry, citizens, poor folk.'

Gilbert Swaile does not seem to regard this as conferring any special knowledge on Jack; looks sceptical, impatient.

'I have spoken,' Jack says eagerly, 'to many of those whose work is multiplied by the sickness.'

'And? Who?' the brewer looks down at his list of accounts, losing interest in Jack.

'The buriers, Job and Jonah,' confident Jack answers. 'Burying the plague dead. They smoke. I mean the buriers smoke to keep the infection at bay. They smoke bags and bags of tobacco. Their pipes break. Buriers here in St Cyneswide and St Tibba, and in every parish struck by the plague, there is a great need of tobacco, of pipes.'

Gilbert Swaile shakes his head, stands up, ready to dismiss Jack.

'Tobacco. There is a glut. Warehouses down the docks full of it. Overflowing with tobacco. No profit to be made there. The buriers can have all the tobacco they need, and more. As for pipes, the pipe-clay monopolists, the men of Westminster, they have a tight hold when it comes to pipes. They'll be the ones who make money out of your Jonahs and Jobs here and everywhere. There is no business for me here.' He generously, and condescendingly, adds, 'for us.' Gilbert Swaile turns away.

'Coffins. Shrouds. Shrouds and coffins,' Jack says promptly, not put off.

'Well? So?'

'William Pickhering, joiner, his workshop in the square. He is making more coffins but supplies of wood are short. I know of a merchant who can provide all the wood that's needed.'

'Who is that?'

Jack ignores the question. 'Shrouds. For those with no money for a coffin – there are many of them – shrouds will be needed. Yards and yards, miles and miles of cloth needed for shrouds.'

'And you can find yards and yards, miles and miles of cloth?'

'Yes, wood for coffins, cloth for shrouds.'

'What are wood and cloth to me? Why tell me this?'

'You will need to look wider than this parish to sell your beer. People are leaving, fewer thirsty mouths, your sales dropping.' Jack gestures, a clever guess, to the accounts. 'I can sell wider for you. I know London far beyond St Cyneswide and St Tibba, even beyond the walls. And,' Jack pauses for effect, 'I've come to you because you are a man of worth, of note, who has the standing to make a corporation which will bring everything together – ale, cloth, coffins, and more – into a venture which combines small enterprises, businesses, workshops, into something greater. More powerful. Wealthier. A joint venture.'

'Is that all I do? No money from me required?'

'Money required from all,' says Jack, 'from all. Spending money to make even more. Money begets money.'

'Who are the all? The all who will spend money to make money?'

'You. William Pickhering. The wood merchant. The cloth merchant.'

'And you?' asks Gilbert Swaile. 'What *do* you bring to the table?'

'I can sell, I can organise, I bring ideas. I can bring people together to their advantage, to all our advantage, to the venture's advantage. And I have time, Walter Hall being gone away–'

'Fled,' the brewer says automatically. 'He has fled.'

'Yes, fled. I have time and I know who to know. I bring all that.' He spreads his arms, all that.

'Only that? You ask me to bring my position, my money. You have told me what you offer and I answer is that all?'

'I can bring money. Some money.'

Gilbert Swaile looks dubious. 'We shall see.' But he does not dismiss Jack. 'So, how will you take this forward? When will you tell how much money you bring? Not now?'

'I will take it forward by getting all who are, or might be, part of this together. There I will present some sums, some calculations of expenditure, of profit. Then there can be talk of who brings what money. How much.'

'Good. You do that. When you have more about this gathering, these sums, tell me.' Gilbert Swaile waves him away.

'It will be soon,' Jack calls. 'No time to lose.'

Jack leaves the brewer and his brewery. He has in his pocket a letter from Walter Hall who has fled. The letter, dated Wednesday 5 July, Syon House, tells him that with Jenkin Williams coming in to St Cyneswide and St Tibba as Minister pro tem, he, Walter Hall, will no longer make quarterly payments to Jack Green the footboy. However, regarding payment, Jack Green is free to make any arrangments with Jenkin Williams that both are agreeable to. Jack Green will naturally understand that there is no question of both Walter Hall and Jenkin Williams paying him. Walter Hall trusts that with God's blessing and protection Jack Green will come unscathed through these difficult times that are currently affecting not just London but the kingdom at large. Indeed, His Majesty and His Court will be removing to Hampton Court and Jack Green will inform Jenkin Williams of this so that any further correspondence can be addessed accordingly.

From what Jack has already found out of Jenkin Williams – a man of limited means with a wife and children – there seems little or no prospect of any payment from him. The best Jack can hope for is to keep his garret quarters in the rectory.

It is a hot night, hot even for this hottest of summers. Then comes thunder and lightning and the storm lasts all the night. Jack in the garret, the rain on the roof, he lies awake with more schemes in his head than those he has opened today to Gilbert Swaile. He will be as wealthy as Sir Thomas Vyner. More so.

* * *

London, Saturday, 8 July 1665
Evening

'Crowded!' exclaims the Church Warden with satisfaction. 'Room's crowded and not all here yet. More to come!' He names out loud, counts on his fingers: 'Thomas Trew, Nathaniel Hale, John Barriffe, Erasmus Bacockie, you young Jack Green, here's William Sutterwhit and Robert Tollinson just come. And all these brave lads from St Matthew Friday Street. Give us your names lads.'

'Raphe Wroth,' says Raphe Wroth pointing to himself, 'Harry Pecke, Christopher Frier, Nicholas Marrett, Edmund Stase. All from St Matthew Friday. All for Bible and no bishops. All have torn the Porridge book.'

'Young ones for the Good Old Cause. Good lads, good men who will overturn the porridge pot. Still waiting on more to come. Chose this room, this big room, at the *Nag's Head*, bigger than the *White Hind*, now I'm not sure it will be big enough. Crowded and still more to come. Anyone seen Anthony Erlam, Zachery Waite? They know to come to the *Nag's*. Jack lad, fetch the pot-boy will you? There are some thirsty mouths here.'

'Zachery Waite,' says Erasmus Bacockie tearfully, 'I fear we'll not see him here tonight. Perhaps never see him again in this life.'

'What do you mean, Erasmus?' John Barriffe asks. 'Why do you say that?'

'Yesterday I took my morning draught with him at the *Hind*. He had the head-ache, complained miserably of it. Looked feverish, and his ale didn't settle well in his stomach. We won't see Zachery Waite here tonight. Or I fear ever.'

The room is silent. There are close looks at Erasmus Bacockie who yesterday was with the ailing Zachery Waite. But the pot-boy brings in drinks and the five St Matthew Friday men set to noisily and show their elders how to drink.

'And here,' says a relieved Frances Barrow, 'here is Alexander Muzzard and, and one other.'

Most in the room know Alexander Muzzard of All Hallows the Great, or know of him. The other, a long bearded and dusty country man in a farm smock, is not familiar.

'If he comes with Alexander Muzzard then he's a Fifth Monarchy Man. Must be,' says John Barriffe.

'I know the face, not the beard, I don't know the beard but know something of the face. It was from some time ago, but I can't find the name,' Nathaniel Hale says.

'A psalm!' Alexander Muzzard uses his parish clerk's voice. 'A psalm before we hear from our friend. Psalm the one hundred and eighteenth. A great enterprise as we shall hear of today deserves a fitting psalm.'

'Commended by Oliver Protector himself, that psalm,' John Barriffe calls out.

'Yes, as I was going to say, a psalm highly praised by the Protector. Let us sing to the praise and glory of God psalm the eighteenth and one hundred, Martyrs' Tune. Not all verses. Follow my line:

> *The Lord himself is on my side, I will not stand in doubt,*
> *Nor fear what man can do to me, when God stands me about.*
> *The Lord doth take my part with them that help to succour me:*
> *Therefore I shall see my desire upon my enemy.*
> *Better it is to trust in God, than in man's mortal seed:*
> *Or to put confidence in kings or princes in our need.*

While Alexander Muzzard lines out the next verse – a verse, like all the verses, that they know word perfect – Nathaniel Hale nudges John Barriffe, whispers a loud whisper, 'Colonel Henry Danvers! That is Colonel Danvers! Always a strong man for the Cause.'

The bearded, smocked country man looks up at this name, his name. Nathaniel Hale sits up straight on the bench, a trooper on parade. Alexander Muzzard charges ahead at a goodly trot over this interuption.

> *They did with force thrust fore at me, that I indeed might fall:*
> *But through the Lord I found such help, that they were vanquished all.*
> *The Lord is my defence and strength, my joy, my mirth, and song:*
> *He is become for me indeed a Saviour most strong.*

'That last verse!' Alexander Muzzard shouts, 'My joy, my mirth, my song! We will sing it again!' They do, to the great satisfaction of all.

'Saints, godly men, God's party. Here is a man not long returned from the Low Country, returned at a time, a most, most opportune time, to carry forward the business of all godly men. Charles the Bastard has fled, fled again as he has done before, fled with his tail between his legs–'

'Between his legs,' guffaws Harry Pecke from St Matthews Friday Street, 'the whoremaster bastard has always something between his legs.' He wags a suggestive finger.

His sally is appreciated by the other young St Matthew men but the interjection is resented by the old troopers.

'Pipe down,' calls Erasmus Bacockie belligerently. Harry Pecke is not abashed. Those from St Matthew Friday Street are prentice boys near the end of their time. Brawling young men.

Raphe Wroth stands up, asks contemptuously, indifferently, 'Will you have us go?'

'These are the ones who last year beat their master, cooper Ireland on Breadstreet Hill,' John Barriffe tells Thomas Trew. 'Beat him. They was taken and put in the pillory. He was one,' he points to Nicholas Marrett, 'him another,' points to Edmund Stase. 'Then all the Cheapside prentices, a great company of them, came and escaped them away and pulled down the pillory. Pillory put back up, torn down again. You remember? Drums beat all up and down the city to raise out the train-bands to quiet the town? Only last year, around this time.'

'I do remember,' says Thomas Trew after thought, 'I do remember. A trained-band here in Cheapside on their guard.'

'That was us,' says Nicholas Marrett, 'and they caught us again and pilloried us again and whipped us back to cooper Ireland's house. We was whipped and beaten but he wouldn't beat us again. Won't. He knows what will happen.'

Christopher Frier, still a small boy, speaks in a high voice, 'Putting prentices in the pillory, that has never been done in the City since it was the City. It ought never to have been done to Nicholas Marrett and Edmund Stase and it won't be done again.'

Edmund Stase stands, says in mock politeness to the old troopers, 'Will you see the lash cuts on my back?'

Nicholas Marrett stands with him, 'You can see where the whip cut my face. See? Here,' he traces a large scar from the forehead down his right cheek.

Nathaniel Hale jumps up, 'We have come to hear of some great business, not to be lectured by prentice boys!'

'And so you shall,' says an exasperated Alexander Muzzard, 'so you shall, you all shall. Now all sit, all sit, to hear of this great business. All take your places.'

Because they will hear of the great business, they do. The prentices genially, Nathaniel Hale angrily.

'This, this country man,' says Alexander Muzzard with a grin, 'as Nathaniel Hale said, this country man is Colonel Henry Danvers, Colonel Henry Danvers his very self, now safely back in England. The man chosen by all to lead the Council of Six. The man–'

'So let us hear the man, Alexander Muzzard, let us hear him!' shouts Nathaniel Hale, still angry.

Alexander Muzzard says, 'Here is the chief man to carry on our design,' sits down, and leaves the floor to Colonel Henry Danvers.

'Spies,' Henry Danvers says very softly.

'I can't hear. Speak up! Did he say lies? Why is he whispering?' Erasmus Bacockie asks in confusion.

'Spies!' roars Henry Danvers, banging down on the table and making the pots dance. 'Spies! Spies are everywhere!' He stops, looks at them in turn.

'Now you,' he points to Thomas Trew, 'look at the man on your left, look closely. All of you, look to the man on your left. Then on your right. Then in front. Then behind. Do it. All of you. If you know that man is loyal, then stay. If you do not know that man is loyal, if you have any doubt, any at all about anyone here then go. Now. And if one goes we all go. If there is a spy here we are all lost.'

They all look carefully around them. No-one moves. No-one goes.

With a solemn nod Henry Danvers ackowledges that the room declares itself to be free of spies. He speaks in moderate, reasonable tones.

'The Good Old Cause. Words we say with a smile, with affection, with pride. Our Cause. The Cause of all the saints, of God's party. It is a Good Cause. But is it an Old Cause?' he asks.

'No!' he thunders out. 'No! It is not! Old means past, means gone, but our Cause is not gone. It is not past. It is our Cause of today, of tomorrow, of eternity! It is the Cause of King Jesus! Remember the cry, King Jesus, and the heads upon the gates? Those heads, those blessed heads, they are still there. Still looking on and waiting. Waiting for us, and now we have come, we are here!'

He has captured his audience, who sit in fierce silence. This is what they have come to hear. This is what they want to hear.

'Good Old Cause. You can retire to memories. Good memories, yes. Comfortable memories. Happy in what once was. Retreat to the good old past. Retreat and let the forces of Babylon have their easy victory. Let their forces of shameful wickedness, sin and apostasy, drag all down into the pit. Into eternal damnation!

'Or you can take up your swords, your butchers' knives, your woodsmen's saws, your tailors' needles, your masons' hammers! Take them up for King Jesus and his Good Eternal Cause! And pray God that he will put an axe into the hands of his servants to hew down king and bishops, root and branch!'

The *Nag's Head* rumbles with approval. The pot-boy, standing by the prentices with two hands full of pots, stands enthralled. There is a pause, all must drink and refresh.

'Thirsty work,' says Henry Danvers conversationally, disarmingly, and finds again his reasonable, calm voice. 'They are mistaken who believe – and there are some who do believe – that the affections of this people, this land, are towards the House of Stuart. Towards the House of Stuart? Towards Charles the Bastard? Beloved only of drunken whores and whoremasters? We will not have the kingdom of Stuarts for there is the kingdom and dominion of our church, of Christ and his saints, to be expected upon this earth!

'The Good Cause. The Good Now Cause! The Good Forever Cause! And now is the time to fight for King Jesus, for all those of a Gospel spirit to fight. We will do God's duty against this Charles, against this poor and beggarly king, against his court, his lords, his bishops. If we do not we will be the most monstrous wretches that ever trampled on the ground through the globe of all the earth. We must not draw back our hands from doing the Lord's work, for it is said by the Lord that one shall frighten one thousand. The enemies of God cannot harm the saints.

'Remember the false idol that Nebuchadnezar saw in his dream. He saw a great image whose brightness was excellent, whose form was terrible. This image's head was of fine gold, his breasts and arms of silver, his belly and his thighs of brass, his legs of iron, his feet part of iron and part of clay.'

'Book of Daniel,' Church Warden Frances Barrow says to Jack the footboy.

'There came a stone in Nebuchadnezar's dream, a great stone which smote the image upon the feet of iron and clay and broke them to pieces. And the iron, the clay, the silver, and the gold were broken to pieces together and became like the chaff of the summer threshing floors and the wind carried them away and no place was found for them.'

Colonel Henry Danvers raises up his arms, 'Christ is the stone that will crush all the powers of the earth. The Stuart, his church, his bishops, his Book of Common Prayer, they shall all be broken to pieces and like chaff will be blown away by the wind and no place – no place! – will be found for them!'

There is a great intake of breath.

'The time has come for King Jesus, for his saints, for the godly.' Now Henry Danvers sounds like a mild school master. 'Who knows the third day of September? Eh? Who knows it?'

'The death day of Oliver Protector,' says Raphe Wroth quickly, getting in before the old men have found voice.

'Yes. Oliver's death day. More?' urges Henry Danvers.

'The great victories, our great victories at the Dunbar fight in 50 and the Worcester fight in 51, both on the third day of September,' Nathaniel Hale, himself once of Oliver's regiment, shows these upstart prentices that they do not know everything. He would also show them his Dunbar medal, flourish it at them, but he has lost it somewhere.

'Every year has a third day of September,' says Henry Danvers. 'This year, 65, there shall be a victory that will surely measure up to, perhaps even outshine, those of Worcester, of Dunbar. A victory that will make the Good Old Cause anew! The Good Forever Cause!'

The room stands and cheers and stamps its feet and thumps its pots on tables.

'There are others waiting to hear him tonight, other gatherings, and we must go,' Alexander Muzzard announces.

As he waves his farewells, makes his way through a hand-shaking, back-clapping crowd, Colonel Henry Danvers says, 'Remember that day, and remember great days past, great days to come. And to come soon! Very soon. You will hear more of this. All you of God's army! More!'

He stops at the door and calls back, 'Book of Malachi, chapter the fourth, verse the third: "Ye shall tread down the wicked; for they shall be ashes under the soles of your feet in the day that I shall do this, saith the Lord of hosts." As ashes under the soles of your feet!'

It is not ashes under foot that Henry Danvers encounters as he leaves at a run but a great gust tearing at the door, heralding a mighty storm of wind and rain.

'Wet out,' says Nathaniel Hale, glad to be indoors talking, drinking, reminiscing.

'Dunbar, those campaigns in Scotland,' says Erasmus Bacockie, 'where we had to carry rations, seven days of rations and they were biscuit and cheese. Biscuit and cheese. After a few days you couldn't tell the difference, what was biscuit and what was cheese. Dreadful dry eating, but better than what the Scots ate! And always in haste, "Lively, you must act lively," that was Oliver in Scotland. And everywhere.'

'What Colonel Danvers said, we here, those like us, we have always been true to the Cause,' Thomas Trew now cannot bring himself to say the Good Old Cause. 'I am true, like my name. Never changed. Those at the top, the lords and sirs, that sort, they can change back and forth and always end up on the winning side. Not so for us.' Thomas Trew is well into his cups.

'Frances Barrow you have a new man at your St Cyneswide and St Tibba, a new man coming in. Who is he?' John Barriffe asks.

'One Jenkin Williams. A man who runs with the hares, hunts with the hounds and always finds a place by the fire.'

'A religious turncoat?' asks Nicholas Marrett who has joined in unasked. 'One of those who will always find himself a living no matter what the times are?'

'Yes,' answers Frances Barrow, 'one of those.'

'Here!' calls Nicholas Marrett to his prentice friends. 'That song, the *Trimming Parson*, St Cyneswide and St Tibba now have one! Do you know the song?' Nicholas Marrett asks the rest of the room. They do not.

'We will give you the chorus first. Christopher Frier is still a boy singer, he will do it best.'

'Sing loud against the storm!' John Barriffe calls.

In his boy's clear, high voice Christopher Frier sings, competes successfully with the rain and the wind.

A Turncoat is a cunning Man
That cants to admiration,
And prays for any side to gain
The people's approbation.

'Lead them through it again,' says Harry Pecke, so he does. All take part. The troopers are quick studies in a song.

'Now the song in full,' Christopher Frier announces. 'Loud voices against the storm!' The prentice boys stand and sing:

I loved no king in Forty One,
When prelacy went down,
A cloak and band I then put on,
And preached against the Crown.

'Chorus!' calls Christopher Frier.

A Turncoat is a cunning Man
That cants to admiration,
And prays for any side to gain
The people's approbation.

I shew'd 'em paths to heaven untrod,
From Pop'ry to refine 'em,
And taught the people to serve God,
As if the Dee'l were in 'em.

A Turncoat, &c.

When Brewer Noll, with warty nose,
The stinking Rump dismounted,
I wisely still adher'd to those
Who strongest were accounted.

A Turncoat, &c.

I preach'd and pray'd for Oliver,
And all his fine abettors,
But curs'd the King and Cavalier,
And cry'd 'em down for traitors.

A Turncoat, &c.

When Charles return'd into the land,
The English Crown's supporter,
I shifted off my cloak and band,
And then became a courtier.

A Turncoat, &c.

The King's religion I profest,
And found there was no harm in't:
I fawn'd and flatter'd like the rest,
Till I had got preferment.

A Turncoat, &c.

I taught my conscience how to churn
Up honesty with evil,
And if the world should over-turn,
I'd side then with the Devil.

A Turncoat, &c.'

'First verse, best verse, sing it again!' calls the Church Warden.

The song is a mighty success, and must be sung several times over. The prentices and the old troopers are made fine friends.

The storm blows itself away, leaving a small rain mizzling down, and the sound of water running over roofs, coursing into the channels.

'Did you catch it all Frances Barrow? Did you William Sutterwhit? A good song to sing in your parish!' shouts Nathaniel Hale.

'I have it all in here!' Frances Barrow bumps his pot on his head. 'In here!'

'In the pot, Frances? Then you will not recall it because your pot will soon be empty!' laughs Thomas Trew.

'So I will refill it. Pot-boy!'

William Sutterwhit, quiet and thoughtful for much of the evening, says reflectively to Jack, 'It was not on Oliver Protector's nose, that wart. Not his nose. He had a large one on his chin. In the middle. And a small one here,' he touches above his right eyebrow. 'I don't know why the song says it was on his nose.' He drinks, thinks, continues, 'Red in the face, Oliver, and a very sharp voice. He had a loud laugh, when he did laugh, and then he roared.'

'He roared laughing when the Scottish lines broke before us at Dunbar, laughed like a man drunk,' says Erasmus Bacockie. 'I will say that it is strange, odd, you should have a Jenkin Williams come to your parish William Sutterwhit. Strange, because there was a William Jenkyn who preached in the godly cause at Christ Church, Newgate Street. Strange. William Jenkyn, Jenkin Williams.' He shakes his head at the oddity of it.

'Colonel Henry Danvers,' Nathaniel Hale says to his new good friend Raphe Wroth, 'He wrote *Mirabilis Annus, the Year of Prodigies and Wonders*. A most important book? Did you know that?'

'No,' says Raphe Wroth, impressed. 'He wrote that?'

'He did. A great book. Great. I have not read it but I have heard it spoken of as a great book.'

'You boys,' says John Barriffe, 'I must go and piss. You good London prentice boys. Here is some counsel, good counsel from an old man. Hear me. Item the first, never hold back a piss. Item the second, never force a fart. Item the third, never waste a stiff yard, day or night. Never waste one. Good counsel.' He wanders off to find a pot to piss in.

'Item the first!' Raphe Wroth calls after him.

'Jenkin Williams, William Jenkyn. Are you sure they are not one and the same? The same man?' Erasmus Bacockie asks the room. The room does not answer.

CHAPTER XVII

'For the comforting of such that delight in music.'

'Dearly Beloved,' says Minister Jenkin Williams to the congregation of St Cyneswide and St Tibba. This is greeted with snickers and guffaws, which he ignores.

'Let us pray.

'Oh Almighty God, who in thy wrath didst send a plague upon thine own people in the wilderness, for their obstinate rebellion against Moses and Aaron; and also, in the time of king David, didst slay with the plague of pestilence threescore and ten thousand, and yet remembering thy mercy didst save the rest: have pity upon us miserable sinners, who now are visited with great sickness and mortality; that like as thou didst then accept of atonement and didst command the destroying Angel to cease from punishing, so may it please thee to withdraw from us this plague and grievous sickness; through Jesus Christ our Lord. Amen.'

Parish Clerk Philip Carter leads the congregation in a fervent 'Amen!'

'That is a most excellent prayer,' says Widow Dorothy Bullen to fellow Keeper Goody Susanna Parsons and to the Searchers and Viewers assembled with her. 'We have never been prayed that prayer before! Most excellent. Walter Hall never prayed us that prayer.' She reaches for her angelica nosegay and holds it firmly.

'Walter Hall was never here, never here to pray that one. And he should have. Should have been here and should have prayed that prayer,' says Widow Lankester caustically, and loudly. Garnering looks approving and disapproving. She cares for neither.

'That prayer, it is in the Book of Common Prayer,' Harry Bosvill says approvingly to John Girling.

'Excellent, Widow Bullen says it is an excellent prayer,' Goody Susanna Parsons says to Anne Abowen, 'it is also – I have been trying to bring to mind the very word and have now found it – it is also a worthy prayer. Worthy.' She nods in satisfaction at the word and at her finding of it.

Widow Margaret Hazard agrees. Worthy is a good word, as is excellent.

The congregation of St Cyneswide and St Tibba have gathered in good number to inspect and to judge their new parson on this his first Sunday in the parish. Many expect to find him wanting, and are looking forward to it. He is already known as the Trimming Parson. The song is sung and hummed and laughed at in the parish streets and taverns. Those strongly of the bishops' party hold him in contempt and suspicion because he was once a dissenter. He is a waiverer. Those strongly on the side of the saints hold him in contempt and suspicion because he was once a dissenter and is now with the bishops. He is a waiverer. A Trimming Parson, a Religious Turncoat. Those not so strong on either side come as if to a playhouse, keen to see how the story might unfold. The church is full with an eager audience.

'Did you see him at church door?' David Smoote asks scornfully. 'Thomas Billington, did you see him waiting at church door as all came in? A low thing to do, like a sectary. Greeting and welcoming and introducing himself. Making himself low. A proper parson would never do that. Walter Hall would never do that, never did.'

'Of course I saw him at church door,' Thomas Billington replies testily. 'I came in that way didn't I? Like everyone else. So long as this new man is faithful, stays faithful, to our king, to our Church of England, to our bishops, and to our Book of Common Prayer then for my mind he can stand on top of the church's mid-most tower every Lord's day and shout a welcome to all.'

David Smoote shakes his head at Thomas Billington's extravagant language. He knows the man has the right views on religion but wishes he were not so obnoxious. John Girling, sitting close by and holding to the same views on religion as David Smoote and Thomas Billington, says, 'So long as he does, Jenkin Williams this new man, so long as he does stay faithful. So long as he does not show himself – again show himself – to be a trimming parson, a religious turncoat. But we shall put him to the proof and wait and see.'

Robert Tomlinson, not sitting by these three but close enough to hear, hums the song's chorus. Mary, his wife, a godly saint for reform like her husband, nonetheless offers him a hard elbow and hisses, 'Not in church! Not that song in church.'

Pained Robert Tomlinson hisses back, 'He is one, a turncoat. Once with us now against us. Turncoat. I don't like him or others the same.'

'It was a surprising and a good thing to first see him there, waiting at church door,' Goodwife Joan Brokefild says to her companions.

'He was gentle, had a soft manner with old Walter Shute. Encouraged him to go through all the streets with his cry that Today is Sunday, Lord's day. So all would know and come to church. Have no excuse not to,' Goody Susanna Parsons says. 'That was a well done thing by this new man Jenkin Williams.'

'No need to worry about the parish not coming,' snorts Widow Lankester. 'All will come to see the new man. And they will see he is not Walter Hall. This new man Williams might be a good man, might not be. Might be like most men, some good in him and some not so good in him.' She looks around to see if this meets with any challenge.

'We will see,' says Anne Abowen, not daunted by their new Viewer. 'I will see. I will make up my own mind.'

'As will we all,' says Widow Margaret Hazard repressively. Widow Lankester has unsettled the ancient women's established ways with each other, but Widow Hazard will not bend before the newcomer's overconfidence. Widow Lankester must earn her place and learn her place.

'Parson's wife, Tomasin Williams, was in before him. He was at church door and she already inside with those three, two daughters, one son.' Beatrix Sutterwhit says to her friend Eppie Smoote. Friends despite Eppie Smoote being for the Book of Common Prayer and Beatrix Sutterwhit a saint. They are more comfortable and content in each other's company than they are with David Smoote and William Sutterwhit. They stare at Tomasin Williams and at Anne, Elizabeth and Arthur Williams. They see Tomasin Williams turn and speak easily to those behind her, to Edward and Ellen Richbell, to Robin Kerton. Tomasin Williams notices the staring women and gives them a polite head-bow of acknowledgement.

Both women, taken in great surprise, make a nod-curtsey in return. 'That is not like Margery Hall, not like at all,' Eppie Smoote says, her wondering voice unsure whether this is a bad thing or a good one.

The time of the singing of psalms is come. The Reverend Jenkin Williams does not leave the church. He moves down to stand on the church floor, on the same level as his Parish Clerk, the same level as the parishioners of St Cyneswide and St Tibba. Those who are not left wondering, not taken aback, by this strange happening are Philip Carter, and Tomasin, Anne, Elizabeth and Arthur Williams.

A message, a summons, for the Parish Clerk the night before. Well after dark Harry Shute at his door, panting with speed and importance. 'The new, the new–' chokes, pauses to catch his breath. 'The new parson, somebody Williams, just come in. Just come into the rectory this night. Says knows this is a late hour, just arrived, come in. Tells me to tell you. Says Parish Clerk to come to the rectory tomorrow before Lord's day service. Says when bell-man – that's William Northage, I told new rector the bell-man that's William Northage,' he looks for praise from Philip Carter, gets none. 'When bell-man gives his last cry in the morning, tomorrow morning, Lord's day, Parish Clerk to come to the rectory.'

'That all?' asks Philip Carter. The boy thinks, begins all over, 'The new parson, somebody Will–'

'So you have just told me. Is there more to say?' Harry Shute thinks then shakes his head. Philip Carter gives a grunt, which Harry Shute chooses to take as approval. The Clerk sees lights across the square in the rectory, candles moving in rooms, a cart unloading outside.

Soon after the bell-man's last cry, and with the coming sun at his back, Philip Carter crutches the short distance to the rectory. Outside the building a stocky man is poking the window jambs with his knife. He turns and says, 'Parish Clerk Philip Carter, here I am, the new rector come in, Jenkin Williams."

Last night he asked Harry Shute to give him the Parish Clerk's portrait so he could recognise him. 'Bad legs. Legs crushed to the bone by a great falling stone,' the boy says. 'Moves by crutches. His legs are no good, but he has a chest like a barrel. And thick arms like a blacksmith. That's Phil – that's the Parish Clerk, his features.' Jenkin Williams recognises his Clerk.

His Clerk takes in the new rector's features. The man has cavalier hair, cavalier moustache, cavalier beard. Philip Carter's first thought: this is a head not at all suited to St Cyneswide and St Tibba.

'These window jambs have the rot,' Jenkin Williams observes.

Why tell me? thinks Philip Carter. Nothing to do with me, rotting window jambs at the rectory. Tell your Church Warden. 'Old building,' he says, 'from the old queen's time.'

'Yes,' Jenkin Williams shrugs. Opens the door and expects his Clerk to follow him inside. He does.

'Walter Hall has told me of the parish. Ha! Told me! I have had one letter. Mostly of his items still here in the rectory, and of money.' He looks pensive. 'We'll talk more of these matters. You and I. The Warden. The Vestry. All the officers of the parish. More talk, but not now. Now I need to know of Walter Hall, his practice on Lord's day. Lord's day. Who is the old man who shouts out loud today is Sunday, Lord's day?'

'Old Walter Shute, grandfather to young Harry Shute, the lad you sent last night.'

'He carried my message well? He must have. Here you are. Here we are. Good. Walter Hall?'

'What to say?' Philip Carter begins cautiously. 'There is nothing particular to say. He had, has, his duties as a chaplain to the king. He could be here in the parish, in church of a Lord's day, or he would be doing his duty in the king's Chapel at Why-toll Palace. Like many men in holy office who have to spread themselves, spread themselves thin across their various obligations. Sometimes here, often not.'

'Spread thin like the miser's butter!' Jenkin Williams laughs. 'Yes, many obligations for many. Not for me. I have no other obligations. Of a sacred nature. So now I am in this parish with its interesting saints, Cyneswide and Tibba. Do you know them?'

'Yes!' says the Clerk, brightening, 'Yes, they are–'

'I am keen to hear, but later. Today's service. What was Walter Hall's practice?'

'When his Royal Chaplain obligations did not keep him from here, he came by coach near church time. Greeted his kin in the rectory, then came over to church.'

'Yes,' Jenkin Williams sits down, gestures to Philip Clerk to do the same. 'Here is a stool near the wall. Can you settle to that? Will your legs let you?'

The Parish Clerk's legs will. He has rarely been in the rectory. Never before been asked to sit. There is silence. Jenkin Williams taps musical fingers. 'Did he sing?'

Philip Carter does not understand the question.

'Walter Hall, did he sing psalms in church?'

Philip Carter gives a shocked laugh, 'No! He never. Left, as they all do when it comes to psalms. Back to the rectory. Left to change from surplice into gown, left as you all – as clergy do. When we finish our psalms I send a running boy to tell him we are done.'

Jenkin Williams taps his fingers again. 'When do you sing psalms?' Jenkin Williams knows when this parish, all London parishes, sing their psalms. Knows this from fellow rectors, who also tell him many parishes are still dominated by dissenters roaring out the psalms – their crude, distasteful Sternhold and Hopkins psalms – sitting on their arses in vulgar worship.

Philip Carter finds this a strange question. All know when psalms are sung. 'As all do, we sing psalms before and after the sermon. As all parishes do.' Philip Carter is uneasy, fears this new man has plans to disrupt, overthrow, their psalm singing.

'Yes,' says Jenkin Williams, 'Yes, that is the custom. Psalms, led by good voiced clerks like yourself, sung before and after the sermon.' He pauses again. More finger tapping. 'Earlier you spoke of the old queen's time. This house being from those days. Do you know her Injunction of 1559, when she brought in new services? Have you heard of this?'

The Clerk has not.

'The old queen brought in new liturgy, but she also made an Injunction permitting music outside the liturgy. Sung psalms. Your sung psalms. *Our* sung psalms. In our English metre. Here are the old queen's words.' He changes immediately into pulpit-voice, reads, enjoying himself:

> *And that there be a modest distinct song, so used in all parts of the common prayers in the church, that the same may be as plainly understood, as if it were read without singing, and yet nevertheless, for the comforting of such that delight in music* – (fine words, for the comforting of such that delight in music) – *it may be permitted that in the beginning, or in the end of common prayers, either at morning or evening, there may be sung an hymn, or such like song, to the praise of Almighty God, in the best sort of melody and music* – (the best sort of melody and music!) – *that may be conveniently devised, having respect that the sentence of the hymn may be understood and perceived.*

Jenkin Williams smiles. Philip Carter wonders how he is expected to respond to the old queen's words, to Jenkin Williams' smile. He says nothing.

'Singing to be at the beginning or the end of common prayers?' Jenkin Williams asks.

Philip Carter can only see trouble ahead. 'This parish, all parishes, we have always sung before and after sermon. Not sing when this, this paper, says.' He can hear pleading in his voice.

'No,' Jenkin Williams' fingers tap the piece of paper. 'Your singing, when you sing, is by custom. Custom. But this,' taps the paper, 'this is law. What church law says. This Injunction of 1559.'

'But–' Philip Carter starts to object, then stops. The parish will hate this change. No matter the law, it is wrong of Jenkin Williams to make the parish change. And an unwise thing for a new man to do, to make changes.

'I am a man who sings psalms, psalms and more,' Jenkin Williams examines Philip Carter's face for a reaction. Sees none. 'I have two items to say, and it it has taken too long for me to say them. Item the first, every Sunday this parish of St Cyneswide and St Tibba will sing its psalms, as it has always done – by custom – before and after sermon. Item the second, I will not leave, I do not leave, when the psalms are sung before sermon. I will stay and sing. Before and after sermon I will stay and sing.'

Phlip Carter fears the parish will find this unsettling, disturbing, intrusive.

'This is a singing parish?' Jenkin Williams asks.

'A very singing parish.'

'Then we will obey both law and custom. The parish of St Cyneswide and St Tibba will on future Sundays sing its psalms, we will sing *our* psalms, before and after sermon, and before and after service.'

Again Philip Carter has no words, needs to think on it.

'But not today, Parish Clerk, not today. Today we will go gently, sing according to custom, and you will announce, when we have sung after sermon, how things will be done the next Lord's day and on all such days. Sing by both law and custom. For as long as I am here. Yes.' This last is a statement, not a question. 'How will my parish, ours,' wide expansive, incorporating gesture, 'How will they like this?'

'They will.'

'Good. What psalms are we singing?'

In church Parish Clerk Philip Carter calls, 'Let us sing to the praise and glory of God psalm the sixty second:

My soul to God shall give good heed, and him alone attend:
For why? My health and hope to speed doth whole on him depend.
For he alone is my defence, my rock, my health, and aid:
He is my stay, that no pretence shall make me much dismay'd.
O have your trust in him alway, ye folk with one accord:
Pour out your hearts to him, and say, our trust is in the Lord.

'A fine voice, a fine tenor voice, the new man.' Goody Susanna Parsons, who wants to be pleased by him, is.

'Do you think so?' Widow Lankester asks dubiously. 'Do you approve of this new man?'

'I do. Do you?' Goody Susanna Parsons asks sweetly.

Widow Lankester makes a throat noise but does not answer.

Goodwife Joan Brokefild suspects Widow Lankester is pondering which answer will cause the most trouble.

'That psalm, good words. My health and hope. My health and aid. Good words for this time of sickness,' says Widow Margaret Hazard. 'Our trust is in the Lord.'

'Yes,' agrees Anne Abowen. 'My defence, my rock, my health and aid.' She and Widow Margaret Hazard exchange satisfying looks of agreement.

'Philip Carter always chooses the right psalms,' adds Widow Dorothy Bullen. 'Strange to see the new man William Jenkin standing there and singing with the parish.'

'His name is Jenkin Williams,' corrects Widow Lankester.

'That's what I said, the new man Jenkin Williams. Strange to have him sing psalms in church is what I said.'

Goodwife Joan Brokefild considers that, of all the ancient women, Widow Bullen is the least fazed by Widow Lankester.

'He looks Welsh. Small, dark hair, sings well,' Barnard Clapshaw says to George Hillcocke and William Pickhering.

'You're no giant, Barnard Clapshaw. Are you Welsh? Jenkin and Tomasin are Welsh names. Their infants have good English names,' William Pickhering says.

'What are they?' asks George Hillcocke.

'I don't know.'

'Standing at church door. Reminded me of Thomas Dugdale. He'd do that. Say some words to us,' Barnard Clapshaw ruminates. 'I thought he would come back with Walter Hall gone.'

'And now we have this Jenkin Williams.'

'Is he really a Welshman? Sounds like a Welshman. I mean his name,

Jenkin Williams, not his voice. His voice is an English voice, not a Welsh voice.'

No-one knows if Jenkin Williams is a Welshman, but he could be.

'This man sings better than Thomas Dugdale.'

'But will he preach better? I say he will not.'

'Health and hope! No health and hope here in St Cyneswide and St Tibba. Not in London. No health, no hope, no people. No one here to buy. A few of us left here who will sell, but no buyers, few buyers.'

'Not so many heads here with hair to cut, beards to trim, faces to shave,' Thomas Conclife, sitting behind, joins in. 'I could cut his hair short,' he throws a thumb at Jenkin Williams. 'Will you go William Pickhering? Leave the city?'

'No.' William Pickhering is firm. 'No, I stay. Will you go?'

He gets no answer from any of them.

'I cannot see Widow Damport,' Thomas Conclife looks around the church. Those with their businesses in the square take a close interest in their fellows there.

'Fled?' asks Barnard Clapshaw.

'Not that I have heard, but not seen for some days.'

This is ominous.

'If it is—' George Hillcocke pauses to find the right words then abandons this beginning. 'Here is a preservative against the pestilence. Take sage, rue, briar leaves, a handful of each, stamp them and strain them with a quart of white wine, put thereto a little ginger and a good spoonful of the best treacle, and drink morning and evening. As I recall it.'

All listen carefully, nodding.

'How do you know these children, Jenkin Williams' children, have good English names if you don't know what they are?' George Hillcocke suddenly asks William Pickhering.

'I was told. And don't ask who told me I, can't remember. But I was told they have good English names.'

Robed for the sermon, Jenkin Williams takes the pulpit. He looks calmly, steadily at his congregation, says, 'From the second Book of Kings,

Chapter the twentieth.' He knows there are those who will take the very word Kings as a provocation.

He reads in a soothing voice, with many pauses, 'In those days was Hezekiah sick unto death.' He pauses. 'And the prophet Isaiah the son of Amoz came to him, and said unto him, "Thus saith the Lord, set thine house in order; for thou shalt die, and not live."' Pause. 'Then he turned his face to the wall, and prayed unto the Lord, saying, "I beseech thee, O Lord, remember now how I have walked before thee in truth and with a perfect heart, and have done that which is good in thy sight." And Hezekiah wept sore.' Pause.

'And it came to pass, afore Isaiah was gone out into the middle court, that the word of the Lord came to him, saying, "'Turn again, and tell Hezekiah the captain of my people," Thus saith the Lord, "the God of David thy father, I have heard thy prayer, I have seen thy tears: behold, I will heal thee."' Pause. 'And I will add unto thy days fifteen years; and I will deliver thee and this city out of the hand of the king of Assyria; and I will defend this city for mine own sake, and for my servant David's sake.' And Isaiah said, "Take a lump of figs." And they took and laid it on the boil, and he recovered.'

A long pause and then in a voice of warm reassurance Jenkin Williams tells his congregation, 'The Lord our God saved Hezekiah, a man sick unto death. Cured his blains, his boils, his buboes. The prophet Isaiah hears the word of our Lord God so that Hezekiah, a man sick unto death, is healed. And it is the same, this very prophet, Isaiah, who brings great joy to us all in his own Book at Chapter the ninth, Verse the second: "The people that walked in darkness have seen a great light; they that dwell in the land of the shadow of death, upon them hath the light shined." And this great light that has come to them, has come to us all, is Jesus Christ the son of God, come to save us all through his suffering, who died on the cross for our sins, who saved us from darkness, rescued us from the land of the shadow of death.

'We have prayed this day, dearly beloved,' there are no sniggers, no laughter, 'as we have prayed today, "Have pity Almighty God upon us miserable sinners, who now are visited with great sickness and mortality; accept of our atonement, and so may it please thee to withdraw from us this plague and grievous sickness; through Jesus Christ our Lord."'

A mighty cry of 'Amen' fills the parish church of St Cyneswide and St Tibba.

There is great satisfaction. The ancient women talk of the curative effect of figs. 'Good for boils on the gum,' Widow Margaret Hazard says.

'For a swelling in the mouth,' says Goody Susanna Parsons, 'I take the juice of wormwood, camomile and skirret, mix them with honey, and with this bathe the swelling.'

'Figs for removing warts,' Wisdow Dorothy Bullen contributes. 'I have removed many warts with the milk from a fig stalk.'

The Parish Clerk announces, 'Let us sing to the praise and glory of God psalm the twenty third:

My shepherd is the living Lord, nothing therefore I need:
In pastures fair, with waters calm, he sets me forth to feed.
He did convert and glad my soul, and brought my mind in frame,
To walk the paths of righteousness for his most holy Name.
Yea, though I walk in vale of death, yet will I fear none ill:
Thy rod, thy staff, doth confort me, and thou art with me still.

The psalm sung through, the Clerk raises a hand to signal he has something further to say.

'By custom we sing, as do all, we sing our psalms before and after sermon. As we have just done. But the law, a law of the old queen, says psalms to be sung before and after service.'

There is a rumble of strong disapproval. The congregation will have their custom over any law. Their psalms. Their custom.

A calming hand from Philip Carter Parish Clerk. 'Pastor Williams, rector Williams,' he ventures a brave personal comment, 'a man who gladly sings the psalms with us, he will have us sing according to custom and law both. So next Lord's day, and every Lord's day, we shall sing,' he ticks the order off on the fingers of his hand held up, 'we shall sing, before service, before sermon, after sermon, and after service. Custom and law both.'

This is a coup, a stroke, a great gift. The congregation are stunned, but pleased, mostly. Pleased because they welcome more singing, but suspicious of any newfangleness. And this is new, despite what might be said about the old queen and her law.

Minister Jenkin Williams returns to the pulpit, takes up some pages of print, reads in his calm, clear voice.

'Brethren, I am to give you Notice, that Wednesday next is a day of public and solemn prayer and fasting, set apart by His Majesty's Authority to be observed by us and the whole Nation, for the averting of God's heavy visitation now upon us in many places of this Kingdom.

> *Upon which day all parishioners, with so many of their families as may be spared from their necessary business, are to resort hither to the Church, and here to behave themselves godly, and reverently, and with penitent hearts to pray unto God to turn these Plagues from us, which we through our unthankfulness, and sinful lives have deserved.*
>
> *All persons (children, old, weak and sick folk and necessary harvest-labourers, or the like, excepted) are required to eat upon the Fast-day but one competent and moderate meal, and that towards night, after Evening Prayer, observing sobriety of diet, without superfluity of riotous fare, respecting necessity and not voluptuousness.*
>
> *The quantity being but sufficient, it is not fit that any delicacy should be regarded. Let no public order be herein breached, nor dissimulation with God committed by pretending godly abstinence, but doing something less.*
>
> *The wealthier sort are earnestly moved to bestow the price of the meal foreborne upon the poor, considering the misery and distress of a number of hungry souls in many places, either almost starving for lack of food, or being sick with eating unwholesome meats.*
>
> *The people are to forbear that day their bodily working, and common buying and selling (necessary occasions, and labourers*

excepted), and to be exercised all the time in holy prayer, godly meditations, and reverent hearing of the Scriptures, either read or preached. And especially they are to take heed that they spend it not in plays, pastimes, idleness, haunting of taverns and ale-houses, lascivious wantonness, surfeiting, or drunkenness, for which, and other sins of our Nation, the heavy displeasure and wrath of God is fallen upon us.

The Fast-day is to be observed in all parts of this realm on Wednesday the Twelfth of this instant July, and on the first Wednesday in every month.

God give us all grace to repent, and in his mercy turn away his punishment from us. Amen.

There is an enthusiastic murmur, another fervent, loud Amen. A Fast day is a solemn act, a physical and spiritual display both, by which the parish, the city, the realm, can show their earnestness in seeking God's forgiveness and his mercy, so may it please Him to withdraw this plague and grievous sickness. The coming Fast day, and all the future Fast days, are welcomed.

'What's he doing now?' asks a querulous David Smoote of no-one, craning his neck as Jenkin Williams moves through the church at the end of the service. 'Going to church door again!'

'Come with me, Parish Clerk,' Jenkin Williams is heard to say, and he waits for Philip Carter, walks slowly beside him to the church door.

'A good sermon,' Beatrix Sutterwhit says to Eppie Smoote as they leave.

William Sutterwhit, nearby, is happy to contradict her. 'Sermon? Much too short. Thomas Dugdale could talk for three hours. More!' William Sutterwhit speaks this to the parish at large, and loud enough for Jenkin Williams to hear.

'I have only come into the parish late last night,' Jenkin Williams responds genially. 'Give me time to prepare and I will talk the very legs off the pews and all those sitting in them. Our good Clerk here has already lost his so he is the only one who will be safe.'

There is a ripple of surprise at this, and pleasure that William

Sutterwhit has been bested by the new man just come in last night. But Jenkin Williams knows what he said is not true. He is bored by long sermons, gets restless, is a restless man, rolls restless, and will never preach for hours. And he knows the strength of a simple, clear homily, one that is not buried in a fog of words, allusions, and examples. The very legs of the parishioners and the pews are all safe.

'Parish Clerk I see these are the ancient women, ancient matrons, who do the parish good service. Give me their names.' Philip Carter does. Obliging to all of them, Jenkin Williams seems particularly taken by 'Widow Margaret Hazard, a Searcher of many years.'

Jenkin Williams looks on her with satisfaction. 'Searchers are to be praised and thanked for their work,' he says.

'Goodwife Joan Brokefild is also a Searcher, also one of many years,' the Widow says sharply, wanting to make sure any praise and thanks are rightly shared.

Jenkin Williams gives them all a God be w'ye, but his eyes remain on Widow Margaret Hazard.

His Parish Clerk draws his attention to Gilbert Swaile, the chief man of the Vestry. Minister and brewer walk together to the rectory. Gilbert Swaile wary.

'Too many people leaving, fleeing,' Gilbert Swaile says, unconcerned that this does not reflect well on Jenkin Williams' predecessor. 'I am a brewer. There is less trade for me and for people like me.' He laughs wryly, 'A Fast day. We all pray for an end to the infection. Soon.'

'There are some matters for us, for the Vestry to discuss,' Williams says.

'An organ for the church?' Gilbert Swaile asks suspiciously.

'An organ? No. More weighty matters than an organ. Why do you ask that?'

'Walter Hall was pressing. He thought an organ a weighty matter.'

'Perhaps it is, but not at this time I think. Not now.'

Gilbert Swaile thinks not ever, but says, 'Vestry will meet after service next Lord's day.'

'Good, the plague is a sufficiently weighty matter for Vestry.' He adds, 'Not an organ. How will you do, how will your business do, with people leaving?'

'The brewing business is down, but I hope for some other opportunities. Some other business as well as brewing.' Gilbert Swaile finds himself wanting to show well before this new man.

'I see. Other opportunities. I know this is not a wealthy parish, and I am a man with no other living to call on to maintain a family. No royal chaplaincy. I am interested if there might be, as you say, other opportunities for business, for me, that will help me provide for a family. I ask you to remember my interest when other opportunities arise.'

Gilbert Swaile does not know what to make of this. The new man is very different to Walter Hall.

'Fast day this coming Wednesday. More psalms – many more! – to sing next Lord's day. Then a good Vestry. Thank you Gilbert Swaile!'

Gilbert Swaile is left feeling bemused, but not discontented.

'This morning, before church time, this new man comes down to my crypt, poking about, looking around,' the Church Warden says angrily to the Parish Clerk, both their pipes aglow. 'Talking about money. All about money. Very affable and hail-fellow. Smiles. Wants to know how much in the collection? Who are the prosperous ones in the parish? Who is the leading man in the Vestry? What's behind this door? Talks to me as if we have been on good terms for years. First time I've met the man!'

Philip Carter can see trouble coming from this. He shrugs. 'I found him, what can I say? Agreeable. Said he will take all services. He has an easy way with him. He had me into the rectory first thing this morning. Even had me sit down! Struck me as a good-humoured man.'

'Trouble. He brings trouble. Even changes how we sing our psalms. Do you like that, Philip Carter? This man will make changes. We will all be the poorer. Him and money.

The King's religion I profest,
And found there was no harm in't:

I fawn'd and flatter'd like the rest,
Till I had got preferment.

The Parish Clerk laughs. 'Perhaps not a great preferment, to come to this poor parish. A sorry reward for flattery.'

The Church Warden unbends a little, joins in the joke. 'He'll find poor pickings here!' But still must say, 'You know the man is a hypocrite. "Woe unto you, scribes and Pharisees, hypocrites! for ye are like unto whited sepulchres, which indeed appear beautiful outward, but are within full of dead men's bones, and of all uncleanness." That is Jenkin Williams, a whited sepulchre.'

'Are we scribes? Clerk and Warden? Are we whited sepulchres?' Philip Carter asks. 'We have all taken the Oath. And so has he. If he is wicked so are we all.' He stops, then says, 'He asked what psalms we would sing. Said he knew them well. He is a good singing man, and rightly left me to do what a Clerk does.'

'Then you talked well together? At ease with each other?' the Warden asks.

'We talked. It was not at all like being given orders by Walter Hall. But yes, mostly at ease. Not like friends and cousins, as the word goes, but still quite easy.'

'So you are all for this new man?'

Philip Carter thinks, says, 'He has not fled. Says he will not. Says he'll stay. I believe he will. That's something.'

'Says.' It is Frances Barrow's turn to shrug, but he does not want to continue at odds with Philip Carter. They smoke out their pipes in companionable silence.

Jack also has met Jenkin Williams. In the late hours of the previous night, Jack, tardily back to the rectory, finds the new man, his family, their chests and bags, all a muddle and a mess.

Jack quickly discovers that he – Jack – had good reason to be absent, 'Called to my father's home. An illness there – not the plague Sir! No, not that, the Lord be thanked. Not that.'

A nimble lad. A clever, reliable one. He quickly shows them into the ancient, labyrinthine rectory, suggests where beds can be made up, helps make them, has chests hefted into appropriate rooms, bags placed handy for when needed. Finds cheese and beer from his own stores. Apologises that he does not have more. Yes, he does have a letter from Walter Hall. Here it is. You see, no mention of when Jenkin Williams and family will arrive in the parish. Had Jack known –

Yes, yes. Jenkin Williams is not annoyed. He understands. He hopes Jack's father will mend well and soon. He has a quick look at the letter, but will read it better tomorrow, when he is more awake. Where does Jack sleep? In the garret? Well, he will talk more with him tomorrow. And although he cannot do more for Jack, yet Jack should know that whatever should be, he can continue in the room in the garret. Sleep well and God be with you.

In his garret room Jack prays he has not ill-wished his father by saying he is ill. He realises he can expect no payment from Jenkin Williams. But he can keep his quarters in the garret. With his roof-high vantage view over the emptying streets to the north and to the south.

CHAPTER XVIII

London, Monday, 10 July 1665

'Where shall we bury him? Carry him to London.
By his grandfather's grave grows a green onion.'

'The word of the Lord came unto me, saying, Arise! Go to that great city and cry against it for its wickedness!'

The ancient women know from his voice that he is a country man, from well beyond London. Just where this might be they have no interest.

'Put on sackcloth and ashes, just as I have done! I have declared a Fast, and declare all shall put on sackcloth, from the greatest even unto the least.' The country man in his crude smock of sacking flings his arm towards the ancient women, 'The least!' he repeats.

He is met with little reverence.

'Woe to the bloody city! It is all full of lies and robbery!'

'Has anything been heard of that Chaukley?' Anne Abowen asks bitterly.

Heads shake. Nothing has been heard.

Another voice approaches. He too gestures towards the ancient women. 'A cure!' he cries. 'Come unto me. My touch can heal our leprous land!' He stretches out both hands, 'Let me cure all!'

Goodwife Joan Brokefild declaims sardonically, 'Oh! Lay that hand on me, adored Caesar!'

The scabby man takes this for an invitation and approaches. The Goodwife scowls and brandishes her red wand to keep him at bay.

'I do not think he, like some in Why-toll, offers a blue ribbon with angel-gold attached when he touches for the Evil,' Widow Margaret Hazard says drily.

'A London man this one is,' says Widow Dorothy Bullen.

'But not of this parish,' Widow Margaret Hazard and Widow Lankester say together.

'When Isaac Brokefild is foxed – and he always is, almost always – he sounds like those lunatics. Speaks Bear-Garden,' Goodwife Brokefild mutters.

The women are relieved to hear the familiar cry of, 'Today is Monday! Today is Monday!'

'Walter Shute is a bufflehead, but those other two are lunatics,' Widow Dorothy Bullen says. 'At least I would say a bufflehead, Walter Shute. But can a man be both? Both bufflehead and lunatic?'

Widow Lankester has a question of her own, 'Where is Isabell Undnay? Shouting in the streets like these crazed ones?'

'Bedlam? Dead?' answers Anne Abowen.

'Dead-lam?' offers Goodwife Joan Brokefild.

Widow Lankester laughs. Goody Susanna Parsons' laugh is a horrified laugh, then she says haltingly, her voice thick, 'If Isabella Undnay is a Bedlam Bitch–'

'She is,' snaps Anne Abowen.

'Then Widow … the Chaukley is even more a Bedlam Bitch, a twice times Bedlam Bitch. She is a traitor to her office of Viewer. She has betrayed the trust of the Vestry, of the parish, betrayed us here, her fellows, who were her fellows. A traitor.' Goody Parsons falls into an angry silence.

The ancient women walk two by two. Viewers. Keepers. Searchers. Two of every sort, thinks Goodwife Joan Brokefild, but not male and female. They are ancient woman and ancient woman. And they are not unclean beasts.

The cries of the shouting lunatics wane, replaced by the piping voices of a small clump of children, boys and girls, playing a funeral game. An interminable argument over whether the game is called Deadman Booman or Booman Deadman is terminated when excited impatient voices cry, 'Let's play it! Let's play!' Little Michael Clapshaw plays dead Booman in the middle of the ring. They sing:

> *Dill dool for Booman, Booman is dead and gone,*
> *Left his wife and his ten children all alone.*
> *Where shall we bury him? Carry him to London.*
> *By his grandfather's grave grows a green onion.*
> *Dig his grave wide and deep, strew it with flowers.*
> *Toll the bell, toll the bell, twenty four hours.*

'Michael Clapshaw plays a fine corpse,' Goodwife Joan Brokefild says from long familiarity with corpses, as the limp child is picked up and carried about, placed down, and his burial mimed.

Michael Clapshaw lifts his head from the ground, smiles at the ancient women, pleased at the praise. 'Lie down! Lie down!' his companions cry. His grave is strewn with scraps of grass and weeds.

'Not many flowers to be found in London streets. Or green onions,' says Widow Lankester.

Michael Clapshaw rises from the dead and the game begins over with a new dead Booman, Annie Carter, lying in the circle.

'We don't want bodies carried to London,' says Anne Abowen.

'Parish did well to get itself the lower churchyard,' Widow Margaret Hazard says. 'Might need more than two. All the burying to come.'

As is now their custom they head for the ancient women's room, up the steep stairs.

'The new man, Jenkin Williams,' says Anne Abowen with pleased anticipation when all pipes are lit.

'He is strong against the plague,' says Goody Parsons. 'That is good for this parish. We have not had that before in this pestilence time. Not in the way this Jenkin Williams is.'

'He is a man of fervent prayer. His praying and preaching. We have not seen or heard this since Thomas Dugdale,' Widow Bullen says, fervent herself.

'Short fervent prayers, and even shorter sermon, this new man,' says Widow Lankester.

Anne Abowen knowing her new friend can be too outspoken, changes the subject, 'Using figs to draw a boil, a blain. I have heard of another cure that you Keepers will know,' she nods deferentially to Goody Parsons and Widow Bullen. 'With smallage, mallows, wormwood and–'

'And rue,' Goody Parsons breaks in, halting Anne Abowen, and fellow Keeper Widow Bullen who would also speak. 'Stamp them well together, fry them in olive oil till they be thick, apply it to the place and let it be until the blain breaks. Then heal it up with a poultice of smallage, wheat flour and milk, applied morning and evening until it be whole. There.'

Widow Lankester will not be diverted, will stir the pot, 'I can hear that song, of a Trimming Parson,' she sings in a fine voice:

When Charles return'd into the land,
The English Crown's supporter,
I shifted off my cloak and band,
And then became a courtier.

'Bah!' says Widow Margaret Hazard. 'This new man is not a courtier. That was the old man, Walter Hall, courtier chaplain to the Scotchman. Jenkin Williams is not a courtier.'

'And we, all of us here, we have all taken the Oath,' Goodwife Joan Brokefild adds mildly, with the same words Philip Carter said to Frances Barrow.

'I have heard three spiders can be used against the plague,' Widow Bullen says.

'How? What kind of spiders?' asks Goody Parsons.

'I don't know that, but I have heard it about three spiders.' Widow Bullen pauses in thought.

'He spoke to all, without regard to rank or station, Jenkin Williams. That was a good thing. A good thing to see. He spoke to me,' says Widow Bullen.

'He stared closely at me,' Widow Hazard says.

'Yes he did,' her friend the Goodwife agrees, 'but not in an unkind way. More of the way of a friend, a kind one.'

'And been seen since on foot, going about the parish,' says Goody Parsons. 'Talking to people. Asking names.'

'His wife, a good agreeable wife. She's of the same stamp as him,' Goodwife Brokefild says.

'So we are all of the same mind?' asks the troublesome Widow Lankester. 'We now have a paragon? Several paragons. Husband and wife, and the children are small paragons, baby paragons.'

Anne Abowen and Goodwife Brokefild laugh tolerantly and wave away Widow Lankester's words, wave away her pipe smoke.

'This Fast, I have been thinking of this Fast day. Eating but one competent and moderate meal towards night, with sobriety of diet, no riotous fare, and respecting necessity not voluptuousness. I can't remember ever eating voluptuous fare. I am thinking of my moderate Fast meal, but I have not yet decided,' Widow Bullen muses aloud.

'Abstinence from flesh meat. Easy enough,' declares Widow Lankester.

'And from wine,' Goody Susanna Parsons adds.

'Not from ale,' Widow Margaret Hazard says.

'Of course not from ale!' Widow Lankester says scornfully. 'Not from ale.'

Widow Dorothy Bullen suddenly sings:

All you good wives that brew good ale,
God turn you from all tears;
But if you put more water in,
The Devil put out your eyes.

Widow Bullen laughs, 'William Bullen sang that, he did. Sang it to me.'

'Sallats are good fasting food,' Goodwife Brokefild says, 'but Isaac Brokefild will have none of it. Asks me if I think he is a hare, a rabbit.'

'Fasting, I will make pancakes,' says Widow Hazard, 'With mace, cloves, nutmeg and cinnamon.'

The ancient women nod appreciatively.

'Fasting,' says Widow Lankester. 'When your belly chimes it's time to go to dinner. Some loud belly chimes coming this Wednesday.'

'No flesh meat. I have decided now on fish with a fine broth,' Widow Bullen declares. 'Some add prunes and dates to their fish broth. I,' she says firmly, 'do not.'

'I love cream and brown bread,' Goody Parsons says. 'Is that superfluity of riotous fare? They are not flesh meat. I would not be one of those who pretend godly abstinence but do something less. I hope cream and brown bread is not superfluity. It is certainly not flesh meat.'

'They are good simple foods. Bread, cream,' Goodwife Joan Brokefild says. 'Who would call cream and brown bread voluptuous?'

'We do not have that Chaukley's recipes for fasting food, the Bedlam Bitch's recipes,' Widow Lankester says.

'Her!' Widow Hazard exclaims. 'What would she know? A woman who does not put angelica and agrimony in her Plague Water! I have no opinion of her. Never did. A wicked woman.'

'Willam Sancroft has fled,' says Goodwife Joan Brokefild.

'William Sancroft? Who is William Sancroft?' Goody Parsons asks.

'Dean of St Pauls,' Widow Lankester jumps in to answer, jealous to know everything before everyone.

'Yes, Dean of St Pauls. Fled to Tunbridge Wells,' Goodwife Brokefild says.

'Fleeing,' Widow Bullen says. 'There are those who have been shut in with the cross on their door who still flee. Not just the Chaukley.'

'We know of fleeing,' Widow Hazard says. 'We searched the Warwin house – Mary Warwin dead of measles – but Francis Wawin thought it plague, and so the family fled. Seen fleeing by neighbour Daniel Maxfilde.'

'Some flee over the roof tops,' says a shocked Goody Parsons. 'I have heard that people have been seen doing this. Over the roof tops. They were reported but it was too late.'

'And smuggled away in boxes,' adds Widow Bullen.

'The dead ones in coffin boxes,' says Widow Lankester, and Goodwife Brokefild laughs.

'No, these were alive but hidden in boxes and smuggled away,' clarifies

Widow Bullen.

'Those who are shut up in a house where the plague is in it, a house with the red cross on the door, those who are members of infected families, if they refuse to remain shut up then they are declared criminals and will be shut up more securely, not in their house but in Newgate,' Widow Margaret Hazard says with righteous satisfaction.

'There is a man,' Goody Parsons says, 'I do not know his name,' she quickly adds before she can be taken to task on this question, 'his servant, a servant of his, was out of the house and fell ill. And I do not know the servant's illness, but his master never suffered him to come back into the house after he was ill. And there are some who will abuse the master for not taking care of his servant, and some who say the master did right and should not let the plague come into his house. It might have been the plague. I do not know.'

'The master should have let his man come back in the house,' Widow Lankester says promptly.

'But if the man has the plague?' asks Widow Bullen. 'Would you let him come in. I would not. That is if I had a servant, which I do not.'

'I think I ... I don't know,' Goodwife Brokefild says.

'If it was someone close, family, a child, a husband, then I would say Yes, come back in. Naturally they would come back inside the house,' Widow Hazard muses.

Goody Parsons nods agreement.

Goodwife Joan Brokefild is still not sure. Instead she says, 'Fasting food:

> *Tis not the food, but the content*
> *That makes the table's merriment.*
> *Where trouble serves the board, we eat*
> *The platters there, as soon as meat.*

This restores the ancient women to good humour.

'I wouldn't eat the platter!' Widow Dorothy Bullen says with comfortable mirth. 'Couldn't.' She opens her mouth to display three remaining teeth.

'Those three spiders. Do you make a poultice of them? No–' Goody Parsons stops a protesting Widow Bullen. 'I know you don't know the answer. I know that. But I am just … thinking how the three spiders might be made a protection against the pestilence.'

'If I knew I would tell you,' Widow Bullen declares.

* * *

London, Tuesday, 11 July 1665

'Hot,' Sara complains from the bed. 'I'm hot.' She has been restless overnight, sniffling, sneezing in the early morning. The Widow wants it to be a mild ague. Wills it to be a mild ague and nothing more. She takes the child's face in both hands. She is warm. Not overly hot. It is a mild ague and it is a hot day, one promising to be hot beyond bearing.

'Do you have the headache?' she asks roughly, still holding the child's face. 'Do you?'

Sara shakes her head.

'Do you?' the Widow insists. 'Answer.'

'No.'

'And no vomiting? I know you did not vomit last night, but yesterday? Did you vomit then? Did you have the headache then?'

'No. I'm only hot.' Sara says crankily. Tries to pull her face away from her mother's hands.

'It is a small ague, a mild fever. I have the cure for that.'

Sara fears it will be a vile mixture that *will* make her vomit, but knows better than to say anything.

Widow Margaret Hazard busies herself with dragon water, rose water, running water, aqua vitae, vinegar. 'And mithridate,' she says to herself, 'half a spoonful, or less, of mithridate.'

Sara baulks at the taste but her mother holds her nose and makes her drink.

'That will cure a mild fever,' the Widow says loudly, with a confidence she does not feel, and takes the child's cheeks in her hands again to see if the fever has fallen.

She feels Sara's body for buboes. She did so, as has become her habit, last night before the child went to bed. Nothing. Still nothing.

Widow Margaret Hazard takes to her knees and pulls Sara down beside her. 'We will pray,' she announces. 'Oh Almighty God we beseech you to bless and care for this child, Sara Potts, a little innocent child of the parish of St Cyneswide and St Tibba. Save her from the ravages of the pestilence and keep her in good health, for ever and ever. We beseech you Almighty God, you who loved your own son Jesus Christ.' The Widow wants to point to the child so there will be no doubt, no mistake, about the Sara Potts she is praying for.

Sara joins her mother in 'Amen,' doing so in their house's own way of saying it thrice, bobbing heads each time, to make sure the Lord has heard and taken note.

The Widow is ashamed that she thought of getting the child physick before she thought of prayer. In any event, the child now has the protection of both.

She says sternly to Sara, 'At the Widow Packe's, her school, tell her nothing of this. If the fever grows worse, if the headache comes, if you vomit, come back here. But say nothing to Widow Packe or to anyone. Do you hear me? Answer.'

Sara nods, 'I hear you. If I have the headache, if I vomit, I come—'

'Or if the fever grows worse.'

'Or if the fever grows worse I am to come back here.'

Widow Hazard does not speak her fear that this could be the coughing and sneezing pestilence, does not show this fear for her Sara who was coughing in the night, and sneezing – only three times, only three sneezes – this morning. And the child rambling in her sleep, but she has always done that, saying nonsense like 'silver play.' She wants to tell the child, order her: do not cough, do not sneeze. She holds Sara's hand tightly but does not speak.

'Parish Clerk says come,' Jemmy Pooly stands at the window, throwing his black wand from one hand to another. Up in the air, catching it. 'Searchers to come Parish Clerk says. Quickly. Says I am to tell him that I have told you.'

'Stop playing with that wand Jemmy Pooly! You have told me Jemmy Pooly that I am to come now go and tell the Parish Clerk you have told me.'

When almost out of sight Jemmy Pooly tosses his wand as high as he can.

Goodwife Joan Brokefild, also summoned, is waiting for her. The Parish Clerk receives them in one of his stern, unhappy humours.

'Corpses to search. Too many. The house of Roger Easewell and Lydia Easewell.'

'Roger Easewell, chimney tax,' Widow Hazard says.

'Hearth tax,' Philip Carter corrects her. 'And three houses you have once searched,' he glares. 'Francis Woodhouse. Henry Gipps,' he pauses. 'Hester Shipley.'

'Widow Shipley is dead then?' Widow Hazard asks. 'The one who would bribe us? That Widow Shipley? She is dead?'

'I don't know of any other Widow Shipley,' the Parish Clerk says sourly.

'Then there is no-one at this Shipley house to try to bribe us this time? Or is there?' Goodwife Joan Brokefild asks. 'Will any Vestrymen care to come with us to search Shipley corpses? John Girling, George Lumme, Emmanuel Bird, they are all welcome to enter plague houses with Widow Hazard and myself. Observe if bribes are offered.'

Philip Carter ignores this. 'There is one more house to search. Close by. In the square here.' He breathes out heavily. 'Harry Bosvill, a good neighbour to his neighbours, reports nothing heard from the house of Widow Damport. Nothing for several days now. Four days.'

Both ancient women Searchers consider four days is a long time for good neighbour Harry Bosvill to wait before reporting, but they say nothing, conscious they have pushed Philip Carter to the limit of his patience on the Shipley widow and her bribes.

'Six in that house,' the Goodwife says. 'Widow Alice, her daughter Dorothy Damport, the Widow's sister Barbara Perwich, her husband John

Perwich, their daughters Bridget Perwich and Em Perwich. And nothing heard from any of them?'

The Parish Clerk shakes his head. 'Harry Bosvill their neighbour says nothing heard. Tells me, I tell you.'

'We will search them first,' Widow Margaret Hazard says, refrains from saying 'for convenience.'

'Yes, search here in the square first. Before he heard nothing, Harry Bosvill heard coughing, sneezing from the house. He thought the ague or something like. Washerwomen in water, in the damp all the time, so he thought the ague.'

'How many days before was that? Widow Hazard asks.

'I don't know! How would I know?' Philip Carter flares. 'Harry Bosvill didn't say.' He waves them away then calls them back. 'Bring your information to me by mid-day. Noon today. Tuesday Parish Clerks' day, Bills of Mortality day.' He says this every Tuesday.

'Mmm,' the Widow says.

'Yes, by mid-day, by noon today, Tuesday,' the Goodwife repeats. Would also repeat 'Parish Clerks' day, Bills of Mortality day,' but knows this would not be wise.

'Sara is good friends with Dorothy Damport,' the Widow says to the Goodwife as they leave. She keeps to herself Sara's fever, her coughing her sneezing, although only three sneezes. If she speaks of these then she might give voice to her fears. She says 'Amen Amen Amen' in her head.

Harry Bosvill is standing outside his soapmanufactory, gazing anxiously at Widow Damport's house, at the approaching Searchers. 'In there,' he calls unnecessarily to them. 'Widow Damport's in there.'

'As if we have just arrived in St Cyneswide and St Tibba from Country Village,' Goodwife Brokefild mutters to Widow Hazard.

'Aye,' Widow Hazard replies in what could be the voice of a woman from Country Village. They wave their red wands at Harry Bosvill in acknowledgement.

'Widow Damport! Widow Alice Damport!' the Goodwife shouts at the door. Knocks loudly. 'John Perwich! Searchers here. Can anyone open?'

No answer. They try the door but it is locked. Widow Hazard bangs with her red wand, calls, 'Widow Damport!'

Foremost among the onlookers gathered at a safe distance in the square is Jemmy Pooly.

'You Jemmy Pooly, call the Constable,' The Goodwife calls. The boy runs off in joyful self importance.

'If it is the pestilence, why did she not call for help? Call Viewers and Keepers?' the Goodwife asks.

'Widow Damport will have her own physick,' Widow Hazard answers. 'Always says she trusts no physick but her own. Recipes she has from her mother, and from her mother's mother.'

The Goodwife raises sceptical eyebrows. Widow Hazard reflects that she, too, trusts her own physick. Did she not give Sara her own physick this morning? There is nothing wrong with trusting your own physick.

The Goodwife, unaware of the Widow's train of thought, says, 'I hope trusting her own physick has not turned dire for Widow Damport.'

Constable Samuel Snow arrives, attended by a capering Jemmy Pooly. Samuel Snow is conscious of the ancient women's status as appointed Searchers of the parish, and acknowledges them, but more conscious of his greater status as parish Constable so his achnowledgement is brief.

Alerted by the helpful, voluble Jemmy Pooly as to why he is needed, Samuel Snow produces his gooseneck iron and tries the door.

The Goodwife offers, 'It is bolted top and bottom. The–'

Constable Snow blocks any further words with an upraised hand. He knows his job – who better? – and he does not need assistance, however well meant, from an ancient woman.

He tries the middle of the door with the end of his gooseneck. The door bows but does not break.

The Goodwife says nothing. Her eyes travel to the bottom of the door, where there is an inside bolt in place, and to the top of the door, where there is also a bolt.

Samuel Snow inserts his gooseneck at the top. There is a crack and the bolt gives. The bolt at the bottom holds until he dislodges that too. He kicks the door open and stands back. The gawkers in the square stare in but come no closer.

Inside the Searchers find corpses, all six. All have coughed up blood. It is the pneumonic pestilence. The disease has gone straight to the lights, the lungs.

Then, as their eyes adjust to the dark room, they see not all six are dead. Not all. Strong Dorothy, lying on a tangled bed of mess, is still breathing, only just breathing. Short, painful, feeble, breaths.

The ancient women stay near the door, a safe distance from her dribbling spit.

There is nothing they can do. She is at the point of death. She cannot see, hear. They hear her take her last breath. Hear the rasping stop.

'God have her in his keeping,' Widow Hazard says fervently.

'In his keeping,' Goodwife Brokefild repeats.

More fervently, silently, Widow Hazard prays, 'God protect and preserve my daughter Sara Potts, an innocent child.' Her mind runs on: Dorothy Damport is, was, an innocent child. And Bridget Perwich and Em Perwich. All innocent children. She prays that Sara Potts has not this week, the week before, been in the company of Dorothy Damport, Bridget Perwich, Em Perwich.

The two ancient women step back. Close the door.

'All dead,' Goodwife Brokefild says to Constable Samuel Snow. 'Widow Alice Damport. Her daughter Dorothy Damport. John Perwich. His wife Barbara Perwich. His children Bridget Perwich, Em Perwich.'

'A cart needed for the corpses,' Searcher Widow Margaret Hazard tells Constable Snow.

'Yes a cart. Later. Tonight,' Samuel Snow replies, and thinks that the parish will need corpse carts. More than one. He says to the excited, bobbing boy beside him, 'Jemmy Pooly, remind me to tell Parish Clerk that Vestry will need corpse carts. For the next Vestry meeting.'

'I can run now and tell Parish Clerk,' the boy answers.

'Jemmy Pooly, boy, listen to me. I say remind me to tell Parish Clerk about corpse carts. Do you hear?'

'Yes,' the boy says. Jack Green the footboy is close by. The two join Christopher Northage and all stand in silent misery outside the stables. There is nothing to say. They stare at Widow Damport's laundry. Christopher Northage sighs, raises his hands in incomprehension, turns back into the stables to tend the horses.

Roger Easewell's corpse has buboes, his wife Lydia's corpse has buboes. Their four dead children have buboes. Their still living son Thomas and still living daughter Margaret have buboes. These two have done what they can to lay the corpses straight, cover them with bed clothes. They sit listlessly side by side, staring at the ancient women.

'You did this?' the Widow asks the children, pointing to the bodies laid out, covered. The Goodwife thinks this a stupid question. Who else did it?

Margaret Easewell nods.

'Well. You did well,' the Widow says.

'The Keepers – you know Goody Parsons, Widow Bullen?' the Goodwife asks. 'They will bring you food and other comforts.'

Margaret looks at the covered corpses, looks questioningly at the ancient women.

'The bearers will come for them,' Widow Margaret Hazard answers. 'Today. This evening. The Keepers will come before. Do you have food in the house?'

Margaret shows her the empty table, the bare cupboard. 'No.'

'The Keepers will come,' Widow Hazard repeats.

Outside in the square Goodwife Joan Brokefild says to her friend, 'Not the coughing, sneezing pest. Not there. Not like at Widow Damport's. Those two children have some chance to live if God so wills it. Some chance. No chance if it was the coughing and sneezing that sits down in the lights.'

The Widow does not reply. Thinks of Sara's coughing and sneezing. Eventually says, 'Francis Woodhouse, his son Edward told the watchman at the door this morning.'

Watchman Michael Pymme stands back a good distance to let the ancient women into the house, calls to them, 'The boy Edward told me—'

'Yes, yes,' the Goodwife says, not unkindly. 'Thank you Michael Pymme.'

Edward Woodhouse looks gratefully at Widow and Goodwife, begins talking and does not stop. 'He died in the night. He must have died in the night. I was asleep and when I woke he was dead. So he must have. I had to sleep. I could not help it. I have been caring for him all these days – three weeks and more. All the time. Sometimes he would rally, sometimes sink, but now he is dead. See? Search him and you will see. It is the plague. I do not have it. Still do not have it. See?' He lifts his shirt, shows his under-arms have no swelling. 'See?' he asks eagerly. Makes as if to show them that the regions by his privy parts are similarly untainted but the Widow stops him.

'We can see you are untouched,' she says. 'You have no fever, the headache, vomiting?'

'No! No! None of that. None of them, the headache, the fever, the vomit. None. It is twenty two days now I'm shut up here. I must be free to go in one week? Eight days? The house to be shut up for one month and that month is soon gone.'

'You have been taking the preservatives? The Plague Water?' Widow Hazard asks.

'Yes, all of them. Whatever the Keepers bring I take it. My father took it when he was able but he already had the pestilence. I did not have it and do not have it.'

The Goodwife nods, 'Yes, you do not have it. We will report to the Clerk, as we always do. The bearers will come for Francis Woodhouse.'

The Widow wishes him 'God be w'ye.'

Edward Woodhouse looks beseechingly at her, at them. 'If you take me to the Clerk now he will see I do not have the pestilence.'

'No,' says the Widow, 'we do not do that,' and closes the door.

The corpse at the house of Henry Gipps has the plague signs, but death has come from a different quarter. The stem of a pipe has gone deep through the palate of the girl Margery Gipps, piercing her brain.

'She was smoking her pipe,' Helen Gipps says.'She was only smoking.'

'She,' Agnes Gipps points furiously at her one surviving daughter, 'she will have us smoke morning noon and night.'

'To better protect us,' Helen Gipps explains plaintively, 'for protection against the pestilence.'

No-one in the room is smoking.

'She tripped, fell and …' Helen Gipps gestures helplessly.

'Tripped over your shoe, your shoe lying where you kicked it off! That is what Margery tripped over!' Agnes Gipps screams at her.

The Searchers can see that Agnes Gipps – exhausted by her outburst – looks worse for the plague. Helen Gipps is still untouched.

The cause of the death of Margery Gipps is self-evident. The Searchers have seen such accidents before.

'The bearers will come for Margery Gipps,' Widow Hazard says perfunctorily and goes to leave.

'The Keepers are coming regularly to you?' Goodwife Brokefild asks Helen Gipps, whose authority, responsibility, weighs too heavily on her. She showed the Searchers in and now takes them to the door.

'Yes,' Helen Gipps answers flatly. She has the unresponsive voice and gaze of one tired beyond endurance. 'Yes, the Keepers come.' As she closes the door she says more to herself than to the ancient women, 'I should have seen the shoe. Should have taken up the shoe.'

The Searchers lean against a resting stone and light their pipes.

'Sara Potts, her reading book, there is a picture of Death holding a spear behind a young boy who falls,' Widow Hazard says. 'The words read "Youth forward slips, Death soonest nips." Mmm.' She breathes a jet of smoke from her good nostril. 'Hester Shipley, Widow Shipley's house next. Next and last. Philip Carter will have the information for his Bill in good time.'

The Shipley door is opened by nervous young girl who points to a corpse laid out just inside. 'Anne Hugget,' she says.

'The cook,' Widow Hazard lifts the shroud, recognises the face. 'So her name is Ann Hugget. And Widow Shipley, where is your mistress?'

'Stays in her room, sees no-one, talks to no-one. We leave her food at her door. Knock and leave. As she told us to.'

'The bearers will come for Ann Hugget the cook,' Widow Margaret Hazard says.

'All searches done,' says the Goodwife, who would walk leisurely back. Her friend will move more quickly.

'Philip Carter will have his informations in good time. We can take our time,' the Goodwife says.

'Mmm. Sara Potts had the ague this morning. It is not the sneezing coughing pestilence, it is not, but I …' the Widow's voice trails off.

Philip Carter sits in the vestry, listens closely to Goodwife Joan Brokefild, then summarises, 'In all fourteen dead of the plague.' He does the additions on his fingers, 'At the house of Widow Damport six; at the house of Roger Easewell also six; Francis Woodhouse at his house; at the house of the Widow Shipley,' he pauses, asks, 'the Widow Shipley herself?'

'Not dead,' Widow Hazard answers. 'Her cook Ann Hugget, the plague.'

'At the house of the Widow Shipley, one, making fourteen plague in all. This Margery Gipps who was not the plague. The description, the cause of death that is listed in the Bill, it is important. "Suddenly" is not sufficient, it says nothing. I do not like "Suddenly," not at all. Although some clerks will use it.' He ponders, 'For Margery Gipps it could be "Killed with a fall," or "Killed by a fall." With or By. Or it might be "Killed by a fall where her pipe pierced the brain." It might be that.'

'Or "Tobacco pipe struck by accident into her brain," it might be that,' the Goodwife suggests.

'Say that again,' the Clerk asks. 'Slowly. Wait till I have pen and paper in hand.'

She says it again and he writes it down carefully. Looks with content at the words.

'Good,' he says to the two ancient women and turns back to completing the Bill of Mortality for the Parish of St Cyneswide and St Tibba for the week past.

Out in the churchyard Goodwife Brokefild will rest and smoke. The Widow turns for home but sees Sara Potts entering the square and calls to her to come.

She takes the child's cheeks in her hands. No fever. Examines her closely, watches, listens, asks, 'The ague?'

Sara Potts shakes her head, still held tightly by her mother, 'No. Gone.'

'The headache? The vomit?' the Widow presses.

'No. We played count the carts, count the coaches, count the carriages, watch the waggons. Tally the, tally the, I can't remember what we tallied,' she holds up her hands and counts off finger by finger. 'You count to ten then start again. The small ones at the school sing that. There are not so many coaches and carriages. Not so many as before.'

'You are well then Sara Potts? Not ill? Well?' her mother asks.

'No, not ill. Yes, well,' the child says, gradually pulling away. Her mother's grip loosens. The child runs off.

Widow Margaret Hazard sinks down onto the churchyard wall beside Goodwife Brokefild. They smoke.

'Do you have Sara smoke?' the Goodwife asks curiously.

'She draws on my pipe from time to time. Enough as needed.'

'The pestilence in the year 25, in the year 36, do you remember?' the Goodwife asks.

'I was not made Searcher until the year 41. I was a maid become a woman in 25. I knew of the plague then, knew it was in London, but my mind ran on other things. Samuel Hazard. In 36,' she shrugs. 'The sickness was not as bad as 25. And 25 was not as bad as we have it now, in 65.'

They hear the vestry door close. Philip Carter turns into Church Lane, his papers in a pouch.

'Fifteen St Cyneswide and St Tibba deaths in his pouch,' the Goodwife says.

The Widow thinks how her friend says things, says them in a way that others do not.

The day continues hot into evening. Widow Hazard sitting at table with her daughter quizzes her suspiciously, for the umpteenth time, 'Your teacher, the French widow, she does teach in English, does she?'

An impish impulse in Sara urges her to reply, 'Mais oui,' but she can see her mother is in no mood for frivolity. 'Yes she does.'

'Take your bible and read,' the Widow orders.

Sara places the bible on the table before her, closes her eyes, opens the book, then her eyes, and reads:

> *And it shall come to pass at that day, saith the Lord, that the heart of the king shall perish, and the heart of the princes; and the priests shall be astonished, and the prophets shall wonder.*
>
> *Then said I, Ah, Lord God! surely thou hast greatly deceived this people and Jerusalem, saying, Ye shall have peace; whereas the sword reacheth unto the soul.*
>
> *And at that time shall it be said to this people and to Jerusalem, A dry wind of the high places in the wilderness toward the daughter of my people, not to fan, nor to cleanse.*
>
> *Even a full wind from those places shall come unto me: now also will I give sentence against them.*
>
> *Behold he shall come up as clouds, and his chariots shall be as a whirlwind: his horses are swifter than eagles. Woe unto us! for we are spoiled.*
>
> *O Jerusalem, wash thine heart from wickedness, that thou mayest be saved. How long shall thy vain thoughts lodge within thee?*

'Stop,' the Widow says, 'stop at those good words, "Wash thine heart free from wickedness, that thou mayest be saved." Good words, words I have heard Thomas Dugdale preach.' She reaches again for Sara's face, feels it is cool to the touch, and is pleased.

'Widow Hazard,' Goodwife Brokefild calls at the door, 'Widow Hazard, one more search to be done today.'

In the evening half light the Widow sees the Goodwife standing with a large man, a face she knows, although he is not of the parish.

The Goodwife says, 'Thomas Micoe, the–'

'Thomas Micoe the dung man, that is who you are.'

He nods genially, 'I am.'

'Thomas Micoe has found–'

'Found a corpse in a bog house, found here in this parish, and have reported it so it can be searched. This way.' He leads them forth to William Billip's house, lifts an old basket he has used to cover something tiny.

The corpse is small. The ancient women can see it is new-born, or at most some few days old.

'Still-born, or fallen from the mother in birth,' the Goodwife says. They have seen this before.

Thomas Micoe, does not say anything but points to the infant's mouth. A small piece of cloth has been stuffed in. Lying nearby is another piece of the same that could have wrapped the head.

'Not a stillbirth,' the Widow says sombrely.

'That is not certain, it might be.' the Goodwife replies.

'No woman brought to childbed in this house,' the Widow says. 'No woman expected to lie-in at William Billip's house. This next house, it is Ned Wattes.'

She looks at the Goodwife, continues, 'Maude Wattes who sells in the street, her time is due. We saw that she was due. Maude Wattes.'

She goes to the house and bangs on the door, calls, 'Maude Wattes! Maude Wattes!'

The house is silent. There are no candles to be seen through the draped window. They look for Thomas Micoe to ask if he has seen anything, anyone, but he has gone.

'I will call the Constable,' the Widow says to the Goodwife. Repeats loudly for the street to hear, 'I will call the Constable on Maude Wattes.'

Nothing from the house. They replace the basket over the corpse, weigh it down with a stone, tell a watchman nearby to watch.

The Goodwife leads her angry friend away, walks with her to the lower churchyard where they can talk privately over their pipes.

'An unnatural mother, Maude Wattes. She has murdered her infant.'

'We cannot be sure of that,' the Goodwife says calmly. 'We cannot be sure. We do not know.'

'She smoothered the infant. Stuffed cloth in the mouth, bound it shut. I saw, you saw, Thomas Micoe saw.'

'Yes, cloth. Perhaps to protect her dead infant, her already dead infant, to protect him from the muck. She has just given birth and the child is dead. Newly delivered mothers are sometimes wrong in their minds.'

'So you say,' the Widow says. 'I will report murder. A mother shall not murder her child.'

'No, she should not. But think of what I say. The child could have been still-born. Maude Wattes distracted in her mind. It could well be. And it is too late to report the death tonight. It must wait until tomorrow and that will give you time to consider. For me, I do not think it murder.'

'Mmm. You say so. This morning I believed my Sara had the pestilence and would die. Sara Potts I saved, all my natural children dead. I do not understand what you are saying about Maude Wattes.'

The Goodwife asks in great earnestness, 'Think, and wait until tomorrow is what I am saying. We will talk then, before the Fasting day service. Tonight, think on't, consult your pillow. Will you?'

The Widow looks steadily at her friend and after long thought nods and says, 'I will.'

At her table the Widow consults her bible. She knows where to find pages that tell of the deaths of innocent children. She weeps for them all.

> *Thus saith the Lord, about midnight will I go out into the midst of*
> *Egypt, and all the firstborn in the land shall die, from the firstborn*
> *of Pharaoh that sitteth upon his throne, even unto the firstborn of*
> *the maidservant that is behind the mill.*

The Widow sheds more tears for the poor maidservant behind the mill and her dead firstborn. No fault of the maidservant that she serves some king, some pharoah. Why should a maidservant, of all people, be so bereaved?

> *Herod was exceeding wroth, and sent forth, and slew all the*
> *children that were in Bethlehem, and in all the coasts thereof, from*
> *two years old and under.*

Herod is a wicked man – another king – but worst of all is the wicked Abraham. Widow Margaret Hazard loathes this Abraham, would have him hanged, drawn and quartered and would rejoice to watch. Abraham is an unnatural father.

Abraham built an altar there, and laid the wood in order, and bound Isaac his son, and laid him on the altar upon the wood. And Abraham stretched forth his hand, and took the knife to slay his son.

If the Lord God himself, wreathed in a ball of blinding light, were to enter her house and order her to take a knife and kill her daughter Sara, she would defy him without hesitation. She is no unnatural mother.

She hears the sound of Sara breathing sweetly, easily, in her sleep. In the street the bell-man walks, tolling his bell and calling the names, from Widow Alice Damport to Ann Hugget.

London, Bills of Mortality for 130 Parishes
from the 4 of July to the 11 of July 1665
Buried, in all – 1268; Plague – 725
Parishes clear of the Plague – 90; Parishes Infected – 40

CHAPTER XIX

London, Wednesday, 12 July 1665
Fast Day for the averting of God's heavy Visitation

'The Lord will smite thee with the botch of Egypt, and with the
emerods, and with the scab, and with the itch.'

'Cures against the pestilence! Come, who buys my cures against the pestilence!'

'Today is Wednesday! Fast day!'

'Prayers and preventives! Trust not so much in the Physick as in the blessing of God, without which all Physick is ineffectual! Prayers and preventives here, both! Come buy!'

'King Death is here! Now hear me, hear me, you London people of St Cyneswide and St Tibba, hear me and see King Death!' The broadside seller displays a fearsome picture held high on a cleft stick, a leering skeleton draped in ermine: crown on the skull, sceptre in one hand, hour glass in the other. The seller bawls out, 'See! And hear! Hear this!

> *Death triumphant cloath'd in ermine,*
> *'Bout whose bones do crawl the vermine,*
> *Doth denote that each condition*
> *To his power must yield submission!*

'Pestilential poesies! Heavenly antidotes against the plague in this time of general contagion!'

Church square is jostling with street sellers who will out-shout each other, out-position each other, and parishioners who will hear each one and inspect his wares. A feverish, near festive, enthusiasm, moves and excites the crowd.

'Have you seen Widow Hazard?' Goodwife Brokefild asks Goody Parsons.

'I think in church. Gone in.'

Widow Bullen agrees, 'Yes, gone early into church. With her daughter. Always with her daughter.'

Anne Abowen and Widow Lankester arrive arm in arm, the Widow vigorously talking food.

'Fast day today,' announces Widow Lankester loudly, unnecessarily. 'At dinner yesterday, and supper, I fortified myself against today. And now on this Wednesday Fast day I will eat one competent and moderate meal towards night, observing sobriety of diet, without superfluity of riotous fare, respecting necessity and not voluptuousness.' She emphasises words 'sobriety,' 'superfluity,' 'riotous,' and particularly 'voluptuousness,' a word she stretches with protruding lips and a final hiss.

Her voice is earnest, but – as always with Widow Lankester – the Goodwife wonders if this earnestness, this scrupulous reiteration of the Order of the Fast, might mask some dismissive mockery. The Goodwife recalls Widow Lankester's tone at Vestry when asked if she would take the Oath: 'Oh yes. Oh yes.'

Anne Abowen, already well used to her fellow Viewer's ways, regards her with silent interest and anticipation.

'Good you fortified yourself,' says Widow Dorothy Bullen. 'I did the same. A Fast can pull you down if you are not prepared. What did you eat?'

'Yes,' Goody Susanna Parsons says. 'What did you have? At your dinner, and at your supper?'

'Olla podrida,' Widow Lankester replies with a shrug. 'That was dinner.'

'All those meats!' Widow Dorothy Bullen exclaims. 'Did you take all of them?'

Widow Lankester does not answer immediately, considering whether to venture a Yes. 'No, not all of them, not before a Fast day. I wished, in advance, to avoid voluptuousness.'

'All those meats in an olla podrida!' Widow Bullen will recite them all. 'Thick gobbets of well fed beef, gobbets of the best mutton and the best pork, gobbets of venison – red and fallow – the foreparts of a fat pig, and a crammed pullet. Then after they have all boiled, a–'

'Yes, yes,' says Widow Lankester testily, feeling elbowed aside by Widow Bullen's volubility. 'Yes, then all the birds. We know.'

'Oh yes, all of them. A partridge,' Widow Bullen continues 'a chicken chopped in pieces, then quails, rails – that is good, quails and rails! – and black birds, larks, sparrows, and other small birds. But if you did not use all of them which meats did you leave out?'

'Most,' Widow Lankester says drily. 'I put in potato roots–' She holds up a hand to stop Widow Bullen from taking over the vegetables. Speaks louder, 'Turnips, skirrets, spinach, endive, succory, marigold flowers, lettuce, violet and strawberry leaves, bugloss, scallions, and–' Again she holds up a hand, 'And sugar, cloves, mace, cinnamon–'

Widow Bullen will not be stopped, joins in, 'ginger, nutmeg, verjuice, salt–'

Widow Lankester speaks faster, 'Prunes, raisins, currants, blanched almonds, and slices of oranges and lemons!'

The ancient women smile, Widow Brokefild and Goody Susanna Parsons titter.

'No levity on a solemn Fast day,' chides the Warden, ushering the parish into church. 'And where is sobriety of diet in this? Is all this, all this food, is this respecting necessity and not voluptuousness? Hear the church bell. Come, all inside.'

Widow Lankester undaunted, replies, 'The parish pension does not provide for poor ancient women to indulge in such food. But now that I am a widow *and* a Viewer will the Vestry pay my pension twice over?'

'We only eat such an olla podrida in our fancy,' the Goodwife adds genially. 'Our fare is not so riotous, but we may talk.'

'Talk you do,' the Warden is dismissive, waves them to the church.

'Driving us like hogs,' Anne Abowen says. 'He is sour today.'

'What *did* you have in your olla podrida?' Widow Bullen asks, 'I want to hear.'

'Beef, a very scrawny pullet, turnip, spinach, skirrets.'

'I call that a pottage.'

'So do I, but I like the words, olla podrida.' She repeats, 'Olla podrida.'

'What will he buy?' Anne Abowen asks. They watch Frances Barrow go over to the broadside sellers. 'I bought this good preventive, it starts with the tops of rue, a garlick head.' She has a small, flimsy sheet covered in print. 'Bought it from that one there, he with not a single hair on his head. Bald like the head of a prentice boy.'

Goodwife Brokefild looks anxiously around the square. 'You're sure Widow Hazard is inside?' she asks.

'Yes, gone in,' Goody Parsons says. 'Gone in early with her daughter.'

'She looks like her mother,' Widow Lankester says.

'How could she?' Widow Bullen asks. 'Widow Hazard is not her born mother.'

'I know that. Everyone knows that. I mean the child sometimes has that long stare, that long silent stare like Widow Hazard.'

'Like mother, like child,' Goody Parsons says.

'She is a good mother to the child Sara Potts,' Goodwife Brokefild says for her friend.

Anne Abowen agrees, 'She is, unlike the child's born mother. Whoever she is.'

'Not from this parish, they always cross to another parish to abandon their infants,' Goody Parsons says.

'Crowded! Our church is full today,' says Widow Bullen. It is, but red wands give them clear passage to where they sit. None will crowd in on them. 'Sit by old St Tibba,' Widow Bullen says comfortably. 'She is a very ancient woman by now, that St Tibba!'

'She is here, good,' Goodwife Brokefild is relieved.

'Who? St Tibba?' asks Widow Bullen, and finds herself amusing.

'Widow Hazard,' Goodwife Brokefild is almost impatient.

Widow Hazard, her eye fixed on Sara who sits with the parish children, turns briefly to her fellows when they sit beside her but says nothing.

'You are here before us,' Goodwife Brokefild says with forced cheer.

She gets a minimal shrug in reply. 'What we saw, searched, last night,' the Goodwife cannot hold herself back. 'You were going to think on it. Have you? Thought on it?'

'Later, we will talk later. Not now,' Widow Hazard gestures self-righteously at the arrival of Jenkin Williams.

'Oh!' The Goodwife is exasperated. The entrance of the minister has never inhibited talk in church.

'I have never seen so many people in church!' Widow Dorothy Bullen exclaims. 'And I have lived in this parish all my born days. Three score years and more.'

Widow Lankester and Anne Abowen exchange sceptical looks.

'Her age is a wandering star, never in the same place,' Widow Lankester says in a loud whisper.

'Dearly Beloved,' Jenkin Williams' voice is calm, carrying, reassuring. There is no smirking, no muffled laughter at his words. The swollen congregation of St Cyneswide and St Tibba wants its church to protect, preserve, save and succour it in this evil time, and is hungry for this Fast day to do so. They say with fervour: 'We acknowledge indeed that our punishments are less than our deservings; but yet of thy mercy, O Lord, correct us to amendment, and plague us not to our destruction.'

'We did not sing a psalm,' Robert Tomlinson mutters to Mary Tomlinson, 'We were to sing before service and we did not. The man cannot keep his word. Still a turncoat and a trimmer.'

'On Lord's day, that is to be on Lord's day and every Lord's day. Nothing was said of how psalms will be sung on special Fast days,' Mary Tomlinson says impatiently. 'You did not listen.'

The Litany is warmly embraced, some of it, this Fast day. All are glad to say, to cry out: 'From lightning and tempest, from plague, pestilence and famine, from battle and murder, from sudden death, Good Lord deliver us.'

But many fall silent, as they do, at the words: 'From all sedition, privy conspiracy, and rebellion, from all false doctrine, heresy, and schism, from hardness of heart, and contempt of thy word and commandment, Good Lord deliver us.'

'I read now from the Book of Deuteronomy, Chapter the twenty eighth, the prescribed Lesson for this Fast Day, as declared here in the Order for Morning Prayer,' Jenkin Williams holds up an impressive bundle of print.

'Walter Hall never did that,' Nicholas Troute says.

'What? Who never did what?' Simon Gurry asks.

'Walter Hall never did.'

'What?'

'Show the Order of Service.'

'Why should he?'

'Pipe down you two,' says a voice, but they cannot hear clearly who said it.

Jenkin Williams reads in solemn, heavy voice:

> *If thou wilt not hearken unto the voice of the Lord thy God, all these curses shall come upon thee, and overtake thee. The Lord shall make the pestilence cleave unto thee, until he have consumed thee from off the land. The Lord shall smite thee with a consumption, and with a fever, and with an inflammation, and with an extreme burning. The Lord will smite thee with the botch of Egypt, and with the emerods, and with the scab, and with the itch, whereof thou canst not be healed. The Lord shall smite thee with madness, and blindness, and astonishment of heart.*

'I have an itch,' Robin Kerton says, scratching.

'Of course you have an itch,' William Pickhering replies. 'You stable horses. You always have an itch.'

'The emerods are a curse,' George Hillcocke says, shifting uncomfortably. 'But many have them. My mother and father both.'

'Let us sing to the praise and glory of God psalm the thirty ninth,' announces Philip Carter Parish Clerk. The teeming congregation follows him in lusty voice.

> *Lord, take from me thy scourge and plague, I can them not withstand:*

I faint and pine away for fear of thy most heavy hand.
When thou for sin dost man rebuke, he waxeth woe and wan,
As doth a cloth that moths have fret, so vain a thing is man.
Lord, hear my suit, and give good heed, regard my tears that fall:
I sojourn like a stranger here, as did my fathers all.
O spare a little, give me space my strength for to restore,
Before I go away from hence, and shall be seen no more.

'That is a very fine psalm. "So vain a thing is man." Very fine,' Beatrix Sutterwhit pronounces in tones that brook no disagreement. There is none.

'Very fine indeed,' agrees Eppie Smoote. '"Take from me thy scourge and plague." Very fine.'

'In church square this day,' Jenkin Williams says, now robed for sermon.

'Church square,' scoffs Thomas Conclife, 'Always been called St Tibba's square. That's what it's called, that's what I've always called it. Why's he say church square? What would a new man just come in know? Knows nothing, that's what he knows.'

'Never,' says Edward Richbell. 'Never been called that. No one calls it that. It's church square, and what else would you call it Thomas Conclife? Square right in front of the church? Church square. St Tibba's my arse.'

'Called that by those in the know,' rejoins Thomas Conclife.

'In church square this day,' Jenkin Williams says, 'There are men selling broadsides, chapbooks, with cures against the pestilence.'

Many in his congregation look at the printed sheets they bought, feel in their pockets for small booklets: wary that they are to be condemned for buying on the Fast day; for buying in front of the church; for taking covert looks at the cures. Fearful that these will be taken from them, they conceal them.

'I have some, bought some,' Jenkin Williams says, to his congregation's surprise and great interest.

'Here is "The Charitable Physician Prescribing Cheap and Absolute Remedies for Prevention and Cure." Here is "A Collection of Seven and Fifty approved Receipts Good against the Plague: taken out of the Five

Books of that Renowned Dr Don Alexes. Secrets for the Benefit of the poorer sort of People." Now, today, here in our church of St Cyneswide and St Tibba, I offer you the best physick of all: Heavenly Antidotes Against the Plague. Hear me, and hear my advice to you to make good use of this medicine.

'Take a quart of true Repentance, mixed with Fasting and Prayer, and put thereto four handfuls of Faith in the blood of Christ, to which add as much Hope and Charity as you can procure. Let a clear conscience be the vessel to receive all these. This done, boil it on the fire of Love till such time as, by the eyes of Faith, you may perceive the dark scum of the love of this world to be obnoxious to your stomach. Then with the spoon of fervent Prayer make all clear, and having added to it the power of patience, strain it altogether in the Cloth of Christ's Innocence, and drink it for your morning and evening's draught.

'Having thus, by holy Meditation, prepared your soul, you may next proceed to use some of those medicines for your body. Yet trust not so much in the Physick as in the Blessing of God, without which all Physick is ineffectual.'

Having listened in rapt silence, the parishioners of St Cyneswide and St Tibba give a great rumbling murmur of approval, of satisfaction, at such excellent preaching, now confident that their recipes for cures need not be hidden away.

The Parish Clerk calls forth, 'Let us sing to the praise and glory of God psalm the fifty first:

Have mercy on me, Lord, after thy great abounding grace:
After thy mercies multitude, do thou my sins deface.
Behold in wickedness my kind and shape I did receive:
My sinful mother at the first in sin did me conceive.
With hyssop Lord, besprinkle me, I shall be cleansed so:
Yea, wash thou me, and so I shall be whiter than the snow.
O God, that art God of my health, from blood deliver me:
That praises of thy righteousness my tongue may sing to thee.

Under the blessed protection and shade of this most powerful Fasting day, the congregation is ready and eager for their Minister Jenkin Williams to speak again. He prays: 'O most gracious God, Father of Mercies, and of our Lord Jesus Christ, look down upon us, we beseech thee, in much pity, and compassion, and behold our great misery and trouble. For there is wrath gone out against us, and the Plague is begun. That dreadful arrow of thine sticks fast in our flesh; and the venom thereof fires our blood, and drinks up our spirits; And shouldest thou suffer it to bring us all to the dust of Death, yet must we still acknowledge, that righteous art thou, O Lord, and just are thy judgements. For our transgressions multiplied against thee, as the sand on the sea-shore, might justly bring over us a deluge of thy wrath.

'The cry of our sins, that hath pierced the very heavens, might well return with showers of vengeance upon our heads. While our earth is defiled under the inhabitants thereof, what wonder, if thou commandest an evil angel to pour out his vial into our air, to fill it with infection, and the noisome pestilence, and so turn the very breath of our life into the savour of death unto us all! But yet we beseech thee, O our God, forget not thou to be gracious: neither shut thou up thy loving kindness in displeasure. For his sake, who himself took our infirmities, and bare our sickness, have mercy upon us; and say to the destroying Angel, it is enough.

'O let that blood of sprinkling, which speaks better things than that of Abel, be upon the lintel, and the two side-posts in all our dwellings, that the destroyer may pass by. Let the sweet odour on thy blessed Son's all-sufficient sacrifice and intercession interpose between the living and the dead, and be our full and perfect atonement ever acceptable with thee, that the Plague may be stayed.

'O let us live, and we will praise thy name; and these thy judgements shall teach us to look every man into the plague of his own heart: that being cleansed from all our sins, we may serve thee with pure hearts all our days, perfecting holiness in thy fear, till we come at last, where there is no more sickness, nor death, through thy tender mercies in him alone, who is our life, and our health, and our salvation, Jesus Christ, our ever blessed

Saviour, and Redeemer. Amen.'

'Amen!' the church of St Cyneswide and St Tibba cries out.

'Wait,' says the Goodwife as the church slowly empties – the parish in exultant mood, convinced that with prayers, remedies and fasting the plague will be vanquished.

The Widow stands still, fixes the Goodwife with a face empty of expression.

'Did you consult your pillow?' Goodwife Brokefild asks with excessive cheer.

'No need. My pillow could not tell me more than I already knew.'

'You said you would sleep on it.'

'I slept well, with a clear conscience. This morning early, at first light, I gave information of Maude Wattes to the Constable and to the Parish Clerk. The murder by Maude Wattes of her new-born infant.'

'Ahhh,' the Goodwife pauses to think, to not say what she wants to say. Says, 'I thought we would talk again, you and I, this morning before, before … Did you think that if we spoke once more you might, might be swayed to my mind?'

'No, I did not think that, but I did not want, do not want, to dispute with you. I know my own mind. You know yours.'

'It is not certain! Not certain it is a murder!' the Goodwife cries. 'Mothers with a new infant can have their minds unbalanced. I have seen it. You have seen it. We do not know if … We do not know!'

'I do not want to be at odds with you,' the Widow says. 'I do not. You are my good friend, but I am not you. You are who you are and I am who I am.' She sharply summons Sara to come and walks away.

'Parish Clerk,' Goodwife Joan Brokefild says. Philip Carter is not hard to find, perched beside the parish chest in the vestry. He looks up. 'Widow Hazard has reported a death we searched last night. An infant.'

'She gave an information to Constable Samuel Snow, and to me, of a child murdered in this parish by the mother, Maude Wattes.'

'The infant is dead. I do not say it is murder.'

'Widow Hazard spoke of cloth in the child's mouth, and other binding that she searched. Not a natural death.'

'I am a Searcher, as Widow Hazard is a Searcher, but I did not see a murder.'

Philip Carter rummages in his chest and shows her a fresh sheet, lettered at the top, 'Bill of Mortality for the parish of St Cyneswide and St Tibba from the 18 of July to the 25 of July 1665.' He points to the sole entry thus far: 'Murdered by the Mother (an Infant) at St Cyneswide & St Tibba.' 'Entered by me this morning.'

'No,' Goodwife Brokefild says. 'No. The death should be listed simply as "Infant," as we see, often see, in the Bills of Mortality. No cause given. No need. Infants die. Or even "Found dead in the street, an Infant." I have seen this too in the Bills.'

'This was not in the street. It was in the privy. Smothered.'

The Goodwife persists, 'Do you have the last one, Bills for all parishes for 27 June to 4 July? Do you have it here?'

Philip Carter is annoyed but wants to know where this will go. He finds the Bill.

'There,' points the Goodwife. 'See. "Diseases and Casualties this week: Infants, 9." They can die, infants. As all know.'

'There is a law, from the time of James, a law to prevent the destroying and murdering of bastard children.'

'This was no bastard!' the Goodwife exclaims. 'What has this law to do with the lawful child of Ned and Maude Wattes?'

'Bastard or lawful, an infant may not be murdered. Maude Wattes did not want to be trammelled with another infant.'

'At worst,' the Goodwife jabs a finger at the entry on the new Bill, 'this must read "Killed by the mother (being Distracted) an infant at St Cyneswide and St Tibba." I have seen such words in the Bills of Mortality. If she killed the child it was while distracted, her mind out of joint. Not a murder.'

Philip Carter is irritated, does not want to hear more. 'Our Company of Clerks, December past we made a high Petition to Sheldon the Archbishop, and beyond to the King, a supplication for reforms to make our Bills more perfect. We wrote, the Company wrote, how the sins of adultery, fornication and bastardy lead to the exposing and destroying of infants. By this, we said, "murders pass concealed and undiscovered." The very Privy Council is to examine and report on it. This murder here in our parish is not a trivial matter to be hushed and put away!'

Goodwife Joan Brokefild says bitterly, 'I would have reported the infant as dead. No more than that. A dead infant, another one, one of many.'

'So you would have, but Widow Hazard came here first. Gave her report. You are off the point. There is no more to be said of Maude Wattes. She has been taken. She is in Newgate. Now leave. Go.'

At the door the Goodwife turns to him, cries, 'Sheldon of Canterbury? The Archbishop? He is no friend to saints. He is a wencher, what men call a wencher. He keeps a woman for lewdness. This is who will remedy the sins of adultery and fornication? A whoring whoremaster! That is your Archbishop!'

'I have heard those stories,' Philip Carter says, 'And he is not mine. I do not choose archbishops, bishops, any bishops. I will have no bishops. You have said your piece, now go.' He knows she has the right of it about Sheldon, he is a whoring whoremaster. As is the king.

'Lot of noise,' the Church Warden says to Philip Carter. 'I could hear it from the font.'

'Shouting ancient woman.'

The Warden waits to hear more.

'Maude Wattes and her murdered infant. Goodwife Brokefild says it is no murder, Widow Hazard says it is. The plague growing on, more deaths every day, and she harps on this one death. I don't know why it sticks in her gizzard. It's bred ill blood between the Searchers. She shouted, I told her to go.'

'Plague deaths,' Frances Barrow says. 'Did you see this? Did you buy one? See: "A table comparing the increase of the Plague betwixt the year 1625 and the present year 1665." Sold in the square this morning. See, compares week by week, twelve weeks from the end of April to the present.

Uses the Bills of Mortality.'

The Clerk is interested, 'Yes, yes, let me see. The year 25 more plague deaths at the beginning, but–'

'And in 25 a thousand more deaths than this year.'

'I was going to say,' Philip Carter says impatiently: this is his work, he is a Parish Clerk with responsibility for Bills of Mortality. 'What I was going to say is that – see, from the middle of June – the deaths in 65 grow more than in 25. We will have it worse. I hear from the other clerks.'

'What do the other clerks say of their ministers? I've heard more have fled. A good thing. Our saints have taken their pulpits, good Independent men.'

> *Now, where's Beloved? Why, Beloved's gone.*
> *No morning Matins now, nor Evening Song:*
> *Alas! The Parson cannot stay so long.*

'Thomas Jacombe, ejected in 62 from St Martin Ludgate, he's found a church with an empty pulpit,' Philip Carter says.

'Thomas Jacombe? Oliver Protector called him Long Tom of Ludgate.'

'Our new man here did well today, Jenkin Williams did. His closing prayer moved hearts.'

Frances Barrow will not have it, 'It was in the printed Order of Service for today. He read it from that!'

'Yes, but he said it well. And a fine sermon.'

'He may well have stolen that from some pamphlet hawked in the square.'

'You will not have him, will not allow him, will you Frances Barrow?'

'I will not. He pesters me, always about money. What are the church rates? Can we make them higher? Wants to see the valuations of the houses, says they are too low. How much was in the collect? Always money with him. And he *is* a trimming parson. Still a turncoat, always a turncoat. I don't trust him. And he will flee, of course he will flee.'

The Parish Clerk changes the subject. 'The sellers in the square, did you buy more?'

'Yes. See this, see this picture of King Death, the Plague. Death wears a crown, holds a sceptre. The dead king. This tells of the coming death of the bastard king Charles Jermyn, that man of blood. And if the pestilence does not kill him, if it kills only the poor, it does not matter because he will soon die. Here is Death, and "each condition to his power must yield submission." Each condition, rich and poor, prince and prentice. There are great things soon to come Philip Carter. Hear me, a great business is in train. The beast is upon his last work. God will blast them all, and the people of God and the Good Old Cause will live.'

'Frances Barrow I pray you are right.'

'So do many others. We will soon see the day when godly men will have their pulpits, have them back, by right, not just because the porridge men have fled.'

They sit in silence.

Frances Barrow lowers his voice, 'Henry Danvers is here in London. Colonel Henry Danvers. Not long to wait. The pestilence has thrown everything, thrown the court and bishops, all out of order, thrown them out of town! The business is in hand.'

They tend their pipes, sit and smoke. The Clerk wonders if Frances Barrow will speak more of Henry Danvers. Wonders if he wants him to. He thinks not.

The Warden stares at the picture of the leering King. 'He was not a perfect man, Oliver Protector. Not always true to his friends, to those close to him, who supported him. Had his rages. Such rages. Would not stomach Colonel Whalley, his regiment demanding their due pay. This was in 49. Had young Robert Lockyer shot in Paul's churchyard: his last words, "I am troubled that so small a thing as contention for pay should have my enemies take away my life." One of Oliver's rages. But he was a good and brave leader in battle and he never took the crown. Did not, even though pressed. Not Oliver. He was not perfect, but only King Jesus is perfect.'

'He hated Henry Vane,' says Philip Carter. 'There was a man who gave a good speech on the scaffold. Said all he did was for the glory of God, prayed for England, for the churches in England, for the City of London.

Said he was sure to be presently at the right hand of Christ, and would see the reign of the saints on earth with Christ.'

'Fasting,' says Frances Barrow, 'a week before Henry Vane his execution, the day of his trial, your Fifth Monarchy Men—'

'Not mine,' Philip Carter breaks in, 'Not mine nor Jane-Pym Carter's, no matter what her family are.'

'The Fifth Monarchy Men had a day of fasting for Vane and Lambert, while they were tried.' He shrugs.

Their pipes are out. The Warden stands. 'This business with the Wattes infant. The murder. What do you say?'

'I say Searcher Widow Margaret Hazard is an honest ancient woman.'

'And Goodwife Brokefild?'

'She is an honest Searcher.'

'And what do *you* say, Philip Carter?'

'I say what my Bill says.' He holds it up and points: 'Murdered by the Mother (an Infant) at St Cyneswide & St Tibba.'

Frances Barrow has nothing to say to this. It is not his business.

'That young Robert Lock, he was—'

'Lockyer, Trooper Robert Lockyer,' the Church Warden says.

'Robert Lockyer, he was right, a man must be paid.'

'Yes, a man must,' says the Warden, but he is thinking of the return of godly men to the town's empty pulpits, and what should have happened here in St Cyneswide and St Tibba if not for this Jenkin Williams. But then, this Jenkin Williams, the trimmer and turncoat, will not stay long. He will do as Walter Hall did and flee. Flee with all the wealthy, the doctors, the lawyers, with all those who can afford to. Flee with all those who have caught the running disease.

Closeted in his room at the far end of the crypt, Frances Barrow's mind runs on a drinking song of the troops, sung in other days in other circumstances, but which fits well today. It is – he works to recall the name – it is *A merry health drunk in wine and beer, not to them that flies for it, but to those that stay here.* The rest of the words come as he sings:

What means our brave gallants
So fast for to fly?
Because they are afraid
That some danger might be,
They car'd not for seeing
The citizens die,
But what is all this to thee or to me?
Since Charles and his brother
First crossed the seas,
To shun the great danger
That they could fore-see;
There's many hath catched
The Running Disease,
But what is all this to thee or to me?
If that all false traitors,
Were banished our land,
And that from all Popery
It once might be free,
Then saints in a band
Might join hand in hand,
Then times will prove better to thee & to me.
Then merrily and cheerily
Let's drink off our beer,
Let who as will run for it,
We will stay here.

Frances Barrow wishes he has a drink in hand, longs for companions to join him in song, but he is sure Jenkin Williams will *not* stay here, and when he goes then Thomas Dugdale will come back in. He breathes a great sigh of nostalgia and exasperation both, and goes to find John Barriffe of the Private and Loving Society of Cripplegate to drink with and sing with.

* * *

'Bufflehead Walter Shute never gets it wrong,' says Goody Parsons. 'If he says it is Wednesday, it is Wednesday. Never wrong. I find it very helpful.'

'Will the Searchers come?' Anne Abowen asks. There are only four ancient women in their room.

'Who knows?' Widow Lankester says. 'They're at odds about the Wattes infant. One says one thing, the other says another.'

'And them good friends,' Widow Dorothy Bullen shakes her head.

'The only thing they agree on is that the infant is dead,' says Widow Lankester.

'Well, they are Searchers, they know best about such things,' Widow Bullen says consolingly.

'If there is evidence of a murder, then it is a murder. If there is no evidence or not enough evidence then it is a dead infant and no more,' Anne Abowen says.

'This preventive recipe,' Goody Parsons shows the leaflet she bought, 'as well as rue and garlic it has half a quarter of walnut and salt. You eat it every morning.' She reads, "continuing so a month together, this is also good against the worms in young and old." That is good to know.'

'For worms, I use half a hazel nut, not a walnut, and aloes socotrine, all wrapped in the pap of a roasted apple,' Widow Bullen offers. 'And here is Widow Margaret Hazard.'

Widow Hazard enters, looks around, says, 'She is not here.'

'No,' Widow Lankester says. 'Not here. Not yet. You two did not agree on the infant Wattes' death.'

'No. Did not.' Widow Hazard sits down, stands up, sits down. Watches the door.

The room is ill at ease.

'The psalm verse, "A cloth that moths have fret." It would sing well here, the moths have been busy here about their work,' Widow Bullen points. 'The baize has been got.'

'And the psalm that sings of a sinful mother,' Widow Hazard stands again, now loud, angry. 'She, Maude Wattes, she was that, a sinful mother. A sinful mother who murdered her infant.'

The ancient women sit and listen, mend their pipes, say nothing.

'I do not take bribes. I do not lie. I do my duty as a Searcher. I tell the truth. I saw a murdered infant and reported a murdered infant to Constable and Clerk. That is all of it, that is the truth of it.'

'The Goodwife did not see it the same,' says Widow Lankester, ever ready to stir a bubbling pot.

'She did not. She sees what she sees. I see what I see.'

'The psalm sings of hyssop for cleansing,' Goody Parsons will steer the room to safer, calmer waters. 'Hyssop water and white wine are good for the lethargy. And—'

'I have had enough of recipes and cures, and all this,' Widow Hazard says bitterly as she leaves.

The heavy silence that hangs behind is quickly broken.

'Angry with Goodwife Brokefild,' says Widow Lankester.

'Why? She got her way, Widow Hazard did,' Goody Parsons says. 'Reported the death as a murder and it is now called a murder, although Goodwife Brokefild says it is no murder. It should be she who is angry.'

'She is,' Anne Abowen says.

'It does not make for a companionable ancient women's room to have two angry Searchers. First the moth has fret and now this,' Widow Bullen says with resignation.

'More room. Two less people in this small smelly room,' says Widow Lankester.

'For me, I *am* interested in recipes and cures,' Widow Bullen says.

'I found out, you hang them around your neck,' Anne Abowen says.

'What?' Goody Parsons is confused. 'What is? What do you do?'

'The three spiders. I asked. Against the plague, you wear three dead spiders on a string around your neck.'

'I would not like to do that,' Widow Bullen says dubiously.

'If it works I will,' Widow Lankester says, turns to Goody Susanna Parsons, asks, 'If you don't know what day it is, how do you know the Bufflehead is right? How can that be?'

Goody Parsons is sure there is an answer to this but she cannot find it.

In the street, Widow Hazard finds the waiting Sara singing to herself, dance-stepping back and forth:

Stepping on the green grass,
Thus, and thus, and thus,
May we have a pretty lass
To come and play with us?

'What is that?' the Widow asks crossly. 'Stop that.' They walk home morosely, silent.

Bread and cheese and beer bring better humour. Sara is a good, dutiful daughter tending her mother at table.

'Tell me,' the Widow says in softened mood. 'Tell me, sing to me, more of that song, the green grass one.'

You shall have a duck, my dear,
You shall have a drake,
You shall have a young man
Prentice for your sake.
Suppose this young man was to die
And leave the girl a wider?
The bells shall ring, the birds shall sing,
We'll all clap hands together!

Sara claps her hands and her mother briefly does too.

CHAPTER XX

'Why should we not, while in this world remaining,
Strive our talents to improve?'

'Here is Jack Micoe!'

Does Thomas Micoe place too much weight on the word Micoe? Perhaps. Does he know that, as far as the London beyond Dung Wharf is concerned, his son is Jack Green?

'Now tell me of the livery life Jack. Is it still the livery life with Walter Hall fled?'

'The new man in the rectory, Jenkin Williams, is not a man for a livery, so I do not wear it. Mostly.' With his father, with everyone, Jack will speak as if he is entrenched in Jenkin Williams' service, doing well.

His father nods. 'Look across the river Jack – what do you see? Do you see a shipyard?'

'Yes,' says Jack cautiously, wondering where this will go.

'Now look here, around you, what do you see?'

Clever, sharp, reliable Jack is sure he knows the answer, has heard it many times, but dutifully waits for Thomas Micoe to give it.

'There a shipyard, here a shit-yard!' Thomas Micoe bellows at his own wit. 'That is excellent! Shit-yard. I might have said it before but if so I have forgotten. Today it is new-minted. And new or old, it is good wit! You are all health in these unhealthy times? Safe and sound?'

Jack throws out his hands. What can he say? He is sound at this moment. 'And you? And Oliver and Richard and Margaret and Joan

Micoe?'

'The dung keeps me sound, keeps us sound. Not everyone in St Anne Blackfriars can say the same. The new Bills give us this last week seven burials, six of plague. Six. None in the weeks before, none, no plague here. Now it is. And Fasting day yesterday, with all to forbear from bodily working and to resort to church, excepting – excepting, hear this Jack Micoe – excepting those who may not be spared from their necessary business!' He laughs his great laugh, 'But everyone must do their necessary business, Fast day or no Fast day, and we gong men have the necessary business to collect it.'

Jack is a small small lad again, laughing helplessly at his father's gong wit.

'Joan Micoe keeps Richard and Margaret and herself shut up. Wants nothing to do with the world so they will stay safe, saved.' It is Thomas Micoe's turn to throw out his hands. What is to be done? 'Here's Oliver, fresh from the river. Growing big, too big. Need to put a great weight on his head to slow him down. Look at those arms Jack, his legs, ready to be in a match of wrestling at Bartholomew Fair! What would he do to those North and West countrymen?'

Good-natured Oliver is happy to give a mock wrestling display for his brother.

'A draught,' Thomas Micoe proposes. 'To *Sampson*. Do you know it Jack, in Paul's Churchyard? We can drink and talk.' If Jack has come for a reason, and Thomas Micoe suspects he has, it might be more easily told over a draught. 'And here, close by, convenient for those who take too much, is Pissing Alley. Some know it well,' Thomas Micoe laughs. He calls for Alderman Byde's ale. 'And a pigeon pie, a big one, for three hungry men who have been solemnly fasting.'

'I have been here before, but not for a long time,' Jack says.

'That would be a Muggleton gathering. Your Walter Hall and your Jenkin Williams and your church of St Cyneswide and St Tibba, not for Muggletonians – here's our church, rooms in taverns, so you would have been here for that. That was before you went over to the porridge bishops,'

Thomas Micoe teases.

Oliver laughs, 'Porridge man.'

Jack takes this calmly, used to family jibes about being a footboy in a rectory.

Thomas Micoe greets the arrival of the pots of ale with a song:

> *My heart it is cheered with wine,*
> *And oil makes my face for to shine;*
> *My God hath prepared me in time,*
> *To meet him in glory divine.*

Sampson's pot boy is confused, 'Wine? I thought you will have Alderman Byde's?'

'Yes, Byde's. The song was for some other business. Do you remember singing it Jack? One of the many Divine Songs?'

'I remember the singing, not that particular song, and how the meetings were ...' He searches for the right words: peaceful? kindly? at ease? Mostly. Apart from the damning. He remembers looking forward to Muggletonian gatherings with the songs, food, talk, games with the other children, the familiar tavern smells.

Jack says, 'I liked the meetings.'

Thomas Micoe nods, satisfied, but corrects his son, 'Gatherings.' Adds in satisfied voice, 'No bishops, no priests, preachers, parsons, vicars, rectors, ministers, or what else you might call them. None.'

Jack joins in, 'No liturgy, no litany, no prayers, no sermons, no homilies, no collects, no communion, no kneeling.'

'Holidays, all in carts or a waggon to a country tavern – we do that, not your churches.' Oliver says.

'To the *Green Man* on Strand Green? I remember that,' Jack says.

His father and brother nod, 'Yes, still go there at times.'

'Lot of talk at the gatherings,' Oliver says, 'and high words from time to time.'

'I don't recall high words, arguments,' says Jack.

'You stopped coming when you were still young, when you went with

Walter Hall,' says Thomas Micoe. 'You must have not have taken note of the arguments and disputations. Not all the time, but sometimes there are high words. Your brother's one who likes to argue,' he says with a mixture of pride and amusement.

This is news to Jack, Oliver speaking out at Muggletonian gatherings. But he must open the business he has come about, so begins casually, 'I am well settled with Jenkin Williams, but would like to do even better.'

'Would you? Yes, all of us would do better,' Thomas Micoe agrees, sings:

> *Why should we not, while in this world remaining,*
> *Strive our talents to improve?*

'Do you recall that one?'

Jack knows that the Divine Songs of the Muggletonians would make a very thick book if bound together. Wonders if his father will sing them all. Perhaps, so Jack must get on with it.

'This infection, the pestilence. You now have plague deaths here in Blackfriars, and there are deaths in St Cyneswide and St Tibba and other parishes. The Bills show forty parishes infected already. With the hot summer it will grow worse and grow worse,' Jack pauses. His father and brother are listening.

'For any deaths there are coffins, winding sheets, shrouds. These are always needed. If there are many deaths then even more will be needed, and for the plague there's lime must be laid in the graveyards, carts needed to carry away corpses.'

'Yes,' says Thomas Micoe, puzzled, not knowing where Jack is leading them.

'Two of these necessaries, the lime and the carts, there may be some business here for Thomas Micoe and sons.'

'How?' Thomas Micoe is still puzzled.

'Lime pebbles by the Thames. Downriver. We saw them from the barge at low water on the river edge. I remember.'

Thomas Micoe nods, 'Down the estuary, by Northfleet.'

'These are the makings of lime for the graveyards.'

Thomas Micoe has caught up, 'Bring them back in the barges? Load of lime stones? Could be money in it. Has to be burnt, the lime stone.'

'If this plague is to be a great scourge, as it looks it will, there will be money in graveyard lime,' says confident Jack. 'And the burning could be here, or at Northfleet. There are kilns at Greenhithe and Swanscombe but we could have our own.'

'Good, good, we should have our own. We could burn it at Northfleet or here. No, not here, burning lime gives a foul smell and we do not want that here, I can't abide foul smells. Better to have our own kilns at Northfleet, or use Edward Brent's kilns – Edward Brent of Kent! – and bring the burnt lime here. Lime is good but I cannot see money for us in coffins or shrouds. Edward Brent of Kent! That is good!' He roars laughing.

'No, but there will be money in carts. Those Carmen who will be free of the Worshipful Company of the Woodmongers and the Coal Trade of London, those Carmen your friend John Sled of the Woodmongers hates, they'll welcome more business.'

'Carrying the dead,' says Oliver.

'And our lime,' says Thomas Micoe. 'More money for the Carmen, perhaps, but what business is there in it for us?'

'Let me find that,' says Jack. 'If you can tell me a name to talk to.'

'A name! I have heard John Sled curse the name. Nicholas Bibbie, his parish St Andrew Undershaft, he is your man in the Carmen. But I cannot see any money in this for us.'

'I'll try,' says Jack.

'And I will see what lime we can get from Northfleet. We'll need men to rake up the lime, kilns for burning.' Thomas Micoe looks pleased, says, 'Like dung, this lime business smells like money, you boys!'

Thomas Micoe looks at them, at the tavern, well satisfied. 'We often gather here, did when John Reeve still lived, and now with Ludo Muggleton. That back room there. A good, private one. John Reeve was always the loud fiery prophet. Ludo is a quiet man, brings peace with him.'

'Except for the cursing, the damning,' says Oliver with enthusiasm.

'Not only damning, blessing as well as damning,' Thomas Micoe says comfortably. 'In your parish two days since,' he says to Jack, 'that dead infant. Oliver found it.'

'The Searchers,' Jack says, 'one of them says it was a murder, the other says not.'

'It was a murder,' Thomas Micoe says. 'I don't need to be a Searcher to see that.'

They stare at the crumbs of pigeon pie on the table.

'God,' says Oliver, a true Muggletonian, 'his interest is not in us, so why prayers, why these Fast days? Will they stop the plague, turn it back?' He picks up the crumbs with finger tips.

'No prayers for us. No point,' says Thomas Micoe genially. 'None of that.' His tone changes. 'You, Jack, you be careful. I've said it before and I'll say it again, the more you stir a turd the worse it stinks. Stick to business, Jack, money business, and you'll do well. Avoid scheming, plotting, politics, like the plague,' he laughs, 'like the plague. If you're not in gong – and you're no longer although we'll have you back if you want – find some other good way to fill your pots with gold. But you know that. There's rumours I hear about plots in the parishes, in your St Cyneswide and St Tibba. Don't you stir the turd.'

Jack nods seriously, wonders what his father had heard, what he knows.

'This business with the Carmen,' says Thomas Micoe. 'I don't want trouble with John Sled, I still do business with him. When you speak to Nicholas Bibbie don't say you're Jack Micoe. Use some other name. You'll think of something.'

* * *

After-noon

Jack will be both bold and clever – join the lion's skin to the fox's tail, as the word has it – but neither courage nor cunning help him win over Nicholas Bibbie, or even meet him.

He farewells his father and brother at *Sampson* – 'God be w'ye' – and with determination, with enthusiasm, sets out for St Andrew Undershaft. Asks a back carrier the way.

'You know where the pole, the shaft, once was?' The carrier asks in turn.

'No.'

The carrier gives an exasperated huff, 'Well it's there, St Andrew Undershaft. Understand? Church, St Andrew, is under the shaft,' he says with slow emphasis, as if talking to some clownish countryman. 'Except the shaft's not there any more. Taken away and burnt, and a good thing that was. That's where the church is. Are you for reform? You are aren't you?'

'Yes, I am,' Jack says. Sure this is the right answer. It is.

'Good lad. It's off to the east. Head east. You'll be right. God be w'ye.'

Jack walks east, and finds the church of St Andrew Undershaft.

He disappoints a street seller – 'Buy a mat for a bed!' – and does not buy a mat, but asks where he can find Nicholas Bibbie, his house.

'How would I know? Ask someone who lives in this parish. Ask her,' he points to a cookmaid weighed down by a basket of alexanders, chibols, marvellous apples, and a manchet, about to enter a house.

Jack, in his best voice, his Walter Hall voice, asks her if she knows the house of Nicholas Bibbie the carman.

She calls into the house, 'Petherick! Petherick! Someone asking for Nicolas Bibbie, his house!'

'Who? What?' a west country voice shouts back.

'Nicholas Bibbie, his house!'

'Who's asking, Honor Garland? Who is it?'

'I don't know! He just asked me. I don't know him!'

A footman, his coat half on, comes to the door, sees Jack, who is not wearing any livery, and impatiently casts off the coat.

'Who wants to know about Nicholas Bibbie? Why?'

'Business,' says polite Jack, 'Carmen business with Nicholas Bibbie the carter.'

'More trouble then. Are you with him?'

'With Nicholas Bibbie? I have business to do with him.'

'So did they who came yesterday. They had business with Nicholas Bibbie. So are you with him, with John Sled? The Woodmongers and Coal Trade John Sled? That John Sled. You are, aren't you? With him?'

'No,' says Jack cautiously. 'No, I'm not with John Sled. My business,' he tries again – this is frustrating – 'my business is with Nicholas Bibbie. I don't know John Sled's business with Nicholas Bibbie, what John Sled's business is.'

'He's big in the Woodmongers and Coal Trade, John Sled,' says the footman.

'Yes, I know that,' says increasingly desperate Jack.

'So you do know him then, John Sled?'

'The name, I know the name John Sled. Woodmongers and Coal Trade John Sled. My business with Nicholas Bibbie is … is, my business. Nothing to do with John Sled and the Woodmo–'

'Yes yes,' says Petherick the footman testily. 'So you say.' He looks carefully at Jack, says, 'Nicholas Bibbie, his house, see that lane by the church? Look in that lane, Offley's Lane, see the broken and burnt carts, see the door by them. That is Nicholas Bibbie, his door, his house. Just as well you are not with John Sled.' Satisfied with how he has dealt with Jack's question, the footman retires.

The cookmaid is gazing at Jack with interest, says, 'My name is Honor Garland.' Raises her eyebrows at him questioningly. Jack already knows her name. Petherick the footman is loud.

Jack thinks that Honor Garland has a very fine name. 'That is a very fine name, Honor Garland,' he says.

'Yes, it is.'

'I am Jack Green, a footboy from St Cyneswide and St Tibba.'

She smiles at him, 'To see Nicholas Bibbie.'

'Yes.'

She continues to smile at him. He says, for something to say, gesturing towards her basket, 'Those marvellous apples are …' he struggles for the right word, 'marvellous.'

She bursts into laughter and pouts her chest out at him, 'Marvellous?' She laughs.

He blushes. She asks, 'Which apples do you mean?'

Jack finds St Andrew Undershaft an unsettling parish. Says quickly, at random, 'The shaft, the pole – St Andrew Undershaft – it was taken down, burnt. When was that?'

She shrugs, shouts, 'Petherick!'

'Yes! What now Honor Garland?'

'The pole! The shaft! When was it taken down and burnt?'

Petherick calls from inside the house, 'How would I know? In the time of the old queen, or her father, the old king. Why?'

'He wants to know!'

'Where was the pole?' Jack asks, unable to stop himself.

'Petherick! Where was–'

'No matter, no matter,' says Jack hastily. 'An idle question.' He mutters 'God be w'ye' and makes for Offley Lane.

Before he has gone far he hears, hopes he hears, thinks he hears, but knows he does not hear, Honor Garland call him and ask him where *he* would put the shaft.

He stops and looks back. She waves her basket of alexanders, chibols, marvellous apples, and a manchet, at him.

The house of Nicholas Bibbie, thanks to Petherick the west country footman – Jack's fingerpost in this odd parish – is not hard to find. Offley Lane is a mess of broken wheels, a burnt cart, and crude dung daubings on what must be Nicholas Bibbie's door. Jack knows dung.

From behind the cart an angry man with a raised club comes at him. Jack has his sword and draws it, says in Blackfriars, 'I have business with Nicholas Bibbie. Business to his advantage and to mine.'

'Then why do you carry a sword and menace me?'

'Because you carry a club and menace me. I am only here on business, good business. Nothing else. Petherick the footman,' Jack points back up the lane, 'he told me about trouble here from John Sled.' Jack waves his sword at the wheels, the burnt cart. 'Nothing to do with me. I have nothing to do with John Sled.'

The club, then the sword, are lowered.

'John Sled hates us carmen. Says we want our own company. Which we do and we will. He was here yesterday with his woodmen. Look at that shit on the door!'

'What is it?' asks Jack. 'Some drawing?'

'Meant to be the bundles of faggots, that's what the Woodmongers have on their guild arms. They smeared shit on Nicholas Bibbie's door to show they were here, show it was them that did the burning and the breaking. They came back and did those shit signs last night. That shit sticks like, like shit on that old door.'

Jack Micoe knows about removing shit from anything, but keeps this to himself. 'You're a carman?'

'Of course a carman! I am with Nicholas Bibbie, we will have our own company, separate from the Woodmongers. Are you with us? For us?'

Jack tries once more. 'I have business with–'

'Well you can't talk to him. He's not here. Gone.'

Jack looks sceptical.

'Bang on the door if you will. Might shake some of the shit off. He's not here. No business for you here today.'

'Tomorrow?' asks Jack, 'Will he …' He gets a silent, despondent shrug in reply. He walks back up the lane, hoping to see Honor Garland the cookmaid. But the door is closed and he is eager to quit St Andrew Undershaft and make a swift return to St Cyneswide and St Tibba.

His way leads him down St Mary Axe into Leadenhall. Ever curious, he takes close interest in the markets, yet these sad days there is little to see: few buyers; some stalls empty; those still open manned by dispirited mongers. They take heart at seeing Jack, a new face, wave him over, call him to come and damn him when he doesn't. The eel man is insistent, 'See my great dish of eels! Who has better fish? Sweet and fresh as new cream, what more could you wish!' Jack does not wish for eels.

Through Leadenhall, into Cornhill, Poultry, finding only a trickle of traffic, few people and fewer carts, the markets shrunk down from their usual shouting, crowded, jostling ways. Even frantic Cheapside is slow and sullen, much of its custom has fled. 'London mongers,' his father would say, 'are the rudest people on God's earth. Street market hectors and bullies. Most coarse of all men, even coarser than watermen, and they are coarse. Not,' Thomas Micoe will add with a guffaw, 'not like those in the gong trade who are gentle folk all.'

The further west Jack goes the more red crosses are seen on doors. Outside these doors are bored or sleeping watchmen. A tavern with its sharp ale smell again brings to mind his father, his brother – Oliver, to his surprise, now a strong Muggletonian – and the songs of the Muggletonians.

Happy Muggletonians who only
True faith have to receive
Revelations ever new,
Gave to great Muggleton and Reeve,
Which makes us to Christ our king
Sweet hallelujahs ever sing.

He sings loudly. Striding into church square he is beckoned over by Widow Margaret Hazard.

'What is that song? I don't know it. Who are great Muggleton and Reeve? What are Muggletonians? Why are they happy? A strange song,' she says sharply.

'A song some people sing,' Jack says as blandly as he can. 'I heard it … heard it somewhere.'

'Not a psalm,' the Widow says suspiciously, 'but you're singing of Christ, singing sweet hallelujahs. What is it?'

'A good song, sung by saints,' he pauses, reluctant to say more but will defend his father, his brother, his family, adds, 'godly men and women all.'

'An independent church then? Not papist, not Prayer Book?' the Widow asks.

'No, not papist or porridge.'

'Good, good. Muggleton and Reeve?'

'Tailors, both of them. London tailors. Good men.'

She nods approvingly, looks to him for more.

'Some say,' he begins cautiously, goes quiet when he sees Jenkin Williams approaching.

Minister Jenkin Williams comes to them with a benign smile. 'Jack, Widow Hazard. I am glad to see you, glad. Good service to the parish Widow Hazard with your information of that infant's murder.'

The Widow nods. This is not the way a minister talks to a Searcher.

Not put off by her silent stare Jenkin Williams offers her tobacco from his pouch, places it in her hand. 'Fill your pipe. The thanks of the parish, and Jack,' he laughs, 'can find his own tobacco, eh Jack?'

The Widow nods her wary thanks, helps herself to tobacco and hands back the pouch. Jenkin Williams beams and goes off with a cheery, 'God be w'ye!' Calls, 'Jack, come with me.'

The Widow lights her pipe, smokes, and thinks. She does not know what to make of Jenkin Williams. He is not like the small bald parson of her youth, not like John Gifford, Angus McManus, Thomas Dugdale, Walter Hall, or any minister appointed to St Cyneswide and St Tibba. She is not at ease with him, he is unsettlingly different. But she was not at ease with any of them, except Thomas Dugdale. And she cannot talk of this to Goodwife Joan Brokefild, who keeps her distance.

'Walk with me to the rectory,' says Jenkin Williams to Jack. 'Two items to talk of.'

Jack looks at Jenkin Williams enquiringly.

'At the rectory, we will talk there.'

Jack, always ready to curry favour, says as they walk, 'Your sermon yesterday, Heavenly Antidotes against the Plague, it moved many hearts: "Yet trust not so much in the Physick as in the Blessing of God, without which all Physick is ineffectual." Many talked of it after.'

Jenkin Williams smiles a small smile, 'Yes, but some would say it was too short.'

'Ah, that's the old people,' says Jack, 'they always want more words than the ear can hear. They judge a sermon to be best if they sit until their … until they are numb. Some will spend all of a Sunday sermon-seeking through the parishes. No fault in them for doing that,' he quickly adds.

'Certainly some will spend the Lord's day in admirable pursuit of wise and holy words of good counsel,' Jenkin Williams says with solemnity.

In the library he offers Jack tobacco, 'The good Widow Hazard only took a widow's mite, so there is plenty here for both of us. Walter Hall gives you a fine report, Jack Green. He says you know London better than most, and that as well as being clever and reliable, you are also brave when needs be. You two fought off a gang of thieves?'

'Drove them away with fire and sword,' says Jack, not a little proud.

'Isaiah Chapter sixty six, verse the sixteenth: "For by fire and by his sword will the Lord plead with all flesh: and the slain of the Lord shall be many." An ominous verse for these times.'

'I meant no comparison,' Jack says hastily. 'I did not have that verse in mind.'

'But you do know it?'

Jack wonders if Jenkin Williams is toying with him. 'Know it because I must have heard it in church, but I could not quote book, chapter and verse, as you can.'

'But you have good knowledge of London, and that is my Item the first.'

'Yes, good knowledge.' Except, Jack thinks, of St Andrew Undershaft, but he knows of it now, some of it.

'Then tell me where a man will find a good gaming house, not a low one, a good one.'

Jack shows no surprise at the question. It is not his position to show surprise, or anything, other than to demonstrate that he is clever, obliging, reliable. '*Speering's Ordinary* in Bell Yard, close by Lincoln's Inn Fields.' It is not so very far from Blackfriars.

'A respectable house?' Jenkin Williams presses.

'Even respectable gaming houses always have–' Jack pauses, says with engaging honesty, 'I have not been inside *Speering's Ordinary* or any other, but I do know London and I have seen entering and leaving all kinds of folk, the best quality, as well as the meaner sort, prentices and idle folk, all of them players. I think only those who have no money are unwelcome at *Speering's*.'

'Even then, good credit will serve,' says Jenkin Williams with a smile. 'So you are not a player Jack? That's good. Yes, even respectable houses take in those who are not so respectable. Money is money is money eh?'

Jack nods vigorously at this, 'Yes.'

'That was my Item the first, my Item the second is that when I visit *Speering's Ordinary*, as I intend to, I will have you come with me. In such places it is always helpful to have a brave man with a sword to hand. Will you?'

'Yes,' Jack answers immediately. Why wouldn't he?

'I ask because I will be winning tonight at play. I know that. Winning handsomely, and will have my winnings safely home. There are always those rooks – do you know the word? rooks? – rooks in a gang who will wait for you as you come out with your winnings, and beat you and rob you.'

Jack nods, he does know the word rook, and what rooks do.

'So here is Addendum the Letter A,' Jenkin Williams is enjoying himself. 'Addendum A to Item the second: you must remain sober, alert, unfoxed, awake. Agreed?'

'Yes, I agree to that Addendum,' Jack, too, is starting to enjoy this contract-making.

'Addendum the letter B: you must watch everything, everyone, closely. There are those who will get drunk a man who is winning, or they will put themselves forward as a good friend, or both – particularly when they see how much ... Well, you will keep them at distance? Agreed?'

'Yes, I agree to Addendum the letter B to Item the second,' says Jack enthusiastically. This Jenkin Williams is an unlikely rector. No sombre, sober cleric. At all.

'Excellent!'

'Will it be, might I ask, will it be cards or dice? Or both?'

'Jack Green! What a question! There is only one game, the most bewitching game, Hazard! You do know it?'

'A dice game. I know that. I don't know how it is played.'

'Most of those playing it don't know that either Jack!' Jenkin Williams laughs. 'A man can win or lose fortunes at Hazard.'

'You said you will be winning?' curious Jack asks cautiously, politely.

Jenkin Williams does not answer directly. 'What you have to look out for – not you, you don't know the game – what I keep a keen eye out for are all the cheating tricks. All the tricks they try to put upon the ignorant, or those they *think* are the ignorant. Palming, topping, slurring, knapping, stabbing. You don't need to know these.'

This is just as well. Jack doesn't know these.

'Jack, I am surprised you haven't asked me what will be the benefit to you in this?'

Quick thinking Jack, 'Yes, the very question on the tip of my tongue. Will there be some benefit to me in this?'

'There will. The parson's benefit, one in ten. Do you call that handsome?'

'I do sir! Very handsome. I thank you.'

'Yes, I agree, it is very handsome. Now, a moot point, is your one in ten to be Addendum the letter C to Item the second, or, Jack Green, is it to be Item the third?'

'Very handsome must be Item the third,' says Jack promptly.

'Yes it must. Now in other towns, elsewhere, play begins at about eight at night. How long to walk there, to *Speering's Ordinary*? We will hackney back if there is one to be had.'

'Half an hour walking will do it easily,' says Jack, who knows London better than most.

* * *

12 at night

'Jack, find us a tavern as quick as you can! A tavern! A tavern!' Exhilarated Jenkin Williams laughs and laughs.

'It will be the *Bear* near here, or the *Bear*,' Jack replies.

'Then let it be the *Bear*! There are two *Bears*? Where is the other?'

'Not so far, but in the wrong direction, too far to the west,' says Jack.

'Then it must be the eastern *Bear*, the near *Bear*.'

They sit on the end of a congenial bench, close by a noisy party of singers.

'Drink, you can drink now young Jack. Not too much, you still have to get me safely back to church square, but have one drink, or perhaps two.'

Jack drinks, says, shaking his head in wonder, 'The poor creature that had played away even his shirt, his coat, his wig! Standing muddled in the corner in his breeches. I've never seen the like.'

'And his doublet, and his waistcoat and his vest! His friend was no help, "Cheer up Theophilus, nakedness is the best protective against a fever. No pestilence for you!" Theophilus did not look happier for this comfort.' Jenkin Williams laughs again, leans back in great content, wants to hear more from Jack, who is eager to talk.

'Men take their losses in many different ways,' Jack says in wonder. 'The whining and pitiful players. The cursing, swearing, angry man with all his zounds, and rogues, and curs–'

'Then curs and rogues and zounds once again. He could think of little else to say, that angry man. He lost most of his words as well as all of his money.'

'And those who lost and shrugged and walked away,' says an amazed Jack. 'Lost twenty guineas at a throw, and then another, and another, and shrugged it off as if it was a groat and nothing more. Without appearing any discontent at all. I wonder at them.'

'Did you see – of course you did – the three who came in drunk and who combined their stocks of gold? One with twenty two pieces, the second with four, and the third with five. And the one with twenty two forgot what it was he had and then argued that he had brought no more than the rest! What sport!' Jenkin Williams splits himself with laughter.

'Did the one who cursed and damned as he left, did he know his bible well?' asks ingratiating Jack.

'He who shouted "There shall be no reward to the evil man; the candle of the wicked shall be put out," and "Let the wicked fall into their own nets, whilst I withal escape," roared out while he escaped? Yes, knows his Proverbs and Psalms. But he forgot "He that hasteth to be rich hath an evil eye, and considereth not that poverty shall come upon him." He did not shout that one.'

Jack considers that he has watched how Jenkin Williams had, this night, himself hastened to be rich and how he has been showered with good fortune. He does not say this, but gives a wise nod and says, 'There were many who hastened to be rich – pickpockets and cutpurses and thieves. Many of them eager to pay their respects to you.'

'A new face is always honey to flies. All the rooks and bullies. I have seen them slice the silver buttons off a man's coat.' Jenkin Williams looks around the tavern room, lowers his voice. 'We did well. Your one in ten gives you twelve of these.' He gives Jack a glimpse of a gold guinea cupped in his hand. 'But let us say fifteen, fifteen for good work. We escaped whilst the wicked fell into their own nets. Yes?'

'Yes to fifteen. Many thanks, my thanks!' says grateful and surprised Jack. 'The wicked fell into more than nets. There were tables overthrown, swords drawn, candlesticks thrown – what a quarrel!' Jack lowers his voice, 'I am grateful, very, for the fifteen.'

Jenkin Williams smiles, 'Men heated with wine, choleric, their money lost, what a brawl! All the House in such a garboyl! Kept the rooks occupied while we made our escape to the stair head.'

They drink, satisfied men. Listen to the singing.

'This catch, this one,' Jenkin Williams says, 'do you sing it, do you know it Jack?'

He does. They join the singers.

My lady and her maid, upon a merry pin,
They made a match at farting, who should the wager win.
Joan lights three candles then, and sets them bolt upright;
With the first fart she blew them out, with the next she gave them light.
In comes my Lady then, with all her might and main,
She blew them out and in and out, and in and out again!

Jenkin Williams laughs immoderately. 'What a wager Jack! A wager at farting! Men will wager at anything. Always a wager. Life is a wager!'

Jack sniggers, 'She blew them out and in and out, and in and out again!' And takes his turn to laugh immoderately.

'Good that it was one of the respectable Ordinaries, *Speerings*. Who knows how the night might have ended had we gone lower. Your hard, fixed stare kept the rooks in their nests. Quite the fierce face.'

Jack is pleased. He has rehearsed his blank, threatening face and is gratified Jenkin Williams noticed. He would like to think he did mighty deeds of courage in Speerings to deserve his fifteen guineas. True, he had looked severe, threatening, his hand hovering on his sword hilt, but most there looked the same. Yet if Jenkin Williams will praise him and pay him fifteen guineas he will not say no.

'Have you heard this one Jack?' Jenkin Williams asks, calls down the table to the singers, 'Here's not a song but a jest, hear this!' He has an audience.

'A gentleman, a married man, is riding in the street, not riding well and his horse throws him. A gentlewoman laughs at his clumsy tumble and he, terribly vexed, says to her, "Madame, curb your laughter! My horse only stumbles when he meets a whore!" She sharply replies, "Have a care then sir that you do not meet your wife, for then you will certainly break your neck!"' He roars laughing, repeats, 'Have a care then sir that you do not meet your wife, for then you will certainly break your neck!'

The host at the *Bear* joins in the mirth. He is challenged by a singer, 'Do you know, John Swaybye, the seven properties belonging to a host?'

John Swaybye has heard this many times but will not spoil the fun, these are all paying customers. Standing by the table, his arms folded comfortably across his apron, the host of the *Bear* says, 'No, Alexander Sibthorpe, do tell me, tell us all, the seven properties.'

Alexander Sibthorpe is already deep in mirth before he has said a word, 'Item the first, a host must have the forehead of an ox.'

To cheers and pots banged down on the table, John Swaybye pulls his hair back from his forehead.

'Item the second, he must have the ears of an ass. Item the third the back of a nag. Item the fourth the belly of a swine.'

To even greater uproar John Swaybye advances his belly.

'Item the fifth the subtlety of a fox. Item the sixth he must skip up and down like a frog, and Item the seventh,' Alexander Sibthorpe pauses, tries to contain himself. 'Item the seventh he must fawn and lie like a dog!'

John Swaybye flicks a cloth at him. The table laughs immoderately.

Jenkin Williams calls for drinks for the whole table, 'And our host to join us!'

On their walk back to St Cyneswide and St Tibba – seeking but not finding a hackney – Jack ventures a question that has been puzzling him.

'How,' he asks if he may ask, 'did you know you would win at Speering's? You said you would, and you did. Handsomely.'

Jenkin Williams does not answer immediately. He nods graciously to bell-man William Norhage who comes up to check who is out in the streets so late. William Northage in turn touches his cap and wishes them well this fine evening. They pass several sleeping watchmen, some have been kicked awake by William Northage but have settled back to sleep once he is out of sight and hearing, he and his bell receding.

They enter the rectory by the kitchen door. 'A secret I will share,' says Jenkin Williams confidentially. 'Searcher Widow Margaret Hazard. The parish Searcher. My Searcher. Her name will tell you, it told me because my game is Hazard. My game, her name. Her blind eye. Her blind left eye. She is a certain of good fortune.' Jenkin Williams speaks with great enthusiasm. 'You know, you must, that the left eye is for bad fortune, the right eye good. She has no left eye, only the right, so Widow Hazard carries good fortune, only good fortune, with her, and her name.'

'You had good fortune tonight,' Jack agrees.

'Yes! It had to be. The delight, Jack, the delight, of sweeping a great pile of yellow-boys from the table! And here is your share of the good fortune. Fifteen guineas. You brought us all back here safely: my one hundred and five guineas, your fifteen guineas, and the two of us. All of us safe.'

Jack is again extravagantly grateful for his fifteen yellow-boys, now resting heavily in his hands.

'I touched her hands,' confides Jenkin Williams. 'The tobacco pouch. Widow Margaret Hazard. When I offered her my tobacco pouch. Touched her hands and that guaranteed my good fortune.'

Jack offers more thanks for his guineas, and they make their separate ways to bed, Jack climbing the steep back stairs.

Deep in his pocket Jenkin William holds his Bristle Dice. Each with a hog's bristle stuck in the corner to trip the dice favourably. 'The newest way,' said the ingenious man Jenkin Williams met on the coach to London, 'of making a high Fullam or a low Fullam.' And the ingenious man was right.

CHAPTER XXI

*'And because Murder of all sins is the most heinous in the sight of
the Almighty, but especially the Murdering of Kings and Nobles,
therefore God punisheth it with one of his severest punishments. I
mean with the Plague.'*

'Many men off to Gilbert Swaile, his brewery' Goody Susanna Parsons says
brightly, hoping a cheerful voice will help lighten the heavy mood of her
friends. 'Here is young Jack Green leading like a bear a large, shambling
man with an enormous wig. What curls! Who is that large man? I don't
know him.'

'Not of this parish,' say Anne Abowen, Widow Dorothy Bullen and
Widow Lankester, in wry, dry chorus.

Widow Lankester, sitting on the right of the perched ancient women,
moves and sits on the left, next to Goody Parsons. 'The better to see into
Brewery Lane,' Widow Lankester explains.

'William Lacie has gone in, I wonder why, and here is William
Pickhering, not far for him to come,' says Widow Lankester who, if ever
she can, will always be mistress of any talk.

William Pickhering lopes past them into Brewery Lane, bringing with
him a waft of sawdust, of fresh-cut wood.

'And why William Pickering or William Lacie,' says Widow Bullen.
'William Lacie to the brewery? Some of those cloth bales of his are quite
comfortable and some are not. All are more comfortable than this stone
wall. Too hard on my old arse bone.' She stands and peers up the lane,
blocking, perhaps intentionally, Widow Lankester's view.

'All your bones are old, not just your arse bone,' Widow Lankester says, nudging Widow Bullen aside. 'Your arm bone, your leg bone, your skull bone.'

'That is so,' Widow Bullen agrees. 'All of them are old.'

'One more coming,' says Anne Abowen. 'It is–'

The four ancient women fall respectfully silent. The one more coming is their rector, Jenkin Williams, also turning into Brewery Lane.

He calls a warm 'God be w'ye!' to the ancient women.

'Not like Walter Hall,' says Anne Abowen approvingly.

'Is he a man too …' Goody Parsons stops to find the word. 'Is he a man who has too much levity to be a good, a good–'

'A good parson, rector, vicar, minister? A good one of those?' asks Widow Lankester.

'Yes,' says Goody Parsons. 'Yes. A good one of those.'

'He does have a fine cavalier head,' Widow Lankester says. '*Now* he has one. I wonder if in Oliver's time, when Jenkin Williams 'Curs'd the King and Cavalier, And cry'd 'em down for traitors,' I wonder if then his hair was shorter, even shorn? I wonder if he did that.'

'Well of course he did,' says Widow Dorothy Bullen complacently. 'Of course he would. It was the way things were done then. All know that. And a bit of levity does not go astray. William Bullen was a man for a bit of levity. Not all the time, only some of the time.' She smiles at the memory of Williams Bullen's occasional levity. 'And William Bullen was no parson or the other things you said. Not at all.'

'Goodwife Brokefild and Widow Hazard still keeping themselves to themselves,' says Anne Abowen, stating the truth evident from the two absences on the wall.

'No deaths? No corpses for them to search? When there are corpses they won't be able to keep themselves to themselves. Have to search together. Must be some deaths soon,' says Widow Lankester.

'Yes, always two Searchers,' Widow Bullen says. 'And two Keepers, and two Viewers. Yes, a death will bring them together. Whether they like it or not. Perhaps they will, perhaps they won't.'

'That will be soon then. Widow Shipley has the signs, and all in her house,' says Viewer Anne Abowen.

'Thomas Dorbridge and Katherine Briggs are both sinking,' says Viewer Widow Lankester. 'Both of them.'

'The family Gipps. The girl Helen still has no signs,' Widow Bullen says.

The perched ancient women sigh together. They have all seen that some get the signs and die. Some get the signs and don't die. Some don't get the signs.

'Poor Goodwife Joan,' says Widow Bullen. 'If there is no searching she will have to keep to her house with that Isaac. The sot.'

'She won't be *there*,' Anne Abowen says confidently. 'She will stay away from *there* as best she can.'

'And she should,' Widow Lankester says.

Goody Susanna Parsons disagrees. 'A wife should submit to her husband,' she says firmly.

'You have heard that from Peregrine Parsons,' says Widow Lankester. 'I heard the same from Ahuzzah Lankester, the presbyter. He had the chapter and the verse. "Wives submit yourselves unto your own husbands." And much more of the same.'

'Yes,' says Goody Parsons, 'in scripture.'

'Ahuzzah Lankester would say his favourite, "Aged women should be in behaviour as becometh holiness, not false accusers, not given to much wine." Often said that to me. Especially about false accusers and not given to much wine. I was no false accuser.'

Anne Abowen raises her eyebrows, which Widow Lankester sees, as she is meant to.

'Always speaking from his bible, presbyter Ahuzzah Lankester. I saw in his bible, on the same page which says aged women should not be false accusers, I read there "Aged men should be sober, grave, temperate, sound in faith, in charity, in patience." I told him I gave him all due praise for being sound in faith. He was sound in faith.'

'And the rest? Sober, grave, patient, the others?' Anne Abowen asks boldly, as Widow Lankester means her to.

'Sound in faith,' Widow Lankester repeats.

'Isaac Brokefild is not a sober man,' Widow Bullen says. 'And none of those other things. Goodwife Joan has on her … you can see what he's done. Isaac Brokefild. I have seen the black eyes she's had from him.'

This is uncomfortable talk. Every household has some closed doors they do not want others – or themselves – to open. Even Widow Lankester.

Even so, Widow Lankester puts her shoulder to the door, barges in. 'Ahuzzah Lankester, we were not long wed. He was angry about – I have forgotten what about – he struck me such a blow above my left eye,' she points, 'here, I cried out in great pain. I scratched and bit him. He sent for butter and parsley for my eye but I had to lay a poultice on it all day. My eye was black for many days, and all noticed. It was at Christmas time.'

The others nod, or stay still, as they will.

'William Bullen,' Widow Dorothy Bullen will speak. 'William Bullen, the worst of William Bullen. I once answered him in some way he did not like. He pulled me by the nose, gave me great pain and I cried a great while. By and by he would be friends again, and we were friends. Most of the time we were. That pull on my nose was the worst of William Bullen.'

Anne Abowen will say nothing of Edmund Abowen. She stares at the churchyard.

As for Peregrine Parsons, Goody Parsons is not unhappy with him. Mostly kind: once in anger he has wiped his dirty shoes on fresh-washed clothes; more often has thrown a trencher when he did not like her food, but not thrown at her. She is patient. What Widow Lankester said of that aged man in the bible – sober, grave, temperate, sound in faith, in charity, in patience – Goody Susanna Parsons recognises herself. Goody Parsons will say nothing here of Peregrine Parsons. She looks at her fellows and sees herself fortunate.

The ancient women stiffly lift their old arse bones off the churchyard wall; leave the square in pairs; Viewers, Keepers.

* * *

'This is all of us. All of us here,' announces Gilbert Swaile, who has had barrels, trestles and planks placed as rough seating.

'If you know who all of *us* are, you know more than I do,' George Crofts says pugnaciously. 'Do you know me? Who I am?'

'I am Jenkin Williams,' Jenkin Williams breaks in, 'the rector of this parish.' Jenkin Williams has chosen to sit next to Gilbert Swaile. 'Tell us who you are.'

'George Crofts, Baltic merchant, shipping-man, wood, timber.' George Crofts stares around the room, makes it clear he is a man of substance, someone to be reckoned with.

'Did not young Jack Green tell you who would be here, tell who might be part of this, this venture?' Gilbert Swaile first looks at Jack with disappointment, then relishes the word 'venture.'

Jack, taken aback, wants to say something in his defence, but George Crofts' voice booms out. 'He said you – you are Gilbert Swaile the brewer? – I can see and smell this is a brewery, although what a brewer has to do with the kind of trading this boy mentioned I don't know. Tell me.'

'In good time, all in good time,' says Gilbert Swaile, ruffled by this naval onslaught. 'Here are men of substance, of note, in this parish. Our rector, Jenkin Williams; an important cloth merchant William Lacie, his business lately much expanded,' William Lacie raises his head. 'William Pickhering who is well-known in this parish as a joiner. A joiner,' Gilbert Swaile pauses, 'a joiner who is a skilled maker of coffins.' Said on a triumphant note.

'Skilled?' George Crofts scoffs. 'Skill is needed to bang a few planks together to hold a corpse? Is yours the small workshop across the square? I have sharp eyes, seaman's eyes.' William Pickhering's apron, wood-shavings, and smell declare him to be the joiner with coffin-making skills.

William Pickhering sees no need to answer, is busy staring at George Crofts' mightily curled wig.

'Jack I already know, footboy as was to Mistress Alice Crofts' kinsman, Walter Hall. He's gone hasn't he, Walter Hall? Fled the town with all those, all of them, at Whitehall? Elsa Hall, Alice Crofts, her mother, she would have Alice Crofts flee. She stayed. Of course she stayed with me. So, why are we here? Why am I here in this brewery of yours, Gilbert Swaile? Is there ale for us?'

Gilbert Swaile calls for ale, turns to Jack and says with exasperation, 'Tell George Crofts, tell us all, why we are here.'

Jack quickly launches into his patter: sad times, bad times, but business must still be done; particular business, particular trades, more in demand because of the sickness; men of enterprise who see the demand, move quickly, spend wisely, will prosper.

Jack speaks well, clearly, finishes with a grand flourish, 'Such men of foresight will be doing a great service to a nation ill-prepared for the onslaught of the pestilence. Will be seen as, will *be*, great benefactors in a time of dire need.'

'Profit and honour both,' George Crofts approves, finds this a good combination, is more comfortable with this meeting.

'Tell us, Jack Green,' says Jenkin Williams in kindly, encouraging tones, perhaps usurping Gilbert Swaile's presiding role. 'Tell us more of the particular businesses, the particular trades that will bring us all profit. And of course honour.'

Gilbert Swaile showily looks at his watch, holds it up close to his eyes. 'We don't have all day. Quick as you can Jack. I for one have work to do.' Shows he has taken the reins again.

Jenkin Williams gestures magnanimously, a wordless 'of course.' George Crofts slaps his knee to drive the horse on, flicks a hand at Jack to continue.

'Dying. People are dying. Death demands coffins and shrouds. Coffins, William Pickhering, shrouds, winding sheets, William Lacie. The more deaths the more coffins and shrouds.'

'Stop,' commands William Pickhering, holds up a hand to halt the galloping horse. 'The parish coffin,' he says sourly. The parish coffin is a grievance of long standing. 'The pestilence is killing the poor. I will not be making more coffins if the parish coffin continues to be used over and over again for the dead poor. How,' he adds, an afterthought, 'will we all make profit then? The parish coffin makes more visits to the churchyard than the rector or the Clerk. Your pardon rector Jenkin Williams, but the parish coffin–' He needs say no more, his disgust with the parish coffin is evident, and already well known.

'There is a Vestry meeting coming and I think,' Jenkin Williams looks enquiringly at Gilbert Swaile, 'I think Vestry may find that in these harsh times of pestilence and infection, may find that the parish coffin is a source of contagion, a danger to us all. Am I right in so thinking?' He asks Gilbert Swaile.

'My very thought,' says Gilbert Swaile approvingly.

'Then there's the wood. All these deaths you're expecting,' William Pickhering says sharply, even accusingly, to Jack, as if he carries some measure of responsibility for the pestilence, for the increase in the Bills of Mortality. 'Many more deaths means many more coffins means much more wood – doesn't have to be good wood, cheap wood's just as good, even better – but I'll need cartloads of it.'

'Leave that to me,' says George Crofts with great satisfaction. 'I am the man for wood.' He is known as a man who imports marine supplies from the Baltic, timber not the least. He is not known – has kept this firmly to himself – as a man who has frequently been bubbled by his suppliers in Stockholm, in Riga, in Danzig, in Bremen, and in Hamburg. It seemed, and perhaps it was the case, that they had taken turn and turn about to cheat him. He changes suppliers, changes ports, and all goes well with the first shipments. Then he finds rubbish wood – splintering, knotted, poor quality pine – stowed underneath good Baltic oak, Scotch fir, Norway white spruce. All billed to him as top quality. It is no comfort that other English merchants complain of the same depredations. George Crofts has a large store of wood perfect for cheap coffins to hold the dead poor. 'I am the man for wood.'

'Here is ale,' says Gilbert Swaile. He has had Giles the prentice boy bring the best brew.

'And about time,' says George Crofts, who is determined to make himself obnoxious, or has no idea he is being so. Jenkin Williams, who is enjoying the meeting, cannot decide which.

'Coffins, wood, that is settled then,' says Gilbert Swaile.

'No,' says William Pickhering, 'it is not settled. Will George Crofts want payment for his wood? He will. Who will pay him? Am I expected to?'

'Payment, money, funding our venture – we will come to that,' says Jack Green confidently.

'Yes, we will come to that,' Gilbert Swaile repeats, hastily grabbing the meeting back.

'We *need* to come to that,' says William Pickhering.

'See a lot of red crosses on doors here in St Coney. Excuse my word parson, St Coney's is a jest in the family. You know family jests,' George Crofts says with a guffaw. In fact the family jest – made only in the bosom of the family of George and Alice Crofts – is to call the parish St Cunny and St Titties, a jest George Crofts makes in the marriage bed when he will visit the saints in Alice Crofts' parish.

'Business, we are here for business,' says William Pickhering. 'Not to talk of red crosses on doors.'

'But that is our business here! The dead are our business here, all those red crosses,' laughs George Crofts.

'Can we also serve the living?' Jenkin Williams asks severely, deciding this is the right moment to show he is of the church, of charity.

'The living? Our trade is with the dead – there are a lot of them and will be more. A good, reliable market, the dead.' George Crofts looks around for agreement, gets it from William Pickhering. 'Do you have more ale in your brewery Gilbert Swaile? This is thirsty work.'

'Business, shrouds, winding sheets,' Gilbert Swaile says while signalling to Giles the prentice to fetch more ale. 'Here is William Lacie, now more than upholstery.'

'Yes, now more,' says William Lacie with great satisfaction. 'The stocks of John Sly linen-draper–'

'Fled,' Gilbert Swaile interjects helpfully.

'Yes, fled. John Sly linen-draper, his stocks, I have them. Bought them.

And Frances Aspiner, tailor, cloth merchant, dead – not of the pestilence –
but dead nonetheless. Widow Aspiner has gone from town. I would not say
fled. Some might. She has gone to family in Salisbury, was glad to sell me
the stock in Frances Aspiner's warehouse.'

'So you have cloth for shrouds,' Gilbert Swaile sums up for those who
might not have understood. William Pickhering is gazing into his ale.

'Ample stocks, of any quality. Cheap stuff for the poor, but still money
in it of course. Which brings us to money. I have the stock, I bought it.
Who here will pay me for it? And why should I not sell it myself? Why do
I need all you? I know my business.'

'Our venture,' Jack is the one who can explain. 'A venture together,
you need this joint venture. We all do. Here in St Cyneswide and St Tibba
we have a small market. A good market,' he hastens to add, 'but small. We
will sell here, but other parishes, less organised, less prepared than ours,
will be in desperate need of shrouds, of winding sheets, of coffins. We will
be prepared, we will have what they need. We can sell to a big market. Big,'
here he looks sad, sorrowful, 'and, alas, growing even bigger. Our venture
will sell to – will help! – as many of the sadly unprepared parishes as we
can because we will have cloth and coffins. I am ready to bring news to the
other parishes of the help we can provide. To go out and sell our help.'

'Money,' William Pickhering looks up from his ale. 'What money for
this,' he brackets the words with suspicion, 'this "joint venture?" Eh? What
money from us here? I provide skill and labour to make the coffins. Does
this "joint venture" pay me?'

'A good point,' Jenkin Williams comes in smoothly, glibly. 'How I
see it, we all – all six of us,' he looks quizzically at Jack, 'we all contribute
the same amount to the joint venture. All have equal shares. If we say, to
suggest an amount, fifty guineas each.'

'Fifty guineas!' George Crofts shouts. William Pickhering and
William Lacie are equally shocked.

'Hear me out,' says calm Jenkin Williams. 'You, George Crofts, get
credit within your fifty for the wood you provide, as will you, William
Lacie, for your cloth, and you William Pickhering for your labour.'

'And skill.'

'Skill!' George Crofts scoffs again. 'Twenty guineas. I say twenty guineas. Six shares here, twenty guineas each. That is one hundred and twenty guineas all told. One. Hundred. Twenty. There, that is what I say.'

'Fifty is much too much,' agrees William Pickhering. 'And how will this "credit" be calculated? Who will calculate it?'

'I am a man of the cloth,' says Jenkin Williams. He knows fifty guineas a man is too much, much too much, but as well as being a man of the cloth he is a man who knows gaming houses and knows how to bluff and when to make a false opening bid.

'A man of the cloth? So is William Lacie here!' says George Crofts, laughing enormously at his own wit. 'So is William Lacie a man of the cloth. And I say again twenty guineas.'

'I hope I can be trusted to do some calculations,' Jenkin Williams continues smoothly, 'to find some figures – in consultation with you all, of course – that will satisfy everyone here.' He knows this is impossible, but there is no point in saying that at this moment. He adds as if making a great concession, 'Then let us say thirty guineas a man.'

'Twenty,' repeats George Crofts.

'Twenty eight,' replies Jenkin Williams, who has always been prepared for somewhere between twenty and thirty.

'Twenty five,' says George Crofts reluctantly.

'Well, if you will beat the sum down so harshly,' says Jenkin Williams, sounding hard done by, 'then let it be twenty five as you say.'

George Crofts, William Pickhering and Gilbert Swaile share a triumphant smile. William Lacie, who has been paying careful attention to the bargaining, thinks Jenkin Williams, cloth or no cloth, is a sharp man who must be closely watched.

Jack has prepared his own set of figures, as he told Gilbert Swaile he would, but he can see it is best that Jenkin Williams make the case here. The words of Jack the footboy will not carry the same weight.

'What of this Jack Green, the footboy? What is he doing here anyway? Can you, Jack Green, find twenty five guineas? Or even one? Are you sufficiently in purse to do so?' asks William Pickhering as unpleasantly as he can.

'I am, I can,' says Jack Green, to the surprise and disbelief of everyone in the room except himself. 'I can bring twenty five guineas to the table. And, more, I will ask no credit for the important, crucial, work I will do selling our shrouds and coffins in other parishes, taking orders from them, serving the joint venture.'

'You have twenty five guineas? We will have to see them,' says William Lacie.

'We will have to see everyone's,' says Jenkin Williams cheerfully.

The meeting relaxes, drinks more.

'The ale to your liking?' Gilbert Swaile asks George Crofts. 'You've drunk enough of it.'

'Swaile's ale?' George Crofts takes another long draught, shoots it back and forth in his mouth. This un-English behaviour is watched closely. George Crofts has been to foreign parts, to the east across the narrow sea, and to the frozen north where they grow only wood and know only winter. 'Drinkable,' he pronounces with a shrug, 'almost as good as an ale wife's brew.'

Gilbert Swaile finds the man impossible, ignores him. 'No time to lose,' he says. 'All are agreed?'

'Yes, I'm sure we all are agreed,' says Jenkin Williams. 'Jack, you have been paying close attention, you can tell us what the Items are from this meeting.'

'I can,' says Jack, thinking quickly. 'Item the first: George Crofts to supply suitable timber to William Pickhering for coffin-making. Item the–'

'Not all at once! Not supply all at once,' says an irritated William Pickhering. 'I don't have space to store great stacks of timber.'

'Cart load at a time?' asks George Crofts. 'Start tomorrow and you send young Jack to me when you need more.'

William Pickhering would like to disagree but can see nothing wrong with this proposal.

'Jack?' says Jenkin Williams.

'Item the first, as amended: wood supplies starting tomorrow, then further as required. Item the second: William Lacie to have ready cloth suitable for shrouds and winding sheets. Cut to size?'

'Of course cut to size,' says serious William Lacie. 'All the same size. As big as a bed sheet, no need for larger. Wrap it around, tie top and bottom. Done.'

'Item the third, funds: agreed twenty five guineas per person present here. Adjustments to this for any credit due; this Item in the hands of Jenkin Williams, rector of this parish, St Cyneswide and St Tibba.

'Item the fourth: Jack Green to market the St Cyneswide and St Tibba coffins and shrouds to all and sundry beyond our bounds. These are the four Items, by my reckoning, that come from this meeting.'

'What will you supply Gilbert Swaile? Your ale? No use to corpses,' says George Crofts.

'My twenty five guineas, my name, and I have three brewery carts. These will come in useful. And I reserve the right to claim credit for their use, like others here have done. I have already supplied ale today to the joint venturers but I do not expect payment or credit for that.'

'You could sell your ale as plague water.' An unexpected suggestion from William Lacie, a man not known for jesting. 'There is money to be made in plague water. Add some noxious tasting herb.'

This idea lingers in the air, mingling well with the smell of the brewery ale.

'I have heard ...' William Pickhering begins hesitantly, pauses, perhaps for effect, perhaps to think further on the matter. 'I have heard of a recipe, a draught for the infection–'

Jenkin Williams laughs, '*For* the infection? Surely *against* the infection, not in favour of it!'

William Pickhering takes no notice. 'A recipe, a draught *for* the infection is to take featherfew, maleselon, scabious and mugwort, same measure of each, bruise them and mix them with old ale – with old ale do you hear? – let the sick drink six spoonfuls and it will expel the corruption. A good, serviceable recipe. With old ale.'

'Swaile's Plague Water Ale?' asks George Crofts.

'Not water, we need not say *water*,' says Gilbert Swaile. 'Swaile's Plague Ale will serve us, serve the joint venture well. What was the recipe once more?'

'I have it down,' says confident Jack. 'I can sell Swaile's Plague Ale in every London parish.'

'The recipe from my mother's mother,' says William Pickhering, now pleased. 'She – Matilda Ridglie, her name – she survived the pestilence of 25. Drank this plague ale – of course it wasn't called Swaile's Plague Ale then, I don't know what it was called – she drank it, whatever it was called, without halt during that visitation and for years after. Never was struck down by the plague, not in 25 or after. Not years later. Never. Scabious ale, did she call it scabious? It would be a suitable name if she did, but I can't recall if it was scabious ale. Perhaps not.'

'Swaile's Plague Ale will sell well,' Jack repeats. 'Sell well.'

'Of course it will,' says William Pickhering. 'And do I get credit for it? For my recipe? I should. Others get credit. How much do I get?'

'If we all get credit for every little thing, every word, every recipe,' this scornfully from Gilbert Swaile, 'our joint venture will be rich in credit and poor in guineas.'

'Little thing! My mother's mother's recipe a little thing that this boy says he can sell all over London. A little thing!'

'Wait. How do we keep track of it all? Moneys paid out, moneys coming in, profit made, loss suffered. With each doing his own line of business, how does our venture keep track? Know what's what? Tell me that?' asks suspicious William Lacie.

'I will do that,' offers Jenkin Williams. Each to keep his own accounts, but – if you will, if you all will? – I will come to each, perhaps once a week, and keep up a book that combines the whole venture. Consolidates each enterprise into the whole. That is, if you agree. Each can call on the common pool, our joint sum of one hundred and fifty guineas to forward their business, then – based on the amounts in the venture book – we can share out profits, share fairly. Yes? It will be,' he says smiling, 'our common wealth.'

'Each keep his own accounts? Yes, that is best, and rector to be the watchman over it all,' William Lacie agrees. He, and the others, can see how this system could be played to their own advantage.

'Good. Agreed, and I will give an accounting at every meeting we have,' says Jenkin Williams.

'A fifth Item,' says Jack. 'Item the fifth, rector Jenkin Williams to keep a book for the whole of the venture. and to give an accounting at our meetings.

George Crofts, who has drunk enough, and more, of Swaile's ale, finds a song.

> *Hey ho, hey ho, heart's delight strong ale is good in winter;*
> *Do a fair maid upon a brass pot and the child will prove a tinker!*
> *Tink, tink, tink, tera,*
> *Tink, tink, tera, tera,*
> *Tink, rink, tinktink!*

The others know it but do not join in out of respect for the cloth.

Walking to the rectory cheerful Jenkin Williams hums, whistles, sings, 'Tink, rink, tinktink!' Turns to Jack walking with him, says, 'You did well Jack Green, very well. Tell me, do you have twenty five guineas? I know you have fifteen at least. Or did have unless you have spent them already. Have you?'

'I will have twenty five when you call for them,' Jack says. He already has more than that. The fifteen, plus the thief's horde found in the house of office by very young Jack Micoe, the dung-pot boy. Kept safe and sound since by Jack Green, the rectory footboy. Who will be as wealthy as Sir Thomas Vyner.

Jack thinks of his father's rich wisdom of the heap, of the rooster who stands on top of the dung pile crowing. Of the roosters he saw vying today it was Jenkin Williams who easily climbed over Gilbert Swaile and George Crofts to win the top of the heap. Jack will watch him closely and learn.

'This pestilence,' says Philip Carter Parish Clerk.

Frances Barrow, Church Warden, mends his pipe and waits to hear more.

'I have read,' Philip Carter has a printed sheet in hand, 'I have read this. And it comes from our own Clerk of the Parish Clerks,' he sighs in deep disgust. 'Listen, from young John Bell on the causes of the plague:

> *This Judgment is laid on us for the sin of Rebellion, which extended much farther than that of the Israelites against Moses and Aaron; for the Israelites only murmured, they touched not the life of either of them, and yet God plagued them for it. Our Rebellion extended to the height of Rebellion; even to the taking away the life of the best of Kings, his late Majesty of ever blessed Memory, whose blood doubtless doth incessantly cry to the Lord for Vengeance.*

'The best of kings! And there is more the same. Hear this:

> *For if the Lord punished the sin of Saul, a King, so severely for shedding the blood of the Gibeonites, who were his Vassals and Slaves, Hewers of Wood, and Drawers of Water, that neither the lives of himself and his three sons, who fell all in one Battle, in one day, nor the three years of Famine in the Land, could appease God's wrath therefore, but that the blood of seven more of Saul's sons must do it.*
>
> *May not then this Nation justly expect God's greatest judgements to fall on the people of it, for shedding the blood of their lawful Sovereign? For their sin therein was as much greater than Saul's, by how much a lawful and good King (over three so fair, large, and populous Kingdoms) is greater than a Vassal or Slave.*
>
> *And because Murder of all sins is the most heinous in the sight of the Almighty, but especially the Murdering of Kings and Nobles, therefore God punisheth it with one of his severest punishments. I mean with the Plague: for God himself accounted three days Pestilence equal to three Months flying before the Enemy, or three years of Famine.*

'Lays it on! A man eager for favour and patronage, John Bell?' sneers Frances Barrow.

'A man wickedly wrong. Young John Bell has got it arse about. The plague is not punishment for the king killed. If kings are part the plague's making, it is because the king's son has come back. A false, heretical, whoremaster, papist king. A scandalous and poor king, rolling from whore to whore. Bell says heinous, the murdering of kings and nobles. Nobles! All buffoons at court. Monarchs and their thrones are hateful. For a good twenty years, and they were a good twenty, this was a nation in the righteous charge of godly saints, and now ... this. If this plague is a punishment – I don't know, don't know if it is – but if so then this king-come-back is why God punishes the nation with the plague, his severest of punishments.'

'Removing this scandalous king will appease God's wrath?' says Frances Barrow eagerly. 'Jesus Christ is our king and we need no other. We get rid of the Scotchman and God will lift his punishment?'

Philip Carter is not sure. 'Yes. I hope so. It *should* be so. I hope that it will. But I am not sure if the plague is God's punishment or a trial we must face. A trial for us all. We are being put to the trial? I don't know.'

'Punishment or trial, we'll have him gone, the whoremaster rogue. It is not the Good Old Cause we have, Philip Carter, it is not old, gone, it is now, our Good Cause is now. Colonel Danvers himself says it.'

Philip Carter Parish Clerk half listens to Frances Barrow, a man sounding fevered in his enthusiasm. Some of the words, some of the phrases, penetrate as Philip Carter ponders punishment or trial. Trial or punishment? He does not know. From Frances Barrow he hears: '... have his head off and cut him small as herbs in a pot ... two hand granadoes to be thrown into ... Monck and Charles hanged together, rogues ... Dunbar, Worcester ...'

'The third day of September,' says Philip Carter, coming out of his reverie. 'Dunbar and Worcester. And Oliver Protector's death in 58. Same day. Seven years now.'

'The same day. The great weight of history, of prophecy, on September's third day. Think on it.'

'I think on the plague! Its numbers, deaths, all growing,' says a dejected Philip Carter. 'I fear it! How long are we all to live? All of us?'

'Who knows how long we live?' says Frances Barrow dismissively. 'I take heart, Philip Carter, and so should you. See what this plague has done,' Frances Barrow lowers his voice, 'the emptying town, the court gone. Take heart from our victories, Philip Carter!'

A commotion in church square draws them to the vestry door. George Crofts, a seaman awash with Swaile's Ale, is flailing at a flotilla of parish children whose game blocks his path.

'And there is a man who can help,' Frances Barrow wishes Philip Carter a warm God be w'ye and hurries to catch shouting George Crofts.

Philip Carter makes himself comfortable leaning against the vestry door, refills his pipe, watches, listens.

> *Rise up, rise up, Betsy Brown, off your poor feet,*
> *To see your dear mother lie dead at your feet.*
> *I won't rise, I won't rise off my poor feet,*
> *To see my dear mother lie dead at my feet.*
> *Rise up, rise up, Betsy Brown, off your poor feet,*
> *To see your dear father lie dead at your feet.*
> *I won't rise, I won't rise off my poor feet,*
> *To see my dear father lie dead at my feet.*
> *Rise up, rise up, Betsy Brown, off your poor feet,*
> *To see your dear sister lie dead at your feet.*
> *I won't rise, I won't rise off my poor feet,*
> *To see my dear sister lie dead at my feet.*
> *Rise up, rise up, Betsy Brown, off your poor feet,*
> *To see your dear brother lie dead at your feet.*
> *I won't rise, I won't rise off my poor feet,*
> *To see my dear brother lie dead at my feet.*
> *Rise up, rise up, Betsy Brown, off your poor feet,*
> *To see your dear sweetheart lie dead at your feet.*
> *I will rise, I will rise off my poor feet,*
> *To see my dear sweetheart lie dead at my feet.*

Parish Clerk Philip Carter weeps, locks the vestry door, goes home.

CHAPTER XXII

'Sing with thy mouth, sing with thy heart,
Like faithful friends, sing "loth to depart."'

'At Barnabas Bloxsom, his house,' says Edward Cary, once Captain, now brewer of Southwark.

'What? Where?' asks Nathaniel Hale, once of the Protector's Regiment.

The large cellar of the *Feathers*, Fish Street, is full of loud people, with more coming.

'At,' repeats Edward Cary in his Captain's voice, 'at ... here is Gilbert Swaile come to join us!'

'Edward Cary,' says Gilbert Swaile, who decides immediately to say nothing about Swaile's Plague Ale.

'Who is this boy with you. You know him? We are talking of spies. Do you know him?'

'Spies?' asks Nathaniel Hale. 'Are we talking of spies? I know this boy from the *Nag's Head*. Seems a good boy.'

'He is Jack Green from my parish,' says Gilbert Swaile, not showing his irritation with Edward Cary. No spy. I can vouch for him.'

'How are we talking spies?' asks Nathaniel Hale. 'What spies?'

They move closer together, the better to hear.

'At Barnabas Bloxsom, his house,' says Edward Cary again, pointing to Barnabas Bloxsom tailor of Southwark, who smiles over his ale and says nothing.

'A gathering of saints at his house, talking of God's work, planning,' Edward Cary says. 'Talk of guns and powder, how many, when one of our number, one Ralph Hichawe, jumps up in agitation to confess he is informing on us!'

Barnabas Bloxsom nods, breaks his silence. 'He did.'

'He did,' confirms Dr Bartholomew Ward. 'I heard him.'

'Then?' asks Nathaniel Hale of Edward Cary. 'What then?'

'Then Ralph Hichawe points his finger at three present and says they are the same. Points at Andrew Hemerford, Thomas Akehurst and Anthony Showry.'

'All of them sitting in different corners of Barnabas Bloxsom's room, playing they did not know each other,' says Bartholomew Ward.

'I think they did not,' Barnabas Bloxsom says slowly. 'Each did not know the others were spies.'

'Ralph Hichawe knew they were all informers. Named them all,' Bartholomew Ward says to settle the matter.'

'No,' persists mild Barnabas Bloxsom. 'They were shocked, all three, when all the names were named.'

'I am with child to learn how you disposed of them,' says Gilbert Swaile.

'The gathering, thirty and seven of us,' says Edward Cary, 'we debated–'

'Total in all,' interrupts Barnabas Bloxsom, 'my house, I counted, total in all six and thirty – counting myself of course – barely able to fit into my big room, which is not so big. Never so big as this cellar. Yes, six and thirty in the room, but take from that four, the four spies you understand, so two and thirty debated what was to be done.'

'Some would have them all killed,' Colonel Edward Cary resumes command.

'I spoke for that,' says Bartholomew Ward the doctor. 'Take them to the river by night and stab them, shoot them–'

'We voted against shooting,' Edward Cary says. 'Waste of shot and powder, no need to shoot. And the noise.'

'So you stabbed them and threw them in the river?' asks Gilbert Swaile.

'There was a vote, after the debate we voted.'

'A long debate, or debates, many talking in small groups,' says Barnabas

Bloxsom.

'True,' says Edward Cary. 'A heated gathering. High words.'

'So you stabbed them and threw them in the river,' repeats Gilbert Swaile.

'No!' says Bartholomew Ward in disgust. 'We did not. We should have done so but we did not. I voted for death.'

'They were beaten heavily and warned never to be seen again,' says Barnabas Bloxsom, who also voted for death but accepted the will of the major part of those two and thirty who voted.

'Over there, you meeting in corners!' calls jocular John Barriffe, militia man volunteer of the Private and Loving Society of Cripplegate. 'What are you plotting?'

'Undoing plots, unravelling plots against saints,' answers Edward Cary, who did not vote for death but does not know why he did not.

'Plots against us hatched south of the river?' asks Thomas Trew.

'South of the river!' there is a rumble of derision for anything that happens south of the river.

The rumble is ignored by Barnabas Bloxsom, Edward Cary and Bartholomew Ward, who are confident of the virtues of Southwark over everywhere else.

'Here he is! Colonel Danvers! Who's that with him?' asks William Sutterwhit.

'Alexander Muzzard,' says John Barriffe helpfully, 'Clerk of All Hallows the–'

'I know Alexander Muzzard, difficult not to know him. The other one.'

'Clement Ireton,' says a woman who turns around to tell them. 'A fine man and close to Colonel Danvers.'

'Who is she?' William Sutterwhit whispers to John Barriffe.

'Mary Rande, writes tracts in our cause, a godly woman.'

William Sutterwhit's curiosity earns him a suspicious glare from a woman next to the godly one. He raises, unobtrusively, uncertainly, a questioning eyebrow to John Barriffe, who closes down his face and does not respond.

'Hear him! Hear him!' Alexander Muzzard bangs on a trestle, sets pots rattling. 'Now hear this man who is come to deliver the country from the tyranny of an outlandish dog!' In the quiet he repeats quietly. 'Hear him.'

Henry Danvers, once Colonel, has now put off his country smock, his long beard, and looks like a middling Staffordshire gentleman, which he is.

'At Dunbar,' he says in the resonant voice of a Member of Parliament, which he once was, 'At Dunbar before the fight, Oliver cried out "Rise up Lord! And let thine enemies be scattered; and let them that hate thee flee before thee!" Oliver prayed, and he bid all take heart, for God had certainly heard his prayers and would appear for our cause – His cause!'

Henry Danvers, soldier, gentleman, once MP, Baptist preacher, faces his congregation in the cellar of the *Feathers*, Fish Street, repeats, '"Let thine enemies be scattered; and let them that hate thee flee before thee." Enemies, them that hate thee, they can be anywhere. Before us, behind us, among us.'

'Among us, yes, they can be among us,' Edward Cary mutters to Bartholomew Ward.

'We see the swarming of the papists, of the church unreformed with its idolatrous liturgy–'

'Porridge!' call out Raphe Wroth and Harry Pecke, prentice boys from St Matthew, Friday Street.

Henry Danvers gives a curt nod to this interruption. He is getting into his stride and does not welcome interruptions.

'Corrupt prelates! The dregs of popery in what they call the church.'

'No king, no bishops! No king, no bishops!' the high voice of Christopher Frier carries well in the cellar.

'No king no bishops,' Henry Danvers agrees, now riding with the tide of his excited congregation. 'This plague is a sign. The sign that the Lord is beginning the destruction of the Antichrist in this year 1665. Next year, next year is 1666, a year of wonders, the number 666 the number of the Beast! The fall of the ungodly comes! They shall die, but the godly, we godly, we will live in perfect health when Christ comes into his kingdom. Yet the day of calamity is at hand for those who persecute the saints, persecute the true believers. They will fly before us as chaff in the wind!' He sweeps an arm, a great wind, scattering the persecutors as chaff.

Feet are stamped, pots banged and banged again.

'Persecutors. They will try to stop us. They will hold up their hands against the wind, but no one can stop the wind, yet they will try. How? By spies, by informers, who set out to undo what we will do. What we do!'

There are those who consider Henry Danvers to be a man obsessed by spies, and there is some exasperation – good-natured exasperation – when yet again he orders all present to go through the rigmarole of vouching for each other. But Henry Danvers is taking no chances – conscious of what has befallen others near to him.

Harry Pecke makes a comedy of it by pretending not to know his fellow prentices.

Their elders take it more seriously. The men from Southwark know each other and many more. Mary Rande and Widow Harding know each other and many more.

'Widow Harding,' whispers John Barriffe softly to William Sutterwhit, 'a very violent woman.'

Those who were at the *Nag's Head* know each other. Newcomer John Beech, tailor, knows Barnabas Bloxsom, tailor. Newcomer George Crofts is known to Frances Barrow and Jack Green, even though he is wigless today, his bald head giving him the appearance of a portly old prentice. Newcomers William Peskell, Edward Riggs and William Hill know each other. The brewers know each other ('Amos Andrews of Limehouse not here,' says Gilbert Swaile to Edward Cary).

'It seems we are safe,' says a satisfied Henry Danvers after all have recognised and been recognised.

'Some of us not here,' pipes Christopher Frier. 'From St Matthew our fellow Edmund Stase dead of the infection, poor boy.'

'John Wigan the same,' says Nathaniel Hale. 'Dead. And Erasmus Bacockie.'

The cellar full of people – those who knew Edmund Stase and John

Wigan and Erasmus Bacockie try to recall the last time they saw them, spoke with them, drank with them.

'Erasmus Bacockie, at the *Nag's Head* he was weeping for Zachery Waite,' says Frances Barrow. 'He'd not long before taken a draught with him he said. Said Zachery Waite had the head-ache, fever. He feared he'd never see Zachery Waite again.'

'Now Erasmus Bacockie himself,' says Thomas Trew. Shakes his head.

'Here is Francis Buffett! Is John Rathbone coming? He is expected.' The newcomer, stern and self-important, is welcomed by a beaming Alexander Muzzard, who leads him to confidential converse with Henry Danvers and Clement Ireton. George Crofts, a sober and sensible bald-headed George Crofts, is beckoned to join them.

'Edward Cary you did not vote for death. Why was that?' asks polite Barnabas Bloxsom. 'It was a close vote.'

'Yes, close. Fifteen hands for Yes, seventeen for No. Even if I had voted Death it would be sixteen sixteen.'

'You haven't said why you voted against Death.'

'No, I haven't,' agrees Edward Cary.

Mild Barnabas Bloxsom, who voted for Death, laughs.

'The people of God can never do the Lord's work until Charles the scarlet whore is stabbed,' says John Barriffe of the Private and Loving Society of Cripplegate in conversation with William Sutterwhit. 'I have been giving thought to how this could be done. It could be easily done in his own bedchamber. "When he is drunk asleep, or in the pleasure of his bed," you know, as said in that play.'

William Sutterwhit does not know what play, has no time for plays, answers, 'Not in London now, the king and his bedchamber. Easier done, stabbing, when he was in bed at Why-toll.'

'London or anywhere, we have friends. And not just his bedchamber and stabbing, some will throw hand granadoes into his coach. That will do the business. The stabbing. Or the hand granadoes.'

'If the voting had been sixteen sixteen, there would be a second vote,' resumes Barnabas Bloxsom.

'Too late for that,' Edward Cary says to his friend.

'Hear him!' shouts Alexander Muzzard once more.

'Good news,' says Henry Danvers. 'Colonel Buffett, our good Colonel Francis Buffett here, he has ten thousand men, horse and foot. Ten thousand!'

Colonel Buffett steps forward and is cheered and hurrah-ed, which he receives graciously, as his due.

'And thirty thousand in Holland our friend Clement Ireton tells, he has heard from letters home that there is an army of thirty thousand men in Holland, all of them ready to sail, to return home, to fight. Ready in regiments under officers from the glory days, ready to gain the heavenly crown in Jerusalem, ready to bring in the reign of saints!'

The cellar roars. Clement Ireton, a gentleman from Middlesex, stands by his friend Henry Danvers.

'With God's army we will blast them,' shouts Henry Danvers. 'Do you know – of course you do! – the cry, the war cry of our army at Dunbar? The Lord of Hosts our cry! The Lord of Hosts! Dunbar, the third day of September the year 1650. Only fifteen years before. Remember that day. The third day of September. Remember Worcester, remember Oliver Protector! Our cry the Lord of Hosts will ring out again, and soon, soon!'

'That is psalm the forty sixth,' calls out Thomas Trew. 'Not that, but the one hundred and seventeenth was sung at the Dunbar fight! So many hot disputes at sword point there. We drove them like turkeys. Like turkeys!' He opens the song in his fine voice and is joined by all the voices.

> Oh all ye nations of the world, praise ye the Lord always:
> And all ye people ev'ry where set forth his noble praise.
> For great his kindness is to us, his truth does not decay:
> Wherefore praise ye the Lord our God, praise ye the Lord alway!

It is sung again and again. The gathering settles into drinking and talk.

'Thirty thousand coming from Holland,' says William Peskell. 'Will they come soon?'

'It must be soon,' says Nathaniel Hale. 'How many days to the third of September? Not many, so it will be soon.'

'What will happen then? What will they do?' asks Edward Riggs. 'Take the Tower? Kill the king?'

'Only they know,' says Nathaniel Hale, peering at the close quartered group of Henry Danvers, Clement Ireton, George Crofts, Frances Barrow and Alexander Muzzard, their heads together.

'No sign of John Rathbone,' says William Hill. 'I thought him to be a man active, leading, in this business.'

'Edward Chillenden, as was Captain, he was to be here but he isn't. The plague, other matters, might keep them. Even so, a fine gathering of saints here!' says Nathaniel Hale.

'The fat man with the prentice head, George Crofts his name Henry Danvers said,' calls prentice Raphe Wroth to Jack Green. 'He is well in there with the colonels. A man of substance? You came in with him and the other one in the front there, the one with the round, flat face. You are all together?'

Jack comes to the four Friday Street prentices, pleased to be asked to join them, pleased to escape the old men and their war stories: men he has only met thrice but whose battle tales he already knows word for word: the claggy wet fields at Marston Moor, the fog at Naseby, 'So thick you could chew it.'

'George Crofts a shipman merchant trader,' he tells them. 'Frances Barrow the other one, Warden at St Cyneswide and St Tibba, once a trooper with the Eastern Association.'

'Action soon?' asks Harry Pecke. 'Third day of September. All these old soldiers. They have their heads together there.'

'There are trepanners everywhere who will run and tell, betray us,' says Nicholas Marrett. 'Henry Danvers and all are keeping close rein on what they say. I would kill a spy. Like that.' He slits a throat, stabs a heart, chokes a neck.

The other prentices agree, and Jack must join in. They peer around, looking for trepanners.

'They will need the prentices, need young blood, these old men,'

Raphe Wroth says confidently. 'London prentice boys, we are a force and they know we are a force.'

'You are,' says Clement Ireton, coming up, 'You are a force, come and talk with me for a minute,' he says to Raphe Wroth.

'Raphe climbing his way up in the world,' Harry Pecke jokes. 'He will soon be sitting with the big men, ordering us about like a master.'

They watch, but he does not sit with the big men, instead has some quiet words with Clement Ireton and comes back smiling.

'Well?' asks Nicholas Marrett. 'Are you made Captain or Colonel?'

'He wanted to know if prentice boys are solid for the Cause and whether there are other lads I can vouch for. I said we have been, we are, and we will be solid, and I can vouch for many more.'

A toast is drunk by the prentice boys to themselves.

'Your friend lashed on his back, he is dead of plague?' Jack asks.

'Edmund Stase, his father, mother, brothers, sisters, all in the house dead. We wept for him, for them, still do,' says a sorrowing Christopher Frier. 'Even his aunt who was not in the same house.'

They must drink some more at this sad news.

'Here is a jest to cheer us. Edmund Stase was fond of a jest,' says Harry Pecke the joker. 'Hear this. A woman, a fishwife selling fish in Friday Street market, always has this to say to men who will cry down her fish to cheapen the price. She says, "As you intend to have some of my *fish* in your belly, so I would fain have some of your *flesh* in my belly." "No," says he, "I can't spare my flesh to such an ugly puss as you." "No, no," replies she, "I don't mean as you mean, oh no, I mean your nose in my arse!"'

'Your nose in my arse!' The boys call out in joy. 'Your nose in my arse!'

The boys linger, raucously farewelling all who leave. 'All good friends here!' Raphe Wroth calls.

'God be w'ye!' Frances Barrow, departing the *Feathers*, Fish Street, calls over and over. Cheerful, pie-faced Frances Barrow. 'What a day, Jack Green, what a day! Things go on the move, our wheels are a-going!'

They walk north, looking about cautiously, back to the familiarity of St Cyneswide and St Tibba. Frances Barrow thumps his heavy club on the cobbles, Jack Green keeps his hand on his sword.

'It is the Tower, always the Tower,' Frances Barrow confides. 'The arsenal there, powder stores. The Tower, and the weapon makers. John Gladman as was Major, and Ralph Alexander, was Captain, now weapon makers. Both New Model men and today in business with arms, sword blades, gunlocks, all manner of weapons. Good friends of the Cause. The Tower and the weapons. There must be our first blow.'

'The first blow is against the Tower?' asks interested Jack.

'Yes, but strange no sign of John Rathbone. He is in the vanguard of it all. Henry Danvers carries it well, speaks as a man inspired, but it is, or was, John Rathbone *and* Henry Danvers. Their plan together.'

'The plague, perhaps it has John Rathbone?' ventures Jack.

'Who knows? It could be. But we are fortunate in George Crofts! He knows the Tower, has entry there because of his trade. George Crofts is our key to the Tower. Henry Danvers is glad of him. Our key. Strange to see him without his wig, bald like your prentice friends. Your nose in my arse!' Frances Barrow laughs.

Night: and corpses are privily carried to burial. Turning to Gracious Street Frances Barrow and Jack Green avoid burdened, stumbling bearers. On the alert, in Poultry they stop, stand back, and give way to a handcart wheeling a corpse from a small alley.

'George Crofts,' muses Frances Barrow as they gain church square. 'Bald George Crofts. A key to more than the Tower, eh? He will do God – and our Cause – and himself – and you – good service Jack Green! Particularly good service to his purse and to yours, and to all who meet at Gilbert Swaile's brewery. God be w'ye Sir Jack Green, Member of Parliament! I must see to my pigeons. Cats will take them if they can.'

In the comfortable presence of his pigeons Frances Barrow's mind turns, as it does often, to a scene he saw as a boy in Dosthorp: a frantic pigeon, caught in trellised honeysuckle, calling and struggling and making things worse until rescued by a determined flock hovering beside it with a ceaseless flapping of many wings until the vine was loosened and all could fly off together. The rustling, cooing pigeons are a solace.

* * *

London, Sunday, 16 July 1665
Vestry Meeting

'It is the most extraordinary hot day that ever I knew,' says George Lumme, glaring around the vestry table. 'Most extraordinary. The sickness putting all out of order, and now this heat.'

'And the bells going always, always the bells,' Emmanuel Bird, too, is annoyed. 'Not just our bell – which is right and proper for the dead of St Cyneswide and St Tibba, our bell should toll – but we must also hear the bells ringing in from parishes not ours.'

'London is in mourning,' Jenkin Williams observes, interested to see that Vestry meetings in St Cyneswide and St Tibba are no different from any other parish. His words are received with dutiful sombre head nodding.

'Vestry Clerk Philip Carter, where is the Oath?' Harry Bosvill is also peevish. 'It was decided at last Vestry – read the Minutes, the Minutes. It was decided–'

'I have the Minutes, and here is the Oath. I was slow finding it in my papers. Here is the Oath.' Philip Carter places the Vestry Oath centre table.

'Read the Minutes!' unappeased Harry Bosvill repeats, more agitated.

'I am the new man here,' Jenkin Williams intervenes, raising his hands slightly off the table, gesturing peace, calm. He is watched closely. All will see how tightly the new man will hold the Vestry reins, if he can hold them at all.

'I am the new man,' he repeats. 'I have led us in prayer, called upon our Lord God to bless our deliberations and guide us in wisdom. Our Clerk has placed the Vestry Oath on the table, as decided last Vestry. We are twelve present. Are there more to come before we go to business? Tell me, I am the new man here.'

'We are not twelve,' answers William Sutterwhit. 'Not twelve at all. We are nine.' He looks for agreement from the table, and gets it. Eleven of the twelve in the room wait to see if Jenkin Williams, the new man, can

416

find his way through this. There is a pause.

'Twelve but nine. Yes,' says Jenkin Williams. 'Yes. Rector, Clerk and Warden all *ex officio*, so nine Vestrymen from the parish. Yes, I see that is the way you count, we count, here in St Cyneswide and St Tibba, and so will I.'

'I do not know *ex officio*,' grumbles suspicious Robin Kerton, who does know that Latin is dangerous, popish.

'I *do* know *ex officio*, know it well,' Emmanuel Bird breaks in eagerly. 'My father was an Attorney. A respected Attorney of great repute, respected and of *great* repute. He knew *ex officio*, knew it very well, and I know *ex officio*.' Emmanuel Bird is exultant, repeats with satisfaction, '*ex officio*.'

'We speak English in this parish, only English,' calls William Sutterwhit. 'English, not popish.'

'What we say here in this parish,' Robin Kerton explains to Jenkin Williams, ignoring Emmanuel Bird and William Sutterwhit. 'What we say is that you, and Clerk Philip Carter and Warden Frances Barrow, you all, you three, you are here because … well, because you are here.'

'Yes,' agrees Jenkin Williams genially. 'We three are here because of the position, the office, we hold. As you say, here because … we are here.'

'I said that, I said *ex–*'

'Windfucker, Emmanuel Bird,' exasperated Robin Kerton whispers to Beavis Piggot, who chokes back mirth.

'The Minutes from last Vestry tell that you were then eleven, but today nine. What do we know of Edward Richbell and Robert Holt? Missing today,' Jenkin Williams asks. 'Vestry Clerk?'

'Robert Holt, his house collapsed when building. His business down, the sickness coming on – it's now scattered almost everywhere, the Bills tell – people fleeing … in short he has removed himself and family to Reading, to kin there.'

'And Edward Richbell?'

'Shut up, Edward Richbell, his family. All shut up with the infection.'

The Vestry is shaken.

'Do you know more?' John Girling asks.

'The coughing, the sneezing, all of them failing fast. The Viewers viewed them, kept their distance,' Philip Carter reports.

'Not long for life,' says George Lumme.

'The infection is all our Items today,' Jenkin Williams has the list before him, as does Philip Carter.

'It should have been all our Items last Vestry, if we had not wasted time and breath on all that foolery about Searchers and bribes and brawling watchmen. Waste of time,' Gilbert Swaile takes out his watch and props it on the table.

'A windfucker Vestry, that was,' Robin Kerton whispers again.

'Clerk Carter has the Item list for us to consider. Several things necessary to consider in this sad time of visitation. Tell the first,' says Jenkin Williams, 'and I ask Gilbert Swaile and his fine watch to watch the time so I do not run this Vestry on too long.'

'It is not Jenkin Williams who will run us on too long,' Beavis Piggot says to Robin Kerton.

Gilbert Swaile is happy to have attention drawn to his fine timepiece, unhappy to be cut down to timekeeper.

Philip Carter has his list of Items. Jenkin Williams strolled into the vestry room the evening before, humming. Surely not humming the *Trimming Parson*? thinks a shocked Philip Carter, but the humming stops before he can be sure. 'Parish Clerk, Vestry Clerk – the Vestry Minutes tell you are both – I will need Items for tomorrow's Vestry on how to address the visitation of the pest.' He lifts an enquiring eyebrow at his Clerk.

Philip Carter already has a list, hands it to Jenkin Williams, who takes a cursory glance and passes it back. 'Good. I will have a copy.' He is given one. 'Again good, good.' He walks away, humming again, but clearly not the *Trimming Parson*, and sings:

> *Sing with thy mouth, sing with thy heart,*
> *Like faithful friends, sing 'loth to depart.'*
> *Though friends together may always remain,*
> *Yet 'loth to depart' sing once again.*

Philip Carter does not know what to make of Jenkin Williams, but does not dislike him. A Trimming Parson, but easier than Walter Hall, far easier. Now, Sunday, Philip Carter takes the Vestry though his list of Items.

'Arranged,' he says, 'from Watchmen to Grave. Item the first, Watchmen.'

'Wait, hold!' calls Emmanuel Bird. 'Hold! We say pro tem, and that is Latin. We said it last Vestry, see the Minutes – read the Minutes Vestry Clerk – pro tem, so we can also say Latin *ex off*–'

'Gilbert Swaile's watch speaks only English,' says Jenkin Williams looking at the timepiece and privately relishing its Roman numbers, 'and it is saying we must hasten with our business. Clerk, Item the first.'

'Item the first is watchmen,' says Philip Carter. 'I have not listed Viewers, Keepers and Searchers. This was done at last Vestry.'

'Done and overdone. We do not want to talk of that again,' says Gilbert Swale. 'And I would say the same of watchmen. Is there any more business to do with them? More brawling?'

'No more brawling. We have watchmen at plague doors, but as the infection gets worse–'

'*If* it gets worse,' insists Harry Bosvill. 'If it gets worse.'

'Bad enough already for the well-born, the very well-born, and the wealthy to flee,' says Robin Kerton. 'It will get worse.'

'More watchmen will be needed,' says Philip Carter.

'Do you have names of those who will?' asks Jenkin Williams, knowing he does.

'Here are names,' Philip Carter takes from his papers another list.

'Is the Vestry agreed that the parish will appoint more watchmen? As needed? From this list? Yes? Good. For the Minutes, Vestry Clerk. Next Item,' says Jenkin Williams.

'Who are they? Who are those on this list?' asks John Girling.

'The Clerk will show you the list after Vestry if you have any names to add, or even names to subtract. Item the second, Clerk,' Jenkin Williams is smooth.

'Item the second, corpse bearers, coffin carriers. Not many will do this willingly, carry plague corpses to burial.'

'Pay them, men will do anything if the money is right. Carry shit away, carry corpses away. Pay them,' says Beavis Piggott airily.

'Do you have coffins, William Pickhering,' asks George Lumme. 'Do you?'

'A point well made, George Lumme, well made, and we will come to coffins in good time, but first the bearers,' says Jenkin Williams, pleased – as are William Pickhering and Gilbert Swaile – that the need for coffins has been raised so soon.

'Bearers,' says Frances Barrow, 'we have two, Richard Rice and Thomas Iny, and two more who say they will, although I have doubts of Jon Veale.'

'Jon Veale,' scoffs John Girling, 'not a man for work.'

'All parishes will need more bearers–'

'*Might* need more bearers, *might*,' says Harry Bosvill.

'All parishes will need more bearers,' Frances Barrow continues. 'Parishes close by here, we can share the cost of bearers, share bearers, so there will be men sufficient to do the necessary business.'

'Are these good parishes?' asks Emmanuel Bird. 'Which parishes?'

'All are good parishes,' says reassuring Jenkin Williams. 'All Hallows on the Wall, St Bartholomew the Little, St Mildred Poultry. All good parishes.'

'St Mildred Poultry is an excellent parish, excellent,' enthuses Harry Bosvill. 'The rector Richard Perrinchief is a man most loyal and learned, both. Loyal and learned. A very strong man for our Church of England, and for no other church. At all. A man who has wrote the most important book, *The Works of King Charles the Martyr.*' Harry Bosvill looks in triumphant defiance around the vestry table. 'I have the book if any wish to read it. All should.'

'We will combine corpse bearers, men and costs, with all these good parishes. A great benefit and great saving to all. We agree? Good, for the Minutes Clerk.' Jenkin Williams marks off Item the second on the list. 'Now we come to coffins. And shrouds. Coffins, as George Lumme rightly said, we must have coffins. Item the third, coffins and shrouds.'

'The parish coffin must cease, stop,' says Gilbert Swaile. 'It cannot be used again and again, cannot become a growing garden, a nest of pestilence, a sewer of sickness, breeding disease. Are we all agreed?' He asks, with a glance at Jenkin Williams.

'Does any Vestryman want to continue with the parish coffin? No? Then we *are* all agreed.'

'I shall have it chained up,' Frances Barrow says. Chaining the parish coffin is greeted with enthusiastic nods.

'William Pickhering, are you able to supply coffins sufficient for the burial of the poor, for the corpses of the poor, now that the parish coffin is in chains?' Jenkin Williams asks.

William Pickhering assures the Vestry that he can do so. The meeting proceeds to shrouds.

'William Lacie, whose cloth business has expanded in recent days, can supply shrouds, winding sheets, all at good price. I know this from William Lacie himself,' says Gilbert Swaile.

'All agreed? Good. Clerk, for the Minutes, Item the third, the parish coffin in chains; coffins from William Pickhering; shrouds and winding sheets from William Lacie. The day *is* exceeding hot,' says Jenkin Williams.

William Sutterwhit absent-mindedly, perhaps, picks up the Oath and fans himself. The room waits for Harry Bosvill to notice.

'The Oath, the Oath, lay it down. It is not to be abused as a fan, it is the Oath!'

'I meant no harm,' William Sutterwhit says. 'The day *is* exceeding hot.' He passes the Oath a few more times in front of his face and places it down carefully, meticulously squaring it centre table.

'Item the fourth, burials,' Philip Carter looks to Jenkin Williams.

'I will not, we as a parish cannot, have plague corpses, no matter how distinguished and worthy the corpse, buried in the church. We cannot worship and say our prayers and praise God on top of a heap of pestilential bodies. And we will not accept, if we ever have – and our Clerk tells me we have not and will not, ever – accept corpses for burial from another parish. Even one as eminent as St Mildred Poultry.'

'Room for graves,' says the Church Warden. 'We have room still for graves in our churchyard, the upper churchyard here, and goodly room in the lower churchyard.'

'That was a good buy, parish was wise to buy that land,' Robin Kerton says. 'Not all supported it. I always said it was a good purchase, would serve us well in time of need. And so it is.'

'Where will we bury the distinguished and worthy?' asks Emmanuel Bird from self-interest. 'If not in church where they should deservedly lie, where will they lie?' Emmanuel Bird has chosen his own place near the altar, but expects he will outlive the plague and will still – eventually, later – lie there.

'Here in our churchyard. Room in the churchyard, the upper yard, will be kept for the distinguished and worthy,' Jenkin Williams reassures him.

'Upper churchyard, as the rector says, for them and none other, I will see to that,' adds the Church Warden. 'Reserved for them until we see where the Bills of Mortality take us.'

'The distinguished and worthy, who decides distinguished and worthy?' asks Beavis Piggot. 'Who decides where those of this parish will rest – upper churchyard or lower – until the trump of God sounds and those that sleep in Jesus arise?' It is a question that many are eager to hear answered.

'Our Clerk, a man of many years' experience in this parish, well knows the worthy and distinguished, and can decide,' answers Jenkin Williams.

'What if he gets it wrong?' asks John Girling. 'What then?'

'Rector decides,' says Philip Carter, paying Jenkin Williams back in kind, and adds, 'Whether for notables in the upper churchyard or others in the lower, the gravemakers must go deeper. We must bury the pestilence deeper, and pay the gravemakers to do so. At least six foot deep the Orders say. *At least* six foot, so we should go deeper than that.'

'An extra two shillings per diem,' says Frances Barrow.

'Two shillings? Per diem? 'Ruinous! It will ruin the parish!' says George Lumme.

'No good having a parish chest clinking with coin if we are all dead,' says Gilbert Swaile.

The Vestry is swayed and supports the ruinous salary for gravemakers.

'Agreed? Good. For the Minutes. The next Item ... what Item are we Vestry Clerk?' Jenkin Williams asks.

'Item the fifth, Brokers of the Dead.'

'Yes, Brokers of the Dead. This will help pay for the gravemakers, George Lumme,' says Jenkin Williams. 'Church Warden?'

'All can see this plague has caused and will cause great cost to the parish. Watchmen, corpse bearers, coffins, shrouds, gravemakers, not to say payment to Viewers, Keepers, Searchers. All heavy expenses for St Cyneswide and St Tibba. Heavy, and possibly ruinous if we are not careful. But we are careful. Property left in plague-struck houses, our Brokers of the Dead will seize that property and it becomes parish property.'

'Seize my property?!' So many voices, difficult to distinguish whose.

'Only the property of those on the parish, of those who cannot afford to pay for their food, their nursing, their coffins, their bearers, their burials.' This speech of reassurance is left to Jenkin Williams. 'All who can afford to pay – all here, for example – your property is safe for your family, your heirs. Brokers of the Dead are only for ... the others. In short, for the poor.'

'Are we to be comforted by that?' asks Beavis Piggot.

'If you will be, yes,' replies Jenkin Williams. 'Church Warden to give names of those who would be such Brokers. Frances Barrow himself will be one '

'*Ex officio*,' says Emmanuel Bird.

'Of course that,' agrees Jenkin Williams. 'Gilbert Swaile's fine watch tells me we must keep on, shouts at me: time is of the essence. Item the fifth and the last, Clerk.'

'It is Item the sixth,' Philip Carter pauses, repeats, 'Item the sixth, Dog-killers.'

This is met with resistant silence.

'The Orders say, order, that "Dogs be killed by the Dog-killers appointed for that purpose." This parish, all parishes must appoint Dog-killers,' says Jenkin Williams, holding up the Orders.

The silence draws on.

'You are all thinking who might best do this business,' prompts Jenkin Williams.

'It must be done,' sighs Emmanuel Bird.

'It must,' agrees Robin Kerton.

'Who will do it?' asks Harry Bosvill.

'And cats, also cats are to be killed,' says Frances Barrow.

The Vestry has nothing further to offer.

'This matter needs thought. It will carry over until next Vestry and we will consider names then, names that will come to you,' says smooth Jenkin Williams. 'We have done our business here and not taken too long to do it, thanks to Gilbert Swaile's timepiece. Our items increased as we talked but the Clerk will make good sense of them in the Minutes.'

'Alas Edward Richbell dead and now his Gnasher,' cries William Pickhering to the emptying room. 'His Gnasher.'

St Cyneswide & St Tibba, July the 16ᵗʰ, 1665

Vestry Present
Rev Mr Williams
P Carter, Parish Clerk
F Barrow, Church Warden
G Swaile
B Piggot
E Bird
J Girling
R Kerton
W Sutterwhit
H Bosvill
W Pickhering
G Lumme
Item – Watchmen: appointed as needed; Clerk's list
Item – Corpse bearers, coffin carriers: combine bearers & cost with p'ishes All Hallows on Wall, St Bart Little, St Mildred Poultry
Item – P'ish coffin not continued, chained

Item – Poor burial: Wm Pickhering coffins; Wm Lacie shrouds, winding sheets

Item – Burials: wthy upper ch'yard; rest, lower ch'yard

Item – Gravemakers: 6 ft or more; + 2ˢ per diem

Item – Brokers of Dead: seize property of poor on the p'ish; Ch. Warden Broker, & to name other Brokers

Item – Dog-killers: next Vestry; names to be proposed

* * *

London, Tuesday, 18 July 1665

The Bellman tolls his bell, calls the names: begins with Edward Richbell, Ellen Richbell, and through all their children; then George Hillcocke, Sissily Hillcocke, and theirs.

London, Bills of Mortality for 130 Parishes
from the 11 of July to the 18 of July 1665
Buried, in all – 1761; Plague – 1089
Parishes clear of the Plague – 76; Parishes Infected – 54

CHAPTER XXIII

London, Wednesday, 19 July 1665

*'The best fritters: To make the best fritters, take a pint of cream
and warm it; then take eight eggs, only abate four of the whites,
and beat them well in a dish …'*

'Jenkin Williams did well at Vestry,' Philip Carter says. 'A lot of business done in good time.'

Frances Barrow grunts. 'Business done in the way alchemists at Bartholomew Fair sell the philosopher's stone. Smooth and glib and too good-natured and you don't know his hand has been in your pocket until you are home.'

'Nothing taken from my pocket,' says Philip Carter.

'Not yet, but you won't know when his hand is in your pocket.'

'Dog-killers, this business of Dog-killers,' Philip Carter shakes his head.

'My pigeons will not be killed,' says Frances Barrow. 'This Order, "No hogs, dogs, cats, tame pigeons, conies be suffered to be kept within any part of the City." Who will be the parish Pigeon-killer? Will our Vestry have one killer for hogs, one for dogs, one for cats, one for conies and one for pigeons? Or will one or two killers club them all to death? Bah.'

'They can leave the city. I mean the hogs and dogs and what-not can be sent or taken out of the city,' says Philip Carter.

'My pigeons will come back,' says Frances Barrow wryly. 'That is their nature. Will you have a brace of pigeons Philip Carter? We will eat our way through the whole cote before the pigeon killers come.'

'No names have been proposed,' Philip Carter says. 'The plague might end before we find anyone who will do the business. I don't know when it will end. People shut up in houses. Locked in. Ill, suffering, dying, shut off from all the world. When will it end?'

Frances Barrow chants:

When cowards shall forget to rant,
Schoolboys to frig, old whores to paint.
When the Jesuit fraternity
Shall leave the use of buggery.

Philip Carter chokes on his pipe. 'I have not heard that before! You are saying it will never end? Is that a trooper's song? It has that ring to it.'

'Better days coming,' Frances Barrow says, suddenly cheerful. 'Better days, and soon. Your friend – and mine too – Alexander Muzzard of All Hallows the Great, he says in his fiery way, "All the world groans under the tyranny and oppression of kings, but all earthly monarchies will be destroyed forever and we will come to a time of peace and riches for all, heralded by the trumpets of doom for the fall of Rome, the whore of Babylon, in this year to come, 1666! The Year and Number of the Beast!" So says Alexander Muzzard, and I don't say he is wrong. He says it in his shouting, excited way. A man of spitting enthusiasm.'

Philip Carter can easily recognise Alexander Muzzard in this.

'The *Zealous Soldier*!' says Frances Barrow, as excited as Alexander Muzzard, and sings:

Some few years since when we behold and see
The fruits of our hard labours, and behold
This Nation flourish in tranquillity,
And God's true worship, as it ought, extolled:
Then shall we say oh praised be the Lord,
That we attained peace have by the sword!

'By the sword,' repeats Frances Barrow. 'I meant it about the brace. I am the man who kills my pigeons and no-one else. That is *my* nature. We'll deny the pigeon killer.' He goes to fetch pigeons for Philip Carter.

'I'm to the lower churchyard,' Philip Carter calls after Frances Barrow. 'I'll be back for the pigeons.'

Edward Richbell and his dead family would take up more room in the upper churchyard than the Parish Clerk deems fitting, and the baker is consigned as worthy only of the lower one. Philip Carter stumps his way past the rectory, past the empty bakery, to the lower yard.

'Did you dig below six foot? Deeper?' he asks buriers Job and Jonah.

'Course we did,' grunts Job. 'Told us to, didn't you? So we did.'

High mounds of earth sit on top of the fresh graves.

'Want us to dig them up so you can check?' asks Jonah calmly. 'Easily done. The soil's still loose.'

'I– what I want is what the Orders of the Lord Mayor and Aldermen of the City of London want.'

'What we want is more pipe money. Chew through a lot of pipes making graves, burying plague corpses,' Job says. Points to the broken pipe stems that have been arranged into small crosses on the new graves. 'And more makers, more gravemakers. If people keep dying from this plague we'll need more men to bury them.'

'If there are any living left to do the burying,' Jonah adds. 'And tobacco as well as pipes. Pipes no use without tobacco.'

'At least six foot deep,' Philip Carter says as he leaves. If most burials are to be here, and they will be, Vestry will have to pay for an overseer at the lower churchyard.

Relieved to back at what he considers *his* churchyard, he checks that the parish coffin is securely chained. It is. Wrestling himself into a comfortable position in the vestry, he looks for Frances Barrow's whore of Babylon and the number of the beast in the Book of Revelation. Wondering if it will tell him his fortune, his fate, wondering if he will recognize it if it does. Reads:

> *Here is wisdom. Let him that hath understanding count the number of the beast: for it is the number of a man; and his number is Six hundred threescore and six.*
>
> *And I saw a woman sit upon a scarlet coloured beast, full of names of blasphemy, having seven heads and ten horns.*

And the woman was arrayed in purple and scarlet colour, and decked with gold and precious stones and pearls, having a golden cup in her hand full of abominations and filthiness of her fornication:

And upon her forehead was a name written, MYSTERY, BABYLON THE GREAT, THE MOTHER OF HARLOTS AND ABOMINATIONS OF THE EARTH.

Philip Carter's face wrinkles in incomprehension and revulsion. He closes the bible, regretting opening it. He knows Alexander Muzzard and the Fifth Monarchy Men find light, enlightenment, prophecy and wisdom here, all leading to the glory of the Fifth Monarchy ruled by King Jesus. Philip Carter sees only darkness and monsters, hears only the Bedlam voices of crazed men who shout in the street.

* * *

London, Thursday, 20 July 1665

Raining.

'You here? There's a change,' Isaac Brokefild is wet, drunk. 'Goodwife Joan Brokefild home, Goodwife Joan Brokefild cooking for her husband, Goodwife Joan Brokefild not wandering the streets, not peering in windows, not listening at doors, not singing to herself. Don't know where you got the name Goodwife. Not from me.' He tugs at his wet shoes. They stick, don't budge.

'No, not from you.'

'Come and do these shoes, they're stuck. Come on!' He thrusts a leg out. 'And the other one! Hurry up! I'm wet. I need a Goodwife, don't have one. Just you. What are you cooking? What's my dinner? Do you want a kick? What is my dinner?'

'Fritters.'

'Fritters,' Isaac Brokefild mutters. Takes up a penny pot of sack and downs it. 'Where's the rest? You didn't get just a penny pot? Where's the rest?'

'Just a penny pot. For the fritters.'

'Fritters. Give me sack and keep your foul fritters. And books again?'
He grabs a chapbook. 'Spend my money on sack, not on this, this–'

'It is mine. Bought from my purse,' Goodwife Joan Brokefild reaches
for her book.

Isaac Brokefild tears it once, twice. Delights in the despair on her face.

'Books! Fritters!' He throws the torn pages on the fire, kicks over the
pot of batter rising on the hearth.

Goodwife Joan Brokefild takes the frying pan, bubbling with molten
lard, waiting for the batter now oozing on the floor, and smashes the heavy
pan at Isaac Brokefild's head. It caves in the right side of his face, smashes
his bones, burns his flesh.

The smell of singed hair, skin, his brief scream, fill the small room.
Goodwife Joan Brokefild stands back and watches Isaac Brokefild twitch,
dribble blood and drool, and bleed on the flagstones: his blood, the batter,
the lard, mingling.

'Fritters,' she says and tries to rescue her chapbook from the flames but
it is gone. Burnt. Dead.

Isaac Brokefild is not yet dead, moans, gurgles. His left eye stares at
the Goodwife. Possibly asking for her help. Possibly asking her not to hit
him again. Possibly both.

She gazes back, looks at what she has done, and sees that it is good.
Remembers the blows; the beatings; the kicks; the insults; the finding fault;
the always finding fault. She wants to remind him of every kick, every
blow. But there is no point in talking to a dying man. She is a Searcher. She
knows death and is pleased it has come to Isaac Brokefild at last.

She can see brains. Knows he will not suddenly sit up, like one of
Widow Hazard's farting corpses, but still she holds the frying pan, a good
heavy pan, her best. She beholds what she has done, and it is very good.

While he dies she scrapes up the sorry mess from the floor, but
keeps the frying pan close. She is sorry about her book, wishes she had
struck him before he tossed it on the fire. Goes back over what happened
and understands that if he had not burned the book she would not have
struck. So perhaps it was just as well. Yes. She can buy another, although

she had grown familiar with, fond of, its blemished paper and its clumsy print: 'Rogues' spelt 'Rogeus'; 'Printed for P. Brooksby in Pye-Corner' was 'Pirnted for P. Brooksby in Pye-Croner.'

It is not so easy to clean up Isaac Brokefild, and she does not want to. She sits by the fire and waits for him to stop breathing. When she thinks he has, she counts to one hundred. Then, to make sure, counts to one hundred again. Wonders if she should count to one thousand. Wishes she has a watch. Gilbert Swaile has a fine watch, it is the talk of the parish.

With a pleased smile to herself she thinks of a verse from her rescued book of poetry, her battered book of poetry, well-hidden, where Isaac Brokefild will not find it. He never did and now he never will.

> *Man is a Watch, wound up at first, but never*
> *Wound up again: Once down, He's down for ever.*
> *The Watch once downe, all motions then do cease;*
> *And Mans pulse stopt, All Passions sleep in Peace.*

She moves closer to the body on the floor. Checks, carefully, cautiously. All motions ceased; he's down for ever; all passions sleep in peace. She does not want peace for Isaac Brokefild. She wants him dead. And he is.

* * *

'A corpse to search,' Anne Abowen, a good woman for reform, standing straight, back straight, neck straight, calls at Widow Margaret Hazard's door. Rain runs off her hat onto her soaking clothes.

'Wait,' the Widow calls: puts on her overskirt, her bodice, her hat, shuffles feet into her pattens, takes up her red wand, opens the door. 'Who is the first finder? Who is the corpse? Did death come while you were viewing? Have you called Goodwife Brokefild?'

'We are going to see her and you will find the answers to your questions.' Or some of the answers, Anne Abowen adds to herself, some.

They walk in silence through the rain.

'An accident,' Joan Brokefild says to her fellow Searcher. 'Isaac

Brokefild, drunk, hurries in from the rain, pulls off his shoes – clumsy, falling in drink – stumbles, falls onto the rising pot, the fritter batter, the frying pan of hot lard. Dashes his brains out.' the Goodwife points out the shoes where Isaac Brokefild tripped, points to the bashed, singed head by the fire, right side down on the flags, now thick with batter and lard and blood and brains.

'You were here, saw it?' Widow Hazard asks.

'Making fritters, his dinner. Fritters. I am here by the fire and see him come in drunk. He takes his shoes off and with haste and drink stumbles over them and falls heavily, very heavily. As you see,' she points.

'A hard fall. Hard,' the Widow bends down by the body, searching the corpse. 'Mmm. Hit his head hard on the stones?' She waves flies away.

'And on the pot, the rising pot with the batter, and on the frying pan. Fell right on the pan, into it, a heavy pan of boiling lard. Hit it with his head, his face. I was making fritters,' she shrugs and points again to Isaac Brokefild, his mess.

'Mmm.' The Widow turns to Anne Abowen. 'You, Anne Abowen?'

'Goodwife Brokefild called out as I was passing. I came in. I could see what had happened but you are the Searcher, one of them, and the Goodwife – her own husband, so she … She saw what happened, was here, saw it all. And I came for you.'

'Mmm.'

Joan Brokefild finds her pipe and the others do the same. They smoke in silence and watch the flies gather on Isaac Brokefild, his head.

'Grabbing for the penny pot of sack, Isaac Brokefild,' Joan Brokefild says in conversation. She gestures with her foot to the pot on the floor. 'I am waiting for the batter to rise and swell before adding the sack but Isaac Brokefild will put the sack into himself. Will snatch up the pot, and in his urgency trips over his shoes.' She shakes her head, can see this plausible pantomime play in the room as she tells it. She is an appreciative audience for this comedy, or tragedy, or farce, *The Fall of Isaac Brokefild, Sot,* and hopes for wider acclaim.

Searcher Widow Margaret Hazard sits, smokes, thinks on Isaac

Brokefild, his death, the how of his death. Killed with a fall. Killed by a fall. Or something other. Had his brains dashed out. By a fall. She bends down once more to search his smashed head. Damage done on the right side. Flesh melted, scorched, singed, burnt, bashed. The right eye badly fried, clagged in a mess of lard and batter. And some grey brain. She sits back and smokes.

An almost comfortable silence joins the ancient women, fills the room, along with the smell of death, food, fat, and Isaac Brokefild's emptied bladder and bowels.

'Killed with a fall? Not for me to say,' says Anne Abowen, saying it.

'No, not for you to say,' replies Searcher Widow Hazard, exhaling smoke. Comfortable smoke.

'Viewing, I have seen cracked skulls on the living. Some skulls as thin as egg shells. Crack as easily, as easily as these,' Anne Abowen waves a hand at the cracked egg shells in the scrap bucket, and is distracted by the number of them. One, two, three, eight eggs. Extravagant. Too many eggs for fritters. She would not use so many. No more than four.

Joan Brokefild's eyes follow Anne's hand to the scrap bucket. For the fritters she was supposed to abate only four of the eggwhites but cannot remember if she did so.

Widow Hazard wonders if some words of comfort should be offered. Wonders what they might be. Whatever words she found would be false, and Joan Brokefild would know them to be false. She cannot say 'Gone to God.' Isaac Brokefild has not. Waits to hear if Anne Abowen will offer solace. She does not.

Anne Abowen stands, shakes her pipe dottle into the hearth, close to Isaac Brokefild's head, says, 'Widow Brokefild, you were a goodwife to Isaac Brokefild, a man killed with a fall.' She takes her leave and says softly, but not too softly, perhaps talking to herself, perhaps to Isaac Brokefild, his corpse, 'His candle put out.' She does not say in full "The candle of the wicked man shall be put out," does not need to. Ancient women know their bible. Anne Abowen knows epitaphs. Finds one in her mind for Isaac Brokefild.

Death levels All, both the wicked and the just;
Man's but a flower, and his end is dust.

A wicked man, Isaac Brokefild, and no flower.

'God be w'ye,' Anne Abowen says genially to her fellow ancient women.

'And w'ye,' the always reassuring reply.

Widow Joan Brokefild thinks of Maude Wattes, formerly of this parish, now in Newgate. Wonders if she is to join her there. Widow Margaret Hazard is no fool, has searched many corpses. Her one eye is a good eye. Widow Joan looks at Widow Margaret.

'Anne Abowen is a stiff, upright women,' Widow Hazard muses. 'A good Viewer. When she was paired with that Chaukley it was Anne Abowen who did all the business. Good for Reform, she is very strong there. A good bible woman. Struggles with the Oath, with Uniformity. Stiff necked. Vestry will still have her as Viewer. The Clerk and the Warden propose she make an act of occasional conformity. Whatever that is.'

'That was supposed to happen some time ago. Is she still thinking on it? She is still viewing,' says Widow Brokefild.

'A good Viewer. And she knows eggshell skulls. No Searcher, but a good Viewer. Says Isaac Brokefild killed with a fall, although it is not for her to say. She is not a Searcher. We Searchers, you and I, we know corpses. Not for her to say.'

Eggshell skull? Isaac Brokefild is, was, a bonehead, a thick skulled bonehead, thinks Widow Brokefild, still not sure how many of the eggwhites she abated. Four? More? Less?

'Do you make fritters often?' Widow Hazard asks in conversation.

'Not often, but I had the cloves the mace the nutmeg the saffron the sugar and cinnamon and apples. I bought cream and eggs and ale barm and the penny pot of sack. I don't make fritters often.'

'Mmm. My mother made meat fritters. Especially mutton. Any mutton left on the joint, carves off the last few slices, batters and fries them. I was fond of my mother's fritters,' says Widow Hazard. Her mother served them with potatoes, boiled; tomato, cut in half and seasoned with basil leaves; and pickled sallats. A simple meal she always said when she served it.

'Mine are sweet fritters, with apple, and before dished strewn with a good store of sugar and cinnamon.'

'Was Isaac Brokefild fond of fritters?'

'He was not a man for fondness. Not in this house.'

'Anne Abowen has the right of it. You were a goodwife to Isaac Brokefild.'

'I was. He was not a good husband to me.'

'He was not a good husband. That's well known. He was not.'

Silence comes again.

Widow Hazard thinks of Maude Wattes, and how she was right to report the murder. That was an innocent babe. Born innocent no matter what rectors and bishops and the Book of Common Prayer and the learned – she pours scorn on the word – the learned, say. Innocent, an innocent new-born. Killed. Murdered by Maude Wattes.

Widow Brokefild thinks of Maude Wattes, and how Widow Hazard was wrong to report the poor distracted mother as a murderer. Wonders what Widow Hazard will do now. What she will tell of this murder.

The pondering in Widow Brokefild's head becomes a play with two speaking parts –

Scene: A room in a poor house in London. A man's bloodied body lies before the hearth. His widow sits, gazing at the corpse.

Enter a Searcher and a Viewer. The Searcher searches the corpse. The Viewer sits silently by the newly made widow.

JB to Searcher: Will you call the Constable for a murder? You did so for Maude Wattes.

WMH: Is it a murder then? Do you confess?

JB: Will you report a murder?

WMH: Maude Wattes did a murder, so I reported a murder. Is this a murder?

JB: What do you see?

WMH: Of course I see a murder. It is a murder.

JB: Will you report a murder?

WMH: A murder is a murder. I am a Searcher. I report deaths, their causes. You know that.

JB: What will you report here?

WMH: What I can see, what I search. I am a Searcher, I report my search.

Widow Brokefild corrects, amends, toys with this dialogue, hopes WMH will give a different answer, a better answer. But it is Widow Margaret Hazard who reported Maude Wattes. Widow Margaret Hazard who takes no bribes, does not lie, who is of honest reputation and of the best sort as can be got in this kind.

Angrily, newly made Widow Brokefild says out loud, 'He would call me whorespawn.' And thinks: in my head I would call him bastard, whoreson, a most wicked, evil man. In my head. Adds calmly, out loud, 'Do you have questions for me? Is there more I can say?' asks Searcher Widow Joan Brokefild of Searcher Widow Margaret Hazard.

'Mmm,' Widow Hazard pauses. 'I cannot think of any. It looks like Isaac Brokefild was killed with a fall. I can see that, even though I have only one eye. Looks like he was killed with a fall, and that is for me to say, and I say it. To you, and to Philip Carter Parish Clerk. And you are a Searcher and you say the same, searching this corpse, husband or no husband?'

'No husband,' says Widow Joan Brokefild. 'Killed with a fall.'

Widow Margaret Hazard waves her pipe in farewell. 'Bearers will come for the corpse. You will have a time of it cleaning up this nasty business,' she gestures to the mess. 'God be w'ye.'

'And w'ye.'

Widow Joan Brokefild is confident, almost certainly confident, that Searcher Widow Margaret Hazard will report death by accident. Isaac Brokefild, in drink, accidentally fell into a fire. Killed with a fall.

But there is Sara Potts' mother. Since Joan Brokefild found, saw, that she had hit Isaac Brokefild with the frying pan, killed him, she has given careful thought to Sara Potts' mother, as well as to Maude Wattes, her fate.

Should she have been bold and said to Widow Hazard: I know who Sara Potts' mother is. Where she is. I know. I have always known. What then? Bargained, cheapened, with Widow Hazard to shrink death by murder to death by accident? You give me my life, I give you Sara Potts' life, and yours, to keep unchanged. We both, you and I, we say nothing. Other than say the Lie. An accident. Isaac Brokefild, his death. An accident.

Yet she could not make herself write this dialogue into her play, or say it anywhere other than at the back of her mind, and so she kept silent. Because. Because she believes, trusts, Widow Margaret Hazard will not speak against her; just as she will not use Sara Potts and her mother against Widow Hazard. She will not, and she will not.

Widow Joan Brokefild crouches down to clean up, wonders if she should try to rescue the mess of batter from the blood and shit. Decides she can't. Her nose is near the ordure and Widow Hazard's words come to her, 'Is my arse beshitt'n?' She works on. She has cleaned up after Isaac Brokefild before.

If she had abated the wrong number of eggwhites, she wonders, would this have spoiled the fritters?

CHAPTER XXIV

London, Friday, 21 July 1665

'When she comes home she'll break our bones,
For tumbling over cherry stones,
We'll follow our mother to market.'

'Dogs! Dogs!' calls a pleased Jack to excited great dogs Dog, Maydog and Third, who leap up barking their greetings. Visiting his family Jack is in his worst clothes, not best: old breeches, old boots, and an old smock covering as much as it will. Clothes that will not object to great shitty dog paws.

'Here is Jack Micoe! Jack Micoe here to spend a pleasant hour with his family! Pastime with good company!' Thomas Micoe waves, almost as effusive as his dogs to see Jack, and with mock dancing steps and genteel hand gestures da da-da's his way through the song's opening notes. Claps Jack on the back.

'They say Jack, men do, this song was made by old king Harry who killed all his wives. Chopped their heads off, the lot of them. Old beast he must have been. No place for kings here in the Commonwealth of Dung, eh Oliver?'

Oliver gives Jack a shrug of here-is-our-father-being-our-father.

'You will be wondering, Jack Micoe, what me and Oliver and Eliezar are doing on this next-door land and what work we are at.'

Jack *is* wondering why they are there and what work they are at.

'This land, its wharf, that fine new barge, all now the property of Thomas Micoe and Son – or Sons if you will – purveyors of fine dung!' As always, Thomas Micoe is the best audience for his own wit.

'Jack, you see us here building a stall, not a lay-stall, but a lime-stall.

Not a lay-stall for dung but a lime-stall for lime, and all set up on our own land, and the lime to be carried on our own barge.'

'So Richard Vyolet sold? He never would before.'

'No Jack, he never would, not to me. De-spised me and my dung. Told me often, to my face, "Thomas Micoe I de-spise you and your filthy dung. Your stinking heaps next to my land, my wharf. Who will load or unload their goods here? Who will do business, trade, next to shit mounds? No-one will, Thomas Micoe." You know the man Jack, a most awkward man.'

Jack knows the man by reputation, by family stories, and by vivid childhood memories of a shouting angry face over the fence, a terrifying face, had not the predecessors of Dog, Maydog and Third been by his side, raging furiously back at Richard Vyolet.

'Oliver did the business. Told him a story how he was splitting away from me to set up for himself and how it would spite me if Richard Vyolet sold to him. Eh Oliver?'

'Not hard,' says Oliver. 'He was breaking his neck to get away from London, afraid witless of the plague.'

'Prices,' says Thomas Micoe. 'Prices, good prices for buyers, anyone who will leave town will sell, sell for a groat or less, sell anything they can't take with them. Richard Vyolet, he couldn't take his land or his wharf. Gone to be a counterfeit gentleman at Reading or somewhere, eh Oliver? Eliezar! Here's Jack! All of us for a draught, wash the dirt down. The *Globe* or the *Devil*? Shall we all of us go to the *Devil*?' Thomas Micoe roars at this fine jest.

'Joan Micoe is well?' Jack asks his father as they go to the *Devil*.

'No Jack, she is not well. She has not been well for some time and is no better, indeed is worse. She is not well, and I will have private words with you. Not now. Later. That lime is horrible dry, chalky stuff. Gets in your throat, your nose. Much worse than dung. But it will make us money.'

They sit, smoke, drink.

'No trouble finding a bench and a table,' says Oliver. 'These plague times, people are dead or fled.'

'Jack,' says Thomas Micoe, 'I have heard a very nasty thing. Hear this.

In Portugal – I heard this from a sailor, Abraham Vandecounter his name, he will be master of our lime barge, a good man who knows the wide world – in Portugal he says they scorn to make a seat for a house of office, they shit all in pots and empty them in the river! Abraham Vandecounter says this is the truth. No work for gong men in Portugal. What a place!'

'Abraham Vandecounter has sailed to many places, many foreign ports,' says Oliver with admiration.

'Foreigners,' scoffs Eliezar, 'everywhere over the sea there are foreigners. Filthy. No seat in the house of! The. Dirty. Bastards.'

'Oliver, Eliezar, I will speak privately with Jack,' Thomas Micoe sets a stern face, shunts his eyebrows. Oliver and Eliezar nod and move away, Oliver sitting so he can see his father.

Thomas Micoe pauses, takes a breath, looks to find his words, creases his brow, says in a whisper, 'She will not see the women here, the Blackfriars women, and the doctors are fled. She keeps to her chamber, day and night, not fit to go abroad.' He stops, struggles to find words he can say out loud. 'It is her months, but she has them all the time, most of the time, her months. And a sore belly, she says it has grown dangerous she thinks. Very ill in bed, in great pain.'

Jack has lived five years in the house of Walter Hall and Margery Hall. He has heard Margery Hall's irritation, complaints, that she has her menses, *ses Mois*, that *ceux là* are upon her. Sometimes Margery Hall would keep to her chamber, but not all day, not every day. He nods, and wonders why his father is telling him this.

'Not well, Joan Micoe is not well.' Thomas Micoe stops again. 'Wasting away.'

Groping for something to say, Jack asks, 'Has she taken physick?'

'Physick. Everything I can find under the Dominion of Venus, anything to stop bleeding.' Thomas Micoe counts off on his fingers, 'Stinking Arrach, Cudweed, Chestnut – good to stop women's terms, Chestnut – Golden Rod, Horsetail – staunches inside bleeding – Tree Moss the same. None of them do the business. None. She's tried them all. Why am I saying this to you, Jack Micoe? Why? Those Searchers in your parish where we found the new-born infant, the murdered one. That Searcher with the eye. She must be a woman who knows things. Knows these things. Will you ask her, or the other one with her, or anyone, anyone outside Blackfriars? Joan Micoe might listen to them. That is why I am telling you this. Will you? Ask them to help a poor suffering woman? She might listen to them because they are not from Blackfriars.'

'Ah.' Jack is taken aback. Affronted. How can Jack Green, after all these years, be expected to introduce his new world of St Cyneswide and St Tibba to this other world, this old world, of Jack Micoe of Blackfriars? Jack Micoe, the dung-pot boy, son of gong farmer Thomas Micoe? He shrinks at the thought. Imagines conducting Widow Margaret Hazard to Blackfriars: This is my father, Thomas Micoe; my father's wife; Joan Micoe; my brother Oliver Micoe; this is Dung Wharf and these are great mountains of dung.

'Good. Good,' Thomas Micoe takes Jack's ambiguous 'Ah' for willing assent, wipes his eyes. Oliver, concerned, comes over.

'Jack will help us, Oliver,' Thomas Micoe tells him. 'He will.'

'Good, then she will get help.' Oliver waves Eliezar back to the table and calls for more ale. 'A song to cheer you father?' he asks solicitously. 'A cheering song?'

'She will get help. It is unjust I should lose a goodwife a second time. Unjust. No, no song for now. Later. Not a time for merry songs now. When she is better.'

'Yes father,' says obedient Oliver.

'Here is some wisdom of the heap,' says Thomas Micoe finding something of himself again. 'Although I am not sure if it is wise. Hear this: "A ripe pear is more likely to fall into the shit than on the ground." What do you make of that?'

'Only the foolish man would spread dung under his tree when pears are ripe and ready to fall,' Oliver answers quickly. 'That would only happen if the pear-man is a fool.'

'Yes,' agrees Eliezar, who has country kin. 'Harvest time the wrong time to spread dung. 'Abraham Vandecounter has that ripe pear story as a saying of the Dutch, or the Belgian. Foreign,' Eliezar shakes his head.

'Back to Dung Wharf,' says Thomas, rising. 'Jack will you see Joan Micoe? If she will see you.'

'If she will see me I will.'

'Oliver, what song was it you would have us sing?' Thomas Micoe asks.

'This one: "Yesternight I was full merry with a cup of claret and sherry. Much tobacco did I take, which made my pate full sore to ache." That one.'

'Ah, that one! When she is well again we'll have that one.'

'Here in the Commonwealth of Gong,' Oliver says, jesting with his brother, 'see we have mountains, we have a mighty sea, and we have taken, conquered, the land of our enemy.' Then whispers to Jack, 'You will help him? Help her? He is at his wit's end about Joan Micoe.'

'I will see. See what I can do,' Jack answers brusquely, irritated at being pressed by his little brother to do what he does not want to do.

Joan Micoe will not see Jack.

'Not well, she is not,' a disappointed Thomas Micoe repeats. 'Next time Jack, see her next time. Did you do good business with Nicholas Bibbie the carman?'

'Fled. No business to be done there.'

Thomas Micoe sighs at the news. 'And I have spoken to John Sled, Company of Woodmongers and Coal Trade of London John Sled. Spoke about carts to deliver the lime. Says he will help me "if he can." If. He is going to be great in supplying dead-carts to parishes, expects to be busy with this. And he will be. So no profit for us in dead-carts. Nicholas Bibbie gone and John Sled all out for himself and his Company. But we will still need carts for the lime, eh Oliver?'

'Buy them when upstream, or down, bring them back on the barges,' suggests Jack. 'Have your, have *our* own carts. There will be countrymen ready to sell carts.'

'Jack! You are as sharp as that little sword you carry! Thomas Micoe and Sons will prosper. And Sons Jack, eh? Oliver! Hear this!'

Oliver is impressed, pleased to have such a thinking brother.

'What an enterprise, Thomas Micoe and Sons! We shall gather our crumbs, Thomas Micoe and Sons shall. What great thinkers are you two.

Lime, our own carts, and our plague water. Joan Micoe, her physick – she will have nothing to do with Blackfriars women, I told you that – Oliver, out finding physick for her, has found–'

'Butterbur,' says Oliver, taking back his story. 'Butterbur, growing in low ground, wet ground, by the river, up river. Seen it from the barge, big broad leaves. The roots to be taken up and then cooked down in a great pot of water. Drink the decoction, serves as a fine protection against the plague and all pestilential fevers.' Oliver looks to his brother for approval, unsuccessfully.

'Provokes the sweating, Jack, provokes the sweating,' says an enthusiastic Thomas Micoe, a cheerful man again. 'We are calling it Oliver's Cordial, a Particular for the Plague. The name will appeal to some, if not to all. And if taken to task by king's men, we will say: here is Oliver Micoe, it is his plague water! Won't we Oliver? What do you say to that Jack?'

Jack will say to himself he has had enough of family, and says to his family he will take his leave now.

'Remember the Searcher with the one eye Jack! She will remember me. God be w'ye.'

'And w'ye.'

Bah! Oliver's Cordial, a Particular for the Plague: Jack much prefers 'A Powerful Palliative and Preventative for all Plagues and Pestilences.' That will sell! He must tell his father this next time. When that will be he is unsure.

Walking back, Jack is not thinking of Widow Margaret Hazard. He is thinking of the rectory with Walter Hall, Margery Hall, and she talking fretfully of her menses, *ses Mois*, the *ceux là* upon her. He learns these words, their meaning. And his thoughts move on to a book. Walter Hall's secret French book, kept in a locked chest in the bed chamber: *L'Ecole des Filles*.

Inquisitive, curious Jack, who understands keys and locks and latches, finds the book. His understanding of French improves. At night, at times, he hears Margery Hall read *L'Ecole des Filles* in her fine French accent to Walter Hall. Never for very long, the reading being soon interrupted by sounds of fucking. When they are absent, Jack unlocks the chest and reads what he can of the secret French book, and each time his prick stands *et décharger*. Now the chest, and the book, and Walter and Margery Hall, have left the rectory.

The book is printed in Bruxelles. Abraham Vandecounter will know where it, and others like it, can be bought. Jack hopes.

Jinny Bosvill is in Bradford-on-Avon, near Bath. Honor Garland is at St Andrew Undershaft: Jinny bath; Honor undershaft.

* * *

London, Saturday, 22 July 1665

'Jane-Pym Carter's great belly goes from great to even greater,' says Widow Dorothy Bullen with keen interest.

'She looks like a country woman with a harvest of parsnips and coleworts caught up in her apron,' snorts Widow Lankester, which reaps small 'Ohs!' from Widow Bullen and Goody Parsons.

'Jane-Pym Carter's crop was sown in December or January, harvest due in two months time. Ahuzzah Lankester was a country-born man who knew when to sow parsnips and coleworts,' Widow Lankester reminisces. 'He would say "You may at all times of the month and moon sow parsnips and coleworts," and some others – spinach, asparagus, radish, and more but I forget.'

'Ahuzzah is not a name I know,' says Anne Abowen.

'Few if any know it. It was the plague of his life. Wherever he went he met cries of "Ah Huzzah! Huzzah! Here he is, Huzzah!" His father,' she shrugs, 'he would choose a bible name for his son that no other man's son had.'

'Jenkin Williams, he will have a maid of all-work,' says Goody Susanna Parsons.

'No, Jenkin Williams, his wife, is to have a maid of all-work. Jenkin Williams has no interest in the business,' says Anne Abowen.

'None too soon to have servants working in that great rectory,' says Widow Lankester. 'She had to beg, Tomasin Williams had to beg.'

'He would first have a cook, and he did,' Goody Susanna Parsons says. 'The cook Bab Pyat, and he told Tomasin Williams there was no need for any other servants, "We are only a small household" he said. We need no more.'

'Tomasin Williams, she said – this was heard, heard in church square, through the window,' sympathetic Widow Joan Brokefild adds, 'said she was a poor wretch, expected to make fires–'

'Fires not needed in this summer weather!' exclaims Widow Bullen. 'No fires needed today, and the cook, Bab Pyat, she will tend the kitchen fire.'

'She said she was expected to make fires,' Widow Brokefild continues, 'wash his foul clothes, all their foul clothes, go to market, keep up the house accounts.'

'Going to market, keeping accounts, that is what a wife does,' says Widow Hazard, 'if the house has enough money to keep accounts. The rectory does. I keep a purse, that is where my accounts lie. And I always know how much I have.'

'Never enough,' says Widow Bullen comfortably. 'Never enough in the purse.' She looks around the ancient women's room. 'William Lacie has moved some cloth, more space but less to sit on. And here we are, all of us again.' She nods at Widow Hazard and Widow Brokefild, side by side, smoking.

'Jenkin Williams, he was careless in his answer,' says Widow Brokefild, who sees no need to acknowledge, and will not do so, any past difference with Widow Hazard. 'He says "Well if you will, you will, I leave it to you," and he leaves the rectory like a man with no cares.'

'Who will she have, Tomasin Williams, for her maid?' asks Anne Abowen.

'She will first have them all before her,' Goody Parsons jumps in, 'Susan Godscall, Lucy Utbar, Doll Maylinge, and one other I don't know. And they all must come recommended. She demands they be recommended, then she will choose her maid from them.'

'To come recommended is good business,' says Widow Bullen. 'If I were ever to have a maid, I would want to have her recommended.'

The notion of an ancient woman with a maid is a ridiculous thought that causes great mirth in the ancient women's room.

'The town is gone very quiet,' says Widow Hazard.

'As in Isaiah,' declares Anne Abowen, '"The whole earth is at rest, and is quiet: they break forth into singing."' Then she announces, 'Psalm the fourth:

> *Sin not, but stand in awe therefore, examine well your heart:*
> *And in your chamber quietly, see you your selves convert.*

If it were right to applaud a psalm, they would, instead they sit in their chamber, quietly, briefly, at rest. This plague has tired them, worked them, not killed them but killed many others. The list for the Bills is growing.

Deaths: they will not speak of Isaac Brokefild; they will not speak of Maude Wattes, likely dead in Newgate; not of Isabella Undnay, surely dead somewhere.

'Is there any more heard of that Chaukley?' asks Goody Susanna Parsons.

'Why would there be? Why would anything be heard of Ursula Chaukley? The veriest confident bragging gossip of all, that is Chaukley. St Cyneswide and St Tibba is well rid of her,' says Anne Abowen.

'Mmm. And Libby Chaukley, it is better for her here, in this plague town, than with her mother, her grandmother,' says Widow Hazard. 'Better here than with a bad mother.'

'Goody Parsons,' says Widow Lankester, 'you are the youngest. And here is a farding, will you–'

'A farding! I will not, whatever it is!' Goody Parsons takes umbrage.

'Hear me out. The farding is not for you. It is for the pot boy. Will you go down those fearful stairs – we others are too old to be always up and down them – and call the pot boy to fetch us more ale.'

'Pot boy! Pot boy!' Goody Parsons at the window bellows until the pot boy comes and she can throw him the farding for his reward.

'Youngest but not young enough to be up and down those stairs,' she tells Widow Lankester.

Smoking, drinking, gossiping, the ancient women enjoy their chamber, although not quietly.

'Jane-Pym Carter is big but carries it, carries herself well,' says Widow Margaret Hazard to common agreement.

They hear the departing pot boy say out in the street, 'Up there, they are all up there, William Lacie's room.'

Heavy footsteps herald a dark haired lad, a polite boy, familiar looking, who says he will talk with the St Cyneswide and St Tibba Searchers if he might.

'You might,' says Widow Joan Brokefild, and Widow Hazard gives a brief nod.

'You are a first finder come to report a death?' Widow Hazard asks him.

'No. No deaths, no corpses, although it was a corpse that brings me here. It is a story.'

'We like stories,' says Widow Bullen. 'Sit and tell.'

There are no bales left for him to sit on and he makes himself comfortable on the floor against the wall.

'I am Oliver Micoe, son of Thomas Micoe gong farmer. You have seen him in this parish – the dead infant in the house of office, the corpse.'

This is met with wary silence, stiffened bodies, hardened lips.

'I am not here for that. Joan Micoe, my father's wife, second wife, is not well and will not see any of the women in Blackfriars – we are in Blackfriars – my father is at wit's end and has hopes women from another parish will find help for her.' He looks at them expectantly.

'Doctors all fled,' says Widow Hazard, 'and not much good even when here, which they aren't.'

'Why will she not see the Blackfriars women?' asks Widow Joan Brokefild.

Oliver shrugs, 'Don't know.'

'How is she not well?' asks Goody Parsons.

Oliver looks at the ceiling. 'It is a women's matter,' he says, hoping this will suffice.

'What kind of women's matter?' asks Widow Bullen. 'There are many. Too many.'

Oliver again seeks guidance from the ceiling, finds it in the floor close to him, mumbles, 'Her those, they keep on.'

This is received with sighs and nods.

'She has pain, great pain?' asks Anne Abowen.

'Yes.'

'Hester Fenner, midwife Hester Fenner, she knows all such things. She is the woman to see Joan Micoe,' Widow Lankester is firm.

Hester Fenner fetched from All Hallows on the Wall, comes rapidly – Oliver Micoe has promised a gold guinea if she will come, now.

Oliver Micoe and the gold guinea: Yesterday, Friday, Jack Green has given much thought to this business of his sure discovery as Jack Micoe if he is to bring the St Cyneswide and St Tibba Searchers to Blackfriars. Since this must not be, he is pressed to find a plan, and does, a plan with the subtlety, the cunning, of John Thurloe.

Jack's plan: He returns in quiet, unseen, to Blackfriars and engages Oliver Micoe in private conversation. Jack explains he cannot mingle his two worlds, self-evidently this will benefit no-one; Oliver is unsure, reminds Jack of their father's urgent plea; we will help him, says Jack, you and I. How? asks Oliver. You, Oliver, will come to St Cyneswide and St Tibba and ask the ancient women for help – a young lad, you will do it better than me. In this way the ancient women will come, poor Joan Micoe will be helped, and we will have done what our father wants us to. He wanted you to, thinks Oliver, but if it will help his father, help poor Joan Micoe, then he will do so. He is about to tell Jack this when Jack pulls out a guinea, a gold guinea, a yellow-boy, and tells Oliver: here is this yellow-boy, for you. Oliver is taken aback. For your trouble, says Jack, for your help; to do with as you will, urges Jack, handing over the coin. Oliver thinks the less of his brother and pockets the guinea.

So Oliver has a gold guinea to urge Hester Fenner to come, and she does.

The progress to Blackfriars of Oliver Micoe, Widow Margaret Hazard, Widow Joan Brokefild and Hester Fenner, midwife, takes them through a boisterous game, the shrieking children scattering before them. Widow Hazard looks hard, squinting her good eye, for Sara Potts, her daughter, but does not see her. Small Libby Chaukley's ears quickly picked up the sound of red wands tapping on cobbles, of familiar voices, and she hurried with her good friend Sara Potts into hiding. Sara, familiar with the business of abandoned children being taken up, cared for, has taken small Libby Chaukley warmly and proprietorially under her wing.

> *We'll follow our mother to market,*
> *To buy herself a basket,*
> *We don't care whether we work or no,*
> *We'll follow our mother on tipty-toe,*
> *When she comes home she'll break our bones,*
> *For tumbling over cherry stones,*
> *We'll follow our mother to market.*

Betty Stopford plays Mother with vigour, chasing, catching and beating her taunting children, to their screams of delight. Widow Hazard and Hester Fenner disapprove.

Oliver Micoe cannot answer Hester Fenner's question whether Joan Micoe is given to fits of the mother. He does not understand it and prefers to walk ahead of the three women, but can still hear Hester Fenner talking of the different colours of the Terms that flow in too great abundance, depending on the offending Humour: whitish and pale; or yellow; or dark coloured black or blue. How waters of plaintain, purslane, shepherd's purse, sorrel, syrup of pomegranates, or dried roses will cool and thicken the blood.

Oliver will hear no more of this, and to fill his ears sings a favourite song:

> *O Father, Son and Holy Ghost,*
> *Triune in titles, never three;*
> *Lord Jesus Christ, denied by most,*

'Welcome to Blackfriars!' calls a grateful Thomas Micoe. He is not surprised by their arrival. Oliver has already explained to him that Jack is much occupied on business in St Cyneswide and St Tibba – 'so Jack says' – and asked him, Oliver, to bring the ancient women. More, 'Jack says' he would rather his parish business not be mentioned; 'Jack says' he has good reasons for this; Oliver adds, 'known only to Jack'; and 'Jack says' best he not be mentioned. At all. Thomas Micoe shakes his head and says 'Jack' and Oliver Micoe nods his head and says 'Jack.'

Jack is not mentioned, at all, during the visit to Blackfriars of the St Cyneswide and St Tibba ancient women, and Hester Fenner from All Hallows on the Wall.

'We call it Blackfriars,' says jovial Thomas Micoe, 'but here we are at Dung Wharf. My business.' He points out the unmissable piles of dung. 'Plague or no, dung keeps coming, but you are not here for this. Joan Micoe has said she will see women who are not from this parish.'

'We are not,' says Widow Hazard. 'We are from St Cyneswide and St Tibba, and midwife Hester Fenner is from All Hallows on the Wall.'

'All Hallows on the Wall. That is a good long way from here. A good long way! Joan Micoe will like that. And your hat, midwife Hester Fenner, that is a fine hat and Joan Micoe will like that. Come! Don't mind all the gong, come!'

'I have left them to it,' Thomas Micoe tells Oliver, beaming. 'She will see them! Joan Micoe is talking to them now. Did not say no. It's well done Oliver. Midwife Hester Fenner is being most attentive, most. I have great hopes of this visit.'

An hour later the three women, not from Blackfriars, emerge. Hester Fenner has many encouraging words for Thomas Micoe.

'The colour of the blood shows fullness is the cause – I have dipped a clout in the blood. Bleeding will help, it will. I opened the liver vein of the right arm and bled her a little. The bleeding needs to be little but often. Also some cuppings to the back and the breast against the liver, right below the paps. That is to draw the blood back. But you must not scarify–'

'Bleeding a little and often,' says Thomas Micoe, breaking her flow. 'Will you come to do the bleeding? Come back here?' He presses a guinea into her hand. 'The wisdom of the heap says muck and money go together.'

Midwife Hester Fenner assures him she will come back for the bleeding. Bids him a cheerful God be w'ye.

'Your song,' Widow Hazard will stay a while to ask Oliver Micoe about his song.

'A Muggletonian one,' answers Oliver. 'We are Muggletonians here. We sit and sing in worship. Not here, not sit here at Dung Wharf, elsewhere.'

'That song, the one you sang. "Father, Son and Holy Ghost, Triune in names, never three." Is that the Muggletonian way of thinking?'

'We sing "Triune in *titles*," but names will serve. There is only one God, Jesus Christ. The others, God the Father, the Holy Ghost, are names and nothing more. He is one, never three.' Oliver laughs. 'Not all outsiders agree. None agree! But we have the truth. It was revealed,' he tells her with pride, 'by the Last Witnesses, Muggleton and Reeve.'

'The Holy Ghost is a name? Nothing more? Just the one God, Jesus?'

'Yes, the others are just names. There is only the one God. Jesus was not sent by God, he is God, and that is that.'

'Mmm,' Widow Hazard will think on it, also on how Oliver Micoe and Jack Green both sing Muggletonian songs. She will think on all this.

London, Bills of Mortality for 130 Parishes
from the 18 of July to the 25
Buried, in all – 2785; Plague – 1843
Parishes clear of the Plague – 62; Parishes Infected – 68

CHAPTER XXV

Wiltshire, Friday, 28 July 1665

'She tipped them, she tossed them, she made them so black,
She put so much pepper she poisoned poor Jack.'

'Are they in hot pursuit? Have they raised the hue and cry?' Uncle Rowland, in full dramatic cry himself, asks in a stage whisper heard throughout the coach. After long deliberation he has chosen a middle seat, inside, as the safest place to hide, but now pushes abruptly past the window passenger to peer out into the dark, a dark so dark nothing can be seen.

He slumps back, bumping the window passenger on one side and Jinny Bosvill on the other. Then leans over to the window again and shouts, 'Coachman! Whip up the horses! Whip them up! We must make haste!'

'Will you have the window, sir?' The window passenger asks frostily. 'Let us exchange places.'

'No!' says Rowland Holmes. 'No. I will stay here where it is safest. I will not exchange places.' He turns to Jinny Bosvill. 'Quick, my plague water, I will fortify myself well before we reach London. Well before.'

'A long way before we reach London,' says the window passenger. 'Must get to Chippenham first.'

'I had rather, much rather, gone over to Bath and caught the coach direct to London,' Uncle Rowland reproaches Jinny Bosvill – it is her fault she has not had him ready in time for the coach to Bath. She has failed him as all others have done.

'Failed me, especially,' he mutters, 'especially Rachel Scudamore, "a kind old woman!" Walter Hall called her a kind old woman.'

Walter Hall who loves his family and will have them all safe during the pestilence despatched them, servants and baggage and all, at his expense to his ancient kinswoman Rachel Scudamore in Bradford-on-Avon.

'Large house,' Uncle Rowland mutters on, 'fine house, fine gardens.'

The house, built in the time of the old Queen, has dark cramped rooms, winding passages leading to strange stairs that go up then go down, to no purpose. Cold even in this hottest of summers. And harshly, despotically, ruled by another old queen, Rachel Scudamore.

Jinny Bosvill has three ways of dealing with Rowland Holmes, she ignores him, she bullies him, or she humours him. In the coach it suits her best to ignore him. But her bullying could not stop his grand dithering over which books to steal, 'borrow,' from Rachel Scudamore's library before they fled, 'broke camp.'

'She will not miss these books. She is no reader, Rachel Scudamore. I have learned that this last month.' He sees doubt, even mirth, on Jinny Bosvill's face. 'My kinswoman Rachel Scudamore will not mind a kindness to a kinsman. She is kin to Walter Hall, as am I, thus Rachel Scudamore and I are kin by marriage. Thus.' Rowland Holmes has satisfied himself on this point.

* * *

On their arrival a month prior, Rachel Scudamore assembled all in the forecourt, family and servants together.

'Here you are as good cousin Walter Hall said you would be while he is with the king God bless him what a good man a fine man to be the king's chaplain he wrote me a fine letter in a fine hand.' She holds the letter on high.

'Is she blessing the king or Walter Hall?' Jinny Bosvill, her large frame prominent among the servants at the back of the company, says to Nan Futrell.

'I am doing what is only my duty in having you here under my roof I hope I will always do my duty by kin I have always done so and I hope and expect that you will do your duty to me you will join the household in prayers three times a day and all will be given work to do there are no idle hands here as the Book says "We hear that there are some which walk among you disorderly not working at all but are busybodies."'

'We are not busybodies! None of us busybodies,' protests an outraged Elsa Hall, much put out and exhausted by the journey from London.

'The Book then says "Them that are such we command and exhort by our Lord Jesus Christ that with quietness they work and eat their own bread" but here you will be eating my bread so you must work to earn it.'

Working for their bread is familiar to cook Nan Futrell, to undercook Jinny Bosvill, to waiting woman Mary James; not so familiar to Godfrey and Elsa Hall, nor to Ingram and Luce Hall; and not at all familiar to Rowland Holmes. Nan Futrell nudges Jinny Bosvill in quiet delight. Jinny nudges her back.

'Now all will come into the house and see what a busy working house this is come come now first.' Rachel Scudamore points to a legend over the front door.

> In all labour there is profit but the talk of the lips tendeth only to penury.

'Where do you find that in the Book? Where? Where?' Rachel Scudamore asks briskly. 'Where?'

'Proverbs?' hazards Rowland Holmes.

'Of course Proverbs,' says Rachel Scudamore impatiently. 'Of course Proverbs which Chapter which verse all know it is Proverbs well?'

There is silence.

'You London folk do not know the Book,' she says in disappointment. In the great hall there is another inscription, this done in poker work.

> By much slothfuness the building decayth and through idlenes of the hands the house droppeth through.

'Idleness through idleness the second l has not been given in slothfulness nor the second e in decayeth and not the second s in idleness that is true idleness! It lives idleness bad work poorly done.'

'Proverbs?' essays Rowland Holmes.

'No! Ecclesiastes of course Ecclesiastes it is.'

Down a long stumbling corridor Rachel Scudamore stops to draw the dispirited Londoners' attention to more poker-work admonitions posted above doors.

'My sons' rooms you are blessed with daughters,' Rachel Scudamore tells Luce Hall. 'I am cursed with sons the room of Charles Scudamore see,' she reads, perhaps Londoners cannot read:

> *He also that is slothful in his work is brother to him that is a great waster.*

'Brothers brother to him that is a great waster this house knows that brother yes here he is,' she points to the second door.

> *The desire of the slothful killeth him for his hands refuse to labour.*

'Henry Scudamore his room he is slothful and refuses to labour that is Henry Scudamore it is you are blessed with daughters and work will be found for them for you all you will see from the writings the many that this is a busy house but not a house for busybodies prayers before breakfast prayers before dinner prayers before bed we pray three times a day in this house we do all do.'

Rachel Scudamore falls silent, slumps, deflated, pokes her lower lip, takes Edith and Meriall under her arms. 'You two good girls will sit by me at table and your mother Luce Hall is it yes Luce Hall and the waiting woman.' She turns to Elsa Hall, 'Do you have daughters?'

'I have a daughter. She will not leave London. She will not. A married woman she will stay with her husband.' Elsa Hall is distraught. She is in this outlandish place, in this strange house with this fearsome woman and her daughter is in London with wicked impoverished George Crofts.

Rachel Scudamore nods, shrugs, 'I will see you at table prayers before table the bell will ring the bell Esther Dickenson will show you …' Rachel Scudamore, her spring of words run dry, points listlessly to her housekeeper and walks away.

'Will we meet her sons? At table?' Godfrey Hall, who has had enough talk of daughters and mothers and girls and being told what to do by Rachel Scudamore, asks Esther Dickenson. 'The brothers?'

'Charles Scudamore is dead. Henry Scudamore might be at table or he might not. He does as he pleases.' Esther says this last with a nod of mild approval.

Godfrey and Elsa Hall are to sleep in the room: 'Love not sleep, lest thou come to poverty; open thine eyes, and thou shalt be satisfied with bread.'

Ingram and Luce Hall are conducted to: 'How long wilt thou sleep, O sluggard? When wilt thou arise out of thy sleep?'

'This work, the lettering, who made that?' asks Ingram Hall.

'Henry Scudamore. The mistress gave it him as an occupation and to teach him,' Esther Dickenson answers. 'His style grew better the more he did.'

'Rowland Holmes who came with us, where is he, which room will he have?' Luce Hall asks.

'The gentleman Mr Holmes has found the library and has made himself comfortable there.'

'Surely he will not sleep in the library?'

'No. I did find him sleeping in the library, but his bedchamber is close by the brothers' rooms. His room is to be "This we commanded you, that if any would not work, neither should he eat."' Esther Dickenson laughs, 'That is a guest's room, as these are.'

Rachel Scudamore leads dinner prayers in the great hall, and takes as her text, 'The first Book to the Thessalonians Chapter the fourth.' She admonishes them all to abstain from fornication, 'That every one of you should know how to possess his vessel in sanctification and honour not in the lust of concupiscence.'

Her eyes focus on the place at the other end of the table, set for the meal but not occupied. She says firmly, wearily, 'That no man go beyond and defraud his brother in any matter but as touching brotherly love ye need not that I write unto you for ye yourselves are taught of God to love one another.'

She ends with, 'And that ye study to be quiet and to do your own business and to work with your own hands as we commanded you. That is what the Book says we will eat.'

Rachel Scudamore looks about with satisfaction as food is carried in, says, 'Eat well but not to excess,' and points to another inscription dominating the table:

> For the drunkard and the glutton shall come to poverty: and drowsiness shall clothe a man with rags.

'Little to eat then,' grizzles Rowland Holmes to Godfrey Hall and Ingram hall, all seated by the empty chair.

Rowland Holmes is wrong. Rachel Scudamore cuts large slices from a pie of pork and veal and tongue and boiled eggs, brought carefully to table by Jinny Bosvill and Mary Sitsilt, under cook-maid in Rachel Scudamore's house.

'I do not think I will come to poverty,' Uncle Rowland tells his nephews through a full mouth. 'Not at all. And here comes a fine cake, and a cheese.'

Also comes a black haired man in a dusty jacket who takes the empty seat. He smiles at the company, says, 'Welcome, welcome,' and is quickly served pie by attentive Mary Sitsilt.

'Here is my son Henry Scudamore,' his mother announces. 'He joins us when it pleases him.'

'I do,' Henry Scudamore agrees. 'I do join you and pleased to do so. My mother says Walter Hall writes a fine letter, and here you are, here you all are. Welcome again.'

'You have not read the letter would not read it,' Rachel Scudamore scolds.

'No need, you read it, said it was a fine letter written in a fine hand, and here we all are. Fine pie, always a fine pie here.'

'Reading my son Henry Scudamore disesteems learning despite me he was not educated to learning but to hawking.'

'St Tibba, she is the patron of falconers,' says Edith Hall confidently.

'Of falconers a patron who?' asks Rachel Scudamore.

'Yes, St Tibba of falconers but no-one knows what St Cyneswide patrons,' Edith Hall says. 'At least I do not and Uncle Rowland does not and he knows many things that most do not.'

'I did not know we falconers had a patron,' says Henry Scudamore. 'Fortune was with me today, perhaps from this Tibba saint although I did not know her until now, some water fowl left this minute in the kitchen. Mary Sitsilt will pluck them,' he smiles at the under cook-maid.

'These saints who are they where are they?' asks Rachel Scudamore.

'Our parish church in town, our church, is St Cyneswide and St Tibba,' Luce Hall hastens to explain. 'Those are the saints that give our church its name.'

'London saints,' Rachel Scudamore nods. 'Yes when you have done cheese we women will be at our work after the pudding our lemons our butter a fine pudding our small beer is stronger than other small beers the small girls are drowsing but they will soon be awake enough to do some work you are clever to know of this St Tibba in this house I esteem learning even I a plain understanding country woman esteem learning doubtless doubtless you men will stay and drink but remember the drunkard shall come to poverty tomorrow there will be work be business for all God be w'ye I have needles and wool for all and linen for working Wiltshire has fine sheep you will find the finest.'

'You are being well cared after? Of course you are. Esther Dickenson will see to it. She sees to everything.' Henry Scudamore has wine brought for Godfrey Hall, Ingram Hall and Rowland Holmes, brought to the sitting and drinking and talking men.

'Esther Dickenson, is she the good-humoured fat widow?' asks Rowland Holmes. 'She takes good care.'

'Yes,' Henry Scudamore laughs. 'Yes she is the good-humoured fat widow. Do not mind my mother, that is how she is, a talking woman. She will have your women and maids doing needlework. Flowers if it is fancy work, she favours flowers, as do I, or mending, there is always mending and she will have all take up a needle.

'A Bleakard this wine, comes in through Bristol. Did my mother's prayers – I am always abroad during prayers – did her prayers have you abstain from fornication? Will she have you possess your vessel?' Henry Scudamore must laugh at this. 'Will she have you possess your vessel in sanctification and honour, not in the lust of concupiscence? Your vessel! I have heard it called many things, but a vessel? Not for a man, although it may suit a woman, her parts, a vessel.'

Tavern humour is not common in Walter Hall's rectory in St Cyneswide and St Tibba, but Godfrey and Ingram Hall are tired, have eaten well, and find the Bleakard easy to drink. Ingram laughs helplessly, and Godfrey vents sharp bursts of mirth that will not be repressed. Rowland Holmes, who has fallen asleep, surfaces at the laughter and as a good fellow joins in.

'Tomorrow she will find work for all. I say my work is to hunt and hawk and bring home fresh kills. Fish, fowl, boar, hare. It is good exercise and profitable, I tell her. You can tell her I asked you to join me. If you will, as you please.'

'I am not made for hunting,' Rowland Holmes murmurs. 'Not at all.'

'Then for you the library. Say you will take charge of the library. You look a reading, thinking stamp of man. She always says the library cries out to be taken in hand.'

Rowland Holmes nods his agreement. He has already found that the library has comfortable chairs.

'I must go forth and empty my vessel,' Henry Scudamore stands. 'Drink on. My mother will not allow a pot in the hall. I said we could have it behind a screen but she says she will not have the smell or the noise of men pissing like stallions. I told her I would not shit in it unless urgently necessary but she still denies me. I am the idle son who does not have a pot to piss in.' He laughs again.

'They have left us, Godfrey Hall and Ingram Hall,' Rowland Holmes tells Henry Scudamore on his return. 'Been carried off to bed by wives who are tired and red-eyed and will have no more of husbands sitting and drinking and smoking and talking coarse. Driven, ridden to bed like Phyllis and Aristotle.'

'I have heard of Aristotle. Who is this Phyllis?'

'His wife. She rode him like a horse.'

'That is certainly a good path to pleasure, having a woman ride bareback on top of you. But I did not know married folk did that, I am surprised. So, now in their bedchambers Elsa is riding on top of Godfrey and Luce on Ingram?'

Rowland Holmes sighs. This man can be puerile. 'No. I mean that in the histories Phyllis will rule her husband Aristotle and to show this she rides on his back through the town.' He is not sure Henry Scudamore understands and explains further. 'Like a child playing on a fond father's back. That sort of riding.'

'Yes yes that is for children, but with a woman riding bareback on a man for pleasure this is best done astride. It would not work side-saddle – the target buried in closed thighs. So these women Elsa and Luce have ridden, have driven their husbands to bed? That is the married state. You are not a married man?' Henry Scudamore asks.

'That happiness never befell me,' says Rowland Holmes comfortably. 'I fear I am too discriminating.'

'It never befell me, and I fear I am not discriminating at all,' Henry Scudamore is laughing again.

'I am fond of Aristotle,' says Uncle Rowland with quiet self-satisfaction. 'I am a man for the Greeks.'

'What? Greek love, boys and bums? That is why you have not married?' asks a surprised Henry Scudamore. 'Surely that sort of thing is only for young scholars who have nothing else on offer?'

'No,' says Rowland Holmes through pursed lips. 'No, not that. I am a reading man, a singing man. A man who is all for leisure. Aristotle says, as you might or might not know–'

'Not know in my case. I never could get the Greek, found the Latin hard enough. Greek couldn't be beaten into me although it was tried. Learning is a cruel thing. The Latin I could master, just. A teacher, a good teacher, Mr Latimer, rector, every time we asked to go forth we had a Latin word from him which we were to tell him again on our return. A good way to learn.' Henry Scudamore gives a great yawn. 'He said of me it was like teaching iron to swim, and so it was.'

'Aristotle says the first principle of all action is leisure,' Rowland Holmes tells him severely. 'Both are required, but leisure is better than occupation and is its end. I follow Aristotle in that, not in, as you put it, boys and bums.'

'That is a fine piece of Aristotle! I like that: leisure is better than occupation. That is the thinking Greeks for you! You must write down that Aristotle and I will do it in poker-work. You have seen all my poker-work? My mother chooses the words, not me. But I will choose this Aristotle. My thanks for that. More Bleakard? More for us both and a toast to Aristotle!'

They drink to Aristotle and his eternal wisdom.

'Strange name, Bleakard,' says Henry Scudamore, holding his glass before the candle, turning it. 'It is not bleak at all. See? A fine colour. It is quite ... un-bleak. Tomorrow your nephews will go hunting with me although my mother would have them dig in her gardens but you are all gentlemen and kin and should not dig in gardens, or pollard trees. Although I do like to pollard trees, and spaliering, especially that. Tomorrow I will show you all those I have spaliered. As a young man, a youth, I spaliered every lemon tree I could. My mother sets great store by lemons. For puddings.' Henry Scudamore goes into an excursus on the best fashion of espaliering while Rowland Holmes goes to sleep.

'Aristotle!' Henry Scudamore elbows Rowland Holmes. 'Your Aristotle, our good Aristotle, our man for leisure, a man who understands the importance, the *primacy*, of leisure. My brother was a man for action, not leisure. What does Aristotle say about hawks? He must know hawks.'

No reply from Rowland Holmes. He is nudged more vigorously.

'Aristotle. Hawks. What does he say of them?'

'Let me think,' says Rowland Holmes, meaning let me sleep. 'Aristotle. Hawks. He says–'

'I knew he would know hawks! Yes, tell me.'

'Aristotle will have ten – or is it eleven, perhaps twelve – of ... the Greek is *hierakes*, hawks.'

'Yes! Hawks! I was sure he would know hawks. Tell me more.'

'I cannot remember them all. There is the *asterias*, the *aisalon* – that is our merlin.'

'Aristotle knows our merlin,' Henry Scudamore falls briefly silent in amazement, in admiration. 'A good small hawking bird, good for quail. I have three merlins. Their names are–'

'Will you hear more of Aristotle? I am tired and will go to bed.'

'Yes. The other names. Yes.'

'The *kirkos*, the *spizias* the, the ... the *phassophonos*. And that is all I can recall. The library will tell you the rest. In the library. I must go to bed now. God be w'ye and good night.'

Henry Scudamore calls after him. 'Good night and my thanks for our good Aristotle! I will ask you – tomorrow will ask you, not tonight – for the Greek for his primacy of leisure and the Greek for all his hawks, however many of them there are.'

Rowland Holmes' footsteps drag down the hall.

'I will,' says Henry Scudamore, contentedly musing to himself, 'I will do them in poker-work. The hawks I will put on my hawk-cote, the primacy of leisure on ... on somewhere. The best copyists are those, the masters say, who do not know what they copy, so they follow the words and letters more faithfully. It will go well.'

He meant to tell Rowland Holmes they will eat bacon froise tomorrow, that will put a spring in his step.

Half dozing, he regrets he did not ask Rowland Holmes, who is a singing man, to join him in a song or two before retiring.

'An old hunting song. He would like that.' Henry Scudamore sings to himself:

> *Blow thy horn thou jolly hunter, thy hounds to revive-a,*
> *Show thyself a good huntsman whilst that thou art alive-a,*
> *That men may say and sing with thee, thou hast a merry life-a,*
> *In pleasure all the day-a, Venus's mate to wife-a.*

He drops off to sleep murmuring, 'Venus wife life.'

* * *

'This is my room, and you will share,' says under cook-maid Mary Sitsilt to Jinny Bosvill, who stops to read the poker-work over the door.

> *And withal they learn to be idle, wandering about from house to house; and not only idle, but tattlers also and busybodies, speaking things which they ought not.*

'Mistress chooses the words, a good lesson to all servants she says, and Henry Scudamore writes them. He thinks it a great jest,' she laughs. 'See how he brings forth the words tattlers and busybodies? When he was burning the letters he asked us who were the tattlers and who the busybodies. We had great sport telling him! We named him as the most idle. He agrees! It was good sport.'

Jinny laughs too. She will find out who are the tattlers and busybodies.

'Here is another,' says Mary Sitsilt. There is more poker-work above the bed.

> *Behold! This was the iniquity of thy sister Sodom, pride, fulness of bread, and abundance of idleness was in her and in her daughters.*

'When we said to Henry Scudamore while he was working this, that if this Sodom has fulness of bread and abundance of idleness we will all go there, he would not stop laughing,' she pauses, looks at Jinny. 'It was me who said that, and then he told me, days after, what this Sodom is and does. I said if there is such a place where such things are done it is not in Wiltshire.'

'What did he say to that?'

'He laughed. Henry Scudamore always laughs. He is not like his mother.'

'He has a brother?'

'Charles Scudamore is dead. The wars I think. Before I was born. Mistress talks always of Charles Scudamore to shame Henry Scudamore but I think he is used to it. They argue all the time, the mistress and Henry

Scudamore, but will not leave each other, Esther Dickenson says it warms them both. Those who knew him, some of them, say Charles Scudamore was proud and quarrelsome. Henry Scudamore is not like that. Oh! Move,' Mary Sitsilt pushes past Jinny Bosvill to get out of bed and drops to her knees. 'Prayers. I forgot to say prayers.'

Jinny joins her.

'At night, before bed, by the bed, I pray for my mother, my father, my brothers, my sisters, all my family, for the mistress and all in the house, for the king and queen, and last ask Jesus Christ our Lord to bless me and God to bless us all,' Mary explains.

'I pray much the same,' says Jinny, and they pray. 'Amen.'

'I cannot go to sleep yet,' says Mary. 'Your feet are cold. Your London plague. We all here are greatly afraid of your London plague. When mistress said you were coming here from London, her London kin, we all said we were afraid. I was. All the house, she had us all stand where she had you stand, when you first came, and she said it was her duty to take in kin and she hopes she would always do her duty, and it was our duty too and anyone who would not do their duty could flee and she would tell the world they were lazy and idle and they would not find a position elsewhere and if they still would flee they should do so now. And no-one did but that night two from the house and three from the fields, they fled.'

Jinny is wide awake, cannot sleep. 'I cannot sleep either. You did not flee. Why not?' she asks, new and unsettled in this strange household but soothed by Mary's chatter.

'Where would I go? My mother, my father, my brothers and sisters and all my family are here in Bradford. Where would I go? I could not leave them. Betty Lyte who was with me before you in this room, cleaning maid, she fled. She was very frightened of you London plague people. What does plague look like? We do not know here. It must be fearsome. Betty Lyte's feet were always warm.'

Jinny is suddenly downcast that she does not measure up well against Betty Lyte's warm feet, would weep, tells herself she is too grown to weep before this small girl in this out-in-the-country house with its unfamiliar soft rumbling burring voices, but still feels the tears trickle down.

'Betty Lyte was not a talker. You are a good talker. She would always be saying "Go to sleep Mary Sitsilt. Go to sleep, stop your chatter." You are not like that, I am glad you are good for talking. Tell me about your London plague.'

Cheered that she is judged a good talker, Jinny talks. 'There is the headache, the fever–'

'The headache and the fever are the plague? I have had the headache and the fever, not now but I have had them. Surely that is not the plague? If so then I have had it.'

'No, there must also be the buboes, sore swellings in the armpit or between the legs that give great grief.'

'Buboes!'

'And blotches and sometimes blains.'

'Buboes and blotches. Then what happens?'

'Most die.'

'Oh! Let us talk of something else – else, the ladies Elsa and Luce in your house, tell me of them.'

'Both can be those words you said, proud and quarrelsome, but not all the time. Elsa will be the foremost because she is married to Godfrey the oldest – Godfrey is very proud, stiff – but Luce is a woman who will push herself forward. The girl Edith is clever but a spy, she watches everyone and everything. She will know everyone's secrets. Meriall is a small, obedient child.'

'You are fond of your cook?'

'Nan Futrell? Yes, I have been with her since a small girl.'

'I fear,' says Mary cautiously, 'I fear she will not have an easy time here. Our cook, Marjorie Plank, is a jealous woman, jealous of her kitchen her cooking her food her larder. Over the larder door, she asked the mistress a good bible saying for over the larder door, and she has "The fool foldeth his hands together, and eateth his own flesh." It is a nasty thing to have over the larder door! Henry Scudamore laughed mightily at that one too. I keep my head down and do as she tells, but I still have endless trouble from

Marjorie Plank. Nothing will please her, and your Nan Futrell with her London cooking and being in her kitchen will not please her at all.'

'Nan Futrell is a most excellent cook!' Jinny protests. 'I know that. I have worked with her, for her, for … for much of my life. An excellent, kind cook! Not at all idle.'

'That will not count. When Marjorie Plank heard your company has a cook she said to mistress, "I will not have her in my kitchen," I heard her say it. And mistress said "Then you will not and she must do something else." She did not say what.' Mary Sitsilt turns on her side, her voice muffled, 'At times in bed I would sing to myself but Betty Lyte would tell me to be quiet.'

'You can sing if you please,' says Jinny Bosvill, 'I do not mind.' There is no answer. She folds herself against Mary Sitsilt's warmth, mutters, 'My feet are always cold,' and sleeps.

* * *

'Are they pursuing us? Are they?' Uncle Rowland demands.

Why would they, Jinny Bosvill thinks, they want us gone, says, 'Why would they? They want us gone.'

'Want us gone! Why would they want me gone? I was a great benefit to that miserable house, in that library! Why would she want me gone? I said I would sing. Would sing for her, that Scudamore, sing for the household to give her, them all, pleasure. The pleasure of song. And I did sing.'

The singing had gone well, at first. Rachel Scudamore was quite taken, at first. Rowland Holmes has a fine voice and the extravagant manner of a player on the stage. He sings the song to her, for her:

> Drink to me, only, with thine eyes,
> And I will pledge with mine;
> Or leave a kiss but in the cup,
> And I'll not look for wine.

It had not ended well, when he sang of the 'rosie wreath sent to thee':

But thou thereon did'st only breathe,
And sent'st it back to me:
Since when it grows, and smells, I swear,
Not of itself, but thee.

'Smells! Smells! Smells of me? What are you saying with this singing? That I have a smell? Are you? Do you?'

'No. No. No! It is the song, only the song by Mr Ben Jonson. His song. You have it in your library. Let me show you.'

'If that "song" as you call it is in my library then it should not be and this Ben Jonson is a very foul fellow to write such things I will have that book out of my library do you hear? And no more of your songs your lewd London songs.'

Rowland Holmes thinks her a contrary old woman counterfeiting outrage at his song, a song he sang so well. But does not say this, dares not.

In the coach they pick at their discontents, silently, or together. Now they are well away from Bradford Jinny fumes, anger replacing fear, at the leering, insults and pawing of the field men and how she had quickly learned to avoid them, to always go in company if she could not avoid them.

'Rachel Scudamore will not be gainsayed in anything. In anything. My work in the library was only just begun. I explained to her again and again I need time to think how best to do the improvements she sought. Lying, sitting, in that chair I was thinking, thinking through it all, the whole library, but she would accuse me of sleeping there, of doing nothing. Nothing! Did you see that lettering she had made? Worked by her feckless son?'

Jinny and the whole house had. Over Rowland Holmes' favourite chair in the library was newly hung poker-work.

Slothfulness casteth into a deep sleep and an idle soul shall suffer
hunger.

'Had that hung above me and called me, called me a, a ... a fillbelly!'

'I would not stay,' says Jinny Bosvill, cutting in to take her turn. 'She would not have Nan Futrell there. Nan Futrell! Would have her cooking done by Marjorie Plank.'

Rowland Holmes will not be interrupted, 'Said she will put me out in the fields! A poor, ailing man, sick to die, out in the fields! My nephew is the king's chaplain. Yes! I said that to her, the king's chaplain my nephew. My hernia, I said to her, I have my hernia that gives me great grief. How can an old man with a hernia work in the fields? But she will not be gainsaid. I am a man hard done by, very hard done by.'

Jinny thinks him foolish to have tried an Uncle Rowland jest with Rachel Scudamore, should not have said to her when she found him asleep in the library for the fourth time, should not have smiled winningly at her and said, 'I cannot work too hard, I have a bone in my arm.' Rachel Scudamore not charmed, not won over, replied, 'That bone in your arm will never be at risk from harm for it never does any work that arm of yours nor the rest of your body a very idle body.'

That was when she called him a fillbelly and had the library poker-work made.

'Too quiet this country,' Jinny complains, now speaking quietly herself, the other inside passengers are showing clear resentment of the criticisms of Bradford-on-Avon, of Wiltshire. 'And at night it is all dark, no boys carrying links, no noise, no lights, no street calls,' she mutters. 'No shouting, no singing, no bell-man crying the hour.' Sounds not heard, never heard, in Rachel Scudamore's remote house.

'If I had stayed that library would have been, have been ...' Rowland Holmes is tired but will search for the right word. 'Would have been ... have been made anew. Yes, would have been made anew.' He grumbles on, 'And I found the Greek, the Aristotle with the primacy of leisure and all the eleven, yes, eleven hawks. That was good work, good library work, and no-one could say it was not.'

The coach is filled with silence and sleep-shuffling and snoring.

Jinny, resentful, thinks how Nan Futrell found a good place in Trowbridge, a wealthy cloth merchant there, but no place for her. Not Nan Futrell's fault. She tried for Jinny, but the Trowbridge clothier would not have any more in the household. So Nan Futrell left, and left Jinny. And Marjorie Plank would not have Jinny Bosvill, the London girl, in the kitchen. 'I am an under-cook,' Jinny had told her. 'Not here, you are no under-cook. The fields for you.'

She had run for solace to Mary Sitsilt, who was comforting but not enough and said when she was a little child she had wanted to be known as one of the finest girls in the field and if Jinny Bosvill did not want that then she did not and she should speak to Esther Dickenson who was kindly and would know how to help Jinny and surely would. But that week Rachel Scudamore was listening to Marjorie Plant, not to Esther Dickenson, so Jinny Bosvill had been told it was the fields for her, Rachel Scudamore saying sternly, in a harsh poker-work voice, 'I went by the field of the slothful, and by the vineyard of the man void of understanding,' and 'The sluggard will not plow by reason of the cold, therefore he shall beg in harvest, and have nothing.' And her field labourers had run because of you London people so Jinny was obliged to replace them in the field.

Jinny did not beg in harvest, but begged Nan Futrell to take her to Trowbridge and Nan asked again at Trowbridge for Jinny and the answer was still no, unless she would work in the fields where there was always work. Mary Sitsilt told her that the men in the fields said London girls will do anything so she should be careful and never find herself alone with them.

One song of Mary Sitsilt in bed was a thread the needle song, a Shrove Tuesday song, when the boys and girls of the town sang and danced along the streets.

> *Shrove Tuesday, Shrove Tuesday, when Jack went to plough,*
> *His mother made pancakes, she didn't know how.*
> *She tipped them, she tossed them, she made them so black,*
> *She put so much pepper she poisoned poor Jack.*

Mary told how, when all the young ones of the town had been gathered into the dance, they went to the church and, hands joined, danced around it three times and then shouted they had clipped the church! Jinny wanted to do it, to clip the church, but Mary was disapproving and said only on Shrove Tuesday and what was Jinny thinking?

Jinny is thinking of another poor Jack, thinking to leave, thinking to go back to London, and says so to Uncle Rowland who says he will leave too and go back to London and he will take her, which she scoffs at, and not quietly, because it will be her taking him.

'Chippenam, Chippenam!' the coachman calls. 'Chippenam and the London coach for all who will!'

CONTINUED IN VOLUME II

ABOUT THE AUTHOR

Rob Wills is the author of the critically acclaimed life of convict James Laurence, *Alias Blind Larry*, praised as 'an absorbing, enjoyable tale underpinned by vast research', and 'a great work of Australian theatre history and a very readable book'. He now gives us a fascinating blend of fact and fiction in *Plague Searchers*.

www.ingramcontent.com/pod-product-compliance
Lightning Source LLC
Chambersburg PA
CBHW060241030726
47493CB00024B/1459